Seven Lost Summers

Broken Oasis Book Three

Eve Campbell

I0735922

Copyright © 2025 by Eve Campbell Author, I. Dream Publishing.

All rights reserved.

No portion of this book may be reproduced in any form without written permission from the publisher or autho under the copyright laws in Australia.

Cover by – 100 Covers

ISBN – 9781923416109 – Seven Lost Summers

Chapter 1

Theo

Five months ago, it felt as if the weight had shifted off my chest, just a little. Scarlet was on stage, alive in a way that made you forget we were still bleeding. That grin of hers—fuck, it glowed, as though she was made for that stage. For a minute, the past didn't pull so hard.

And ten days later, Xander and Poppy announced they were having a baby. A fucking baby.

I wanted to be happy. I did. Nate and I both smiled, clapped, gave them that nod... fuck yeah, man, congrats, you did it.

A whole future stretched out in front of them. The kind we once believed we'd have too, back when we were still stupid enough to believe in forever.

We smiled. We laughed. Said we were happy. But underneath it all, we were collapsing in on ourselves.

Nate and I have been carrying the same fucking weight for seven years. The kind that latches onto your ribs and festers, until you forget what it ever felt like to breathe without it.

We're not living. Not really. We've just been surviving without her. And some days, even that feels like a fucking lie.

Maybe it's just today. Or maybe it's this time of year—how it cuts into me like it has a score to settle. Every time, it finds the softest part and tears me wide open all over again.

Seven brutal fucking years bleeding without her.

Bianca... the girl who transformed me. She pushed me to stop hiding from the world. She fit into our hearts as if she'd been made for us. The universe got one thing right, only to rip her away and watch us burn.

I can't remember what it feels like to have anything but this hollow, aching void where she used to be.

Today, on the anniversary of when everything fell apart, it slams into me as if it's happening all over again.

Seven long years without her laugh, her smile, or the way she could walk into a room and quiet every storm in my head. She was my anchor. Now I'm adrift, fighting to stay afloat beneath the weight of everything she left behind.

But life doesn't stop. It doesn't give a shit about the wreckage it leaves behind or the lives it shatters. It just keeps moving. All I can remember is how her laughter made everything seem a little lighter. And I'd give anything for just one more fucking second to hold her again.

She's gone. Taken from us. Ripped out of this world and no matter how many years pass that truth never gets easier. It lingers, an unbearable loss pulsing beneath my skin.

When Nate kills the engine silence swallows us. We don't move. We can't. It's the same brutal routine over and over. We sit here, trapped in this unbearable limbo, both of us knowing the second we step out of the car and walk to her grave it's over. There's no stopping it. No holding back the flood of pain waiting to drag us under.

We don't want to see her name carved into that cold, unyielding stone. Or face the reminder of everything we've lost. The weight of that day, the silence that roars when memories come crashing in, the heartbreak so sharp it threatens to tear us in two. We're not ready to confront it. Hell, I doubt we ever will be.

So we sit here, paralyzed, clinging to the delay of the inevitable. We hold on to these last fragile moments of numbness before the storm breaks loose and tears us apart all over again.

I turn my head and catch Nate staring through the windshield, his jaw tight, throat working as he swallows hard. His hands grip the steering wheel as if it's the only thing holding him together.

When he finally turns to meet my gaze, no words are needed. He gives a slight nod and that's all it takes. It's time—to stand before her and pretend we're strong enough to face this.

In the days after her death, this place—her graveside—became a second home to us. We spent hours in the grass, staring at her name carved into the cold stone, desperate for a sign. Anything to prove she wasn't really gone, that she was still here with us somehow. We couldn't bring ourselves to leave her; the thought of her lying alone in that cold, lifeless ground was unbearable.

Now, things are different. We only come twice a year, because the pain is still too raw to face any more than that. Once on her birthday, to honor how she lived. And again on the day she was taken from us. Each visit feels like dragging ourselves back into the fire, just to be burned all over again.

And Nate... he changes. Days like this rip him apart in ways nothing else can. He goes quiet, folding in on himself as if he could disappear; as if hiding long enough might let him escape a world without Bianca. He locks himself away in his room, curtains drawn, the air thick with all the words he'll never say.

I let him be. I don't push for answers or ask questions.

Sometimes I lie beside him, our heads close on the bed, the only sound being the quiet rhythm of our breaths. The silence heavy with everything we don't say. It's my way of telling him I'm here. That somehow, everything will be okay... even when it feels like it never fucking will be.

Most days he's my rock, the strong one who catches me when I'm falling apart. But during those two days we spend with Bianca, the weight is too much, even for him. On those days I become his anchor, steadying him, even while I'm on the verge of breaking myself.

No one understands this pain except us. Not Xander, Ace, or Kit. Not even Scarlet. They see the cracks. The hollow stares, the way our voices fall to whispers. But they don't know the ache that never fades. The wound that keeps bleeding no matter how much time passes. This grief is ours alone, a scar we carry in silence, the two of us, year after year.

I clutch the bouquet, a chaotic mix of vibrant, mismatched flowers, just the way she would've wanted, and shove the car door open, slamming it hard enough to rattle my chest. Nate is already ahead of me, his steps quick, shoulders rigid, moving with purpose. It's as if he's desperate to reach her, to feel her presence, to find even the smallest trace of her left here that might ease today's heaviness, if only for a moment.

Nate pauses ahead, his steps faltering as if the weight of her name is too heavy to bear. I feel it too. That suffocating ache, the air thinning until I'm left gasping for a breath that never comes.

That cold headstone will never capture who she truly was. It can't hold the warmth she radiated or the way her laughter lit even the darkest corners of our lives. It can't contain the depth of our love for her, every ounce of it carved into us. No piece of stone could ever carry that. And standing here now, it feels as though we're losing her all over again.

We were just kids back then, naive enough to believe in forever. We thought we were untouchable, invincible. But the day we lost her, that illusion shattered. Hope didn't just fade... it fucking died. Now it lingers only as a ghost, something we can remember but never hold again. A dream slipped too far beyond our reach.

Nate stands frozen at the foot of her grave, body rigid, eyes locked on her name as if he could will her back to life. I watch him, catching the way his jaw tightens, his fists clench and unclench, every movement screaming how close he is to shattering. For a second, I wonder if this will be the moment he finally breaks. If we both will.

Quietly, I step around him and crouch by the marble headstone. I set the bright, chaotic bouquet down beside the others already there. I don't need to read the card—I know they are from her mother. The woman who loved Bianca with everything she had, who shattered the day she lowered her daughter into the ground. Her grief-stricken sobs from the funeral are still etched into my mind, a sound so broken and raw that even now, all this time later, it still tightens my chest.

With the flowers laid, I step back to stand beside Nate. He's motionless, silent as stone, and the weight of him presses into the air between us. He doesn't need to speak. I can feel every bit of what he's carrying without a single word.

I grab his hand, my fingers curling tightly around his. He sucks in a sharp breath and flinches as his grip turns crushing, holding on as though letting go would shatter him into a million pieces.

His touch is everything. It grounds me, a silent reminder that we're not alone in this hell. The vibrant happiness we once knew feels distant now. Buried deep beneath our feet.

Memories of her, our beautiful, wild girl with bright eyes and tangled hair, flood my mind, like a reel stuck on an endless repeat. With her guitar slung low, Bianca's fingers blurred as she tore through the strings, music pouring straight from her veins. She didn't just play; she commanded, owning it in a way that left the rest of us stumbling in the dark. She lived for those moments. For the way the world bent to her will when she held that guitar.

I don't doubt that if she were still here, she'd be bigger than both Nate and me combined. Hell, bigger than anything we've ever fought to achieve. She was a true fucking star—and now she's gone. And here we are, stranded in the ruins of everything that might have been, still wondering how we're supposed to move on without her.

One thing I know for sure: if she were here, Nate and I would never have crossed paths with Xander and Ace. We wouldn't have put ourselves through hell searching for a way to numb the pain. Broken Oasis wouldn't exist, at least not in this form. Maybe it would have happened anyway because Xander and Ace were too driven to let anything stand in their way. But for us, we wouldn't have needed it.

As much as I love those guys and how they've pulled us back from the edge more times than I can count, I would give it all up. Every note we've ever played, every stage, every ounce of fame—it's nothing compared to her. I'd trade it all, burn it to the ground, just to hear her laugh again. To see her eyes light up with that spark of life only she carried.

She was our beginning—everything to us before any of this existed. Even now, after all these years, she's still the one thing I'd give anything to bring back. No music, no tour, no sold-out crowd will ever fill the void she left behind. Nothing ever will.

Nate's grip tightens around my hand, his knuckles white, fingers digging in as if I'm the only thing holding him together. The silence hangs heavy with all the words left unsaid. We used to talk to her. God, we shared everything. In those first years, we'd stand at her grave, the cold earth biting against the warmth of our tears as we poured out our hearts, begging for a sign, a whisper, anything to prove she was still with us.

That ended a long time ago. Now silence is all we have. We don't just stay quiet with her, we've gone quiet with each other too.

I don't even say her name in front of Nate anymore. I can't. I see the way his body stiffens at the sound of it as if bracing for impact, his eyes darkening under the weight of memories that are still too raw. So I keep the small pieces of her to myself. They sneak up on me when I least expect it. Her soft humming while her fingers danced across the guitar strings, or the stupid, cheesy jokes that had us laughing until we couldn't breathe.

God, I want to talk about her. I need to.

I want to say her name without feeling like I'm shattering something inside him, or inside myself. I want to believe that if I say it loudly enough, she'll come back, even for a moment. I want to share the stories, to relive every piece of her. The way she'd bite her lip when she was focused, how her fingers tapped against her thigh when she drifted into thought, the way her presence could turn chaos into something that finally felt right. With her, we weren't just surviving, we were alive.

Still, I keep them buried, even as they eat me alive from the inside out, locked away where they can't hurt Nate, where they can't crack the fragile shell we've built just to keep from falling apart.

The sharp crunch of gravel breaks the silence, and Nate and I both look up. It's Quinn Thomas, Bianca's best friend. She was part of our tight little crew once, back when we thought forever meant something and time couldn't touch us. I often think of Quinn, remembering her grinning behind that damn camera, always snapping photos as if she knew we'd need them one day. Maybe she knew more than we did.

She's walking toward us, head down, her hair falling like a shield around her face. It's been years since we last saw her. And like us, she's not the same. The weight of it all clings to her, carved into her and weighing down on her shoulders. And yet, even with all that pain etched into her, she's breathtaking. The kind of beauty that hits like a punch to the gut, wrapped in too much hurt and too many memories.

Seeing her pulls Bianca into my mind, and I can't help but wonder what she would look like now at twenty-five. I bet she'd be every bit as beautiful as Quinn. Bianca was stunning, wild, untamed, a presence that demanded attention. Quinn, standing here now, is just as striking, but in a different way. She's softer, quieter, her beauty shaped by the weight of the pain she's carried all these years.

As I watch her walk toward us, I can still hear the echoes of their conversations. Quinn and Bianca side by side, dreaming about the future as if nothing could hold them back. They couldn't wait for the day they turned eighteen. "No more asking Mom for permission," Bianca would grin, certain she had the whole world figured out. They'd talk about tattoos and piercings. Every wild plan they could imagine. Their laughter was loud, bold, untouchable, as unapologetic as they were. Back then, we all believed life would always be that simple.

When Quinn finally looks up and sees us, her eyes flicker with something raw... recognition, regret, maybe even fear. I feel it, the hesitation coiled around her like chains, every link dragging at her feet. For a second, I think she might turn and walk away. But she doesn't. She steps forward, then another, each footfall hesitant, as if the ground itself might give way beneath her.

She finally reaches us and kneels at Bianca's grave. Her hands tremble, a fragile betrayal of everything she's trying to hold in. She sets down a bouquet of bright lilies at the base of the headstone, her fingers lingering against the stone a moment too long.

"I'll just put these down and leave you with Bianca," she whispers, her voice thin and trembling, as if the floodgates could burst at any second.

Before I can answer, Nate's voice breaks the silence, quiet but certain.

"No, Quinn. Stay," he says, the words so soft they sound fragile, as if they might splinter if spoken any louder. "You were her best friend. You deserve to be here."

Quinn doesn't lift her head right away. Her gaze stays down, her breath unsteady, as if she's trying to hold herself together but can't. For a moment, even time feels suspended, waiting with her. Then, slowly, she raises her eyes, and it all crashes down. Pain. Loss. That suffocating grief that transforms you, reshapes you into something you can't ever outrun. It's all there in her eyes, the same way it's buried deep in us.

She gives a small, hesitant nod, uncertain if she can face what comes next. Her hands tremble as she reaches into her bag and pulls out a photo. Leaning forward, she places it gently against the cold stone, her fingertips brushing over it before lingering there, shaking, desperate to hold on to the remnants of a past that keeps slipping further away.

I look down at the photo, and it feels like my chest splits open, ribs splintering as everything inside me spills out. My breath hitches. The air turns razor-sharp, each inhale cutting like glass.

It's us—Nate, Bianca, Quinn, and me—frozen in a moment so perfect it fucking hurts.

We had no fucking idea.

I've never seen this photo before, and it tears me apart.

We look so young, so carefree, untouched by the weight of the world. We didn't know the truth then. We didn't know how fast everything could slip through our fingers, how quickly the people we loved could be ripped away. Less than a week after this picture was taken, the ground split beneath us, and we fell fucking hard.

Bianca was gone, and nothing, no stretch of time, no desperate prayer, could bring her back. We didn't just lose her that day; we lost pieces of ourselves. The versions of us in that photo... wide-eyed, clinging to foolish dreams, died with her.

Quinn stands there, silent and still, her head bowed. I watch her and wonder if, in her mind, she's speaking to Bianca, whispering secrets only the two of them would understand.

When she finally looks up, her eyes meet mine, and something sharp drives into my chest, twisting deeper the longer she holds my gaze. My throat tightens, dry as sandpaper, but I force the words out anyway, even though they burn like acid.

"That photo, Quinn... can I get a copy of it?"

It's a foolish request. Selfish, even—as if a picture could ever mend what's been broken. But I need it. I need to see who we were before the world split open beneath us. I need that glimpse of a life untouched by tragedy. I want to hold on to a piece of something unruined, something still whole before Bianca was gone.

A flicker of surprise flashes in Quinn's eyes, gone before I can catch it, replaced by something softer. It's as if she understands why I'm asking, why I need this.

"Of course," she says gently. "I have others too, if you want them."

I nod, swallowing hard.

"I do." My voice sounds steadier than I feel. I want every photo, every fragment of her I can hold on to, because this is all that's left. All we'll ever have.

Quinn's gaze drops to the ground, her fingers fidgeting with the strap of her bag. A faint smile tugs at her lips, but it never reaches her eyes.

"Do you remember those days when the three of you used to jam in your room?" she asks softly, her voice fragile and wistful.

I don't have to answer; I can hear it all. The crash of the drums, Nate's laughter when he missed a beat, Bianca shouting at us to play louder because she didn't give a damn about the neighbors. And Quinn, clapping along, grinning like we were unstoppable.

Nate chuckles softly, and for a moment his laughter cuts through the heaviness, a fleeting spark of warmth. His eyes brighten as he drifts into the memory, and for that instant it feels as if Bianca is here with us again, laughing, teasing, making everything seem lighter.

"Yeah," he says, his voice softer now. "Bianca always pushed us to try every song we could think of. Even the ones we had no clue how to play. I remember she made us do 'Wonderwall' because it was her favorite. We absolutely butchered it."

He laughs, shaking his head. "But she didn't care. She was singing at the top of her lungs, arms thrown around us like it was the best performance of her life."

I can almost hear her voice, off-key and unapologetic, filling the room. I can see her hair falling into her eyes as she danced. She had this way of turning the shittiest moments into some of the best times of our lives.

That part of him, the wild, reckless Nate who used to feel just as untouchable as the rest of us, flickers through in his laugh. And it breaks me, because I miss him. I miss her, but I miss him too. I miss the Nate who didn't carry that constant shadow in his eyes, the Nate who didn't sometimes feel like a stranger to me.

"Her laugh was the best part," I say. It's the one thing that hasn't faded, the only piece of her I still hold on to.

Quinn bites her bottom lip, her jaw trembling just enough to show she's fighting to hold it together. But she's losing. I see it in the shine of her eyes, the rapid blinks as she tries to force the tears back.

"I have some photos from those days," she says, her voice cracking. "They're back at my apartment. You can come by and I can show you."

I nod, but what I'm really holding isn't relief—it's desperation. I need those photos, need to cling to whatever remnants of her are still within reach. Because if I keep losing pieces of her, I'm terrified there won't be anything left of me either.

"I'd love for you to have them," Quinn says. "I can make more copies, but those photos... they're treasures. They caught the happiness we had before everything fell apart."

Nate and I lock eyes. No words pass between us. None are needed. The silence says everything.

"Yeah... we'd love that," Nate says, his voice soft, cracking just enough to show the vulnerability beneath it.

I nod, the knot in my throat choking me. My gaze drops to the photo Quinn placed at Bianca's grave. Our sweet girl. The one Nate and I loved so deeply, so easily as if it had been written into our bones, as if she was always meant to be ours.

And she was... until she wasn't.

CHAPTER 2

Theo

We follow Quinn back to her place, Nate behind the wheel, trailing her little blue shitbox of a car. The one that rattles like it might fall apart with every turn. I don't know how the fuck it still runs, but Quinn drives it like it's a Ferrari.

What surprises me most is that Nate wanted this, wanted to go to Quinn's place, knowing Bianca would be the only thing we'd talk about. Normally, after we visit her grave, he shuts down, locks everyone out.

I turn my head and watch him—the frustration in his jaw, the way his hands strangle the wheel like he's two seconds from snapping it in half. And yeah, for a moment, I wonder if this is going to be too much for him.

But fuck that.

I love him, no question. Still, if this is too much, he can stay in the car, because this isn't about him.

This is about her.

She was the girl who taught me not to hide. The one who saw me when no one else even looked. She made me believe I could be more than the mess everyone else decided I was.

We turn left into the industrial district. The streets are cracked, buildings half-dead, rust bleeding across metal, windows smeared with grime or shattered through. It all looks abandoned, even when it's not. Groups linger on corners, eyes dull, movements sluggish, as if they've got nowhere else to go and nothing left to want.

A pair of boots dangles from the power lines, swaying lazily in the breeze like some fucked-up omen—a warning not to get too comfortable. Every wall, dumpster, and sidewalk is drowned in graffiti. Layers on layers, names and phrases painted over each other until the walls are nothing but noise. Nobody's tried to scrub it clean. This place gave up on being saved a long time ago.

As we crawl through in our shiny, too-clean car, heads turn. Not curious. Not welcoming. Just watching, measuring us, waiting to see if we're here to start something or if we'll keep driving, chased off by the weight of their stares.

I lift my hand, offering a small wave to a kid slumped on the curb, legs sprawled, hoodie shadowing half his face. He doesn't move. Doesn't even blink. Just stares through me, like he's already seen it all and knows exactly how this story ends.

And I wonder if he's been passed around the way I was. If his fists ache from fighting ghosts that won't stay dead. If he's holding out for someone to drag him from the wreckage the way Wes and Rose did for me. Or maybe he already knows the truth. That most of us don't get out.

Quinn pulls up in front of a run-down apartment block and kills the engine. Nate rolls in beside her, slowing to the curb, his eyes fixed on the building.

The place is a fucking mess. Cracks split the concrete like old scars. Blankets hang over windows in place of curtains, shutting out more than just the sun. This isn't just a shitty building… it's a graveyard. The kind of place that eats people alive and doesn't bother spitting out the bones.

Quinn steps out and makes her way over. I hit the button, rolling the window down.

"You can pull in behind me," she says, calm, like this place doesn't rattle her. "It's safe. No one's gonna touch it."

I glance at Nate. He doesn't speak, but the muscle ticking in his jaw says enough.

Safe? That's a word people use when they've never had everything ripped out from under them.

Nate pulls into the lot and cuts the engine behind Quinn's car. We climb out without a word. The silence between us stretches tight, heavy with everything we're not saying.

Quinn leads us up two flights of concrete stairs. Our footsteps echo through the stairwell, sharp and hollow. The railing is rusted, paint peeling in strips. The air reeks of stagnation. The dead weight left behind by too many lives passing through without ever really mattering.

We step into a long, narrow hallway swallowed by shadows. A single bulb flickers overhead, buzzing like it's dying a slow, miserable death.

Each door we pass leaks noise—a woman screaming, a baby wailing, a TV blaring some crap loud enough to shake the walls. This is the kind of place where no one looks up, no one makes eye contact. Where silence isn't peace, it's survival. Where people already know too much to bother asking.

Quinn stops at a door with a dent so deep it looks like someone once tried to kick the whole thing in. She mutters under her breath, digging through her bag until she finds the key, then shoves it into the lock and twists.

Nothing happens.

The door stays shut.

She sighs, like it's just one more bullshit inconvenience stacked on top of a hundred others.

"It gets stuck sometimes," she mutters, shoving her shoulder into the frame.

The door bursts open, slamming against the wall. Darkness waits on the other side, staring back at us.

Even though it's mid-morning, not a trace of daylight gets in. The blinds are clamped shut, sealing the place like a tomb.

Quinn steps inside without a flicker of hesitation, like none of this rattles her. Just another room full of ghosts.

Nate and I hang back, letting our eyes adjust, instincts flaring like alarms that won't shut off.

Suddenly, Quinn yanks the heavy curtains open. Harsh light floods the room, driving the shadows into the corners. She turns back to us, her figure framed in the glare.

"Come in," she says, tossing her bag onto something half-buried under clutter. It could be a pile of forgotten crap, hard to tell. Nate and I stay in the doorway, stuck there like two useless fucks hovering in the silence.

I step across the threshold, and Nate follows. The moment we're inside, Quinn slams the door shut behind us.

My eyes sweep the room, my pulse finally easing off the edge. Black-and-white photos cover the walls—stark shots of twisted metal, crumbling buildings, bridges disappearing into fog. Every frame feels deliberate, as if Quinn caught the last flicker of something fading and trapped it before it disappeared for good.

That's when I see it... and everything stops.

One photo. Larger than the rest. Framed in black.

The four of us, caught mid-laugh, faces lit with something close to joy.

I remember that day. Quinn shoved the camera into Scarlet's hands, muttering that if anyone was going to take the damn photo, it sure as hell wasn't going to be her. Scarlet rolled her eyes so hard it was a miracle they didn't get stuck, then spent ten minutes fumbling with the buttons like the thing was some alien device sent to ruin her life.

It took three tries. Scarlet had the skills of a blindfolded drunk with a personal vendetta against focus.

Each time, Quinn got up to check, muttering curses under her breath before barking at us to move left, tilt our heads, stop blinking. We groaned, swore at her, called her a psycho, but we still did it anyway.

Back then, it was nothing more than another moment, just another dumb photo to roll our eyes at.

Now... I'd stand there a thousand more times. Say the same shit, laugh the same laugh, suffer through every retake, if it meant holding onto that one second a little longer.

The burn hits before I can brace myself.

There she is... our girl. Hair tumbling around her face, that smile that always seemed to know too much, as if she could read every twisted piece of us and still want in. And those fucking eyes. I could've drowned in them. I still do.

I blink hard, tearing my gaze from the photo just long enough to find Nate.

He stands frozen, staring at the photo like it's reached off the wall and ripped his chest wide open. His hands shaking. And that look on his face... fuck, I know it too well. It's the same one that surfaces every time the memory of her cuts through him.

The silence is brutal. Full of everything we should've said, everything we never fucking got the chance to.

"Do you guys want something to drink?" Quinn asks, her voice softer than usual, as if she knows we're already drowning.

"Yeah, what do you have?" I ask.

"Water, juice, beer."

"I'll take a beer," I answer without hesitation.

Quinn turns to Nate. "And you?"

He doesn't answer. Just stands there, eyes locked on the photo like it's choking him, pulling him under. His breathing is wrong. The twitch in his jaw says everything. He's back there. With her.

I step closer, voice low. "You want a beer or something?"

This isn't about the drink. It's about giving him something to hold on to before the fucking grief swallows him whole.

He finally looks at Quinn and gives a small nod. "Yeah. Thanks."

His voice is steady, but his body's still taut, wired tight with everything he's not saying.

Quinn nods and turns for the kitchen. She doesn't speak or look back, just moves with that calm, collected air she's always had, like she's seen this kind of broken a thousand times and knows better than to try to fix it.

She yanks open the fridge—a battered old thing humming loud enough to smother a thought. The door groans, worn out, like even it's tired of this place. She leans in, grabs three beers, the bottles clinking in her grip.

Quinn turns, sets the bottles on the counter, and pops the caps. The metal tops clatter against the surface, one spinning off and disappearing somewhere behind the microwave.

She walks back over, no rush, no fuss. Just Quinn, steady as ever.

"Here," she says, handing me a bottle before passing the other to Nate.

I take the bottle. The chill steadies me for a moment, enough to keep me from falling apart. Nate doesn't drink, doesn't speak. He just stares, eyes locked on the label like there's some secret carved into the glass, answers hidden beneath the condensation. As if staring hard enough might tell him how to fix the shit none of us knows how to survive.

Quinn nods toward the couch. "Go on, take a seat."

Nate and I trade a look before sinking onto the worn cushions, the springs groaning under our weight.

Quinn doesn't sit. She lifts her beer, takes a slow pull, then sets it down on the coffee table beside her.

"I'll be back in a second," she mutters, already turning away

She heads for the closed door off the kitchen, pushes it open, and flicks on the light. A wash of red spills out, flooding the space.

A darkroom.

It's the kind of space where silence clings to the walls. Where Quinn pulls memories out of the shadows and pins them down in black and white. Where moments that should've died still linger, refusing to be forgotten.

I lean forward, catching a glimpse inside.

Rows of photos hang from a string, clipped with tiny pegs, swaying as if they're breathing. Black and white shots. Fragments of her world, pieces of what she's seen.

I only get a second to look before Quinn steps back out, a large box cradled in her arms. And just like that, the air shifts, because whatever's in that box... it fucking matters.

Quinn steps forward and lowers the box onto the floor in front of us. The cardboard is worn. The edges frayed, creased from being opened, closed, carried, and shoved aside more times than she'll ever admit.

She grabs her beer from the table and sinks onto the floor behind the box, legs crossed, settling in like she knows this is going to take a while. Another slow drink, then the bottle rests at her side. Her fingers hover over the lid, pausing. Instead of opening it, her gaze lifts, shifting between me and Nate—searching, measuring, making sure we're ready for whatever the fuck waits inside.

Quinn finally lifts the lid from the box and sets it aside.

Nate leans in right away, elbows braced on his knees, eyes locked on the box as if it might hold a piece of her that hasn't already slipped through the cracks.

Me? I don't move. My eyes snag on the photo sitting right on top, and it's already got me by the throat.

Bianca stands there, guitar slung over her shoulder, that smile tugging at her mouth—the one that cut through the darkest fucking days. She had that untouchable magic, carried the whole goddamn universe in her hands, and dared anyone to take it from her.

The sting hits fast, brutal, unforgiving. I blink hard, fighting to hold it back, but the wave crashes in anyway. Because she's still here. Caught in this photo. Out of reach.

Quinn reaches into the box, her fingers stalling at the edge of the photo, hovering as though the touch alone might split her open. She exhales, steadies herself, and lifts the worn image, placing it in Nate's hands.

"Do you remember when this was taken?" Her voice barely carries, softer than usual.

Nate takes the photo, his grip tightening until the corners bend, knuckles whitening under the strain.

That's when I catch it. The shift. His whole body goes rigid, a flicker of something sharp and raw burning in his eyes. The tension carving itself into every line of him.

He swallows hard, thumb drifting over the photo's edge, tracing it as though he could etch every detail into memory. When he finally speaks, his voice is low and rough, cracked open by whatever the picture dragged to the surface.

"Yeah... I remember."

Quinn reaches back into the box, her fingers skimming over ghosts, over fragments of a past that refuses to stay buried. This time she doesn't falter. She lifts a photo and passes it straight to Nate.

He takes the memory in his hands, and the instant his eyes lock on it, something in him cracks. His brows knit tight, breath torn from his chest by whatever that photo holds.

And then I see it too.

Bianca's on Nate's bed in the photo, guitar slouched at her side, that crooked smirk pulling at her lips. Her eyes are bright, daring, carrying the kind of spark that made it seem like she had the whole damn world figured out. Her hair's a mess, strands curling across her cheek, windblown and wild, exactly how she always was. And now she's nothing but a photo in a fucking box.

My vision blurs before the burn even hits. I blink hard, but the heat only climbs higher. A tear breaks free, hot and fast, and I lock my jaw so tight it feels ready to snap. It doesn't matter. Pain's pain. And this... this fucking shatters me.

"You okay, Theo?" Quinn asks softly. But she already knows the answer, I'm not.

Nate turns, his eyes locking on mine, and for a moment the weight of it all nearly crushes me. Then his hand finds my leg, solid, steady, and fuck, that touch is everything. That quiet way he always knows when I'm about to fall apart. He doesn't say a word. He never has to.

He's been doing this for years—holding me together without ever asking for anything back. No questions. No judgment. Just him.

I don't say a word. I grab my beer and take a long pull, hoping the cold will cut through the burn in my chest. It doesn't. Nothing ever fucking does. But his hand stays, steady, and for now that's enough to keep me from breaking apart.

Quinn's fingers trace the rim of the box, slow and careful, as though every memory inside might scorch her if she moves too fast. She hesitates, eyes darting between us, her mouth parting only to close again.

Then she exhales.

"Bianca told me once she was happiest when she was with you two."

Both Nate and I look up. Her voice is steady, but the words slice straight through.

"She said being with you made her believe she could do anything... be anything. That even when the world felt too heavy, having you both beside her gave her the courage to chase what she wanted."

Nate blinks, and a softness flickers in his eyes, cutting through the weight of it all just enough to let a little air in.

And me? I cling to Quinn's words like they're the only thing keeping me from coming apart at the seams. The ache shifts, just a fraction, knowing we gave her something good. And for the first time since opening that box, it almost feels like enough.

I look at the photo again. That smile...unforced, unposed. Real. Real in a way nothing else is anymore.

Quinn reaches back into the box and lifts another photo, its edges worn soft with time—the kind that wasn't just kept, but held. She turns it over in her hands, a small smile tugging at her lips before she finally shows it to us.

"Oh shit, I forgot about this," she says, her voice lighter now, threaded with an edge of fondness that cuts a little too close.

Bianca's swallowed up in one of Nate's hoodies, sleeves hanging past her fingers, the fabric drowning her. She's grinning, all teeth and trouble, like she knew exactly what she was doing.

Nate exhales, the sound closer to a memory than a laugh. His eyes stay fixed on the photo.

"I always wondered where that hoodie went."

Quinn chuckles, shaking her head. "She didn't take the hoodie. You gave it to her. She was freezing, remember?"

Nate nods slowly, as if he recalls every damn second of that night. "Yeah. I did."

And just like that, the moment moves on.

Quinn keeps digging through the box. More photos, ticket stubs, scraps of a life that would mean nothing to anyone else, but to us, mean everything.

Each piece hits with a memory, a second when she was still here. Breathing. Laughing. Owning every fucking room she stepped into.

Nate starts talking, his voice lighter than it's been in days, shoulders easing as he spills story after story. All the dumb shit she used to say. All the times she got away with murder because of that damn smile.

Every laugh Nate lets slip, every half-smile tugging at Quinn's mouth, drives one truth home, Bianca wasn't just a loss. She was a light we were lucky to stand in, even if only for a while.

For the first time in forever, the silence in my chest doesn't feel so fucking hollow.

So I let the stories pull me in. Let their voices stitch over the cracks. Let time slip past as we do the only thing left for us to do—the only way we can still keep her.... and that is... to remember.

CHAPTER 3

Theo

Age: Thirteen

"Fuck this shit!" I scream, my voice breaking, as it rips through the air. My father stands there-smug, towering, acting as though he fucking owns me.

I had a few weeks where I could almost breathe, where the walls didn't close in every time I blinked. Nate's place gave me that. A quiet space, something close to fucking peace. But the second he saw me on the street everything was over. No warning. No words. Just his fist tight in my hair, dragging me back, a piece of trash he forgot to throw out. I remember exactly what he is... every cruel word he carved into me, every promise he set on fire, every twisted fucked-up reason I had to run in the first place. I didn't leave to be dramatic. I left because staying was a slow death. And now I'm back under his roof, choking on the same poison I bled to escape.

Fuck him. And fuck the sluts he drags through that front door night after night. Same giggles, same dead eyes, same high-pitched moans ripping through the paper-thin walls like clockwork. I've been hearing the same sounds for years. Lying in bed stiff as stone, pillow crushed over my ears, counting the seconds between the headboard slams and his grunts, pretending I'm anywhere but here.

He dragged me back into this shit as though nothing's changed, like the last few weeks away didn't mean a goddamn thing. Back into the stench of weed and whiskey. Back into a house that reeks of sweat, smoke, and silence.

I used to wait for him to be more than this lowlife with a temper and a hard-on for power. But he never was. Not with the way he uses his fists. Not with his words or the parade of hollow replacements for the woman who left before he could ruin her too. His anger doesn't come in bursts; the rage seeps into the air, into my fucking bones. Every word he's ever spat at me still echoes, a loop I've been forced to live in since I was old enough to understand that love doesn't live here. Only rage and control. That's who he is.

And my mother... Fuck if I have a clue where she is. She walked out as if I were nothing. No note. No goodbye. Straight-up vanished. Left me in this godforsaken hellhole with him. I'm just a worthless piece of shit she forgot to take with her.

What kind of mother does that? What kind of person abandons their own kid to a man such as him? She fucking understood what he was like. The drinking, the yelling, the busted walls and broken bones. She was aware of the pills and the cash he stashed behind the drywall. Hell, half the time she was worse... sprawled out on the floor, needle still in her arm, eyes glazed over like she'd already decided this world wasn't hers to live in. And still... she left. Left me here with the devil and called the whole damn thing mercy.

After she left everything got worse. The door never stopped swinging, one junkie after another stumbling in, reeking of booze, smoke, and whatever they were shooting up that night. Chasing a high, a fight, a reason to forget they existed. They'd scream, smash shit, bleed out on the tiles, too wasted to notice the kid huddled in the corner, knees pulled to his chest, biting down hard enough to taste blood to stay quiet. Fighting to survive. He kept his eyes shut tight, like that would stop the fists, the groans, the sick thud of knuckles meeting skin. And when the silence finally came, there was no peace; only the kind that presses down on your chest and whispers, "no one's coming to save you."

Every time some strung-out loser pounds on that door, another crack runs straight through what's left of my sanity. The pressure building inside me, coiling tighter with every second I'm trapped here. I watch them stumble in, dead-eyed and twitching, chasing the next hit, the next escape, while I sit frozen, hoping to hell none of them looks at me the wrong way, like so many have before. Every knock has me flinching. Every slammed door's a loaded threat.

When my father fucks up, I'm the one who pays the price. They don't go after him. Never have. They come for me, thinking putting their hands on me will somehow get through to him. Believing that beating the shit out of me will make him care. As though I was the one who blew the cash, missed the drop, fucked up the deal.

I want out. For years, I've clung to the thought of Nate's place. That it's some distant world where the walls don't bleed and the air doesn't smell like fear. Where a knock at the door doesn't mean danger... where people talk instead of scream. Where I'm not bracing for pain every time the floorboards creak. A place that seems like maybe, just maybe, I could breathe without it hurting.

But I'm not there. I'm stuck here in this fucking nightmare, suffocating in it, chained to this life I can't wait to escape. One day, I swear I'll tear myself free. I'll rip these chains off, burn this place to the fucking ground and never look back.

Bass rattles the walls, loud and angry. The sound floods the house, seeps into my bones, drowns out everything that still hurts. He's high again. He's been twitchy as hell ever since he dragged me back here, restless, paranoid, snapping at shadows. Something's going on. I can sense the truth in the way he moves, the way he won't look me in the eye. Knowing him, he's fucked up again. Screwed up something major. Somehow, I'm certain I'm the one who's gonna bleed for this.

With him distracted, I sense this is the moment. My shot. My one fucking chance.

I slip into my room without a sound, heart in my throat, and shove the window open. Cold air hits my face like a slap. My hands tremble against the ledge. I get one leg over. My pulse hammers in my skull, louder than the fear, louder than the voice screaming, "don't". Freedom's right in front of me, close enough to taste, burning on my tongue like something I was never meant to have but might steal anyway.

The door slams open like a fucking explosion.

A crash. A shadow. The weight of everything I'm trying to outrun shoves its way into the room.

My heart stalls, but panic kicks harder. I lurch forward, scrambling to lift my other leg, to throw myself out the window before the chance is gone. But it already fucking is.

He's on me in seconds. Charging across the room like something feral, unhinged. I barely catch the frame before his fist snatches a handful of my hair and yanks me back so hard the room tilts sideways. Everything spins... light, shadow, ceiling... ending with a thud.

My back hits the floor. All the air is knocked clean out of me. I can't breathe. Can't move. My body screams, but I stay silent as he drags me across the room by my hair. Every nerve burns, every inch of my scalp is on fire. His grip tightens, twists, punishes. The pain is sharp enough to blind me, to drag a sob straight from my chest. But I swallow the scream. I won't give him the fucking satisfaction.

I've been here before. I understand how this plays out. Screaming feeds him. Fighting gives him something to swing harder at. And I'll fucking die before I give him that power.

So I clench my jaw until the bone threatens to snap, swallow the cry choking its way up my throat. Every nerve is screaming, every muscle begging for the pain to stop, but I don't make a sound. I shove the sensation down. Bury it deep where he can't reach. Lock it behind everything I've already had to become to survive. Because if I push through this, I might still have a chance to get the fuck out.

One day. I whisper the words in my head like a curse, over and over. A broken prayer, a promise laced in blood. This won't last forever. Eventually, he'll be the one on the floor, choking on the same fear he's forced down my throat. Someday, I'll be the one standing over him while he begs—just like I used to.

By the time we hit the living room, he's breathing like a fucking animal—heavy, uneven—but his grip doesn't slip. His fist stays locked in my hair, knuckles bone-white, like he needs to hurt something just to remind himself he's still in control.

He halts beside the busted coffee table, grabs a half-empty beer bottle with his free hand, and downs the drink in one long, messy pull. Foam spills down his chin, soaking into the coarse stubble along his jaw. When the bottle's dry, he hurls the glass without a second thought. I don't need to see the impact—I hear the sharp, splintering crash as the bottle explodes against the wall. Another mess. Another piece of him I'll have to dodge.

Next comes the joint. He lights up as if it's a ritual; the flame flickering long enough to catch before the tip glows red-hot. He takes a slow drag, savoring it like peace is something he can inhale. Smoke spills from his mouth in thick, curling tendrils, drifting toward me, sinking into my skin, my clothes, my lungs. It pollutes the air, thick enough to drown in. And I'm stuck there, forced to breathe it in—his poison, his power, his fucking way of reminding me I'll never be free.

As though the thought only occurs to him that he's still got a hold on me, he leans in. Too close. His heat bleeds into my skin as his breath ghosts over the back of my neck, reeking of cheap liquor and rot. It coats me like a sickness, crawling across my nerves, leaving everything inside me recoiling. My stomach twists, bile burns at the back of my throat, and my skin prickles, begging for space I'll never get.

I shift my gaze, and that's when I see the tiny bag of coke sitting there. Waiting. Daring me. Whispering the same promise the powder always does: escape. Oblivion in powdered form.

I've thought about it more times than I can count. One breath. One goddamn sniff. And I'd be gone.

No more pain. No more past. Drowning in the same hollow, fucked-up world that's already swallowed him whole. Some nights, the weight almost passes for mercy. To stop the fighting. To stop clawing at the walls when every path out of here, leads straight back to him. I want to let the rot crawl into my bones, let the numbness smother everything until I don't have to feel, don't have to remember all the shit that's been done to me. Let it pull me under until I disappear completely. No more screaming in my head. No more bruises I can't cover. No more waking up and wishing I hadn't. Where I don't have to be me anymore.

But then, always, without fail, Nate's face cuts through the dark. And suddenly, I can't.

Nate, my best friend, my anchor. The only person who knows the truth. Every bit of the story. Who's seen me broken, bleeding, wrecked and never once looked away. He doesn't flinch at the bruises. Doesn't pretend the scars don't exist. He just stares straight through the mess and looks at me like I'm still worth something.

That's why he's the only thing that feels real. The only thing that cuts through the static. He's my out when it all gets too loud. My grip on the edge when I'm one breath from letting go. He's my escape... my fucking lifeline. The last thread holding me above water while everything else drags me under.

Nate's the one who tells me I'm more than this. More than the shit my father beat into me. More than the rage I've swallowed. All the blood I've choked down and the numbness I've learned to live with.

So I fight, because of him. Even when it fucking hurts. Because Nate is the only thing keeping me from shattering.

A fist bangs hard on the front door—the kind of knock that doesn't ask. It slices through the room, straight down my spine, leaving the air strung tight and ready to snap. Another follows. Louder. Meaner. The door jumps in its frame as if it's barely holding back the storm behind it.

I freeze. Breath caught. Muscles locked. That sound isn't just noise; it's a fucking warning. And I feel the vibration everywhere. In my chest. My teeth. My bones.

I see him flinch. Quick. Subtle. That split-second crack in his mask. A flicker of panic in his bloodshot eyes before something colder rolls in and buries it. He knows and so do I that someone's here to collect.

And in that sick, twisted mind of his, I know the decision's already made. I'm not a son. I'm a fucking transaction. The debt. The payment.

There's some hollow-eyed, desperate bastard on the other side of that door, broken in all the worst ways, and he's about to throw me straight at them.

Some of them didn't want me. Some did. The ones who liked little boys. Their hands, voice and God their fucking eyes. They still live inside me, buried in my skin like splinters I can't dig out. Crawling. Infecting. Rotting. They steal the air from my lungs. Poison the silence. Hijack every quiet moment and twist it into something filthy.

No matter how many times I drag my nails down my arms, across my throat, over my chest, scratching, clawing, trying to scrape them off. I never come out clean. Never come out free. Their dirt stays. Their stains are too fucking deep.

Now I know exactly why he dragged me back. He fucked up, and he was certain only a matter of time remained before someone came knocking. The guys he owes are done playing nice. Empty promises and blood-stained IOUs don't cut it anymore.

He needed someone to toss to the wolves when they arrived.

"Stay the fuck there," he snarls, and before I can blink, he shoves me. My body jerks sideways, useless against the force, and my head whips back before cracking against the hardwood of the coffee table with a sick thud.

Pain bursts through my skull like a flashbang. It's white-hot, disorienting, shooting down my spine, locking up every nerve like I've been short-circuited. I'm gasping, blinking, trying to stop myself from slipping under, jaw clenched so tight my teeth ache.

Every instinct inside me roars to move. To crawl. To drag myself to the fucking window and disappear before that door gets kicked in and it's too late. My fingers twitch. My lungs stutter. Everything in me begs to run.

But I don't. Because I already see how this ends. There's no getting out. No fighting back. No waking up. Only me on the floor, waiting for the next monster to walk through that door.

So I stay down. And I do the only thing I've got left.

I fucking pray that today isn't the day he hands me over again. That I don't get shoved into the arms of another fucking monster with dead eyes and hungry hands. That I don't lose whatever fight is still flickering inside me as I think of Nate.

Please let me survive this. One more time. That's all I'm asking.

The pounding gets worse. Louder, more intense, each one hits like a fucking gunshot. My breath seizes in my chest, pulse thundering in my ears as my father storms toward the door like he's ready to rip it off the hinges. I stay down. Frozen. Muscles pulled tight, every part of me wired and shaking.

The door bursts open.

I don't move. I can't. That's when I see him.

Wes. Nate's dad.

And I'm torn between crying and crawling toward him.

He barrels in like a fucking storm. Wild and unstoppable, too big for these rotting walls to hold. The second he steps inside, the air shifts, like the entire room knows who's in charge now.

My chest loosens like I've been drowning for years and finally broke the surface.

"Where the fuck is he?" Wes roars, voice burning with a rage that doesn't whisper or simmer. The fury devours. The fire wraps around everything, swallowing the fear, the silence, the stench of control.

And for the first time in a long fucking time, I'm not the one who's scared. He is.

Wes is a force of nature—a wall of muscle and ink, his tattoos screaming stories no one dares to ask about. Violence. Survival. Shit, you don't come back from clean. You feel it before he speaks. He doesn't need to raise his voice to own a room. The ink, the scars, the weight of everything he's survived — it speaks louder than any words ever could.

I've never told him what goes on behind these walls. Never let a word slip. But I think he knows. Maybe he's seen the truth—in the way I flinch when someone moves too fast, in the bruises I try to laugh off like they don't mean shit. Maybe he hears the cracks in the way I go quiet when I should speak. How my voice never carries the way it's supposed to.

Or perhaps this place is to blame. This whole fucking neighborhood full of cowards who know exactly what happens here and do nothing. They turn away. Whisper behind locked doors. Pretend the screams are TV static; the bruises nothing more than bad luck. They're too scared to cross the man who's kept me caged my whole life.

But not Wes.

Wes doesn't flinch.

He walks straight into the fire like he's been waiting for this moment his whole goddamn life.

My eyes snap from Wes's fury to the doorway where Nate stands. His face is tight, shoulders tense, worry carved into every line. His eyes find mine, and in that split second, I know.

He told him.

Nate told Wes everything. Laid it all bare, every sick, fucked-up thing my father's done, and the reasons as to why he probably dragged me back here.

For once, I'm not ashamed. I'm not small. Not some broken fucking secret.

I just feel... relief. Like I can finally breathe, and now I don't have to carry this weight alone anymore.

My father steps into Wes's path, puffed up and pretending he can stop him. As if he's some immovable force instead of the pathetic, worthless piece of shit he's always been. But he doesn't stand a chance.

Not against Wes who doesn't even blink. His arm swings out, shoving my father so hard his knees buckle, and he crumples to the floor in a graceless heap of shit. No fight. No power. Just a man who was never as strong as he pretended to be.

"Come on, son." Wes's voice is steady. Solid. Iron in a place built on splinters. His hand wraps around my arm, firm but careful, and pulls me to my feet like I'm something worth holding onto instead of some broken thing meant to be thrown away.

For the first time, there's something solid beneath my feet. Something that isn't cruel. It's safe.

Wes has never treated me as if I'm nothing. Not once has he ever made me feel like I was only the fallout of someone else's fuck-up, the scraps left behind in a life I didn't choose. With Wes, there's no flinching, no pretending. Only this solid presence that makes it harder to keep pretending I don't need it. Around him, I'm not merely the bruises or the silence I carry. I'm something more than I ever thought I could be.

"He's not your fucking son!" My father's words slur, thick with rage and the stink of cheap booze, his breath curling in the air like poison. His eyes are wild, burning with a fury that's all show-because deep down, he knows the truth. He's a coward. He has always been. All bark, no fucking bite.

He staggers forward, still pretending he has a shot at stopping this, but Wes tightens his hand around my arm, a silent promise, solid as steel, and then he moves. Pushes right past my father like he's not even there. As if the pathetic, washed-out bastard blocking the doorway is nothing more but a shadow.

"That's my fucking son. Get your goddamn hands off him!" he snarls, spitting the words like they still carry weight.

Wes lets go of my arm, and I bolt. Feet moving before my brain catches up, tearing across the room toward the only safe thing I've ever known. Nate's standing in the doorway, wide-eyed, frozen—and all I want is to reach him. To fall into something that doesn't hurt.

Behind me, I hear Wes's voice tear through the room, each word soaked in venom.

"You're not a fucking father. He's thirteen, you sick fuck. Not some fucking debt you get to hand over."

The words drop heavy, and for once, my father has nothing to say. No comeback. No threat.

Just silence.

"You touch him again," Wes growls, voice feral, shaking with restraint he's barely holding onto, "and I swear on every grave I've ever dug, I'll fucking rip you apart with my bare hands. I'll break every bone in your body, while you choke on your own teeth."

He steps in, chest to chest with my father, eyes black with rage.

"You think I haven't dealt with worse pieces of shit than you? You ever lay a finger on Theo again and I'll end you so violently they won't find enough of you to scrape into a fucking box." He doesn't blink. Doesn't back down. "Theo's not yours. He's mine to protect now even if it means ending you right here. Come near him again. I fucking dare you."

He turns away as if my father isn't worth another second of his time.

My father stands frozen, mouth twitching like he wants to throw out some drunken threat, but nothing comes. No slurred curses or snarling comeback. Only silence. Because he fucking knows. Wes isn't bluffing. This isn't a warning. It's a death sentence waiting to be cashed in. And if he so much as breathes wrong, the next time won't come.

Wes turns and starts toward us, no hesitation in his stride, only that same quiet fury simmering beneath the surface. Nate and I move without thinking, instinct pulling us apart to let him pass. He doesn't have to say a word. We follow.

Our footsteps echo behind him as he hits the front steps like a man on a mission. My legs move but everything else in me is hollow. The adrenaline's still buzzing under my skin, but it's thinning out, leaving behind nothing but the crash. That deep, bone-heavy exhaustion that wraps around my ribs and pulls me down.

All I want is a quiet corner, somewhere to sit and let this whole fucked-up mess settle, to untangle the knots twisting in my head. And yet, through the chaos, one thought refuses to let go. It presses in, over and over.

Nate's family has always been there. I never understood why. I still don't. I'm the fucked-up kid with too many bruises and not enough reasons to be loved. The waste of space my father made sure I believed I was.

But Wes. The man who steps between you and hell without needing a reason. He didn't ask. Didn't wait. He was the shield I never earned, but he gave it all to me the same.

Rose with the gentle hands, tired eyes, arms that wrapped around me the first time like I wasn't broken glass. She didn't flinch or pull away. She held me soft and steady, and for a second, I wasn't rotting from the inside out.

Even Scarlet, Nate's annoying little sister, always in my face, pushing my buttons, showing up when I never wanted her to, but somehow she knew exactly when I needed someone there. She never let me disappear, even when I wanted to.

Just being in their house, breathing that air is enough to know I've been claimed. And it terrifies me. Because for the first time in my life, I'm not invisible. I'm seen and I don't know how to live with that.

They're not blood but they're something stronger. A constant in all my chaos. A lifeline I never expected, never let myself hope for, but somehow, against every fucked-up odd, they're mine.

I can't say where I'd be if I hadn't met Nate that day when I was sitting on the curb, hollowed out, barely breathing, feeling like the world had chewed me up, spat me out, and forgot all about me. I remember them—Nate and Scarlet riding their bikes, laughter spilling out of them. No weight in their voices or bruises behind their eyes. Pure freedom.

Then Nate stopped. He slammed his brakes on, tires skidding to a halt right in front of me like the universe paused for one fucking second and said, here. Somehow, that pause gave me him.

He didn't look at me the way the assholes at school did —with disgust, or the way their eyes darted away like I was contagious. He knelt down, stared right at me and asked why I was crying. The moment hit so hard I nearly broke.

I wanted to tell him everything. All the suffocating secrets, the pain, the shit that had been eating me alive for as long as I could remember. The things no kid should ever have to carry.

But I didn't, not that day. I couldn't. Not at that point. Not for a long time.

Those secrets... they were mine to bear. My burden. My fucking curse. I locked them so deep inside that they felt like part of me, like if I buried them far enough, maybe-just maybe I could pretend they weren't real. That they hadn't shaped me into this broken, fucked-up version of myself.

But Nate, even back in those days, didn't push. He didn't pry. He sat down next to me, like sitting shoulder to shoulder with a stranger unraveling on a sidewalk could somehow make the world a little less cruel. For a second, the world softened.

Now he knows everything. Every sick, twisted fucked-up shit they did to me, the kind of hurt that steals pieces of you that you didn't even know could be taken. Things I never wanted to say out loud. Things I was never supposed to survive.

He knows what it was like for me to be used. To be stripped down to nothing but fear and skin. To be touched by hands that took without permission and left bruises that never healed. And now it's out there. No more hiding behind half-truths and shrugged shoulders. He sees it. All the damage. All the shame I've choked on for years. And somehow... he's still here.

Even now, with him knowing every fucked-up detail, there's still this part of me that's scared. I'm terrified that one day he'll wake up and realize what I really am. Not just broken. But worthless. The damage that sinks deep and poisons everything it touches. The mess you can't fix no matter how hard you try to love it clean.

When that day comes, and fuck, I know it will; I don't think I'll survive it. Because he'll walk. And he'll have every right to when he realizes I am nothing.

Wes stands at the curb, waiting. Still as stone, backstraight, tension bleeding off him in waves. His whole body's coiled, like he's seconds from detonating. Fists clenched so tight the veins bulge, jaw locked. That kind of quiet fury that doesn't shout.

But with all that anger, even with the intimidating ink staining his skin and the scars that tell the story of a life that's never gone easy on him, I've never been afraid of Wes. Not once.

The first time I saw him, I knew he was a man who didn't need to raise his voice to command a room. A man who could break you without lifting a damn finger. When Nate dragged me off the curb that night, my body beaten and used, my face streaked with tears, Wes didn't say a word. He didn't ask what happened. In that silence, he gave me something I hadn't had in a long fucking time. I was safe, and I was home.

I remember watching him with Nate and Scarlet. The way he carried himself like nothing could shake him. But underneath all that muscle and grit there was something else. Something warmer. In the way his eyes softened when they spoke, even if the rest of him stayed steel. They were safe. Wes would burn the world down before letting anyone touch them.

Fuck, I used to sit on the curb, watching the scene like a movie from a life I'd never get. Wishing I could understand what it was to be protected by someone who wanted nothing in return.

I never thought I'd be on the receiving end of that. But somehow, against all odds, Wes gave that same love to me. A broken, silent kid who didn't know what the fuck to do with it.

As we get closer to the house Wes turns. Rage still burns under his skin, but he keeps the fire caged for me. "Are you okay, Theo?"

"Yeah," I lie, the word barely making it past the tightness in my throat. I force a smile, but the attempt falls flat.

He steps closer, his hand landing on my shoulder, like he sees right through my bullshit.

"Are you sure you're okay?" His voice is soft. "Because it's okay not to be okay."

The words hit hard, knocking the air out of me. I swallow the ache, fight the lump in my throat, blink fast, bite the inside of my cheek—anything to stay steady. But the wave's already crashing.

Before I can pull it together, Wes pulls me in. One arm around my shoulders.

"You're strong, Theo," Wes says. "Stronger than most. But even the strongest break, and sometimes... sometimes, it's okay to let it hurt."

Then his gaze shifts to Nate.

"Take him home, Nate," he says, voice firm, leaving no room for argument. "I'm not finished here, yet."

CHAPTER 4

Theo

Age: Eighteen

I sink into the shadows, jaw tight, a scowl carved deep across my face. Eyes locked on the new girl. Something about her crawls under my skin in the worst way. I don't need distractions. I don't want them. But she's got this pull I can't shake, dragging my focus without even trying. The whole thing pisses me the fuck off more than I want to admit.

And of course, I'm not the only one. Nate's already eyeing her. The bastard can't help himself. That messy blonde hair, the smug grin—nothing less than a cheat code. A single glance and they're handing over their hearts, their numbers, their goddamn dignity. And he takes everything every time. No shame. No strings

But I'm not him. I don't fuck just to kill time or forget the noise. I don't fuck at all. Not because I don't want to. Hell, sometimes the wanting burns so bad it hurts. But wanting and doing are two different things.

Something in me breaks down every time the moment gets close. A switch flips. A wall slams down so hard the shock tears through my whole body.

Nate's got it easy. No demons clawing at his ribs. No memories slicing through him when hands start to wander, when mouths press too close. No weight pressing on his chest, ready to blow the second he lets someone in.

He's the fucking heartthrob of the school. The golden boy. That smirk alone could start a riot. With one snap of his fingers they're lining up, desperate to be the next one to sink to their knees and make him forget everything but the moment.

And me? I'm the guy in the corner. I fight to breathe. I try not to fall apart every time someone steps too close.

With my eyes still on her, I lean back; the joint already burning down in my fingers. I pull in a deep hit, trying to chase the chaos out of my chest, but watching her just fans the goddamn flames instead.

Normally, I don't see people. I tune out without trying. But something about this new chick makes my head snap up like I caught a shot of lightning straight to the brain.

Her black hair's wild, untamed, catching light as though soaked in midnight. She stands across the field, all edge and a fuck-you attitude. Not giving a shit if someone looks at her the wrong way.

And that's the goddamn problem.

She's not supposed to mean shit. Not supposed to make my pulse jack like I'm already fucking hooked, or my fingers twitch, jerking off some reckless-ass idea I know I'll regret. But fuck me sideways, something in her pulls at me.

I lift the joint to my lips and drag hard. My fingers squeeze that fucker, the last tether keeping me from losing my shit. I keep the smoke low and hidden. Getting caught again would be more than a dumbass mistake. Not now. Wes and Rose have already had to pick up my broken, fucked-up pieces more times than I can count. I owe them better than this endless spiral I keep crashing into.

Nate drops onto the bench next to me, all swagger and zero fucks given. His boots drag against the ground as he leans back, sprawling out as though he owns the fucking universe and everyone else is background scenery. He catches my gaze, and that sharp, cocky grin slides across his lips, smug as hell, convinced he already knows what's up.

"Who you got your eye on?" He asks, voice lazy but dripping with way too much confidence.

Without waiting for an answer, he reaches over, snatches my joint, and pulls a slow, deliberate drag like it's his goddamn right. He holds the smoke deep in his lungs then blows it out. Nate couldn't give a rat's ass about rules. Consequences? That shit's for everyone else to sweat over. He's been suspended twice this year already, and if they kicked his ass out tomorrow, he'd probably throw a goddamn party on the way out.

Me? I don't have that reckless fire burning in me. But, fuck, some days, I wish I did.

"If it's her?" Nate jerks his chin toward the new girl. "Goodluck, man. She doesn't look like the type who plays nice."

I roll my eyes and snatch the joint back. "Since when the fuck do I give a shit about nice?"

Nate smirks with that cocky, infuriating grin of his—the kind that makes every girl here lose her damn mind and every guy want to take a swing at him. He's untouchable and he knows it. Not because he looks like a saint, though he'd sell that lie in a second if the chance worked to his advantage. His shield is Wes.

Wes isn't just a name. He's a fucking legend. Ex-biker, ex-trouble, a man people whisper about but never face. Most guys would rather chew glass than cross him. But they've never seen the man who fixes broken furniture or who taught me how to throw a punch so I wouldn't get my ass kicked again.

He's a beast wrapped in steel with a heart bigger than this whole town. Nobody else would believe it because to them Wes isn't a person. He's a reputation. A shadow that follows me. No one in their right mind fucks with his kids.

I keep my eyes locked on her like some fucking obsessed idiot, tracking every step as she cuts through the crowd of kids milling around outside. Her long black hair sways with every move, that perfect ass wrapped tight in jeans like they were made for her. Voices bounce off the brick walls and concrete paths as she heads toward the big doors. Why her? Why the hell is she the one who gets under my skin, fucks with my head when no one else ever has?

I don't waste my time on chicks. I don't have that fuck-it-all drive Nate's got, banging anything with a pulse just for kicks. But, fuck, there's something about her. Something that's jammed itself deep in my ribs, fucking with my head, twisting every damn thought. And I don't have the patience to untangle that shit.

I flick the joint to the ground, grinding the ember under my boot, the only damn thing I can control right now. I yank the hoodie up over my head, push to my feet, and jam my hands deep in my pockets, trying to choke down the itch crawling under my skin before the urge fucking devours me.

"Where are you going?" Nate's voice cuts through, amused as hell.

"To check out the new chick," I mutter, trying to convince myself it's no big deal. "See what she's up to."

Nate chuckles. That asshole knows exactly what's up. I don't slow down, don't break my stride. He slips in beside me, moving fast like he's ready for whatever shit's coming next.

Every girl we pass can't help themselves. Their eyes lock on him, wildfire blazing through, impossible to ignore, and they're nothing more than sparks caught in the heat. Nate drinks the attention in like oxygen. He flashes that lazy grin promising every kind of chaos and trouble they're dying for. He moves through the crowd as though the whole place were built for him. Confidence rolls off him in waves—effortless, unshakable, the way things have always been. He owns every inch of this shit without even thinking twice.

But me... I'm the shadow in the corner. Hoodie pulled low, head bowed like I'm trying to disappear. Their eyes don't latch onto me with hunger the way they do with him, but every glance still scrapes across my skin. The whispers follow me, smoke twisting around a dying flame. I fucking hate the attention. Hate that they're always watching, always judging. I don't want that spotlight. Because if anyone stares too closely, too hard, they'll see the cracks beneath the surface. The pieces barely hold me together. The mess I'm desperate to keep hidden. They'll see how fucking broken I really am, and I'll be damned if anyone gets close enough to learn that.

We step into the long corridor. The place is nearly empty, with only a few cheerleaders scattered by the lockers. Lydia stands in the center, flicking her hair as though she's rehearsed the move a thousand times in front of a mirror. Something she's sure will make every guy here drop to his knees.

She turns at the sound of our footsteps, eyes locking on Nate like a fucking spotlight. Everyone knows she's had a thing for him for years. Nate has already had her twice. First in the backseat of his car, second at some lame party last month. I witnessed the first time, sitting in the passenger seat like an invisible ghost. Heard Nate work his charm and smooth-talk her into spreading her legs, only to laugh afterward, reducing her to another notch on his belt. Another story for him to brag about.

Nate, that cocky bastard, talked her into giving me a blowjob as though it were some fucked-up favor. I should have told him to fuckoff, shut that shit down the second it started, but I didn't. I let the whole thing happen. The way Lydia's eyes cut into me like I was some diseased freak, made my stomach twist into knots. I sat frozen, numb, as if I wasn't living in my own skin. Watched her mouth move, doing its job, but I felt nothing.

I fucking hated the whole thing. How my skin crawled under her touch, dragging all the old shit to the surface, trying to choke me with the past. I couldn't fucking breathe. Nate knows better now. He doesn't pull that shit anymore because I can't stand the pressure pressing down on me.

Lydia's eyes are desperate and full of hope as she steps in our way. She acts like he's some goddamn savior instead of another guy who'll fuck her and toss her aside like yesterday's trash. Nate grins, that arrogant, unapologetic smirk nailed to his face. I catch the look. He's already scheming, figuring out how to keep her hooked enough to get off on the control.

But when her eyes catch mine, everything flips. Her face twists with disgust. I'm still the bitter taste stuck in her mouth that won't go away.

"Hey, Lydia," Nate says, his voice smooth as silk, lazy like he's about to wreck her whole fucking day. "You see where the new girl went?"

Her smile flickers, barely visible, but still enough. I catch that shift in her eyes—the quick flash of jealousy she tries to hide but can't. She covers the slip with fake, bored indifference, but I recognize the glare. I've seen the same thing every time Nate's attention drifts away. That bitter, shitty edge of desperation clawing its way out.

"Theo's looking for her," he says, the lie sliding off his tongue so smooth it might as well be the truth.

"Oh," she says, her voice rising sugary and bright. Her fake-ass smile snaps back into place like nothing happened. She's trying to convince herself she didn't stumble, didn't get knocked off balance by the thought that Nate's focus isn't on her. She leans in, pushing her chest out, tits begging for his attention.

I grit my teeth and move forward so she can't see me flinch from her cold cutting stare. But every step drags harder with all those fucking eyes behind me, Lydia's crew watching, pressing in, trying to strip me bare, tear me apart piece by piece.

"Yeah, she went into the music room, I think," Lydia's voice sounds behind me, her voice soaked in that fake sweet shit she thinks works on guys. All purr, no soul. "You wanna hang later?"

"Nah," Nate says, already walking away.

A moment later he's next to me, slipping into step the way he always does.

He's a dick to chicks.

Doesn't fake a thing, doesn't care.

Fucks around, forgets their names, and moves on. Yet still, they smile at him like he's some gift they didn't deserve.

We head for the music room, footsteps heavy in the quiet. I wonder if the new girl's into music. Not that it matters. Music's the only thing that doesn't fuck you over. Music doesn't lie or leave. The sound is the only thing that makes the noise in my head shut the hell up.

Nate's a natural on the drums. Doesn't even have to think. It's in his bones. The sticks move and the rhythm follows. Like breathing. Like he was born with a beat under his skin.

Wes and Rose gave me a bass for my sixteenth birthday. A brand-new black Fender. Shiny as hell. Too shiny for a kid like me, the kind who grew up sifting through pawn shop leftovers. They offered lessons, said they'd cover it, but I couldn't take more than I already had. A roof, food and safety. That was enough. So much more than I deserved.

So I taught myself. Spent nights in the garage, fingers torn up, skin split open from the strings. Played until the noise finally turned into music. Kept going until the pain dulled and the sound became something real.

I remember watching Nate and Scarlet go at it on the drums. Beat battles that sounded like war. Loud, relentless, like they were throwing punches with sound, trying to say shit only the other could understand. There was nothing soft about it—only fire, only fight. I wanted that, too. Something real that was mine.

So I claimed the sound, note by fucking note. And for a little while, when I'm alone with my guitar, I can almost believe I belong. That maybe I'm not as broken as they all think I am.

We reach the music room and I freeze. My heart is on a rampage, slamming into my ribs like it's trying to break free. I fucking hate the feeling. Hate how my chest locks up like I'm walking into a war no one else can see. Same old shit. That sense of never fitting, of being too much and not enough at the same time.

Nate doesn't even blink. He just pushes the door open, calm as ever. It's always easy for him.

"You coming or what?" he throws back.

I step inside, and, like always, the room shifts. It tilts straight toward Nate, pulled by that quiet, magnetic thing he carries without even trying.

We move to the back, and I let out a breath, my pulse still uneven. I force my eyes up.

And that's when I see her.

The new girl.

She's sitting, untouched by the noise, the chaos never reaching her. She's calm, unbothered. Her posture says she doesn't need to prove anything, proof she's been through worse and walked out the other side without breaking.

Her hair falls in waves down her back, long and dark, catching the light. Her face is sharp and soft in all the right places, a kind of beauty that grabs you by the throat and doesn't let go.

And fuck, it hits me right in the chest. My heart trips over itself and I hate that it does.

She's beautiful. The kind of beauty that screws with your head. The kind that makes you forget your own name for a second.

I stand frozen, barely breathing, pulse stuttering in my throat. My gaze lands on the guitar in her grip and something shifts.

She doesn't just hold it—she commands it. That guitar belongs to her in a way that makes the rest of us look like we're playing pretend. Her fingers settle on the strings with this quiet confidence, shoulders loose, posture unshaken, as if she could tear the roof off this place with one chord and still look bored doing it.

There's an awe, sure, but it's wrapped in something real and fucked up. I need to hear her play. Need to know if the sound she makes feels as dangerous as the storm she's already kicked up in my chest.

She's talking to Quinn Thomas—one of the few girls Nate's never managed to crack. And fuck, has he tried. Every smirk and smooth line. Every well-timed joke he usually pulls to get girls falling at his feet. He threw them all at her.

Quinn didn't bite.

She never does. Never even looks twice. Doesn't laugh, doesn't flirt, just stares him down with those unreadable eyes and that deadpan voice that slices through the bullshit. Like she's already decided she's not here for anyone's games. Especially not his.

I've always respected that. Not that I'd say it out loud. But while the rest fall over themselves to hand Nate whatever the hell he wants, Quinn holds her ground. She's solid. Real. The kind of girl who knows who the fuck she is and doesn't give a shit if anyone else does.

The new girl tilts her head, looks up at Nate, and her face doesn't move. No fluttering lashes. No nervous smile. Not a single fucking flicker that says she gives a shit who he is. She has a steady calm, watching him like she's running the numbers, working out if he's another loudmouth with pretty hair and nothing underneath.

Her gaze moves, locking onto me.

And fuck.

The world jerks sideways. Time warps. My lungs forget how to work. There's this weight in my chest, like someone jammed their fist straight through and started squeezing. I can't fucking breathe.

Her gaze pins me. Cold, steady, sharp as glass. Not judging—just seeing. Not my face alone, not the hoodie pulled low, but what's underneath. The shit I bury. The cracks I pretend aren't there. She doesn't look away. She sees me, as though she already knows what's hiding behind all the silence.

I fucking hate what's happening.

Hate how fast that panic claws its way up my throat and strips me bare. That stare—I've seen the same expression before. The second the truth creeps out from behind my eyes they always pull back. As though I'm less because I'm broken.

I want to drop my gaze. Disappear into the wall, the floor, anywhere but fucking here. But I don't. I stay.

Even though every instinct is screaming at me to vanish, I can't tear my eyes off her. She's all I can see, and for once, the noise in my head goes quiet.

It's just her.

She has a pull no one's ever had over me. Not once. After everything that happened, all the ways the past fucked me sideways, I've never craved closeness. Never wanted someone in my space, under my skin.

But her... Fuck, this isn't only the urge to touch her, though even that thought sparks through me like a live wire. What I feel goes deeper. Like my body's wired to her somehow and I can't figure out how the hell to shut the pull off.

Her lips twitch into a smile. It's small, fleeting. Maybe she doesn't mean to. But fucking hell it lands, right in my chest, and its cares the shit out of me.

But as quickly as it comes, she turns away. That smile disappears, gone like it never existed.

Her head drops. She zeroes in on the guitar, fingers wrapping around the neck with the grip that says she's done this a thousand times in the dark. Her thumb brushes the worn wood, slow and sure, and the moment shifts. Everything pulls tight.

Then she plays.

The first note lands and everything inside me stutters. It's not gentle. The next note follows, fluid and sharp, like a secret slipping from her mouth without permission.

She plays as though she was born for the music.

Fingers dancing over the strings with a deadly kind of grace, every chord pulled from somewhere buried deep. The sound isn't practiced. The rhythm isn't polished. What drives her is instinct—pure, wild instinct. Every move is precise but messy in the best way, all emotion and ache, like she's pouring pieces of herself into the sound and letting the music destroy her.

And fuck, she's good.

So fucking good the sight hurts to watch.

Her eyes are closed, brows pulled in, lost to the music. She doesn't even realize we're watching or she doesn't fucking care. The rest of the world could burn and she'd still be in that chair with the guitar, still spilling her soul into the strings like the sound is the only thing keeping her upright.

I can't breathe. What guts me isn't only her talent—it's everything I've never had the courage to say, everything I've never let myself experience, pouring out of her hands like the music was made for me. My chest hurts under the weight of the sound.

I've never wanted anything so fucking badly. Not only the girl. But the feeling. That goddamn freedom.

"Fuck me," Nate says beside me, voice low and rough, like the words ripped out before he could catch them.

I don't meet his eyes. I don't have to because I already know what I'll see. He'll have that same stupid expression stamped across his face too. He's eye-fucking her, same as me. This girl we understand nothing about. No name. No backstory. A presence that grabs you by the throat and refuses to let go.

She hasn't said a word and I already know we're both fucked. The kind of fucked you don't crawl back from.

Her fingers ease off the strings, dragging out the last note until the sound stretches thin, trembling in the air like the whole room's being held hostage. No one breathes. No one fucking dares.

A single clap breaks the silence—one slow hit of palm to palm from somewhere off to the side. It barely lands before another follows. More join in. Louder. Faster. The sound builds, rolling across the room, chasing away the stillness she left behind.

Chairs scrape, feet shift, bodies move toward her, as if pulled by something they don't understand. I stay still, shoulders locked, watching them circle in—like she's the flame and every one of them is too dumb to notice they're already burning.

Then I fucking see him. Jared Ross. That smug piece of shit with his too-white teeth and that lazy grin he flashes like a goddamn weapon. He's the worst kind of predator—the kind who hides behind charm and a letterman jacket.

He doesn't only screw girls over. He records every touch, every moan, every second they think belongs to them. Later he shares the footage with his boys, passes the clips around the locker room like some twisted highlight reel. He laughs about the whole thing, rates them, talks about those girls as though they're nothing but warm bodies and open legs.

Nate's already laid him out more than once for running his mouth about me, but the prick never learns. He still walks around like he's untouchable. My fists curl without thinking, heat crawling up my neck, jaw clenched so tight it aches. Every part of me is screaming to get between him and her. To show him exactly what happens when he thinks about dragging her name through the same filth he spreads like a virus.

I hate the way his eyes crawl over her, slow and greedy, already claiming her in that arrogant, twisted head of his. He steps closer, shoulders cocked, all that fake confidence rolling off him in waves. Entitled. Smirking. Acting as if the world owes him her attention, her space, her fucking soul.

His voice drops low, smooth and practiced, the kind of tone that's gotten too many girls to fall for his lies. It's a sound meant to coil around her, to trap, to pull.

She looks up, and I fucking catch it. That fake smile stretched too tight, the twitch in her shoulder, the way she shifts back in her seat enough to pull away from him without drawing attention. But I know what that means. She senses the sick, crawling weight of him getting too close.

My whole body tenses as the blood roars through my ears. Fists curling, twitching, burning to move. I want to fucking hurt him. To destroy that smug face before he lays one filthy word on her.

But I don't get the chance.

Quinn Thomas is already reacting.

She stands, shoulders squared, eyes locked, pure fucking fire in her veins. Quinn storms across the room like a damn wrecking ball, steps between them, and slams her hands into Jared's chest so hard he stumbles back with a grunt, all that fake charm wiped right off his face.

"Get the fuck away from her, asshole."

Her voice cuts clean, with no room for doubt, no fear in the way she throws her words. The sound slices through the noise, silencing the room. She spits each line like venom, every syllable loaded.

She doesn't need anyone's help. She's handling this asshole just fine.

Quinn holds her chin high, shoulders squared, eyes locked on Jared as though daring him to come closer. There's this eerie calm rolling off her, the kind that makes your skin crawl—the moment before a storm cracks the sky wide open.

Jared shifts, trying to play it cool, tossing out that loud, cocky laugh that sounds too sharp, too fake.

He knows everyone's eyes are on him.

"Damn, girl," he says, dragging his gaze over Quinn, voice all swagger and poison. "Just 'cause I won't give you my dick doesn't mean you gotta go full psycho. Don't get all twisted when a guy won't chase a tease."

He grins like he's landed a punch, soaking in the attention.

Quinn doesn't flinch. She stares him down like he's gum on her fucking shoe. Her voice is calm, but sharp enough to draw blood.

"Aww, still pissed I wouldn't blow you in the janitor's closet freshman year?" She steps closer, smirking now, like she's enjoying twisting the knife. "Here's the thing, Jared. I don't fuck boys who jerk off to their own highlight reel."

I fucking smirk. Quinn Thomas… a goddamn storm packed into five feet of fury. All fire and razor-wire, mouthy and mean, and tougher than every dick-swinging asshole in this school combined. Step into her space and you don't walk away clean. You crawl.

Jared stumbles, ego limping, face twitching as he tries to recover. He opens his mouth and I already know it's about to be some weak-ass attempt to flip the script.

"I wasn't talking to you, you frigid bitch," he snaps, voice loud and bitter, throwing it out for the crowd. "I'm interested in your friend."

The new girl stands up, slow, as if she's not in a rush for anyone. Jared's eyes snap to her, zeroing in like she's prey.

She turns to Quinn, voice casual, but her grin is lethal. "So this is the guy? The one with the walking ego and the limp dick?"

A tiny laugh slips out before I can stop myself. The room holds its breath, waiting to see whether he'll swing or crumble. But fuck, the whole thing is almost art—watching them strip him down with nothing but words. No fists. Only sharp fucking wit and a glare that could slice through steel.

Jared's face cracks. That cocky grin slips, ego shattering right in front of us. I don't even try to hide the satisfaction curling in my chest.

Quinn and the new girl laugh. It's not sweet its fucking savage. A laugh that slices straight through pride and leaves his ego bleeding on the floor.

The new girl turns back to Jared, not even trying to soften the blow. "Yeah, so no, I'm not interested."

Jared's face twists. That cocky mask slips, all desperate eyes and bruised ego trying to find solid ground.

"Fuck you," he snaps, voice cracking under the weight of every eye on him.

Quinn steps up. "Please. You couldn't get a girl wet in a fucking thunderstorm."

The new girl smiles, all teeth and venom. "Poor thing's probably confused, his dick must be still buffering."

The room fucking explodes. Laughter, gasps, chairs scraping. Jared's done. Burnt to ash before he even knew he was on fire.

I flick my gaze to Nate. He's watching too, a smirk dragging slowly across his face. He's enjoying this fucking shitstorm as well, drinking in every second of it.

Nate turns his head, his stare catching mine and for the first time, I can't read him. That quiet thread that's always tethered us is gone—fraying, splitting.

She's already between us and we don't even know her fucking name.

That thought alone guts me. Because if this goes the way I think it will, if we both keep slipping deeper, I'm not just gonna lose the girl. I'll lose him too.

The one constant I've always had. The only person who's never walked the fuck away.

But if that happens, I don't know if I can come back from that.

Chapter 5

Nate

Her name's still a mystery, but she's already under my skin. She played that guitar with a focus I've never seen. Not only skill, but control. Every note carried weight. She didn't care who was watching, yet somehow, she commanded that entire fucking room. Including me.

Now I'm stuck on her. She's in my head, turning the volume up on things I rarely let in. I keep replaying the way her fingers moved, the way the sound slammed straight into my chest. This pull isn't the usual kind. It's something I don't have any words for.

Maybe that's what unsettles me the most.

I need to find out who the hell she is.

Quinn Thomas is the only one who might give me the right answers, but getting anything out of her is a fucking challenge. She's propped against the lockers, phone in hand, scrolling like the world is on mute. There's chaos everywhere and she's tuned it all out without blinking.

She knows exactly what kind of attention she attracts. How many guys would crawl through glass just to get a glance. But Quinn doesn't give a shit. She doesn't chase approval. She doesn't need anyone to like her, especially not me. That's what makes her dangerous. She plays her own game...always has.

I step up to her and Quinn doesn't even pretend to care. She lifts her eyes only enough to skim over me, that flat, bored stare already cutting. The one that says I'm old news and barely worth her time. Normally, she'd shut things down fast by walking off or telling me to fuck off. She never plays along. Never bites. But this time I don't lead with a cocky smirk or some half-sleazy line.

"The new girl. Who is she?"

Quinn arches a brow, dragging it out like she's already decided this is her entertainment for the day.

"Why?"

I clench my jaw. Swallow the urge. Keep cool. What I want is answers.

She holds my stare a beat too long, those sharp green eyes digging in like she's peeling me open, deciding whether I'm worth the answer or should be made to fucking grovel for the truth. After that comes the smirk that always shows up when she's got the upper hand.

"Bianca." She drops the name casually.

I nod once. "Okay."

After that, I turn away.

"What, no sleazy pickup line today? No charming little ego boost for yourself?" Quinn calls after me, her voice dripping with mockery.

I keep walking, smirking. "Not in the mood to be rejected."

She laughs. "You disappoint me, Reynolds."

As I walk away, I remind myself to keep my guard up. The problem isn't that Bianca is already in my head, stirring things I rarely let through. I need to be considerate of Theo.

For the first time, Theo actually gives a shit about a girl. That never happens. He doesn't do that, or reach out to anyone. Doesn't do crushes or chase. He's the opposite of me. He holds himself back from everything, afraid that if he lets anyone in, they'll see the fucked-up mess he's spent years trying to hide.

The only time I've seen him let someone touch him was the night I talked Lydia into dropping to her knees. I thought he'd want that.

But the second she pulled his cock out I noticed the shift. His whole body locked up. Not in a good way. Not the tension that comes from being turned on. This was something fucking else.

His jaw clenched. Eyes shut tight. His breathing turned ragged.

When her lips wrapped around him, the whole thing didn't look like pleasure. More like he was fighting to survive the moment... his mind had already slipped somewhere dark.

And fuck, I knew exactly where he went.

I told her to stop because whatever the hell was going on in his head, the moment wasn't about pleasure. It was pain. And I should've fucking known better.

That's why this Bianca chick's fucking different. There's something about her that's got him chasing someone for once, instead of standing in the shadows while the world moves on.

I've always thought Quinn was beautiful. Anyone with eyes would. But she's never given me the time of day and I got used to that. Brushed it off. Moved on.

But this new girl? Bianca? She's something else entirely. It's not only that I want to fuck her. It's deeper than that, messier. What gets me is the way she exists. She doesn't give a shit if anyone notices her, but you can't tear your eyes away.

She's the kind of beautiful that fucks with your head. Makes every other girl blur out, every name vanish, every cheap fuck seem even more meaningless than before.

I stood frozen like a fucking idiot, staring at her. Couldn't breathe, couldn't think. All I caught was her and the way she held that guitar, the way her fingers moved as though they carried every intention of the damage they were about to do.

She started to play and the sound wasn't only music. It was a fucking takeover.

I followed her into that room only because of Theo. I caught the expression in his eyes when he spotted her—the kind that strips a guy down to his bones. She had him. Completely.

So yeah, I went after her. Told myself it was nothing more than curiosity. Only an attempt to figure out what the fuck had him hooked.

I head toward the back of the school where Theo always sits behind the gardener's shed smoking and hiding from the world. Before I can reach the spot, three girls cut me off. Two of them I've fucked before. Easy lays with nothing but lip gloss and fake moans. Serena's front and center, always the boldest. Her shirt's unbuttoned enough to give a peek at what she thinks will get her what she wants.

"Hey, Nate," she purrs, voice dripping in that breathy way she uses when she's trying to score another round. She licks her lips, eyes dropping to my belt, and I can already tell exactly what she's offering. I should be all over the offer—used to be. Hell, I've had my dick in her mouth behind the gym more times than I can count.

I open my mouth ready to toss out one of my usual lines, something filthy and easy, but the words die in my throat.

Serena steps in closer, resting her hand on my chest. "What, you forget how to speak?"

I peel her hand off me slowly. "Nah. Saving my breath for someone who doesn't moan on autopilot."

She reels back a little, blinking. "Are you fucking serious right now?"

I lean in, voice low. "Dead fucking serious. Go practice your gag reflex on someone who still gives a shit."

The two girls behind her shift uncomfortably. Serena's mouth opens like she wants to argue, but I'm already done. I brush past her, not bothering to glance back.

That's when I catch sight of them.

Across the quad, Quinn and Bianca head toward one of the bench seats. Quinn's got her usual don't-fuck-with-me stride, sunglasses shoved on her head. Bianca moves as if she's got nothing to prove, only that calm confidence.

She doesn't realize the effect she has, the way she shifts the air when she walks.

Yeah, I'm already fucked. Already pulled in.

Theo's voice from last night won't shut the hell up in my head.

It was late. The two of us in our room, the lights were off except for the glow from the hallway light spilling in.

He was sitting on the edge of his bed bouncing that damn rubber ball off the wall again and again. That sound cutting through the silence. His fallback habit when shit gets too real. When talking means opening wounds.

Scarlett had finally left us alone for the night and I couldn't stop myself. I brought her up, the girl with the guitar.

The second the words left my mouth I caught the change. The shift. Theo's whole body stiffened. His fingers clamped around the ball, held on too long before launching the thing at the wall again. No smart-ass comments. No eye roll. Only silence. Heavy as hell.

I know him. I understand that silence speaks louder than anything he ever says. The way his jaw locked, the way his eyes flicked to mine for half a second. He was already bracing himself, already on edge. And that told me everything. Not to fucking cross that line with her.

I pull out my phone and fire off a quick text to Theo.

Nate: I'm on the rise near the statue in the quad. Meet me here.

I shove my phone back into my pocket because Theo won't reply. He never fucking does.

Mom and Dad keep telling him to use the damn phone they bought him, but saying that is like yelling into a void. He won't. Flat-out refuses. One night, when I called him out, he muttered something about not wanting to be a burden. Said he didn't want to rack up their bill. As if they'd ever give a shit about that. Truth is, he still thinks he's temporary. Still waiting for someone to decide he's too much to deal with and send him packing.

They'd never kick him out. Not in a million years. I only wish he could fucking realize that. Wish he believed how much they love him. But he's scarred deep, and no matter what we say, it's like the damage is permanent. Always waiting for the rug to get yanked out, bracing for goodbye.

I take a few steps closer, hands buried deep in my pockets, keeping enough space. Bianca and Quinn are locked in their own little bubble, talking low and fast like the rest of the world doesn't exist. I hang back, eyes shifting between them and the path I'm certain Theo's about to walk.

Bianca laughs.

My head snaps back, catching her with her head tipped, lips parting, eyes lit up with something wild and unfiltered. For a second, I can't look away.

I don't understand or fucking want to. But the pull still crawls through me. That slow-burn chaos of wanting something I'm certain I shouldn't touch.

At that moment I notice movement past the statue. Theo. Hood dragged so low the shadow cuts across half his face. His shoulders are caved in, hands shoved deep into his pockets as though he's holding himself together by force. He looks half his size, as though, if he makes himself small enough, he can stay the fuck off everyone's radar. Make himself invisible. But I catch the truth for what's there. He's trying to slip through the world without anyone noticing he was ever fucking here.

When he reaches me, he finally looks up. I nod toward Bianca and Quinn.

He turns. Lifts his head.

In that instant, I catch the shift.

The way his spine straightens. The slow drag of his hand out of his pocket. He pushes the hood back only enough to catch her. His eyes lock on Bianca and I watch it happen, the tension on his face shifting, the twitch at the corner of his mouth softening.

For one second, he lets himself want.

"She's beautiful," he mutters.

I don't even realize I'm staring at him until his gaze flicks to mine.

"You wanna go over?" I ask.

Theo doesn't answer right away. His eyes stay locked on Bianca, and I catch the war playing out behind them. He wants to. But he's fighting the urge...fighting her, fighting whatever the hell's coming apart inside him.

"Not if you're gonna open your mouth and ruin it with one of your sleazy pickup lines," he mutters, cutting me a sideways glare.

"Hey, they work."

Theo rolls his eyes, but I catch that flicker of amusement, the reluctant twitch of his lips he tries to bury. "Yeah, and hand jobs work too. Doesn't mean they're satisfying."

"Got me a few dirty favors." I add, my smirk widening, knowing full well that I've got him. Every dirty detail, I've told him all of them. Every meaningless fuck. He knows.

He exhales through his nose, shaking his head. "Yeah when girls suck your dick just to shut you the fuck up it doesn't count."

I laugh out loud. Can't help myself. That's the thing about Theo; he barely says shit, but when he does, the words are fucking gold. Dry, filthy, and sharp enough to cut through whatever heaviness is hanging in the air.

I clap a hand on his shoulder. "You're such a dick, you know that?"

He grins up at me, one of those rare smiles. The kind only Mom or Scarlet usually pull from him.

"Come on," I say, stepping away, heading for the table where Bianca and Quinn are still deep in conversation.

Theo follows and I fall in beside him, his shoulders still curled inward like he's trying to disappear into himself. I keep my eyes on Bianca, trying to figure out what the fuck about her is throwing me off.

Quinn spots us first. Her sharp, knowing gaze snaps to mine, eyes narrowing like she's already bracing for impact. She's waiting for my smirk, the cocky line, the lazy drawl I always throw her way, designed to get under her skin long enough to test whether I'll push my luck with her.

But today, she's not the one I'm focused on. Today, it's Bianca.

Right as we reach the table, Theo's steps drag, only enough to hover on the edge of hesitation. He stops short of awkward, but I catch the shift. The way his body stiffens. The way his fingers clamp the hem of his hoodie like that fabric's the last anchor holding him steady.

Quinn's gaze shifts to him and something in her expression softens.

"Hey, Theo," she says, her voice smooth and casual, like she didn't catch him glitch.

I watch him fidget and the truth sinks in—he's way out of his comfort zone. This isn't small talk for him. This is a fucking war. Every second he stands here, he's battling himself. Wrestling with the instinct to turn around and walk the fuck away before anyone sees too much.

Suddenly Bianca looks up.

First at him.

After that, at me... and fuck.

Her dark brown eyes meet mine and the hit lands as hard as yesterday in that room. That quiet, unreadable expression tells me she already sees through every part of me and couldn't give a fuck whether or not I approve.

I don't even realize I've stopped breathing until Quinn speaks.

"Bianca, this is Theo."

Theo hesitates. Only a beat. After that, he does something I've never seen him do. He drags his hand out of his pocket and holds it out to her.

"Hey, Bianca," he says. His voice is steady, but I can hear the strain. That tight edge underneath. The way speaking costs him something simply to stand there. "Great guitar playing yesterday."

She smiles. Not some forced, polite bullshit. Not the kind you toss out to be nice. The smile is real. Warm.

"Do you play?" Bianca asks, voice effortless. Her eyes stay on Theo, waiting for him to answer.

But he doesn't get the chance.

"Theo taught himself bass," Quinn says, cutting in before he can open his mouth.

Her comment throws me. How the fuck does she know that? I didn't think anyone besides our family did.

Bianca smiles. "We'll have to jam together sometime."

Theo nods. "Yeah, I'd like that."

Quinn looks at me. "And this is Nate."

Her tone is flat, like she's bored just saying my name. And fuck, it shouldn't bother me, but it does. I glance at her, catching the flicker in her eyes she tries to hide. She knows exactly what she's doing.

"That's it?" I say, my voice low. "No smart-ass comment? No warning label?"

She shrugs, lips twitching like she's fighting back a grin. "Didn't think you needed one. You usually do a good enough job ruining your own reputation."

I force a grin and reach for Bianca's hand.

The second we touch, fuck, it feels like something short-circuits inside me. Static races up my arm, heat pulsing through my chest, burning into places I never realized existed. This isn't only chemistry. It's heat behind my ribs. Something waking up that's been buried too damn long. A hit straight to the system.

Quinn smirks, all teeth and knowing eyes, like she finally caught the first crack in my armor. "I was warning Bianca who to stay the fuck away from."

I shoot her a slow grin. "Let me guess. I'm top of the list?"

She tilts her head, lips twitching.

"Not yet," she says, voice laced with amusement. "Still deciding."

"Good to know," I murmur, dropping into the seat beside Theo.

Bianca tilts her head, curiosity flickering in her eyes. "Are you two friends or brothers?"

I open my mouth to answer, but Theo beats me to it.

"Brothers," he says. "Not by blood, but in every other way that matters."

My eyes shift to him. He never says stuff like that.

Bianca watches him and a flicker runs through her eyes. Not pity, but something real.

"Teaching yourself bass is pretty impressive," she says.

Theo shrugs, dragging a hand over the back of his neck. "Most of the time, it sounds like shit."

"I'm sure it doesn't," she replies, and that's when it happens.

He laughs.

And I haven't heard that sound in a long fucking time. Not since the day I fell out of a tree and broke a bone in my foot, when he stood over me, laughing his ass off while I cursed him out. Or when Scarlet wipes the floor with me in our drum battles and he laughs like he's bursting with pride.

But this? This isn't the same laugh.

The sound comes softer.

Almost like the laugh slipped past his guard. And the way Theo's staring at her...fuck. This isn't only about the laugh being different. He is the one who's changed.

I glance at Quinn, catching the way she's watching Theo, her lips curving slightly. It's the look that says she sees him too.

But then her eyes flick to me and whatever softness was there disappears in an instant.

The smile's gone. Her expression hardens. That cold, steady stare she saves for me locks into place, and I meet it without flinching.

We hold the stare, tension stretched tight like a wire ready to snap. Something lingers in the space between us, and neither of us calls it out, but we both fucking feel the pull. It shows in the way she challenges me without speaking. In the way I push back without trying. Some twisted line we keep toeing but never cross.

Bianca's voice cuts through the silence, dragging my attention back.

"I don't know too many people here, so it'll be good to jam with someone," she says, her gaze still fixed on Theo.

Her gaze shifts to me.

"Do you play, Nate?"

I barely get a breath in before Quinn answers.

"Yes to both those questions," she says, voice smooth, almost sweet, but laced with something sharper underneath. "He plays the drums...and he plays the field."

And there it is. That bite. That smirk buried in her tone like she's practically daring me to rise to the challenge. Daring me to deny it.

"I don't have anything going on most afternoons so I'm free anytime you want to jam," Bianca says.

"We can do this afternoon if you want?" Theo replies, eagerness creeping into his voice. He rarely sounds like that. Open. Hopeful.

"Yeah, that sounds great. Where do you live, Theo?"

His eyes drop to the table. Fingers twitch at the hem of his hoodie like they always do when something unsettles him.

I am certain of what's running through his head. He doesn't want her to judge him or catch the parts of his life he's spent years trying to outrun.

"Theo lives at Nate's place," Quinn answers, as if sensing the shift in him too.

I can't help wondering how much Quinn really knows about Theo's life. What they really talked about at those parties, when I'd catch them tucked in some dark corner while I was off drinking and chasing the next girl to fuck.

He told her he taught himself bass. That's not nothing. That's a crack. What else did he tell her? Did he talk about the life he left behind? The shit he never says out loud to anyone.

Does she know about the nights he can't sleep, when the memories get too loud and too heavy, and he slips into my bed without a word? Just needing to be close to someone. To feel like he's not completely alone.

"Okay," Bianca says, turning her attention back to Theo. "So that'll be bass and drums. Do either of you sing?"

Theo lifts his head and for the first time since this conversation started, the tension bleeds from his shoulders. Relief softens his face, glad she didn't push and dig into shit he doesn't want to talk about.

"Nah," he says. "We both sound like shit. Honestly, I think the neighbor's dog has better range than us. Hits a solid high note every time the mailman shows up."

Bianca bursts out laughing, her head tipping back as she gasps for air between the cracks of it. Tears gather at the corners of her eyes, and she clutches her stomach like she's genuinely in pain from laughing too hard.

"Fuck, Theo," she says, still wiping her eyes. "You just made my whole shitty day better. Seriously, I needed that."

Quinn's laughing too.

Smiling, I turn to look at Theo and his whole face shifts. It's like her laughter cracked something open in him. He's not carved in on himself anymore, not bracing for the next thing to go wrong. He's here. In it. Holding on to the fact that he's the reason she just laughed.

Fuck, maybe it's nothing. But the way he's looking at her...it sure as shit doesn't feel like nothing.

Chapter 6

Theo

Fucking hell, my leg won't stop bouncing, this constant twitch giving away everything I'm trying to hide.

Nothing about this feels okay, no matter how many times I lie to myself and say it's just another jam session.

Truth is, my body's calling bullshit before I even finish the thought.

Clammy hands smear against my jeans, useless attempts to wipe away the nerves. Knots twist tighter in my gut, each one pulling me closer to losing it completely. Time keeps dragging, the clock ticking so fucking loud it might as well be screaming. Every second stretches, taunting me, dragging me deeper into this anxious pit.

Bianca's not even here yet and already I'm coming apart at the seams.

There's this weight pressing down on my chest refusing to let up.

All I can do is fucking wait. Wait for her to walk in, for this ache to ease. But I know it won't. And maybe the worst part is, I don't think it ever will.

It's not that I haven't played in front of people before.

Nate's family doesn't count. I've played in their living room more times than I can remember, running through the same setlist, headphones on, trying to pretend the world doesn't exist.

Those moments were different.

They were safe. Nothing about it left me exposed. Pressure never crawled under my skin. Judgment didn't hang in the air, waiting for me to fuck up.

Back then, if I missed a note or slipped on a chord, it didn't matter. There was no shame in getting it wrong. Nobody stood there measuring me against someone who plays as if she was born with a guitar in her hands and gasoline in her veins.

That's what Bianca brings. Fire. Chaos. Brilliance. She doesn't simply play. She burns the whole fucking room down while I sit here with my training wheels on, hoping not to fall flat on my face.

And now I'm supposed to sit across from her, bass in hand, and pretend I belong in the same fucking room.

Every part of me wants to bolt, disappear before she even plugs in her guitar.

Before I can spiral any further, Scarlet's voice crashes through the house like a goddamn foghorn.

"She's here?" She yells loud enough to wake the whole fucking neighborhood.

Nate groans, dragging a hand down his face.

"Scar, for fuck sake." He shakes his head, muttering under his breath, "I swear, that girl's gonna be the death of me."

I smirk. "She's just getting you back for that shit you pulled with Ben today."

Nate rolls his eyes, but he knows I'm right.

We've both seen it—the way guys at school have started watching Scarlet. Like she's a prize they can win, something to claim and brag about.

And Nate?

He made damn sure Ben understood real fucking quick that Scarlet isn't some chick he can add to his rotation.

Cornered him behind the gym, looked him dead in the eye, and told him if he so much as glanced her way again, he'd be drinking through a straw. And if he ever laid a hand on her, losing his spot on the football team would be the least of his problems.

And knowing Nate... He fucking means every word.

Before he can say anything else, the doorbell rings.

My stomach twists hard. Fuck. Alright, this is happening.

Scarlet bolts past, already halfway to the door before Nate even opens his mouth.

Nate shouts after her, but it's pointless.

She throws the door open with a flair that deserves a spotlight and a fog machine.

"Welcome to Casa de Embarrassment, where my brothers will be your personal idiots for the evening," she declares, waving her arm like she's presenting a game show prize nobody asked for.

Bianca laughs, full-on belly laughs, her head shaking as if she's already regretting her life choices.

"Good to know," she says, eyes narrowing playfully as she turns to Scarlet. "You're Scarlet, right?"

With arms crossed and a dramatic tilt of her head, Scarlet fires back. "That depends. Are you here for the music or to witness the circus these two call a personality?"

Bianca smirks, her gaze flicking toward Nate and me. "Mostly here for the second-hand embarrassment. The music's a bonus."

Scarlet grins. "Excellent. You'll be overwhelmed in minutes."

Bianca arches a brow and steps inside with a smirk. "Perfect, I brought snacks and zero expectations."

Scarlet lets out a sharp laugh, tossing her hair over her shoulder. "Damn, I like you. What the hell are you doing wasting your time on these two idiots?"

Bianca grins, shifting her guitar case and eyeing us both like we're about to juggle or burst into song. "Still running tests to determine the exact cause of my poor judgment."

"Wow. Brutal. Right in the ego." Nate says, hand to his chest, stumbling back like he's been personally victimized.

"Please. You'd need a soul for that to sting." Scarlet snorts, arms folded, sarcasm loaded.

Nate flicks her a glance, lips twitching. "Says the girl who held a funeral for her broken drumsticks."

"Grief is a valid emotion. You wouldn't get it, robot boy." Scarlet shrugs.

Bianca lifts a brow, clearly entertained. "You play?"

"Drums. Better than my brother, too." Scarlet smirks.

"For fuck sake, Scar," Nate says. "Do you ever shut up?"

"Only when I'm asleep. And even then, I snore insults." She smirks at Nate before turning to Bianca with a mock flourish. "Well, shall we?"

Nate cuts in, hand dragging down his face. "Oh no. Absolutely fucking not."

"What? You scared I'll outplay or out-charm you? Which one is it?"

"No, Scar, I'm scared you'll sit there and talk shit the entire time."

"And I fail to see the problem." Scarlet raises a brow.

Bianca turns to me, smirking. "Are they always like this?"

"You should see them on a road trip. I considered throwing myself from the van," I say.

Scarlet stares at Nate, waiting for him to cave and get her way like she always does, most of the time. One look, one smartass comment, and he usually folds. Today, though, he doesn't flinch. Still as stone, he stands there, stubborn as ever.

Scarlet huffs, throwing her hands up.

"See what I have to deal with? Fine. Enjoy being boring." Spinning on her heel, she storms down the hall, but not before tossing a parting shot over her shoulder. "Try not to suck too much, boys."

Nate groans shaking his head.

"Every fucking day, I have to put up with this," he mutters.

Scarlet disappears down the hall and the quiet hits harder than it should.

Something about the way the room shifts makes my skin crawl. My breath sticks in my throat. My pulse slams through me, each beat louder than the last. It's only the three of us now, but it's like every spotlight in the world is aimed at me.

Fuck, I wish Scarlet had stayed.

I shove my hands into my hoodie pocket, like that's gonna hide not knowing what the fuck to do with them. I shift my weight, trying to look normal, but fail miserably.

They're both staring and suddenly I'm flayed open.

Bianca steps up, close enough that I catch it. Vanilla, the scent that doesn't ask permission before it fucks with your head. It lingers. Clings. Makes it harder to think straight.

She glances between us, all calm and collected, like I'm not standing here trying to remember how to breathe.

"So," she says, like this is no big deal, "where are we setting up?"

I wish I had a cool answer. Instead, my brain's static and my mouth's wired shut.

"This way," Nate says, already moving down the hall before I can get my shit together.

I follow, pulse pounding so loud it almost drowns out Bianca's footsteps.

Nate pushes open the door to our room and steps back, nodding for her to go in first.

I hang back, still trying to get my heartbeat under control.

Bianca steps in, eyes scanning the room.

Two beds. Dirty clothes. Instruments scattered across the floor, with no real order to any of it. Amps stacked in the corner, cables tangled in a way that says no one's ever bothered to sort them.

She says nothing at first.

Instead, she tilts her head, taking it all in, absorbing every detail without a word.

Nate brushes past me, unfazed, treating this as if it's another regular jam session.

I'm still rooted to the spot, questioning every fucking decision that landed me in this moment.

He drops onto his bed with a lazy grin and kicks a stray shirt onto the floor. "Welcome to the mess."

Bianca doesn't even blink. "I've seen worse."

She heads straight for my bed, drops her guitar case down without hesitation, moving with the ease that says she owns the space even if she's never stepped foot in it before.

Pressure builds low in my ribs, like something's pressing from the inside out. I flex my fingers at my side, but the nerves won't shake loose.

She pops the latches on the case. That's when it appears—her guitar. Built to stand out. Nothing soft or subtle about it. It demands attention the second it shows up. So does she.

She lifts it with one hand, swings the strap over her shoulder like it's second nature. No thought. No effort. Every move she makes is clean, controlled, sure.

Meanwhile, I'm standing here, wired too tight, wondering what the fuck I'm even doing in the same room.

Whatever this is, whatever thing she has, it's not something you learn. It's something you're born with. And I wasn't.

I shift on my feet, eyes landing on my bass propped against the wall, the same one I've played a hundred times before. Still, I don't move. The idea of picking it up now turns my spine to jelly.

Playing in front of her isn't simply pressure; it's paralysis.

She makes it seem so effortless, so instinctive, and I can already sense the distance between us widening with every second.

I walk to the corner, grab an amp, and carry it over to her. The motion gives my hands something to do, gives me a moment to hide the fact that I'm falling apart in slow motion.

She plucks a few strings and my confidence caves in on itself. This isn't just stage fright. It's the brutal awareness that I don't belong here.

For years, I've convinced myself I could do this, that I belonged in this world. That music wasn't something I clung to, but something that lived in me too. But now, with her standing across from me, that lie unravels.

She's about to hear me play, and nothing in me seems ready. I'm seconds away from every flaw laid bare, every ounce of fake confidence stripped down to what I really am — someone who's been bluffing his way through all of it. One wrong note and the whole thing will fall apart. Every hesitation, every rushed chord, every slip of my fingers will give me away. She'll hear it all. She'll see I don't belong in her world and exactly how much of a goddamn joke I really am.

I swallow hard, jaw tight, and grab the amp cable, shoving it toward her before I can think too much about it.

She takes it without hesitation, fingers brushing mine for half a second before she plugs it into her guitar.

The amp hums to life.

Nate pushes up from the bed and crosses the room, stepping behind his drum kit near the window.

He doesn't sit. Doesn't even glance at his sticks. Simply stands there, eyes locked on me.

He knows something's off. Known me long enough to recognize when something shifts. There's no hiding it from him, not when he can read me better than I read myself. This isn't nerves, and he can see that. He knows I'm completely fucked up over this.

"So what songs do you play?" Nate asks.

She shrugs, adjusting her guitar strap with the same calm confidence that never seems to crack. "Anything you want to play, shout it out and I'll see if I know it."

Nate nods, casual as ever, but his eyes flick to me for half a second before turning back to her. "Theo and I have been working on Seven Nation Army by The White Stripes. Are you familiar with it?"

For the first time since she walked in, something eases. Relief creeps in. Nate fucking knew I needed this. Something solid that doesn't make my stomach churn.

I know that song better than I know my own goddamn name. We've run it so many times I could play it in my fucking sleep.

All I hope now is that she knows it.

I turn my attention to Bianca.

She meets my eyes and then fucking smiles.

"Yeah," she says, fingers flexing over the strings like she's already halfway inside the song. "It's one of my favorites."

And just like that, something inside me finally fucking breathes.

Nate grabs his drumsticks and drops into his seat, spinning one in his fingers like he's already hearing a crowd scream his name. Cocky fuck. Could probably fall into a trash can and still stick the landing with a wink and a drum solo.

I head for my bass, trying to act like my heart isn't currently stage-diving without a safety net.

My hands are sweaty as I slip the strap over my neck. It settles across my shoulder and I take a step back. Not towards Bianca, but just out of range of whatever spell she's fucking casting with those fingers.

Nate's smirk is already locked and loaded.

"You gonna plug it in, genius?" he asks, eyebrow raised.

I glance down at the bass, still unplugged. "Nah. Figured I'd go acoustic today."

He chuckles, tapping a stick against his thigh. "Bold move."

"Wait 'til you see the interpretive footwork I've planned. Shit's gonna change lives."

Nate shakes his head, grinning. "Just plug it in, rockstar."

Bianca laughs, and straight away Nate and I both snap our heads toward her. Fuck. She's smiling at me.

"You've got good timing, Theo," she says, tucking a loose strand of hair behind her ear. "Sharp mouth too. I like that."

My brain short-circuits for a second. I cover it with a shrug, casually gripping my bass like it's the only thing holding me together.

"Careful," I say, trying not to sound like I've just forgotten how to function. "You compliment me again and I might start thinking I'm charming."

"Too late," she grins.

And just like that, I'm totally fucked.

"Alright. Enough talk," Nate says. "Let's play. Or do I need to file paperwork to make this a stand-up gig?"

I snap my head toward him, heat crawling up my neck. "Fuck off."

Bianca grins. "Don't be salty, Nate. Not everyone can pull off being hot and hilarious at the same time."

Nate laughs under his breath, shaking his head.

My mouth's shut tight, but my ego's doing backflips. Mostly because hot and hilarious completely short-circuited my entire system.

I come back to reality when Nate taps his sticks together. One, two, three, four.

I dive in, fingers locking down on the strings, sending that first low thrum out into the room. It's tight. Clean. The rhythm that doesn't ask for permission. It just takes over. My fingers dig in, pulling deeper with each note, my foot tapping along to Nate's rhythm. The air shifts. The walls hum. My bones fucking vibrate.

But the whole time, I feel her.

Bianca.

A few feet away. Fender slung low. Watching with that calm, unreadable expression that somehow still manages to set every nerve in my body on fire.

Then she joins in. Not stepping into the song but setting fire to it.

Fuck me, the second her fingers hit the strings, everything changes.

The rhythm I thought I had under control slips straight through my fingers. What was tight becomes electric. What was solid turns volatile. The sound sharpens, digs in, like it's hungry now and chasing something.

She flips the balance. Rewrites the rules mid-song. Takes control as if the music were hers all along and we've just been keeping it warm.

I feel the shift crawl across the floor, climb up my legs, and settle in my chest. Every beat bends toward her, pulled in until the room forgets we were ever here first.

I glance up, and she's already looking at me, lips curled into a smirk like she knows exactly what she just did.

She glances over at Nate, a small smile tugging at her mouth, and I see it. The way his whole face shifts.

That usual cool, untouchable expression is gone. He's as fucking mesmerized as I am. And the second that realization hits, it lands harder than the kick of Nate's own drum.

Because Nate doesn't look at chicks like that. He fucks them. That's it. No promises. No feelings or giving a shit past the unzip.

But right now, there's something different on his face.

That's a fucking problem. Because if he's falling too, I'm not simply screwed, I'm fucked.

Nate can have any chick he wants. He always has. I am nothing compared to him. I'm not the one people notice or the one girls smile at. I know I don't stand a fucking chance.

Movement near the door yanks my focus. I look up, pulse still throwing punches in my throat, and there they are.

Quinn's got her camera up, shutter going off like gunfire, catching it all before it disappears into the ether. Scarlet's beside her, all teeth and chaos, wearing that smug little grin like she knew this moment was coming and we're just lucky enough to live in it.

They're watching us. Quinn's freezing it. This exact second where the world felt right for once. Proof we didn't dream it. That this high wasn't just in our heads. That we existed right here, in this loud mess of sound.

The last note hits the walls, clings for a breath like it doesn't want to leave, then slips into silence.

For a second, nobody moves. Nobody speaks.

Then I hear it.

The clapping. Just two pairs of hands cutting through the quiet.

Bianca's head snaps toward the sound, eyebrows lifting like she forgot the world existed outside this room. Nate looks too, and I see it hit him. That flicker across his face when he realizes we weren't only playing for ourselves.

He was too wrapped up in Bianca's orbit, too busy eye fucking her to notice we had an audience.

"That was so fucking good," Quinn says, stepping fully into the room, camera hanging around her neck.

Scarlet follows, all sharp edges and raised brows. She levels Nate with a cool, pointed stare, the kind that carries enough heat to tell him to back off.

But Nate doesn't bite. He's still watching Bianca like she just hung the fucking moon.

CHAPTER 7

Nate

Fuck, four weeks have passed since that first jam session in my room, and she's been in my head ever since.

We've played almost every day, and still I haven't thrown a single pick-up line her way. Which is insane, considering she's got a face I can't stop staring at and a body that turns my brain to static. That smile hits me square in the fucking chest every time. And when Bianca's got that guitar slung over her shoulder, all attitude and rhythm, the game's already lost. Still, I play it cool. Pretend it's only music. But the truth is, my jerk-off sessions in the shower have turned into a daily ritual. Sometimes twice.

Even Theo's been taking longer, and I know I'm not the only one thinking about her when the water's running.

Bianca's not only under my skin. She's under his too. Got both of us twisted up, and she hasn't even realized.

I used to fuck without thinking. Now I can't even glance at another chick without measuring her against Bianca. She's the girl you want to lose yourself in and forget the rest of the world exists.

Every part of me wants to make a move; fuck, normally I would have by now, but Theo's the reason I haven't.

I see the way he eyefucks her when he thinks no one's paying attention. That isn't some throwaway glance—it's carved-in, laser-sharp focus. I've never seen him stare at anyone like that before. The way he looks at her, feels new.

Whatever this is building into, she's in the center of it, and we're both too far gone to stop.

If she said yes, I wouldn't hesitate. I'd wreck her with him, and still want more.

Theo's starting to open up with Bianca, more than I've seen with anyone. He's looser around her, cracking jokes, slipping into that laid-back charm that usually takes months to show.

Every time she laughs at something he says, I see the way she gets to him. The way his whole face lights up, like that sound from her is some kind of reward.

Maybe she's pulling something out of him the rest of us never could.

Today, only Theo and I are home. The place is too quiet, missing Scarlet's non-stop mouth. She's over at the motorcycle repair shop. It's our dad's place. He's been running it before any of us existed. Grease-stained floors, classic rock always playing too loud, tools scattered everywhere. Scarlet's always been down in the garage with him, watching from the sidelines, passing tools, wiping grease off her jeans without a second thought.

Theo and I have been chilling in our room waiting for Bianca to show up for our usual jam session. She always shows up around this time, give or take a few minutes, and we've both been pretending not to check the clock, counting down the seconds until we hear that knock on the door.

The second we hear the knock, I lift my head and glance at Theo.

He freezes for a moment, shoulders tight, jaw clenched, like his entire body instantly locked up on instinct. He exhales, and something shifts in him. He doesn't say a word. Simply takes off toward the front door, moving like he's been holding his breath all fucking day waiting for this.

I stay where I am, keeping still, letting him have the moment. Trying to act like none of this matters. As if my chest isn't buzzing and my heart isn't kicking against my ribs simply because she's here.

But the truth is, I wanted to be the one who got to her first. Opening that door simply to catch that smile meant for me.

I toss the cable I'd been half-heartedly trying to untangle and move across the room, dropping onto the edge of the bed.

Their voices drift down the hall, the conversation easy, and I stay frozen in place, listening.

The second they step into the room, I lift my head.

"Hey," Bianca says, her voice casual.

Her eyes land on me and hold for a second too long. The heat behind that stare is quiet, but fuck, I can feel it.

She shifts her attention to Theo, her gaze carrying the same weight.

I track the way he shifts on his feet, subtle but telling, like he senses that pull too. He swallows hard, eyes locked on hers, and for a beat, the air between them tightens. Whatever passed between me and her is still hanging in the air, but now the tension's wrapped around him too. She's got both of us off balance, and she fucking knows the effect she's having.

I can't take this anymore. Every second she holds that stare, the heat slams through my cock, my chest, every part of me that's been straining too fucking hard to stay in control. I'm done pretending any of this is casual. Done acting like I don't want her. I'm done holding back.

Fuck it.

My eyes track her as she crosses the room and drops her guitar case on Theo's bed, the same spot she always claims without thinking.

My eyes drag down her body, settling on that short black skirt that's been in my fucking dreams more times than I'll admit. I've imagined slipping my hands underneath that skirt, just to see if she'd stop me—or pull me closer.

Doesn't matter what we're doing, my head's gone the second she walks in wearing that. She has no idea what that does to me, or maybe she fucking does.

She turns around and faces us. That heat in her eyes... pure goddamn invitation.

I step toward her. Her gaze lifts, locking on me as I close the distance. When I stop in front of her, we're so close I can feel the heat roll off her skin. Our bodies aren't touching, but fuck, they could be. One more inch and I'd have her pressed up against me, right where I want her.

Her breath hitches, chest rising enough for me to know she wants it too. I can see it in the way her eyes darken, the way her lips part.

Fuck, I want to touch her. I want to grab her hips, shove that skirt up, and find out if she's as wet as I've imagined every goddamn day since she walked into my life.

But I don't. I stand frozen, drinking in the way she falls apart from nothing more than the space between us.

Before she can say anything, I grab her face and crash my mouth into hers. There's no hesitation, no holding back. It's pure fucking hunger. Weeks of wanting her, of dreaming about her under me, coming out all at once in a kiss that's rough and messy.

Her lips are soft, but the way she kisses me back is anything but. She's all tongue and heat, like she wants to tear me apart and swallow the pieces. My hand slides into her hair, tightening, tilting her head so I can kiss her harder. My other hand lands on her hip, fingers digging in.

My cock is rock hard, pressed right into her stomach, and I swear she gasps when she feels it. I don't let her pull away. I chase that sound, that sharp little breath, like I need it to fucking breathe.

She clutches my shirt, fisting the fabric in both hands like it's the only thing keeping her upright.

I break the kiss briefly, long enough to breathe against her mouth.

"You feel that?" I growl, rocking my hips into her. "That's what you fucking do to me."

Her eyes are glassy, pupils blown, lips red and swollen from my kiss.

I don't move away. Instead, I keep her there, trapped in the heat between us, our bodies pressed so close not even air could slip through. I want her ruined. I want her saying my name with that same breathless voice she was using to moan into my mouth right now.

And fuck, I'm only warming up.

Her gaze shifts. I turn my head in time to catch Theo lowering the amp near her guitar. His jaw's tight, his movements clipped, too fucking careful, like he's barely keeping it together.

Without a word, he turns and walks away.

Shame crashes over me, hot and choking. My skin still burns from her touch, my lips still swollen from the kiss I stole. The taste of her hasn't even faded, and already, the weight of what I've done to him settles deep. I feel like a fucking dog for doing that, while he walks away from the girl we both want. I know I've already fucked it all up.

Bianca brushes past me, the heat of her body dragging against mine for half a second before she moves across the room.

"Theo," she calls out, her voice sharp, like she already knows what's about to happen if she lets him go.

He stops. Two steps away from the doorway. Head down, his back stays towards her.

She steps in front of him, her gaze moving over his face and something shifts. The way she looks at him isn't the way she looks at anyone else. There's a gentleness in her eyes, a steady calm that wraps around him without demanding anything back. Like she sees past all the noise in his head, past all those walls.

She doesn't flinch at his silence. Doesn't try to fill the space with words. She just waits, reading him, steadying him, knowing how to hold him together without touching a single piece.

She doesn't rush him. Just stands there, waiting, patient in a way she's never had to be with me. When he finally looks up, something passes between them, quiet, unspoken, and then she steps in close. The kiss she gives him is soft as breath. Barely there at first. Her hand touches his cheek gently, and I swear the whole fucking room slows down. It's not heat or fire. It's something else entirely. Something that sinks into him, into me, into the silence between us.

She kisses him as if he matters. As if she sees every broken piece and doesn't flinch.

When she pulls back, her fingers brush his hand, threading through it. She guides him forward gently. It's so intimate it almost hurts to watch. A moment later, her gaze shifts.

Those eyes hit mine, and it's fucking different. No softness. Pure heat. Full-blown, fuck-me fire that slams into my chest and knocks the air right out of me.

I watch her walk Theo toward me; her steps slow, steady, almost protective. She stops right in front of me and lifts her eyes to mine and holds. That look alone could drop me to my knees.

She turns around and faces Theo. I step in close until I hear her breath stutter. Fuck, standing this close, with her trapped between us, has my cock straining and my head spinning.

I glance at Theo and catch the way his throat works as he swallows hard. It's his first time being this close to someone, willingly stepping into something that is this charged. I don't think Bianca knows that or how massive this is for him.

He watches her with a quiet hunger. It's different. There's no retreat in it. No hesitation.

She reaches up and moves her long black hair off to the side, and that's all the fucking invitation I need. I move in, my mouth finding the soft skin of her neck. I kiss her hard, sucking enough to leave a mark, letting her know exactly where this is going.

I grind my cock against her ass, and the moan that slips from her mouth... Shit. Pure fucking music to my ears. She presses back into me, arching enough to let me know she craves this as much as I do. I snake my arm around her waist and yank her tighter, her back pressed to my chest, ass snug against my cock. I hold her like I fucking own her. All I can think about is how wet she's gonna be by the end of this.

I kiss along her neck. It's slow and filthy, tasting the soft skin under my lips. When I scrape my teeth across her throat, she fucking shudders. Her breath catches, and she presses back into me, hips rolling like her body's already begging for more.

Theo hasn't moved. He's standing there, eyes locked on us. Watching every movement, listening to every fucking sound. He's devouring it with his eyes, soaking it in like it's the only thing that exists. But he's hesitating. Still stuck in that space between wanting it so bad it hurts and being too fucked up to reach for it.

I lift my head from her neck and look straight at him. He meets my gaze, and there it is. That need. He's burning with desire for her. But fear's holding him back, anchoring him in place. He's terrified of what comes next.

I bring my lips back to Bianca's ear and whisper, low enough so only she hears.

"He's never done this before," I say in between kisses. "You're the first one he's ever let in."

She nods. A mere tiny movement, like she understands. She shifts her attention to Theo.

I slide my hand off her waist and watch as her fingers slip under his hoodie. He flinches. It's fast. That instinct to pull back and shutdown. But he doesn't. He stays still, like he's forcing himself to let it happen.

"Is this okay, Theo?" she asks, soft like she's scared to push him too hard.

His eyes lock on hers, searching. After a beat, he gives the smallest nod before saying it out loud.

"Yes." His voice is low, but there's weight behind it. Like it cost him something to get the word out.

Bianca grips the hem of his hoodie but pauses, waiting for permission.

When he gives it, he lifts his arms without a word. She moves carefully, slowly, easing the fabric up his chest, taking his shirt with it. Her hands don't rush. They don't fumble. She treats him as if he's fragile.

She pulls the hoodie and shirt over his head, her hands slow, careful, then lets them fall from her hand to the floor.

Theo stands there, bare chest exposed, his breathing shallow, controlled, but barely. He doesn't look away from her. Not once. His eyes stay locked on hers, as if everything holding him together depends on her staying right there in front of him.

"Is it okay if I touch you, Theo?" she asks.

Fuck. If she said that to me, I'd already be stripped to nothing, cock in her hand, begging for more. Her mouth, her body, anything she'd give me. I'd take it all, ruin myself for it. But with Theo, she slows it down. She's watching every breath he takes, every twitch in his jaw, making sure he doesn't disappear into himself before she ever gets the chance to touch him.

He nods, just once, letting her know it's okay.

She leans in and presses a slow, lingering kiss to his chest. I watch his eyes flutter shut. It's not panic. Not the ghosts creeping in. He's feeling this. His breathing changes, deeper now, heavier, his body pulling toward her without even thinking.

When his eyes open again, there's nothing soft left in them. No fear. No doubt. Just fucking hunger I've never seen.

I glance at the door. It's still wide open. If Scarlet comes home early and Theo hears her, everything will fall apart. He'll shut it down. His walls will go up. He'll shut me out. It'll all turn to shit.

I move. Quick and quiet. Cross the room and close the door and twist the lock. No one's getting in. Not when we've come this far.

I step in behind Bianca. My cock's rock hard, straining against the zipper, and all I can think about is how fucking good it's gonna feel buried inside her while he watches. While she moans for both of us. When she falls apart in our hands.

I slip my fingers under the hem of her shirt. Her skin is so warm it makes me hiss and fuck, I lose a second just touching her. My hand drags the fabric up her stomach, over her ribs.

She straightens, breath hitching, body arching into mine like she fucking needs this.

I pull the shirt over her head and toss it to the floor, not giving a shit where it lands. Her hair falls in messy strands around her shoulders, and she just stands there in that black bra, caught between me and Theo.

She's stunning. Dangerous. Fucking lethal.

I want her writhing under me, under us, begging for cock, begging for more, saying our names until her voice is wrecked and her body's shaking. I want to ruin her and worship her in the same goddamn breath.

I press my hand to her hip, grinding my hard cock against her ass, needing some kind of pressure, before I lose control entirely.

Because if she asks for it, I'll give her every filthy, fucked-up piece of me.

Theo's eyes are all over her, dragging across every inch of skin, fucking starving, drinking her in as if she's the only thing that exists. His breathing shifts, chest rising hard.

I unclip her bra. The clasp pops, the straps slide down her shoulders, and then fall from her arms before the bra drops to the floor.

His eyes lock on her tits. His lips part, breath caught in his throat, eyes wide with something between awe and desperation.

A wave of jealousy tears through me. Theo's getting the first fucking glimpse at what I've been aching to touch. What I've been fantasizing about, fist wrapped around my cock, too many fucking nights to count.

I lean in, reach around, and cup her tits in both hands, my palms molding to her soft, perfect skin. Fuck, she feels unreal. Warm, full, made for me. I kiss along her neck, dragging my mouth across the place her pulse pounds, and she melts, pressing back until her ass grinds against my cock. Every slow roll of her hips is a fucking tease, and she knows it. She knows exactly what she's doing to me.

My thumbs brush over her nipples, every nerve in my body lights up from the sensation of her.

It takes everything I have not to shove her down onto the bed, rip the rest of her clothes off, and bury myself inside her.

But I hold back. Grit my teeth. Cling to some sort of control. This isn't about me. Not tonight.

This moment isn't mine.

It's his.

Theo fucking needs this. He needs to know what it feels like to let go without falling apart, to sink into something that doesn't cut him open. He needs to feel what it's like when sex isn't a scar. It's fucking electric. Mind-blowing. Something that sets him free instead of breaking him down.

And Bianca... she's the only one who can give that to him. The only one he trusts enough to touch the places no one else has ever been allowed near.

I move closer, lips up to her ear, my breath hot against her skin.

Theo watches, his eyes dark, fixed on every fucking move I make as I slip my hand beneath the hem of her skirt, pulling her panties off to one side. My fingers slip through her soaked slit. She's fucking ready. Her body's begging for it. I circle her clit, dragging soft pressure across it until her breath catches.

She bites down on her lip, trying to stay quiet, but her body gives her away. She wants all of it. Me. Theo. Every filthy, tangled part of this.

My mouth finds her ear, breath hot, voice dropping to a rough whisper just for her.

"I want you to fuck him," I say, fingers still moving over her clit. "He's never fucked anyone before. Show him how good it can feel."

She shudders, her body tightening under my touch.

I pull my hand away, fingers drenched in her slick.

I look to Theo and hold my fingers out, coated in her arousal.

"Suck," I say, voice thick with want. "Taste how fucking ready she is."

His eyes lock on my fingers, chest heaving, lips slightly parted. He's frozen, but I can feel the want bleeding off him. He's never had anyone dripping for him, ready like this.

He leans in and wraps his lips around my fingers, sucks hard, tongue dragging slow over my skin like he's desperate to savor every drop she left behind. It's messy. Wet. So fucking filthy.

His eyes stay locked on her, drinking her in, showing her exactly what he's doing with the slick she gave him.

He looks at me. Eyes dark. Lips still wrapped around my fingers. Tongue still moving.

And fuck me... something punches through my gut so hard I forget how to breathe. My cock twitches, my pulse stutters, and everything in me coils tight. I wasn't ready for this. For him. For that look. That mouth. That heat.

The curl of his tongue around my fingers sends a jolt straight to the base of my spine. I should pull away, but I don't. I stand there, cock aching, chest fucked up, watching him suck my fingers like it's the most natural thing in the world.

And I don't know what the fuck to do with that.

Theo lets my fingers go with a soft pop, the sound fucking obscene in the quiet. My hand falls to my side, still tingling and wet from his mouth.

I swallow hard, jaw tight, breath ragged, and when I finally speak, my voice scrapes out of me.

"How does she taste?"

Theo's eyes flick between us, and a grin curves at the edge of his mouth.

"Fucking perfect," he says, his lips still shining.

I move my arm from her waist, forcing myself to let go and give her the space to fuck Theo. But then she turns back to me. Her hands slide up my chest, tugging at my shirt like she can't stand the space I just gave her. And before I can even think, she kisses me.

Her mouth's hot, desperate, tongue sliding against mine like she's starved for it. Everything in me lights up, savage and filthy and loud. She moans into my mouth, and I nearly lose it right there. If she keeps kissing me like this, I swear to fucking God, I'll fuck her first.

Bianca pulls back, breath shaky, lips swollen from the way she kissed me. She turns, grabs Theo's hand, and pulls him toward the bed like she hadn't set me on fire and left me standing in the middle of it.

I watch them go, cock still pulsing, a brutal reminder of what I want and can't have. Not yet.

When they reach the bed, Bianca tilts her head up and kisses him again.

Theo hesitates for just a second. Then his hand comes up to her neck, fingers threading into her hair like he can't risk letting her slip away. It's not soft this time. It's needy. Desperate. And I watch the way she melts into it and lets him take control. Her body shifts, her lips part, and she gives herself over to him. Heat crawls under my skin, and I swear I can feel every fucking second of it.

When she finally pulls back, Theo drops onto the bed, his chest heaving, breath jagged and raw. His eyes are wild with want. Bianca sinks to her knees in front of him. Theo's gaze never leaves her.

Bianca doesn't rush. She reaches up, fingers skimming over his stomach, tracing along the faint lines of muscle there. Theo sucks in a sharp breath, his body tensing under her touch.

She leans in, pressing a kiss just below his ribs, then another lower. Theo's chest rises and falls faster, his fingers twitching at his sides like he wants to grab onto her.

"You're fucking beautiful, Theo," Bianca breathes, her lips brushing against his skin.

Theo shifts back onto his elbows as he tilts his head back, eyes closing tight, swallowing so hard it looks like he's choking on the words he's trying not to say. And then I see it. The exact moment when he lets go. One hand moves, threading through her hair, his grip testing, hesitant but powerful.

Bianca presses another kiss lower, just above his waistband, her fingers dragging along the edge like she's testing him, waiting for the word to stop or the command to keep going. But no words come. She glances up at him, her mouth hovering just inches from where I can see his hard cock straining beneath his jeans.

"Is this okay?" she breathes.

Theo exhales sharply. For a second, I think he's going to pull back. Old habits, old fears trying to take control, but then he grits out, "Yes."

Bianca smiles before unbuttoning his jeans, the motion torturously slow. Theo tenses, his body fighting it, but he doesn't stop her.

She tugs at the zipper, dragging it down slowly, then glances up at Theo again, giving him one last chance to back out. But he doesn't.

The way he watches her, the way his fingers stay tangled in her hair, it's a goddamn sight I won't ever forget.

She slides his jeans down, just enough to expose the outline of his cock, thick and straining against his boxers. My eyes are glued to it, but then Bianca leans in, pressing her lips to his hip, just above the waistband—and fuck, I barely register the touch. My eyes are too busy watching her ass.

That short fucking skirt, riding up just enough to put her tight ass on full display. The way it curves perfectly, every inch of her body teases me as she kneels in front of him. That black thong barely covering her pussy? It's an invitation, a goddamn tease.

It takes every ounce of control I have to not step forward, rip that piece of fabric off her, and bury myself inside her right fucking now. Instead, I press a hand against my jeans, stroking through them, desperate for relief as the ache in my body grows. I want her, need her, and I'm not sure I can wait much longer.

I take a step, my body moving before my brain can catch up, ready to close the space, ready to take what I fucking want, but I force myself to stop. My gaze snaps back to Theo. The way his stomach tightens, his fingers twitching.

Bianca runs her tongue over his abs, and Theo's lips part on a sharp exhale, barely holding himself together. His eyes are shut tight, but I can still see the struggle in his face, the way he's fighting against everything that wants to snap.

Bianca shifts, pressing her lips lower, dragging the kiss over his skin a little longer before she hooks her fingers into his boxers and tugs them down, enough to free his hard cock. Theo's breath stutters, chest rising and falling.

His eyes open and they find mine.

For a second, Theo stares at me, frozen.

I give him a small nod. A quiet promise that he's okay.

I move closer, sitting next to him on the bed, my body brushing his as I lean in, close enough to catch the heat rolling off him. Without thinking, I press a kiss to his shoulder. It's soft, lingering, something I've never had the urge to do before. It's unfamiliar, but somehow, it seems right.

Theo turns his head, and something in his expression shifts. His eyes drop to my mouth, lingering there a beat too long. My heart skips a beat, and for one second the urge to kiss him slams through me. But then, a sharp hiss breaks through the air, pulling his attention away. Theo jerks and I hear him moan.

I glance down to see Bianca's lips wrapped around the head of his cock, her mouth sliding down his shaft, taking every inch of him. She moves with perfect rhythm, taking him deeper with every stroke.

"Fuck," Theo says. His whole body shudders.

And for a while I just watch him unravel, watch the tension in his body slip away.

CHAPTER 8

Theo

I've never wanted anything the way I want her. Food doesn't fill it. Sleep doesn't touch it. Air barely keeps me standing. She's still on my tongue, soaked into every breath, every thought.

I love the way her slick clung to Nate's fingers, the way he looked at me when he held them out, daring me to move. And I did. Fuck, I didn't hesitate. I simply gave in. Let it happen without a second of logic. No pause. No breath. And now there's no crawling back from this.

She's kneeling in front of me, her mouth on my cock, her lips sliding down over the part of me I let no one touch. And all I can do is sit here and take it, legs tense, fingers buried in her hair, my whole fucking world narrowed down to the heat of her mouth and the way Nate is breathing next to me.

Every sound Bianca makes, every drag of her tongue, every time her throat flutters around me, has got my heart pounding like it's trying to tear through my ribs. My hands grip harder, not to control her, but to anchor myself. Because I'm fucking floating, untethered, lost in something I don't understand how to survive.

This is so much more than I imagined.

Filthier. Hotter.

Messier in all the ways that leave me fucked and wanting more. It's not only her mouth. It's her. The way she looked at me before sinking to her knees, eyes full of something that cut right through the damage and didn't flinch. Her hands on me with this steady need, as if every scar made sense to her.

And suddenly there's Nate beside me, close enough that our arms keep brushing. That should shut me down. Should have me pulling away, pretending none of this is getting to me. But it doesn't. It tightens everything. Nate heats it. Twists it into something I don't want to fight.

His eyes are on me. Burning through the space between us. Watching. Wanting. Every time she moans around my cock, his breath stutters. Fuck, that does something to me. I'm certain I couldn't do this without him here next to me.

I turn my head and catch him palming his cock through his jeans, as if he's barely holding on. I can tell how close he is to losing it. The hunger's right there, eating through whatever's left of his control.

I want to witness him fall apart. I've never thought that before, especially about him. But now I want it. I need to see her mouth on him the way it's wrapped around me. Watching him come undone in the heat of it is all I can think about.

I drop my gaze back to Bianca as she slides down my shaft, her hand wrapped around the base of my cock, stroking what her mouth can't reach. Her eyes hold mine, filled with heat and something that hits dangerously close to affection.

I bite down a groan, my head tipping back, breath catching as she speeds up, her rhythm steady and fucking perfect. I want to tell her to stop so it lasts. But I'm too far gone. One more stroke. One more second.

Nate's voice cuts through. "Are you okay?"

I manage a nod, barely.

"Yeah," I breathe. "Fuck... yeah."

He leans in closer, mouth near my ear, and that alone nearly pushes me over the edge.

"She looks so fucking good on her knees for you," he whispers, voice dripping with something dangerous. "You should see your face right now."

I groan, head tipping forward, eyes fluttering open barely enough to catch Bianca still working me over like she wants to own every piece of me.

All I can think is... I never realized it could be this good, and we've barely started. Her mouth is heaven and sin all at once.

I'm not only hard. I'm fucking throbbing. Every nerve under my skin is on fire, and I can't stop staring at her. The way she moves. The way she holds me in the back of her throat.

She moans around me, and I groan, the sound ripping straight from my chest.

I glance to the side.

Fuck, Nate's beautiful. I know now why chicks fall over themselves to get close. I get it. And it's messing with my head more than I want to admit. I don't understand why that thought hits me now. Maybe it's always been there, buried under years of looking away. But now, with Bianca on her knees, her mouth full of me, and Nate right beside me... I can't escape it.

He glances over and our eyes meet. His lips part slightly. His breath catches. There's this moment that hums between us.

I wonder what it would be like to kiss him. The thought comes so fast, so violently, I nearly flinch. My body tenses, cock twitching in Bianca's mouth, my pulse hammering in my throat. I shouldn't want that. I don't even understand what that means. But I do. I fucking want it. Not instead of her. But with this. With her. With him. It scares the fucking shit out of me.

I groan, loud, my free hand clutching the edge of the mattress like I need something to hold me down.

My whole body seizes as I come hard, hips jerking, a ragged, helpless groan ripping from my throat. My eyes lock on Bianca as I fall apart, and it's like something inside me explodes. My orgasm rips through me, hard and hot, and I can't breathe, can't think, can't fucking hide.

My cock pulses, spilling into Bianca's mouth. Her hand still works me, drawing every drop out as if she knows I've experienced nothing close to this. My thighs shake as my stomach caves. My mouth opens, but nothing comes out. I drop back onto the mattress, wrecked in a way I never imagined was possible.

Nate leans in and presses his palm flat against my chest as though he needs to be sure my heart's still beating. He's close enough that I can sense his heat, his smell, that's been driving me insane since this whole fucked-up thing started.

He says nothing. His hand stays there for a second, before he moves, lowers his head, puts his mouth to my skin and presses a kiss, right over my heart.

His lips stay there, and I swear I forget how to breathe. My heart's going fucking wild, beating straight into his mouth, telling him everything I'm too much of a coward to say. I stare up at the ceiling, ribs heaving, my cock still twitching, still sticky with spit, and I bite down on the thing in my throat that wants to come out. I'm too scared they'll fuck everything up. Too scared that once I say it, it will break everything we are.

Nate pulls back barely enough to meet my eyes.

"I told you," he says. "It's good, right?"

Bianca shifts between my legs, dragging her mouth from my cock, lips swollen and wet, breath coming out hard. She crawls up my body, straddling my hips with that slick heat between her thighs pressed against my stomach.

Nate hasn't moved yet; he still rests on one elbow staring at me, one hand stroking his cock.

Bianca leans down and kisses me. Her lips crash into mine, and I taste myself on her tongue. Her mouth is open, greedy and hot. She kisses me like she wants to crawl inside my fucking mouth and live there.

I kiss her back, fingers digging into her waist as I groan into her mouth, already fucking gone.

Suddenly Nate moves. His arm brushes mine as he reaches for something. She doesn't stop kissing me. Her body grinds against mine; that slick pussy over my abs makes me moan again. My head's spinning. I'm not only ready for more. I'm fucking desperate for it.

Bianca pulls back and sits up. I turn my head to see Nate. He's holding out a condom.

"You want her?" he asks.

My hand shakes as I take the condom from him.

"Yeah," I whisper. "Fuck, yeah, I do."

Bianca laughs as she lifts off me. I sit up ready to open the packet, but Nate stands and moves in front of her, his presence pulling gravity with it. He doesn't look at me. All of his focus is on Bianca now.

I take in the way he kisses her softly, his lips lingering before he pulls back. His fingers trail along her jaw, his thumb grazing the corner of her mouth, and she sighs into it. His hand keeps moving, sliding down over the curve of her ass before finding the zipper of her short skirt and tugging it down,

The second it falls around her feet she steps out of it.

My eyes drop to her ass as he sinks to his knees in front of her. His hands grip her thighs high above the knee, sliding upward in a slow, deliberate path until they reach the tiny black thong, soaked straight through. He hooks his fingers beneath the fabric and looks up at her. She nods without a word.

He peels it down inch by inch, dragging the fabric over her thighs, past her knees. She lifts each foot for him, and he slides it off before tossing it carelessly aside.

Nate stays there, hands planted firmly on her thighs, thumbs stroking slow circles as his gaze fixes on her bare pussy. He leans in, nose brushing against her, eyes fluttering shut as he drags in a breath. The sound that rips from his chest is raw, almost inhuman.

"Jesus," he mutters.

She shudders.

He kisses her inner thigh first, then the other. His mouth trails higher, tongue drawing a slow line up her skin, so close to her pussy it makes her twitch. A breathy moan slips out of her as her fists clench tight at her sides.

Nate grips the backs of her thighs and drags her closer, guiding one leg over his shoulder before lowering his mouth to her. His tongue makes one slow, flat stroke from the base of her cunt to her clit.

She moans.

I do too.

His tongue drags again—slower, firmer. His fingers press her thighs wider, holding her steady as his mouth sinks into her. He flicks at her clit, light and teasing, until her hips roll forward on their own.

"Fuck," she breathes. "Don't stop."

He doesn't. His tongue drags up and down her slit with purpose, circling her clit before flattening to savor her again. His lips seal around her, sucking gently, tugging on that swollen bundle of nerves until her legs begin to shake.

I groan, stroking my hard cock, the condom still unopened in my palm. I should move. Should do something. But all I can do is stare.

Nate flicks her clit with the tip of his tongue, once, then again, faster, until her breath stutters. A moan spills out of her, her hand flying to his hair.

He groans into her like he's addicted to her taste. His tongue flattens, dragging slow through her folds, tracing every inch as if he wants to memorize her. Then he sucks her clit into his mouth, harder this time, and I catch her knees nearly giving out.

"Fuck, Nate," she moans. "Holy shit, don't stop."

He pulls back for a second, mouth wet, lips red, and his eyes find mine.

"She's so fucking sweet," he rasps, before diving back in, burying his face against her.

This time he goes deeper, tongue slipping lower to tease her entrance, and she moans so loud it echoes off the walls. He fucks her with his tongue, one hand gripping her ass while the other glides up her stomach to her breast. His palm closes over her tit, rolling her nipple between his fingers as he licks and sucks, tongue-fucking her until her whole body trembles.

I stroke my cock harder, eyes locked on them. It has to be so good—Bianca's eyes are closed, mouth open, chest heaving. She looks gorgeous. As if she's hanging by a thread, and Nate's the only thing holding her up. A gasp tears out of her as she grabs his hair with both hands and clings on, her whole body shaking.

Nate groans again, louder this time, sucking hard on her clit. She's trembling so badly I think she's about to come already, but he pulls back. His mouth is slick, lips swollen and red, his face flushed.

She's gasping, on the edge, already swaying from the force of what he's done.

"Go fuck him," Nate says. "I want to watch you take his cock."

Bianca stares at him for half a breath, lips parted, before shifting her gaze to me.

My hands shake as I fumble with the condom wrapper, my heart pounding hard against my ribs. My cock is heavy, the tip flushed red and leaking from watching what Nate just did to her.

The foil tears in my hand, and the moment the wrapper's open, I feel it—their eyes. Both of them.

I glance up and catch Bianca at the end of the bed, skin flushed, lips parted like she still hasn't caught her breath. Her hair's amess, cheeks pink, chest rising fast. Her eyes stay locked on me as I roll the condom down over my cock, that kind of focus making my skin burn.

Nate's there too, still on his knees, eyes fixed on my hand around my cock. His jaw is tight, shoulders tense, his chin glistening with the slick he just licked from her pussy.

Both of them are locked on me, watching my hand slide over my cock as I adjust the condom. My fingers work slow and tight around the base, stroking once, twice more, trying to get it right, trying not to fall apart from the way they're looking at me.

Bianca's eyes meet mine first, and fuck, she's beautiful like this—desperate, unguarded, still chasing the edge of an orgasm she hasn't come down from. Her gaze is hazy, heavy with want, lips parted like she needs more of us just to survive.

Nate's eyes find mine next. His chin is still slick with her, his gaze hungry, focused, wild in that quiet way that makes you want to hand over every piece of yourself just to see what he'll do with it.

He doesn't look away.

Neither do I.

I stroke my cock, it's thick and aching, already hard for more.

Bianca crawls up my body, her skin blazing against mine. Her lips are slick, her cunt still dripping down her thighs. She crashes her mouth to mine, tongue pushing in before I can breathe, and I groan into her.

Her pussy grinds along my stomach, leaving a wet, hot trail I can't ignore. My hips jerk up on their own, my cock thick and aching again, trapped between us and desperate for more.

She shifts, and I catch the wet drag of her clit over my shaft. It's fucking brutal. She lifts her hips, hovers over me, and I'm about to line myself up when I sense him.

Nate. His hand wraps around my cock and I nearly choke on my breath. Firm, warm fingers stroke me once before holding me steady, guiding me to her pussy.

"Slide down," he orders her. "Take him deep. I want to see you split open for him."

Bianca lowers herself onto me slowly, as if she knows we're all going to break from this. The head of my cock pushes into her soaked entrance, and Nate's grip tightens around me, holding me steady as he lines it up just right.

She moans as she sinks down on me, inch by inch, and I take in every brutal detail—the stretch, the heat, the slick, the perfect drag of her pussy pulling me deeper. Her walls clamp around me like she doesn't want to let go, like her body's just as desperate for this as mine.

I groan, hands flying to her hips, fingers digging into soft skin as I fight to stay grounded while she fucks me open with every inch.

"Fuck—" The word rips out of me, the rest lost. "She's so tight."

"She's fucking perfect," Nate says, his voice low, heavy with something darker.

Behind her, Nate shifts, the bed dipping with his weight. His hands trail up her back, pressing her forward before sliding down over the curve of her ass. His thumbs part her cheeks, spreading her just enough to see where I'm buried inside her. He groans, the sound rough, almost pained.

"She looks so fucking good like this," he murmurs, eyes locked between her legs. "You feel her?"

I nod, jaw clenched so tight I swear I can hear it crack.

Bianca lifts her hips a fraction before sinking back down, and I almost lose it. My cock's buried to the hilt, pulsing, twitching with every drag of her body. Her pussy grips me tighter, like she's already trying to milk me dry.

I stare up at her—hair a mess, mouth parted as she rides me, dragging me through every sweet, brutal second. I can't breathe.

"Look at her," Nate says. "Fucking dripping down your cock."

I thrust up, can't help it. I need it, desperate for more of this brutal rush of her pussy on my cock. Fuck, now I get why Nate was always chasing pussy. The drag, the heat, the fight to keep from blowing too soon.

Nate leans in, kissing the back of her shoulder before trailing lower, dragging his mouth across her spine. His tongue flicks out, tracing a wet path down her back. She shudders, head tipping forward, a moan caught in her throat.

Every time she lifts off me, it tears me apart. Every time she sinks back down, I forget how to fucking breathe. Her tits bounce with every movement, her mouth spilling soft little gasps as her thighs tremble around me, caging me in.

I groan at the sight, the sound ripped straight from my chest. And fuck, I know it—she wants me. I catch it in the way she moves, the way she tightens when I thrust up to meet her, the way she whimpers when I grip her hips harder and grind into that spot that makes her whole body shiver.

I sense Nate shift behind her, catch the way he's watching us—hungry, like he's barely holding on. Then he steps away from the bed.

My eyes track him as he crosses the room. A drawer slides open, and seconds later he's back, naked. My brain stalls. His cock is hard, flushed, thick and heavy in his hand. His chest heaves, mouth parted, jaw tight, a condom packet already clenched in his grip.

He doesn't open it gently. He tears it with his teeth, ripping the foil in one sharp motion before spitting the wrapper aside. I watch his mouth fall open as he rolls it on, his eyes never leaving Bianca's body.

He kneels behind Bianca, his hands gliding up her back before sliding down to her ass. He spreads her wide, staring at the way I sink into her, her slick cunt stretched tight around my cock.

I catch the shift in her breathing. She tips forward, chest pressing to mine, lips brushing my neck. Her hair spills over my shoulder as her fingers clutch at me like she needs something to hold on to.

Nate shifts closer behind her, his knees sinking into the mattress. He leans in and spits—the sound wet and obscene in the quiet. The slick lands on her ass, and his fingers trace slowly over the tight ring of muscle between her cheeks.

Bianca whimpers.

Nate works his fingers through the slick trail, spreading it in slow, deliberate circles. He smears it over her hole, teasing, and she moans loud, her body jerking on top of me. Her pussy clamps down hard around my cock.

I groan, burying my hands in her hair.

The way her body reacts to him hits something deep in me. I catch every twitch, every tremble. My cock throbs inside her, and I swear I can feel her heartbeat in the way her cunt squeezes me.

Nate takes his time. He spits again, smearing the slick across her with his fingers.

Bianca shudders as his fingers work in careful motions. He shifts behind her, lining his cock up with her ass. I tilt my head, catching him through the curtain of her hair, the rigid line of his jaw, the way his breathing comes broken and uneven.

Nate shifts forward, chest heaving, his cock hard in his hand, condom stretched tight. He strokes himself once, eyes gone dark as he presses in. The tip pushes against her tight entrance, and her breath catches on my throat. Her thighs clamp around my hips, her nails digging into my chest.

I catch the flicker of fear in her eyes, but beneath it there's still want.

Nate pushes forward again. She flinches, her body jolting.

I grip her tighter, my mouth at her ear. "Are you okay."

She nods, pressing her forehead to mine.

Nate closes his eyes, savoring the stretch as he pushes deeper into her ass. I know it's his first time fucking a chick there. He would've told me if he'd done it before. We share everything. His grip tightens on her hips, and when his eyes open again, they lock on mine.

"She's so fucking tight," he groans.

"Take it slow," I tell him.

He nods and holds still for a beat before easing forward, inch by inch. His mouth falls open, no sound at first, just shaky, ragged breaths.

Bianca gasps, her back arching.

"Tell me if it's too much," Nate says.

She shakes her head, lips parted.

"Keep going," she whispers.

He pushes deeper, her body stretching around him as her pussy clamps down on me again. I can't think past the way she's taking both of us.

Bianca exhales, breath breaking into fast, shallow waves as Nate sinks further in. Her body trembles, loosens, then tightens again, fighting and yielding all at once as she struggles to take it.

"God," she gasps. "I feel both of you."

Nate pauses halfway in, one hand pressed to her back. His mouth finds her shoulder, kissing her there, soft, steady, anchoring.

"You're taking both of us so fucking well," he mutters.

Then he pushes the rest of the way, slow but relentless, until his hips press flush to her ass and we're buried inside her together. She's stretched to the limit, cunt and ass stuffed full, and I don't know how she's still breathing.

She starts to shake.

Not from pain. From the weight of it, from the way we're both inside her, connected, full, and feral.

I reach up and brush her hair from her face. Her eyes open, dazed and glassy, lips parting.

"I've never felt anything like this," she breathes. "I didn't know it could be this good."

"I didn't either," I admit.

Nate pulls back a fraction, and she lets out a soft, wrecked sound. Her cunt flutters around me, and I nearly lose it.

Nate moves first.

"Fucking hell," he groans, eyes squeezing shut as he relishes the tight drag of her around him. He braces, gripping her hips harder, steadying his thrust. His pace stays slow, giving her time to adjust.

Bianca cries out, her face buried in my neck, lips open against my skin. She trembles between us, gasping for breath, body stretched to the edge, and I've never seen anything so fucking beautiful.

Nate opens his eyes, glancing down at her back before locking on me. His jaw is tight, and I can see he's barely holding it together.

I start to move, slow at first, hips flexing up, testing how much she can take. My cock drags through her soaked heat as Nate pushes deeper behind her. She tenses above me, then moans, her head thrown back between us. She's dripping. Nate grinds into her ass, as his hands slide over her body.

Her hips roll forward, then back, caught in the rhythm we've built around her. Each thrust drives her down onto me, her body yielding, taking everything. She doesn't hold back. She moves with us, chasing the rhythm like she can't get enough. Her thighs tremble, muscles tightening as she rides the wave, matching every shift of Nate's hips with her own.

She shifts back, arching into Nate's thrust, her hands braced on my chest for balance. Every time she rocks forward, she clenches around me, that perfect, pulsing grip. Each movement is so fucking good it rips the air from my lungs.

She's not just taking us. She's using us, wringing out every ounce of her pleasure. She moves with intent, chasing the friction, the stretch, the brutal fullness of it all. Her breath stutters as she finds her angle, spine curving, ass pressing back against Nate while her pussy clamps down on me. She rides us like she can't get enough, like we're the only thing holding her to this world.

And fuck, watching her like this—shameless, beautiful—it's almost too much. Nate groans behind her, his rhythm faltering, and she flutters around me again, her body on the verge. Her moans break into gasps as we fuck her slow and deep, dragging her closer to the edge with us.

Nate leans in, his voice rough against her ear.

"You want more?"

Her breath catches, and for a moment I think she's about to fall apart. But she doesn't. She lifts her head, eyes wild and dark with need, and says it without a flicker of hesitation.

"Fuck yes."

That's all he needs. His hand slides to her front, down between us, until his fingers find her clit, slick, swollen from everything we've done to her.

The second he touches her, a broken moan rips out of her. Her whole body jolts, head dropping forward as her back arches between us.

Nate starts slow, building her up.

She whimpers, gasps, then moans so loud it slams into my chest. She grinds against his hand, chasing it, desperate, needy.

"Fuck," I grit out, barely able to keep thrusting into her. "She's gonna come."

Nate doesn't stop.

"Watch her," he says, voice steady, like he knows exactly what he's doing to both of us. "Don't miss it."

His fingers move faster, tight circles over her clit, slick sounds filling the room as her moans climb higher.

She cries out, thighs shaking.

I catch the tremor rippling through her, and then she breaks.

A scream tears out of her, and her pussy clamps down so hard I swear I see stars. She shudders, hips jerking, the orgasm ripping through her in brutal waves. Her legs give out, her body collapsing forward, held up only by Nate's arm around her waist and my cock still buried deep inside her.

She doesn't stop shaking. Her nails dig into my skin as her whole body gives out.

"Fuck," I whisper, too stunned to move. "She's unreal."

She's still moaning, breath ragged, clinging to us like she can't tell where one of us ends and the other begins. And I can't stop staring—fucked out and trembling, she's the hottest thing I've ever seen.

Bianca lies boneless against me, breath stuttering at my throat, skin slick with sweat, body still shaking. She's wrecked from coming, but she keeps moving with us—grinding, dragging me deeper like she doesn't know how to stop.

And I can't stop either.

My hands shake against her hips. Every time Nate thrusts into her from behind, he drives her forward, slamming me deeper.

"Shit," I choke out, my voice breaking. "I can't—fuck, I'm gonna—"

I break.

My head snaps back, one hand clutching her waist, the other clawing into the sheets. And I fucking come.

It slams through me hard. My whole body locking as I spill inside her, thick and hot, my cock pulsing with every surge. A sound tears out of my chest, guttural and helpless. She whimpers when she feels it, face still buried in my neck, taking every drop.

My thighs quake, my stomach caves, and my vision goes white.

Behind her, Nate groans.

"That's it," he pants. "Fuck, Theo. You feel that?"

I can't even speak. I just nod, breathless, still half-lost in it.

But Nate's still going. His grip clamps harder on her hips, his other hand sliding down her back to press her lower, opening her wider for him. He drives into her rougher now, sharper, his groans coming faster. He's chasing it—his own high. I can hear it in every breath, every thrust, the way he fucks into her like he needs to drown in it.

I turn my head just enough to catch her face—her mouth falling open, eyes fluttering shut as she moans with every thrust. Every sound she makes sinks under my skin.

Behind her, Nate tenses, his breath hitching.

He groans her name. "Fuck—Bianca—shit—"

His hips stutter, rhythm faltering for half a second before he slams back into her, hard and deep. The bed shudders with it. His grip on her waist tightens, holding her steady as he buries himself again. Then he stills, head dropping forward—

And I see it.

He's coming.

His whole body locks up—chest heaving, muscles straining. His jaw clenches so tight the veins in his neck stand out, and he groans again, louder this time, broken and breathless. The sound lodges in my chest.

I watch his shoulders sag forward toward her as he stays buried deep, coming hard. I don't have to ask, I know she feels every brutal pulse of it. Fuck, he's beautiful like this. He's still spilling, dragging his cock slowly out of Bianca's ass before pushing back in, riding it out like he can't stop. As if he needs to empty every last drop.

Bianca whimpers on top of me, her body twitching between us.

I take in the way his hand sprawls across her back, the way he groans one last time before going still. His breathing is rough as his gaze stays locked on where we're joined.

Slowly, he pulls out, his breath catching with a sharp hiss and a muttered, "Fuck."

His hands linger on her hips, thumbs pressing into the curve of her ass like he doesn't want to let go.

Bianca's chest heaves, hair falling around her face in a sweaty halo. She's trembling, and I can't tell if it's from what we did, or from how hard she came.

Nate leans over her, dragging his mouth along her spine, kissing the back of her shoulder.

"You were fucking amazing," he breathes. "The way you took both of us."

I nod, still stunned.

"You're fucking perfect," I rasp.

She lets out a soft sound, something between a laugh and a broken moan, but doesn't lift her head.

She lands on her back between us, legs still spread, pussy slick and swollen, eyes glassy and blown wide with whatever the fuck we just gave her. I can't stop staring.

While Nate crosses the room to toss the condom in the trash, I reach out, pushing her hair back from her face. My fingers tremble.

She looks at me, and something in my chest cracks open.

And I kiss her.

It's not rushed. It's everything I haven't figured out how to say yet.

She sighs into my mouth, one hand brushing over my chest.

And fuck, I don't want to stop.

When I finally pull back, I rest my forehead against hers and breathe her in.

I get it now. Why Nate chased pussy as if it were oxygen. For a year, he tried to drag me into his world. Told me to stop wasting my dick. Said it would fix the fucked-up shit in my head. Promised the scars wouldn't burn every time someone got too close.

I told him to fuck off. Every time. I didn't want it. Didn't see the point. But now I fucking get it. Now I know what it means to lose yourself in something too good to survive. To finally let go.

This isn't only about sex. This is her. The way she sees me. Pussy was never the missing piece. It was always her.

And fuck, now I can't stop thinking about doing it again.

When the kiss breaks, Nate's already climbing back onto the bed. He drops beside her, pressing a kiss to her shoulder, then another to her cheek. His hand drifts over her ribs, and he looks at her like she's something sacred.

"You were fucking amazing," he says, his voice more honest in those four words than I've heard in years.

Bianca smiles, turning her face toward him. Their foreheads touch, breaths mingling, and for a moment I can only stare at them.

I push off the bed, pull off the condom, and head for the trash can, my body still thrumming, my cock still half-hard, refusing to believe this is over.

When I turn around, they're still there, tangled, silent. Nate's hand rests on her hip, his other tracing slow circles down her spine. She's tucked against his chest, fingers curled into him as if she belongs nowhere else.

For a moment, I wonder if I should move. Walk away. Give them space. Pretend I'm not standing here, still reeling, still hard, still caught in everything we just did.

But I don't.

I climb back onto the bed instead, moving slow as if any sudden shift might break it. My hand finds the outside of her thigh, still trembling. I press my chest to her back, bury my face in the curve of her neck, and breathe her in.

Nate shifts, and he stays silent, his hand finds mine where it rests on her skin.

We stay there. Three bodies, tangled together, and for the first time in a long fucking time, I don't feel so alone.

CHAPTER 9

Theo

It's been four fucking months of Bianca owning every corner of my world, and I'm still here like a starving idiot, waiting for scraps. I'm knee-deep in a madness I never expected, and now it's the only thing holding me together. Most days I can't think straight, and the rest I don't want to.

Last week, I told her I loved her.

I didn't mean to. Didn't plan it. No sweet bullshit with candles and stars. No speech that sounded rehearsed but wasn't.

I said it mid-fuck, with my cock buried deep inside her, Nate's cum still warm on her tongue. She looked at me like I was the only thing in the room that mattered.

And I completely fucking lost it. I pulled out, flipped her over, dragged her hips back against me, and slammed into her like I needed her to know just how far gone I was.

The words spilled out before I even knew they were there, torn straight from my chest.

"I fucking love you."

And for the first time, the truth didn't fucking scare me. It finally rang true.

She didn't flinch. Her mouth curved into that soft, beautiful smile, as if I hadn't already handed her my heart mid-thrust.

She said it back—told me she loved me too. She made it sound easy, as if choosing me wasn't chaos or a storm she wanted to walk away from.

Nate hasn't said it to her. Not out loud. But he's told me—he loves her.

It was two nights ago. One of those nights when the silence felt full. The room still carried her scent, skin and sweat, the kind of heat that lingers long after it's over. We were stretched across Nate's bed with a half-finished bottle between us and a joint burning slow in my fingers.

We'd all fucked earlier. The kind of sex that leaves your limbs useless and your head spinning. The house was dark, and everyone else had already gone to bed.

"I love her," Nate said as he reached for the joint. "And it fucking terrifies me."

He drew in a slow hit, holding the smoke in his lungs like the burn might be enough to drown out the truth. His eyes stayed pinned to the ceiling, never once shifting my way, as if meeting my gaze would make it real.

And I get it. We're both addicted to her, obsessed as if she's the only thing keeping us alive.

I live for the sounds she makes when she comes—the hitch in her breath right before everything shatters. The split second her body goes still, needing that pause before it explodes. The drag of her nails across my skin. The way her mouth falls open.

Now I love fucking. I don't wait for someone else to make the first move. When I want it, I take it. One glance at her, one caught breath, one flicker in her eyes, and I'm there. I pin her to the wall, press her into Nate, and drive my cock into her to whatever track is pounding through the speakers. I chase every gasp with my mouth and swallow every moan like it's the last I'll ever taste.

We talk about the future now. Nothing polished, nothing fake. Just the raw truths that spill out when she's lying between us, sweaty and wrecked, too full of whatever this is to hide behind lies anymore.

Six months left of school and then we're out. No second thoughts. No safety nets. Just gone. We've been looking at places. Nothing serious yet, but enough to picture it. Enough to start sentences with when instead of if.

Crappy little apartments with peeling paint and paper-thin walls that rattle when we play, when we love her so hard she forgets how to breathe. The kind of place where the neighbors bang on the walls and we don't even pause. Where we don't have to explain who we are or why this works. Where it's only us, loud and reckless and finally free.

Music's different for us now. We play like we're building something, maybe a band. It's messy and loud and doesn't always work. But when it does, when it finally locks into place, it feels like something the universe made just for us.

Bianca always says what's meant to be will come. I never bought into that shit. I don't trust anything I can't see, touch, or fuck up with my own hands. But something about her makes me want to believe. If fate's real, there has to be a reason she found us. A reason she stepped straight into the chaos and didn't flinch when she saw me. She could've run. Instead, she stayed.

She chose both of us, as if she was made to fill the space we never realized was missing. And if I let myself trust that, it means the future we keep talking about isn't just a dream. Maybe the late nights, the shared beds, the music echoing through some too-small apartment we'll call ours are only the beginning. And now I'm ready to let it find us.

Nate and I slump against the rusted railing out front of the school, same spot as always. A cigarette burns slow between my fingers, our backpacks dumped at our feet, while we watch the flood of students push through the gates like they've actually got somewhere worth being.

Scarlet's already inside, slipped through the doors without a word. She left us a while ago, head down, headphones on, pretending she doesn't notice the guys staring at her.

My head's a fucking mess. My stomach's knotted tight in that familiar way it always is on mornings like this, knowing I have to walk through those gates. Certain of what's waiting for me inside. Heads turning. Voices dropping. Smiles tightening like they've swallowed something foul and can't spit it out fast enough.

Nate doesn't say a word. He just stands beside me, arms crossed, eyes fixed on nothing. His silence is both a comfort and a curse. He knows me too well to waste it on small talk. He plucks the cigarette from my fingers and takes a drag without asking.

I glance toward the walkway. Instinct now, scanning the path the students take, hoping to catch a glimpse of Bianca before the noise in this shithole swallows everything.

Up ahead, I spot Quinn Thomas.

Her head is high, moving with that steady, no-bullshit stride that dares the world to test her. Black jeans torn wide at the knees. Shirt slipping off one shoulder, her clothes done playing by the rules. She's beautiful. Not the sweet kind. Not the kind that makes you want to write poetry or bullshit love songs. She's chaos with cheekbones. A storm with eyeliner and chipped black nails. Everything about her says she doesn't give a fuck what anyone believes. She doesn't have to speak; you feel it in the way the space shifts when she moves through it. Half the school fears her. The other half wants to be her.

Quinn knows more about me than most people ever will. One night at some shitty party, Nate was off getting high or getting laid, possibly both, and she found me sitting off to one side trying to hide in the walls, when she sat down next to me and asked, "You good?"

That was all it took. I let it spill. Said way too fucking much. Gave her the kind of truth that usually makes people run.

But not Quinn.

The next time I saw her, she just handed me a drink and sat down beside me, as if I hadn't spilled my guts all over the floor a week earlier. No awkward glances. No pity. Just that same dry wit and fuck-you stare that is Quinn Thomas.

And it was exactly what I needed. She never once treated me like I was broken. That's when I knew she was solid. That I could trust her.

Every guy who walks past gives her that same fucking stare. Eyes dragging down her body as if they have some goddamn right to it. As though her ass is up for auction and all they need is a smirk and a line to win her over. They don't get it. Quinn isn't theirs to claim. She isn't some easy lay waiting for validation from a guy who thinks confidence is enough. She's fire and a thousand broken things stitched together just tight enough to keep breathing. She's built walls no one's getting through. Not them. Maybe not anyone.

As she closes in, her eyes lift to mine, and a slow, knowing smile spreads across her lips.

Nate holds out the cigarette. I watch her lips close around the filter as she inhales, then hands it back to him and exhales a slow stream of smoke.

"Hey, Theo," Quinn says.

"Hey. Where's your camera?" I ask, my eyes flicking to her chest. It's always there, part of her. Seeing her without it feels wrong.

"Eye piece was fucked," she says. "Sold one of my shots online and used the cash to get it fixed."

Nate frowns. "You actually make money off your photos?"

Quinn shrugs, nudging a rock with the toe of her boot. "Not really. Just a couple landscapes. One finally sold."

Nate gives a small nod. "Still impressive."

Before Quinn can answer, the air shifts.

I don't need to look to know it's Bianca. My pulse gives it away, hammering the second she steps closer.

Her long black hair is pulled into a slick ponytail, every strand in place as if she stepped straight out of a fucking movie. Sharp. Effortless. She doesn't even have to try, and still she knocks the air out of me.

She smiles. Not big, not fake. Just a slow curve of her lips that lands dead center.

"Hey, girl," Bianca says, sliding in beside Quinn. Their shoulders bump, and Quinn's mouth twitches into a rare smile.

Bianca turns to us, eyes lit up. "Did you hear she sold one of her prints?" Her voice is full of pride, as if it's her own win.

"Yeah," Nate says with a nod. "We were just talking about that. Pretty solid."

Bianca bumps Quinn's shoulder again, grinning. "Told you it was a big deal."

Quinn rolls her eyes, but she's smiling, the kind that never comes easy.

I watch them, the ease between them undeniable. Best friends. No question.

"Hey, Theo," Bianca murmurs, and before I can process it she rises onto her toes and presses a quick kiss to my lips. It's soft, but my whole fucking body reacts. My heart flips, stumbling hard enough I swear it misses a beat.

Almost as fast, she turns to Nate and kisses him too. Unbothered as ever. No hesitation. No second-guessing. She doesn't give a single fuck who's watching. Let them talk, whisper, judge, stare. Seconds later, she's back in front of me, her eyes locking on mine, searching.

Her gaze lifts slowly, dragging over the hood pulled low across my head. The one I never take off here. It isn't just clothing. It's the only thing that lets me breathe when the world won't stop staring, the thin barrier between me and everything I don't want to face.

She lifts her hands, and before I can react her fingers hook the edge of the fabric. She eases it back, slow, as if she's unwrapping something fragile and broken.

I stand there with my throat tight, heart hammering, every part of me screaming to yank it back up.

But I don't. Because in her eyes, she sees every fucked-up piece of me and doesn't even blink.

Her hands frame my face as she says, "You don't need to hide behind anything, Theo. Let those assholes see how beautiful you really are."

I swallow hard and give a small nod. It isn't much, but it's enough to tell her I'll try.

Her smile spreads, and her hand slips into mine. Fingers lace tight, claiming. She's mine. I'm hers.

We move. Step after step through the chaos of this place, through every stare waiting to rip us apart.

Behind us, Quinn says something as she falls in beside Nate. Their words trade back and forth in an easy rhythm, too casual for how heavy the air feels.

The stares hit before we even reach the steps. Heads turn. Eyes lock on us. Whispers crawl up my spine. Every glance lands like a shove, judgment cutting into my skin.

I tense, my grip tightening. Part of me waits for her to pull away.

But she doesn't. She leans in, her breath brushing my jaw.

"Let them watch," she says. "Let them judge. Fuck what they think. That's their problem, not ours."

We step into the hall, and everything in me coils tight. My chest locks, heartbeat pounding louder than it should.

The hallway swallows us whole. I used to keep my head down. Today there's no hood to drag low, nothing to shield me from the stares that always find me. I feel exposed. Skinned alive.

The noise crashes over me. Locker doors slam, the echoes rattling down the corridor. Shouts bounce off the walls, voices overlapping, every word scraping across my ears.

A textbook drops somewhere behind us, followed by a burst of laughter. Overhead, the fluorescent lights buzz and flicker, throwing everything off.

Each step seems too heavy, too exposed.

Reflex has me squeezing Bianca's hand harder than I should, desperate to anchor myself in her skin.

Everything around us moves in slow motion. Groups crowd the lockers, eyes dragging over us. Conversations cut off, mouths frozen mid-sentence. Heat crawls up the back of my neck.

Someone's backpack brushes my side and I flinch. Every glance seems targeted. Every laugh seems meant for me.

A girl with blonde braids watches from the water fountain, her eyes flicking to our joined hands before her lips curl.

Further down, the jocks sprawl against the walls, shoving each other just enough to show off. Shoulders broad, voices raised louder than needed. Alpha bullshit. Their stares crawl over my skin, dragging nails I can't shake.

They don't need to say a word. They've said it all before.

Psycho. Fuck-up. Freak.

They decided who I was in this hall a long time ago. Shoved me into a box I never asked for, branded by wisecracks and cheap shots in the middle of crowds. Sideways looks that said more than words ever could. Their laughter always carried loud enough for me to hear—because that was the point. They wanted me to.

I heard it all. Every name. Every word.

And now I'm walking straight into their line of fire with no armor.

My grip tightens.

One of them chuckles under his breath and grabs his crotch, making sure I see it. That's all I've ever been to them—an easy target. A quiet punchline. The guy who keeps his head down and takes it.

For years, I let them think I didn't care. Let them believe their shit didn't land. But it did. Every fucking time.

Up ahead, one of the cheerleaders drifts to the side, all hairspray and hollow smiles, held together with lip gloss and lies. Her perfume hits hard, sweet enough to rot teeth and thick enough to choke out anything honest.

She leans into her friend, whispering behind her hand, all fake nails and faker friendship.

The other one laughs out loud, a sound sharp enough to bruise.

They brush past with choreographed indifference, all hips and attitude, plastic confidence cracking at the edges.

We're almost past the stairwell when I hear it.

"Well, fuck," Jared Ross calls out, his voice carrying off every locker. "Didn't know Theo knew what to do with pussy."

Jared pushes off the wall, loud and smug, dripping with the same cocky swagger he's worn since freshman year. His letterman jacket hangs open, school colors on display, ego stitched into every step. Every inch of him screams spoiled jock who's never been told no.

"Seriously, man, thought you only had eyes for Nate," he calls out, louder this time. "Guess I got that wrong. You finally gave up on Nate and went for an easier target, huh?" He shrugs. "Guess you're just a freak. Closet case with a new toy."

A few of Jared's buddies snort, one of them clapping him on the shoulder.

Heat crawls up my spine. I say nothing. I can't. My body's stuck between freezing and exploding.

Quinn is the one who steps forward, planting herself between Jared and me, standing dead center with her hands loose at her sides.

"Oh, this is rich," Jared says, rolling his eyes. "What, the frigid bitch here to babysit the broken boy?"

"You've got a loud mouth for someone whose only experience with pussy comes from porn and his own fist." Quinn doesn't blink as she closes the distance. "You run your mouth like you've got game, but every girl you've touched had to fake it so hard they deserved Oscars."

She tilts her head, her voice dropping cold. "Maybe if you spent less time mouthing off about other people and more time figuring out what to do with a real girl, they wouldn't bolt the second your pants hit the floor."

Jared barks out a laugh, fake and forced.

"You still talking, Thomas?" he says. "No guy wants to fuck a mouth that bites back. Maybe if you dropped the attitude and opened your legs once in a while, you'd matter."

He smirks, but the laugh in his throat dies before it can make it out.

Nate steps forward. One second he's behind me, the next he's in Jared's face. His fist slams into Jared's jaw, the crack sharp, clean, beautiful.

Jared crashes into the lockers on his way down. Blood smears his lip, his spit turning pink, and he doesn't get back up.

Nate looms over him, eyes dead cold. "You open your mouth about Theo or Quinn again, and I'll break every fucking tooth in your head."

Jared spits blood onto the floor.

"You're all fucked," he mutters, wiping his mouth. "Every single one of you."

Nate tilts his head. "You fucking done?"

"Nate Reynolds. Principal's office. Now."

The hall freezes. Mr. Hanley stands there with his clipboard, his scowl, the same tired bullshit.

Nate doesn't move. He just stands there, blood drying on his knuckles, fury still burning in his eyes. Slowly, he turns his head, his gaze landing on me first.

"You good?" His voice is steady, that rare version of him that only comes out when shit gets real.

I nod. "Yeah."

His eyes move to Quinn. "You alright?"

She shrugs, a small lift of her shoulders. "Fucker had it coming."

Nate's mouth twists into a smile that never reaches his eyes. Then his gaze shifts to Bianca, watching her for a beat.

"You deaf, Reynolds?" Mr. Hanley barks again.

Only then does Nate turn and step away.

The hallway parts around him, students pulling back as if he might swing again. Jocks step aside. Cheerleaders hold their breath. Every eye tracks him, heads turning, too scared to look away. He walks straight ahead, spine rigid, silent.

Bianca pulls me forward, and my legs move on instinct. We leave the hall, leave Quinn, leave the echo of Nate's punch and the burn of a hundred stares behind us.

We slip down a side corridor, out of sight. Past the lockers and peeling posters, until we're tucked behind the stairwell, hidden from them all.

Bianca lifts her hand, her fingers brushing my jaw. I freeze.

"Do you know what I see?" she asks.

I shake my head.

"I see someone who's been surviving for too fucking long. Someone who's been told he's nothing so many times he started to believe it. But you're not nothing, Theo. You're everything."

My throat tightens. I stare at her, frozen, unable to speak.

"Do you even see it?" she whispers. "What I see when I look at you?"

"No."

"I wish you did. I wish you could see yourself through my eyes for one fucking second. You'd never believe you were nothing again."

She steps closer, and her necklace shifts with the movement, swinging forward—silver angel wings, tarnished at the edges. The chain catches the weak light spilling through the high windows.

She always wears it. I've seen it a hundred times. Wrapped around her throat in class. Tucked into her shirt when she plays. Catching against her collar bone when she laughs. It's always there. Always part of her.

"You're beautiful, you idiot," she says, almost laughing, though her eyes shine. "And you're funny. So fucking funny I can't wait to hear what comes out of your mouth next. Quinn sees it. Nate sees it. The only ones who don't are those fuckers who were never worth a damn anyway."

She notices my eyes on the wings and a small smile tugs at her mouth.

Without a word, she reaches behind her neck, fingers working the clasp until it gives. The wings slip into her palm. Then she steps back into my space, close enough that I forget to breathe.

"I want you to be exactly who you are," she says. "Not the version they shoved you into. Not the shadow you think you have to become just to survive this place. I want you to be spectacular. Beautiful. All of it."

She lifts the chain and settles it around my neck, her knuckles brushing my skin as she fastens the clasp. I feel every second of it.

I close my eyes for a moment. I want to believe her. I want to be the boy she sees when she looks at me. The one who isn't broken. The one who isn't scared.

"I'm not giving this to you because I want you to keep it," she murmurs. "I'm giving it to you so you can remember. Every time you start to shrink. Every time you want to fade. This is proof that someone fucking sees you."

My throat burns. Something cracks beneath my ribs. I stay frozen.

Bianca steps back, her eyes on the angel wings now hanging around my neck. "One day, when you finally believe you're worth more than you think... you'll give it back."

"I..." My voice splinters. I clear my throat. "I will. I promise."

"I love you, Theo." Her voice softens. "I just wish you'd learn to love yourself a little more."

She leans in and presses a gentle kiss to my mouth. When she pulls away, that smile is there—the one that asks for nothing, the one that tells me she sees all of me. Every scar, every shadow, every dark corner.

CHAPTER 10

Quinn

The photos are piling up. Stacks of prints cover my desk, my bed, even the floor under the window. I keep telling myself I'll sort them, label them, slip them neatly into sleeves. But every time I try, I get distracted.

There's a photo of Nate, eyes closed behind his drum kit, sticks suspended mid-air. Sweat clings to the curve of his neck, his mouth parted, chest heaving. You can't hear it, but you can feel it in the shot—every beat he hurls into the silence.

There's one of Theo strumming chords, his shirt riding up just enough to reveal the scar across his hip. He's caught mid-story, and Bianca's laughing, her head tipped back, mouth wide open, the sound spilling out of her as if it belongs to both of them.

The camera stays close these days. Close enough no one notices anymore. They've grown used to it. To me. To the way I move through their noise, catching what slips through the cracks. The four of us, bound by sound and chaos. Bianca tangled up with the boys in a way none of us dare name.

She's become my best friend.

I've never really had one before. I always kept people at arm's length, far enough they couldn't reach the parts of me I wasn't ready to explain.

The guys only ever wanted one thing. None of them gave a shit about the girl behind the lens, the one with something real to say. And the girls... they smiled with their teeth, then tore each other apart the second backs were turned. All glitter and venom.

So I kept to myself. It was easier that way. No pressure to perform. No need to prove I was worth the space I took up.

But something's changed.

I feel it when we're crammed into Nate and Theo's bedroom, music buzzing through the air. I see it in Nate's crooked grin mid-jam, in the way Theo looks at Bianca like she's his next breath. I hear it when Bianca leans in to whisper something meant only for me, and my laugh slips out before I can stop it.

I belong, to this chaos, to them. The four of us, loud, messy, untouchable. And for the first time in my life, I don't want to keep my distance.

We eat chips off the amp case and argue about pointless shit. Theo never says no when I ask to shoot him. Nate calls me Annie fucking Leibovitz and swipes my camera when I'm not looking, probably to fill it with fifty blurry crotch shots and one close-up of his left nostril. Bianca pulls faces at the lens and swears she's going to start charging me.

Some nights we stay too long, sprawled across the back lawn with takeaway containers and shitty jokes. It isn't perfect. But it's ours.

For now.

And I've caught all of it on film.

Today I was supposed to spend the afternoon in the darkroom. I had a plan—music low, gloves on, chemicals biting into the paper until those moments turned into something real.

Instead, I'm in a mall changing room, wrestling with a pair of jeans that feel five sizes too small. The zipper won't budge, and I'm pretty sure I'm about to either suffocate or snap the damn thing in half.

"Quinn?" Bianca's voice cuts through the curtain. "You alive in there or what?"

I peek out to find her sprawled on the bench, scrolling through her phone.

"B, these jeans are ridiculous," I groan. "Why the hell did I think this would work?"

She looks up from her phone, tilts her head, and studies me as if I'm a puzzle missing a few pieces.

"Ridiculous?" Her smile curves, all sweetness. "You're not ridiculous, Quinn. Just a little too adventurous with your choices."

"Adventurous? That's your nice way of saying dumb as shit, isn't it?" I grunt, yanking at the waistband, but it's a lost cause.

Bianca snorts. "They aren't that bad."

"They're skinny jeans, B. I swear one of my ovaries begged for mercy."

She bursts out laughing, then gets to her feet and saunters over. "Alright, drama queen. Step aside. Let me handle this."

I poke my head through the curtain like a nosy meerkat, watching Bianca prowl the store with the focus of someone on a life-or-death mission. She tears through racks of denim as if she's judging contestants on Project Runway: Jeans

Edition. Every so often she pauses, squints, then discards a pair with a shake of her head that screams, absolutely not, how dare you exist.

Then her hand stills.

She pulls a pair from the rack and holds them up to the light, eyes narrowing in thought. Slowly, she nods, as if she's just uncovered the Holy Grail of ass-lifting denim.

A moment later she returns, looking victorious, a pair of jeans draped over her arm. "I found them. These are perfect for you. I swear, you'll look so good even I'll be jealous."

I shoot her a skeptical look. "Jealous? What, are these jeans spun from unicorn hair and fairy dust?"

She grins, planting her hands on her hips. "These jeans will do things to your ass that'll have pedestrians walking into traffic."

I snort. "Perfect. I've always wanted to be a public safety hazard."

I close the curtain and shimmy into the jeans. They slide over my hips as if they were made for an actual human body instead of a Barbie doll. Snug. Soft. Not suffocating.

For once, something fits.

Bianca's laughter explodes outside the curtain.

I freeze, glaring at my reflection in the mirror. "I haven't even stepped out yet and you're already laughing at me?"

"No!" she wheezes through the curtain. "God, no. It's Theo. He just sent me the dumbest thing."

I raise a brow. "What kind of dumb are we talking? Naked dumb, or accidental-poetry dumb?"

"Somewhere in between." She snorts again, her voice light and playful. "He's got this way of being funny without even trying. I don't know how he does it. It's just... Theo."

I tug the waistband into place and glance at my reflection, my voice quieter. "What's it like? Having both of them—Nate and Theo. When it's just you and them. What's that feel like?"

Bianca goes quiet. For a beat, all I hear is the silence pressing through the curtain, gears turning in her head. Then, after a moment, she speaks.

"With them, it's more than I ever thought I'd have. It's this low, steady thrum in my chest, wild and calm all at once. It's the kind that makes your heart ache in the best way. Theo's intense, wound so tight you feel like you have to hold him together with your bare hands. But underneath all that? He's soft. Scared, sometimes. It kills me, the way he's gentle when he lets the guard drop, the way he's terrified of not being enough. And I'd burn the world down to protect that part of him."

She pauses, and I catch the soft exhale.

"And Nate... he's calm. Solid. He always knows when Theo's spiraling, always knows exactly what to say. That boy's got a mouth on him, I tell you." Her voice tilts into a grin. "He's the one who'll drag the orgasm out of you while whispering filthy things in your ear."

I blink. "Jesus. That's... a lot."

She laughs. "Yeah, well, you asked."

"You know Nate used to be a fuckboy. He collected girls the way Theo collects guitar picks," I say, giving the waistband one last tug. "Figured he picked up a few skills in that department."

Bianca snorts. "You have no idea."

I take a deep breath and tug the curtain open.

When she sees me her whole face lights up.

"Told you," she says, twirling her finger in the air like she's summoning a fashion runway. "Turn around. Let me see that ass."

I roll my eyes but spin anyway, fighting the smile tugging at my mouth. The jeans fit. Not just my body, somehow, they fit me.

I glance at the mirror, still half-convinced the reflection isn't mine. Then her voice cuts through the doubt.

"I'm not joking. Those jeans are perfect. Criminally perfect. They should come with a warning label."

A laugh slips out of me before I can stop it.

She pushes off the bench, phone still in her hand, mouth already halfway to another compliment. "No, seriously, Quinn. I can't believe how—"

The words cut off. Something shifts.

Her face goes slack, the smile gone. One foot edges back, half an inch. Her body wavers, unsteady, and her hand lifts, fingers twitching toward me as if reaching for a railing that isn't there.

"Bianca?" My voice scrapes its way up my throat.

She sways again. Less controlled this time, less steady. I take a step forward, heart kicking hard in my chest.

She blinks once, slow and unfocused, as if her brain is buffering and her body's losing signal.

Her fingers slacken and the phone slips, tumbling in slow motion, screen-first to the floor. It smashes against the tiles, skidding across the polished surface until it spins to a stop, the glass fractured into a spiderweb of cracks.

And then she crumples.

Her knees give first, the rest of her body following, collapsing like a marionette with its strings cut. Her arms hang loose at her sides, head tipping forward as gravity drains the strength from her, folding her into something broken and small.

She hits the floor in slow motion, limbs twisted beneath her—a ragdoll dropped by careless hands.

One moment she's standing, vibrant and laughing.

The next, she's on the ground.

Silent. Still. Terrifyingly fragile.

I move before my brain can catch up.

My knees slam the floor, pain shooting up my legs, but I don't feel it. My hands find her arms, her face, anywhere I can touch, anywhere I can prove she's still here, still breathing.

"Bianca," I choke, my voice shaking. "Hey, Bianca, come on. Talk to me. Fuck, say something."

Her eyes flutter open, slow and unsteady, lashes trembling as she looks up at me. Her gaze is clouded, unfocused, searching my face as if I'm a stranger. Her lips part, moving without sound, words trapped somewhere deep in her throat.

She gasps, shallow and uneven, her chest rising and falling too fast. Under the harsh store lights her skin looks too pale, sweat gathering on her forehead, dark hair plastered to her temple. She looks fragile, nothing like the fierce, vibrant girl who was laughing with me only moments ago.

Her eyes slide shut again, as if sleep is pulling her under.

"Bianca!" My voice cracks apart, panic tearing through it. I whip around, vision blurring, heart slamming in my throat. "Somebody help us! Please, someone!"

Shadows shift around me, voices muffled at first, then suddenly closer, urgent footsteps rushing in. A woman shouts, cutting through my panic: "Oh my God, someone call the paramedics!"

Another voice echoes, already on the phone, words spilling too fast—an ambulance, an address, everything sounding impossibly far away.

Footsteps close in, bodies pressing closer. A store clerk drops to her knees, hovering at Bianca's side, eyes wide, hands trembling as she reaches out but hesitates.

"Is she breathing?" another voice demands, sharp and tight with fear.

"Yes!" I shout, but it tears out of me half a sob, my throat raw with terror. "I—I don't know what's happening, she just collapsed... I don't know—"

My voice shatters, choking off, tears spilling down my cheeks, blinding me as I clutch Bianca's hand, my fingers trembling violently.

"I'm right here," I whisper fiercely, squeezing her hand tighter, as if I could force my strength, my life, into her.

Around us, people move frantically—phones pressed to ears, voices raised, panic swirling. I can't breathe. I'm trapped here, gripping Bianca's hand, waiting, begging for her eyes to open again, for her lips to move, for the wail of sirens to cut through this suffocating silence.

I've been standing on Nate's front porch for twenty minutes.

The wood creaks under my shoes when I shift my weight, but I still can't lift my hand to knock. I just stare at the door.

I swipe at my face again, but the tears keep coming. My cheeks sting from it, my head throbs, and my chest feels caved in, crushed under the weight of everything I can't fix.

Every time I close my eyes, I see her.

Her face, pale and still. Her fingers limp in mine. Her eyes not really seeing me. The way her body just gave out, as if something inside her snapped and there was no time to catch it. No way to stop it.

I watched her chest go still. Watched the color drain from her face. Felt the silence settle when no one pressed down on her chest anymore. When the paramedics looked at each other and didn't need to say a word.

I had never screamed like that before. I didn't even know I could.

I was the one who called her mom.

That call will haunt me forever. I could barely breathe, couldn't force the words out. I just kept saying her name. And on the other end, her mom broke.

And now I'm here, my fingers twitching at my sides, desperate to do something, but all I can do is stare at the fucking door.

The house is quiet. Too fucking quiet for what's about to hit it.

My stomach churns because there's no right way to say it. No version that won't split the ground open.

Bianca is gone. And it's on me to hand that truth to them, wrapped in broken pieces and silence. To take the memory of her laughter, her fire, all that fucking light she carried, and crush it with three words.

Bianca is gone.

The words claw at me, tearing me apart before I can even force them out.

My hand hovers near the door, but I don't knock. Because the second I do, this stops being the worst day of my life and becomes the worst day of theirs.

They don't know yet. Inside that house, Bianca still exists. In their world, she's still alive. And I'm about to end that.

I close my eyes for half a second, but all I see is her face. I swallow hard, my throat burning. She was everything to them, to me, to us.

She held all our jagged edges together and never once asked for anything in return. And now I have to tell the boys who loved her that she's never coming back. There's no right way to break someone's heart.

I drag in a breath that barely makes it past my ribs and lift my hand to knock. The sound echoes too loud, cracking through the stillness like a warning shot.

The second my knuckles leave the wood, I want to take it back. Swallow it down. Pretend I was never here.

But the door swings open anyway. And there they are, Nate and Theo. Side by side. Smiling.

Their joy slams into me like a punch.

Nate's smile falters first, his brows pulling tight.

Theo's halfway through some smartass comment, but it dies the second he sees me.

I don't even realize the tears are still falling until I catch the way their expressions shift. I swipe at my face, but it's too late.

"Quinn?" Nate's voice drops, heavy with worry. "What happened?"

He steps forward without waiting, his hands half-reaching out, like he can't decide if I'm hurt or about to collapse.

My heart pounds against my ribs as I fight for words. My hands won't stop shaking, and I wipe at my eyes, desperate to control the tears that keep spilling over.

"I..." The sound cracks before I can form the words. I swallow hard, but the knot in my throat doesn't budge. I don't even know how to fucking say this.

Nate's eyes stay locked on mine. Theo's flick back and forth between us, restless, searching.

"We were at the mall," I start, my breath hitching. "Bianca made me try on these stupid jeans, and we were laughing, and then..."

My eyes drop to the ground, because saying it out loud makes it real. "She just... she just dropped. Mid-sentence. Her phone hit the floor and then she did too. It was as if someone flipped a switch and shut her off."

My fingers press to my forehead. "I thought she was messing around. For a second, I thought it was a joke. But her eyes—oh God, her fucking eyes—they didn't look like her. And I kept calling her name, but she didn't answer. She didn't move. She was right there, and she didn't fucking move."

Theo's brows pull tight, his jaw clenched.

"Wait, what are you saying?" His voice jumps. "She fainted? Passed out—"

"No." I cut him off, shaking my head. "No, it wasn't that." I force myself to look up. "She never opened her eyes again."

The air goes still. Nate stumbles a step back, as if the ground tilted beneath him.

Theo blinks hard. "No." His voice is thin, breaking.

I press my fists into my sides to stop the shaking. "The paramedics tried. They said there was nothing they could do. It was already..."

The word won't come. It doesn't need to.

Theo's hand slams against the doorframe, gripping it like he needs it to stay upright. "No. No, you're wrong. She's fucking fine."

"She's gone, Theo." My voice splinters, breaking the quiet. "She's really gone."

The look on their faces, God. It isn't just shock. It's devastation.

"I'm sorry." My throat tightens, strangling the words. "I don't even know how to explain it. I couldn't... I couldn't do anything."

Theo stumbles back a step as if I slapped him, as if he can still wake up from this. Nate doesn't move. His chest rises once, sharp, then again, slower. And suddenly, he's there.

His arms wrap around me on instinct, tight and desperate, as if he's afraid I'll disappear too. I collapse into him because there's nowhere else to go. My fists clutch at the back of his shirt, sobs tearing out of me, ugly and loud.

He's shaking. I feel it in the way his arms clamp around me, in the way his fingers knot into the fabric of my jacket like it's the only thing holding him up. His breath shudders against my hair, fast and uneven.

"She... she's not okay," I whisper, the words scraping my throat. "Bianca... she didn't make it. She died, Nate. Before the paramedics even got there. She was already—"

The breath rushes out of him. He doesn't speak. He just buries his face in my shoulder and clings, and I cling back, both of us crushed beneath the weight of her loss.

Beside us, Theo sinks to the floor without a sound, his hands tangled in his hair, his eyes vacant, as if the world has slipped out from under him.

He doesn't say a word. Just pulls his phone from his pocket with shaking hands. His fingers fumble against the screen, clumsy, foreign. He taps her name.

The call screen lights up. Ringing.

One ring.

Two.

My heart stutters, because I know exactly what he's doing. I know what he's hoping. If he can just hear her voice, even for a second, maybe it won't be real. Maybe this is all some kind of mistake, some nightmare we'll wake from.

Three rings.

He presses the phone harder to his ear, his jaw clenched so tight it looks ready to crack. Nate reaches for him but stops. We all stop.

Four rings.

I hold my breath. I don't know why I expect silence, but I do.

"Come on, Bianca," Theo whispers, his voice breaking apart. "Pick up. Pick up the fucking phone."

Her voicemail cuts in. That familiar tone, then her voice—casual, sweet. *"Hey, it's Bianca. You know what to do."*

The call ends. Theo stares at the screen until the first tear slips down his cheek. Then another. And another.

He blinks hard, as if he can stop them, but his body begins to shake. The phone slips from his hand and clatters to the floor. His shoulders fold inward, and for a moment he looks like a kid who's just learned the world isn't fair. That good people die. That love can end in a fucking shopping mall dressing room.

"No." It rips out of him—a word, a scream, a prayer. "No. Fuck, no—"

His fingers dig into his jeans, gripping hard as his body shakes. His spine curls inward, shoulders collapsing. His face crumples in a way I'll never forget, as if every piece of him is shattering under the weight of her being gone. The sobs tear through him, full-body, violent, ugly. He drags his hands over his face, but it's useless. The sound of him drowns out everything else.

Nate moves first. He hauls Theo into his arms like his life depends on it.

Theo's falling apart in front of me. Nate's holding him like his arms alone could stop him from unraveling. But I see it in Nate's face. He's breaking too. His chest rises too fast, his jaw locked tight, holding in a scream that wants out.

His eyes flick around, landing on nothing, and still he's trying to be the strong one for Theo.

I press a hand to my chest. My legs won't move. My throat won't open. I feel like I'm underwater. No light. No air. Just grief swallowing us whole.

I want to reach for them, to hold them both, to crawl into their pain and carry it on my back if it would stop them from breaking. But I can't move. I'm frozen, watching something unfixable unravel right in front of me.

Then Nate looks up.

And fuck, that look. His eyes are bloodshot, wet, wide with too much emotion and nowhere to put it. The second we lock eyes, I see the moment it shatters him. His mouth parts, just slightly, like he wants to speak, but nothing comes. He doesn't need to. I see it in his face—the same pain, the same loss, the same fucking helplessness.

Nate reaches out, his hand closing around my wrist, tugging me forward as if he can't take another breath without pulling me into it too, into the grief that belongs to all of us.

And I go, because I can't hold myself up anymore either.

He pulls me down, my forehead pressing into his shoulder as the tears come. Theo shifts, one hand still clinging to Nate, the other fisting the back of my jacket.

The three of us fold into each other, wrapped tight in a silence that only exists when something permanent has been ripped away.

We don't speak. We don't move. Just the three of us, holding on in a silence so heavy it feels like the world itself is holding its breath.

And I know, with every part of me, that nothing will ever be the same again.

CHAPTER 11

Nate

It's been five days since Bianca died. Five days of pretending the world hasn't ended. Five days of dragging my body out of bed and walking through a life that doesn't feel like mine anymore.

The sun still rises. People still talk, and none of it fucking matters.

I keep thinking I'll wake up. That one morning I'll open my eyes and the air won't seem this heavy. That I won't ache like I'm drowning in a room full of oxygen. But every day bleeds into the next, and she's still gone. Still not texting me. Still not walking through the door with her iced latte and that smile that made everything seem less broken.

I keep catching myself about to say her name. About to send her a meme. About to tell her something Theo did that would've made her laugh until she snorted.

And then I remember... she's not here to laugh anymore.

Everything I do seems pointless. I eat, but nothing tastes of anything. I sleep, but I don't rest. I breathe, but the breath is shallow, my body doing this out of obligation, not from want.

I sit here, trying to stitch myself back together with threads that keep snapping.

I can't remember who I was before her. I realize that's stupid, given the amount of time we had together. Eight months of loving her, and I can't tell who I'm supposed to be without her.

All I understand is this: Bianca is gone. And the world keeps turning as if that's not the most fucked-up thing it's ever done.

Theo's barely here. He disappears now, vanishes into silence and shadows as though that's the only place he can breathe. Sometimes he's gone for hours. Other times... it's days.

No messages. Only absence.

I don't understand where he goes. Fuck, I can't tell if he even wants to come back. But the worst part now is I no longer know how to reach him anymore.

I used to be able to pull him out of the dark by saying something stupid. Elbow him. Remind him that he's still here, that he's still loved. He'd roll his eyes, call me an asshole, and let the wall crack just enough for me to squeeze through.

But not now.

Now it's concrete. Cold and solid. He's locked behind the wall and I don't have the fucking key.

I want to reach out and grab him and shake the pain out of him. Tell him we're in this together. That I feel the same way too. That Bianca's name still echoes in my chest like a bruise that won't stop blooming.

But the truth is... I'm barely keeping my own head above water. How the fuck am I supposed to save him when I'm drowning too?

I stand in my bedroom, staring at the spot where she used to sit, cross-legged, grinning, some smartass comment always locked and loaded. But it's empty now. Her laugh is stitched into these walls, taunting me with a ghost I can't touch. She's...

Gone.

I still can't make peace with that word. The word doesn't fit her. She was fire. She was fucking stardust. And now she's... nowhere.

I press the heel of my hand into my chest, trying to push back the weight settling inside. The weight's too heavy. Too cruel.

My fingers reach into my pocket the same way they have a thousand times these past five days, curling around the smooth, worn edges of her guitar pick. The pick's mine now. Or perhaps I belong to the pick. I've been clinging to the thing as though the pick can anchor me to the version of myself that existed when she was still here.

I rub the pick between my fingers, and for half a second—for the tiniest, most fucked-up heartbeat—I almost convince myself I'll catch her voice behind me. Sense her brush past, rolling her eyes, calling me dramatic.

But there's nothing.

Just the silence. And me, choking on everything I never got to say.

I never told her I loved her. I wanted to. The words sat on my tongue more times than I can count, pressing against the back of my teeth, begging to be let out. But I never gave them air.

I thought I had time. That I could wait until the moment seemed right. I kept telling myself that day would come. Another chance. I thought I could hold the truth in a little longer and the delay wouldn't matter.

Now it fucking matters more than anything.

She's gone, and I'm standing in the ruin of everything I never said. She didn't realize. She had no idea that I loved her.

And that truth is fucking killing me.

I haven't seen Quinn since the day the whole thing happened. Not a word. Not even a fucking text.

The reason is I don't know how to face her.

Every time I go to pick up my phone, my hand just fucking hovers there, frozen. My thumb over her name, heart in my throat, and then nothing. I tell myself I'll text her tomorrow. I'll call her later. But later never comes. What the fuck am I even supposed to say? Sorry you watched the person you love die. Sorry you were alone in that.

She lost her best friend. The one who knew her better than anyone. She's drowning in the same fucking grief that's tearing me apart. I want to reach out. I want to knock on her door, pull her into my arms, tell her she's not alone in this. But I can't. How do I help Quinn breathe when my own lungs are collapsing?

I'm flat on my back, staring at the ceiling, when the bedroom door creaks open.

I turn my head, and Theo is there. He doesn't speak. He doesn't even lift his head. He simply stands in the doorway, hands shoved so deep into his pockets. His hood's up again, pulled low, trying to hide the mess underneath.

He appears as if he hasn't slept, hasn't eaten. Hasn't fucking existed since the moment she died. Just floats through time, eyes blank, breath shallow, held together by nothing but the thinnest thread of force, and even that's giving out. He still won't meet my gaze. Maybe he can't. Probably knows the second our eyes connect, he'll fall apart all over again when he sees the same truth in my face. The bloodshot eyes. The cracked lips. The hollowness carved so deep into my chest I don't even bother trying to scrape the weight away anymore.

I want to say something but the words rot in my throat before they ever make it out. Nothing exists that I can give him that he doesn't already carry. The truth's carved into both of us, plain as day.

We're not fucking okay. We're never going to be.

Theo steps further into the room, his eyes flicker to mine for a moment. The pain in them hits hard, sharper than anything I've felt since this whole thing started. He opens his mouth like he wants to speak, but nothing comes out. His jaw works, throat tight, but whatever he was about to say dies before it's born.

"Where the hell have you been?"

The words tear out of me, hoarse and jagged, like they've been stuck in my throat for days. I don't mean for them to sound so harsh, and I hate that it sounds like blame when all I really carry is the ache of missing him.

Theo looks at me. I see it—right there in his eyes—the fight to hold it together, the silent scream behind the silence.

I rise from the bed, the space between us suddenly unbearable.

A few steps closer to him, and everything becomes clear. His eyes are shining, tears pooling at the edges, held back by nothing but sheer force of will. His jaw is tight, shoulders rigid, the emotion is present. He's barely holding himself together, and I see every fractured piece. He too is dying inside, much the same as me.

I pull him into a hug before he can pull away. He doesn't resist. He crumbles into me, his body heavy with grief.

"I don't understand how to do this, Nate," he whispers. "I can't figure out how to live in a world where she's not here."

He crumples forward, chest heaving as he folds into me, fists bunching in my shirt as though this is the only thing tethering him to this fucking earth. The first sob tears out of him as if it had been waiting for years, and suddenly it hits, wave after wave. Shaking. Shuddering. Falling the fuck apart in my arms.

I grip him harder, locking us together, trying to hold all his pieces in place.

My own eyes blur, throat closing around the words I'm barely getting out.

"I don't either, man. But we're gonna have to figure it out. Together. Because I can't—" My voice catches. "I can't lose you too."

He clings tighter, fingers digging into my back like he's scared I'll disappear too.

"You can't keep doing this, Theo." My voice stays even, but everything in me seems to be cracking open. "You can't keep vanishing every time things get too hard."

He doesn't meet my eyes, only keeps gripping my shirt.

"Please," I push, voice shaking now. "You're my fucking brother. I can't let you keep hurting yourself just to feel something."

I pause, swallowing the lump rising in my throat.

"She wouldn't want that. You know that. She hated when you tried to make yourself small."

Theo pulls back slightly. He scrubs a hand down over his face like he can wipe it all away. The tears, the pain, the truth of it.

"I can't figure out how to stand at that spot tomorrow, Nate and watch them put her in the ground." His whole body trembles, shoulders caving. "I can't face this. I can't say goodbye."

I pull him back into me, holding tight, holding steady, as though I can shoulder some of the weight for him.

"I'll be there," I whisper. "You won't have to do it alone."

His breath shudders against my shoulder. His fists stay bunched in my shirt as his sobs shake both of us.

I don't let go.

I stay rooted, arms locked tight around him, anchoring us both. Because when someone means the fucking world to you, you hold on. No matter how hard things get. No matter how much it hurts. You hold on until they can breathe again.

The sky's too clear for a day this cruel. Sunlight spills over the cemetery as though the world is clueless, and doesn't give a shit about the girl we're about to bury. Clouds should be crowding the horizon. Thunder. Something to match the storm ripping through my fucking chest.

Each step toward the gravesite is heavier than the last. My boots crunch over gravel, before grass, but I barely register the sound. Everything blurs together. Only noise under the weight pressing down on my shoulders. My lungs keep tightening, as though they're being squeezed by something I can't shake off.

Theo walks beside me, silent. He's a shadow of himself—shoulders hunched, eyes locked on the ground, fists shoved deep into his pockets. His jaw's clenched so hard I can see the muscle twitch, but he doesn't speak. Doesn't blink. He's holding everything in, sealing himself shut so nothing leaks out, and the weight scares the shit out of me. Because I know what happens when he does that. I've seen where it leads.

Scarlet's on my other side, barely holding herself upright. Her eyes are red, her hands shaking, and her lip keeps trembling like she's one second from falling apart. She stares straight ahead, but her gaze is empty. Hollow. I want to reach for her, to tell her it's okay to break, but I don't have the words. I'm barely holding myself together.

Behind us, I hear Mom sniff once, sharp and broken, and I know Dad's got his arm around her. But there's nothing they can do. No words. No prayers. No fucking eulogy is going to fix this.

Bianca's gone. And we're walking toward the moment it becomes real... permanent... final.

I don't want to take another step, but I keep moving, because she deserves that much.

Nothing remains of her but memories. And even those don't seem safe anymore. Every time I try to hold on to one, it cuts me open. Her laugh echoes in my head, and it seems wrong—too far away, too fragile. Her voice used to ground me. Now she's only a fucking ghost.

I thought I broke the day Quinn showed up, her face pale, her mouth trembling as she spoke the words that shattered everything. But this is worse. This is standing in front of a white fucking coffin, knowing she's in there. Knowing that's it. That's where she ends. No more late-night texts. No more smirks across the room. No more her.

My chest aches. I want to scream. I want to rip the world apart for doing this to her. For doing this to us. But I stand there. Useless. Fucked up. Broken in a way I'll never come back from.

Because this grave, the silence, this fucking pain that won't quit is all I have left.

The cemetery is full of people. Some I recognize. Some I don't. Faces blur into each other—dull eyes, forced sympathy, hands reaching out with condolences that mean fucking nothing. Every murmur seems wrong. Every goddamn whisper lands like a slap. No one knows what to say, and even if they did, I wouldn't want to hear it.

I'm standing still, but it feels like I'm floating outside myself. Everything's muted, like I'm underwater, the pressure building in my chest with every second that ticks by. My feet are planted in the grass, but I swear the ground could crack open beneath me and I wouldn't flinch.

Bianca's mother stands near the coffin, her body shaking as though she's about to shatter. She keeps rubbing at her eyes, trying to scrub away the grief, but the effort's fucking useless. There's no fixing this. No undoing a damn thing. Her sobs tear through the air, and I feel every single one of them hit.

This is what the end looks like. Not some poetic goodbye. Not a soft fade. Just endless pain.

Finally, I lift my eyes to the coffin.

The flowers sitting on top are too fucking bright. Reds and yellows, pinks and purples bursting as though they're clueless about where they are. The whole display insults me in a way, with how cheerful they are. As if someone thought they could dress death up in color and make it easier to swallow. They're loud. Bold. Over-the-top.

She would've hated them. I can already catch her voice full of that dry sarcasm, laughing and shaking her head. "Who the hell picked these out?"

She'd turn to Theo with that wicked glint in her eye, that grin that always meant trouble, and throw him the line. "Alright, Theo. Hit me with your best line about these tacky-ass funeral flowers."

And he would've done it. He always did so she would smile. Would've said something like, "These flowers look like a clown went on a vodka bender and threw up in a garden."

And Bianca would fucking laugh. That loud, unfiltered kind of laugh that made everyone stop and stare. Eyes shining, head thrown back, chest shaking as though she couldn't hold the sound even if she tried. And none of it would matter if Theo's line was half-baked bullshit—she'd eat the words up anyway, make them sound like the funniest thing she'd ever heard. That was her.

But now, all we have is silence.

Movement pulls at the corner of my eye, and when I look up, I see Quinn. She's moving toward us, sunglasses on like they can hide the pain underneath. Her cheeks are blotched red, streaked with tears she's not even bothering to wipe away anymore. Her lips pressed together so tight they've turned white. There's no hiding this kind of pain. I've never seen her look so small before.

She stops a few feet away, her arms wrapped tightly around herself, as if she can keep in the pain. Her chin trembles, and I can see her breathing start to hitch.

I lift my hand and hold my palm towards her.

"Come here," I whisper.

Slowly, she takes a step. Then another. By the time she reaches me, she's already falling apart.

She crashes into my chest, arms around my waist, face buried in my shirt. Her body's shaking, and I can feel every fucking ounce of pain pouring out of her.

I hold her tighter. Let her fall apart in my arms, since there's nowhere safe left to fall.

Then a voice sounds. The priest begins to speak, his voice rising just enough to carry over the wind. Words about loss, about peace, about eternal rest. All delivered in that calm, practiced rhythm meant to comfort the grieving.

The words are distant, floating in the background, but all I register is the steady weight of Quinn leaning against me. She doesn't make a sound, but I can sense her falling apart in the way her weight leans harder with every word spoken.

This is the end. This is the moment when everything we believe about life stops. I swallow, trying to push the ache clawing its way up my throat, but the pain sticks inside me. That white coffin stares back, daring me to accept what's inside. Daring me to let her go.

But I can't.

Time warps into something broken. Seconds stretch and snap, looping in on themselves. I'm lost in a fog that doesn't have an end or a beginning. Everything feels disconnected, as if I'm watching the events playout through glass. Distant echoes in a world that's caved in. Nothing feels real. Everything hurts.

And that fucking coffin just sits there, holding all the pieces we'll never get back.

A sound breaks through the haze. A mechanical hum, as it begins to lower her coffin into the ground.

When the fuck did they take the flowers off?

My eyes snap to the coffin. That white box, inching downward, swallowed by dirt and finality. I blink hard, but nothing changes. I only keep watching the coffin move slow, as though the world's being cruel on purpose. Every inch the box sinks, something in my chest tears deeper. My heart feels stalled, caught in the space between beats, and all I can do is stand rooted and watch her disappear.

Theo inches forward, pulled toward the grave as though gravity's got a hold on him by the throat. His body moves on instinct as if he needs to be closer to her. He keeps his eyes locked on the coffin as the box lowers, as though he's trying to memorize every fucking inch of the wood before the sight disappears. He's following. Step by step. Closer to the edge. For a second, I swear he's going in after her.

Then Mom slips past me, and reaches for him. Her hand gently curls around Theo's arm. She doesn't say anything, just holds on. And somehow, that's enough. Enough to keep him here.

The machine comes to a sudden stop.

The silence that follows isn't peaceful. It's a chokehold. Pressed down on all of us like grief decided to grow teeth.

Then it happens. The first thud of dirt hits the coffin.

The impact slams through me, tearing straight into my chest. A sound I'll never fucking forget. That dull sound of soil against wood. Brutal in a way no one prepares you for. The blow wounds. The noise screams finality. No softness. Only the earth swallowing her whole, one savage shovelful at a time.

Beside me, Quinn flinches. Not once. Every single fucking time. Her body jerks like each hit is landing on her instead. I wrap my arm tighter around her, try to shield her from it, but I can't. None of us can.

That sound keeps coming, and with every drop of dirt, it's like we're being buried too.

I register the weight of a hand on my shoulder, familiar. My Dad. He doesn't speak. He never does when it matters most. He only stays beside me, solid and quiet, a lighthouse in the middle of my storm. And fuck, I'm tired of drowning.

Mom is the first one to speak.

"Sweetheart, the time has come to go," she says to Theo. That same tone she always uses with him. From that first night when he came to our house, sat at the table to eat, eyes hollow, trying to disappear inside himself.

He blinks, and for a second, I think he hasn't heard her. Then Scarlet's there too, slipping her hand into his. She doesn't say anything. Just links her fingers with his and waits. Not forcing him. Not pushing. Just holding steady.

Theo exhales, and he lets Scarlet lead him back one step at a time.

Then Dad's voice sounds behind me. "Come on, Son. It's time to go."

It's only then that I notice there's no one left at the graveside.

Just us.

Mom and Scarlet lead Theo past us without a word.

Quinn lifts her head. Her eyes meet mine, and fuck, the pain festering there knocks the air out of my lungs. I reach up and brush a strand of hair from her cheek. My fingers catch on a tear slipping down her skin.

Neither of us speaks.

We turn and walk away from the grave, leaving the only girl I've ever loved in the fucking ground. Cold. Gone. Forever. Because the hardest part isn't letting go—

It's knowing you never really can.

Chapter 12

Theo

Now

We're at Xander's place, scattered around the pool, the sun beating down like it's got something to prove. Chlorine clings to the air, thick with sunscreen and the smoky bite of whatever Xander's cooking on the grill.

It should be easy. Beer in hand, feet up, the pool cool enough to cut the heat. One of those rare fucking moments where time slows and nobody's bleeding out on the inside.

I take a long sip of my beer, letting the sound of splashing water, lazy conversation, and laughter I'm not part of settle into the space around me.

It's been a week since we were at Bianca's grave, and for once, it hasn't felt like I'm drowning.

The grief still sits in my chest, but it's quieter now. Less of a storm, more like a shadow. I still see her everywhere. I saw her in Quinn's smile, reminding me of the echo of those nights the four of us couldn't stop laughing. I see her in the songs Nate plays without realizing they used to be her favorites.

I guess talking about her with Quinn, saying Bianca's name out loud instead of bottling it up made a difference. The box of photos Quinn gave us helped too, at least for me.

Nate, though... I'm still not so sure. I know being at Quinn's place got to him.

It hit him every bit as hard as it did me. We spoke long about it on the way home. The way it seemed walking back into her world, seeing the way she's living, how fucking different it is from the life we've built.

Every day since we got home, I've gone through that box of photos. Sorting through the pieces. The kind of shit that shouldn't mean much but somehow means everything.

There's one photo Quinn took at that backyard band concert Bianca begged us all to go to, swearing the overpriced tickets were worth it. She dragged all three of us, anyway. Me, Nate, and Quinn, promising it'd be a night to remember.

She wasn't wrong. Worst fucking concert of my life.

The band sucked.

The speakers blew out halfway through.

I'm pretty sure the drummer was high off his ass, barely able to hold a beat.

But when Quinn pulled that old, crumpled ticket stub out of the box, none of that mattered.

Because suddenly, I was back there. Watching Bianca laugh so hard she could barely stand. Back to her dragging us all into a makeshift mosh pit with fifteen people, swearing it was the best night of her life. Back to the way she made everything feel bigger. Louder. More alive.

The second Quinn showed us that stub, we fucking lost it. We laughed until our ribs ached as we remembered that night.

That's what Quinn gave us. A reason to remember. To hold onto the happy stuff, instead of drowning in the day that we lost her.

My gaze drifts toward Scarlet and Ace, tucked away at the far end of the pool, wrapped up in each other like nothing else exists. She's on his lap, her body pressed tight against his. They're making out, completely unbothered by the world around them.

Ace's hands grip her waist, holding her like he's fucking addicted.

It's almost too much, the way they make it appear so damn effortless.

A smirk tugs at my mouth as I set my beer down, the beginnings of an idea creeping in. One I already know I won't ignore.

Time to piss off Ace.

I shove up from my seat, roll the tension from my shoulders, and dive headfirst into the pool. The cold slams into me, dulling everything for a moment. I break the surface beside them, close enough to make my presence known.

Ace barely reacts, too busy with his tongue down her throat to notice anything else. Scarlet's fingers are tangled in his hair, his hands still glued to her waist.

I slick my wet hair back, water dripping down my spine as I smirk.

"Damn, Ace," I say, loud enough to make sure it lands. "You're kissing like you're trying to lick the inside of her lungs. We celebrating something, or just horny on a Tuesday?"

"Fuck off, Theo."

"I would," I shoot back, all grin and no apology, "but I'm kinda worried she's gonna need CPR if you keep sucking the life out of her like that."

Ace turns his head toward me, the kind of slow that says he's already cataloging every brutal way he could take me out and still make it look like an accident.

Which means...

Mission fucking accomplished.

I grin, stretching out along the pool's edge as if I've got all the time in the world.

"Don't stop on my account," I add, smirking, every word a dare.

Ace opens his mouth, ready to put me in my place, but before he can fire off whatever smartass comeback he's got loaded, someone cuts him off.

"Uncle Theo!"

The tiny voice cuts through everything. I turn in time to see Alex waddling over, floaties strapped tight to his arms. His eyes are locked on me like I'm the most important person in his world right now.

Ace clenches his jaw, swallowing whatever insult he was about to throw my way.

I flash him a smug smile and push off the wall, drifting out, waiting for Alex. His tiny arms churn hard, floaties bouncing with every splash as he kicks toward me, determined as hell.

"You made it, kid," I say when he finally reaches me, breathless and beaming.

Alex grins proudly, pushing wet hair out of his face, chest puffed as if he swam the entire ocean.

"You wanna play a game?" I ask, smirking.

His eyes light up. "Yeah! What game?"

"Who can splash Uncle Ace the most?"

His mouth parts in surprise, eyes wide with awe. A slow smile spreads as he nods, arms already pulling back, ready for war.

"Theo, I swear to God—" Ace mutters, already regretting every decision that led him here.

I cut him off with a dramatic sigh, shaking my head as if the whole thing exhausts me.

"Man, you're no fun anymore. Not that you ever were," I add, floating backward, just out of range. "Seriously, let the kid live a little. Don't crush his spirit before he even hits double digits."

Alex doesn't wait for a green light. His hands crash into the water with the fury of a pint-sized hurricane, spraying wild, chaotic splashes straight into Ace's face.

Ace recoils with a sharp curse, water streaming from his lashes as he scrubs at his eyes.

Scarlet bursts out laughing, nearly doubling over. Alex beams like he's unlocked a brand-new life achievement.

Ace looks ready to decide if murder is worth the jail time. "You're a dead man, Theo."

I grin, smug as hell, all teeth and no remorse. "Bring it, rockstar. But you'll have to catch us first."

Alex lets out a delighted shriek and takes off paddling as if his life depends on it, arms flailing, water churning behind him like a damn speedboat.

But before I can make my great escape, Ace is on me. One swift move, a solid grip—and I'm under. Fuck.

When I resurface, gasping and shaking water from my face, Alex's giggle cuts through everything, echoing across the pool like music.

Ace is already on the hunt, slicing through the water with one target in sight. Alex.

Alex kicks harder, desperate to escape, but he doesn't stand a chance. Ace catches him with ease, gripping the floaties, but this time, he doesn't drag him under. He holds him steady instead, chest heaving, water dripping from his hair, and for a second, he looks... calm.

He lets Alex go but stays put. Big, broody, grumpy-as-fuck Ace, floating in the water with a kid who thinks the sun shines out of his ass.

I push through the water and drift over to Scarlet, stopping beside her. Neither of us says a word. We just stand there, staring.

Alex laughs, splashing at Ace, who barely reacts, just smirks and flicks water back at him.

For all the shit I give Ace. For every time I've made it my mission to piss him off, this is who he is. The guy who plays gruff and untouchable, yet lets a kid cling to him as if he's the safest place in the world.

"What's up with Nate?" Scarlet asks, her voice low enough that only I can hear. But I know her. She's been watching.

I shift my attention to where he stands by the grill, arms crossed, watching Xander flip whatever the hell he's burning.

I shrug, not because I don't care, but to pretend it doesn't hurt seeing him like that.

"You know... it's the time of year. Usual stuff."

Scarlet keeps her gaze on Nate. "He said you guys went to Quinn's. How is she?"

I shift, eyes lingering on Nate a second longer before I answer.

"She's still Quinn. Strong. Beautiful. Tough as hell." My voice drops. "The trip to Bianca's grave didn't hit as hard as the other times. Seeing Quinn there brought it all back. Reminded me of how it used to be when the four of us were only... us."

Scarlet glances over, a hint of a smirk tugging at her lips. "Five of us, sometimes."

A grin tugs at mine. "You did tag along more than a little."

She shrugs, casual, though something softer flickers in her expression. "I liked being around you guys. Quinn and Bianca were—" She cuts herself off, clears her throat. "It felt solid back then."

I nod. "Yeah. It did."

We both go quiet, memories pressing heavy between us. The silence says it all—we're all carrying the same ghost.

"So what's lover boy going to do when you start touring next month?" I ask, shifting the conversation.

Her face lights up instantly, that effortless, excited smile taking over. She glances toward where Ace is still hanging with Alex.

"Ace is flying to London to meet up before you guys start touring," she says, her voice softer now, a quiet joy settling in her chest. "He and Xander have been at the house all week, working on new songs. They're good." She looks back at me. "Are you keen to get back in the studio tomorrow?"

"Yeah," I say, smirking. "Gives me a chance to annoy the big guy."

Scarlet laughs. "Try not to get kicked out before lunch this time."

The smile lingers on her face, and I catch myself watching longer than I mean to. She's different now. I've never seen her this happy—not until Nate and I finally pulled our heads out of our asses and stopped giving Ace hell. He makes her happy. And that's what matters.

We both glance over when Poppy steps to the edge of the pool, one hand on her growing belly, the other shoving her wild hair from her face. She's glowing. Pregnancy suits her, even if she still gives Xander shit for treating her like she's made of glass.

He told me the other day how much he fucking loves seeing her pregnant. How it wrecks him in the best way, watching her body change, knowing she's carrying their child.

He missed it all the first time. Now he's here for everything: every scan, every craving, every midnight freak-out. And you can see how much it means to him, finally being able to show up.

"Lunch is ready," Poppy calls, her voice carrying across the pool.

I push off the edge, grinning up at her. "You coming for a swim, Spitfire?"

She snorts, arching a brow. "Yeah, let me squeeze in a quick cannonball."

I smirk, arms spreading wide. "Hey, weight distribution could work in your favor. Might even give you some serious height."

Scarlet chokes on a laugh while Poppy shoots me a look that says she's debating if I'm worth the effort of smacking.

Ace is already lifting Alex out of the pool, the kid grinning like he's just conquered the deep end.

Poppy's gaze shifts to them, her expression softening the way it always does when she looks at him.

Scarlet and I push out of the water, shaking off droplets clinging to our skin. Ace sets Alex down, ruffles his soaked hair, then drops a towel over the kid's head, earning a muffled protest.

Together, we head for the house, wet footprints trailing across the patio behind us.

Xander and Nate are already at the table. Nate's got a beer in hand, while Xander sits close to Poppy, watching her the way he always does, protective, calm, ready to step in if she so much as reaches for a plate.

I walk to the fridge, swing the door open, and grab three beers. Nothing for Poppy. I already know Xander's handled it. He's probably made sure she's got water, juice, or whatever the hell she's craving today. He doesn't miss a thing.

That's who he is now, the guy who looks after his family without being asked. The one who always seems to know what someone needs before they say a word.

There was always something missing in him. He had the music, the fame, the wild nights and noise. Groupies lined up to fuck him, offering anything he wanted—but none of it ever settled him.

His eyes gave it away. Restless. Haunted. Like he was chasing something he couldn't name.

One night, after too many drinks and way too much weed, he spilled it all. How he fucked it up. How he left his heart back in that fucked-up town. How he should've stayed. Should've stood up to her mother.

He said it like a confession, but the truth was already carved into him.

I get it now. I get what he was missing.

It was her.

Poppy.

Spitfire.

She anchors him in this life, and not in some fairytale, perfect kind of way. She drives him crazy at times, calls him on his shit, keeps him honest. But she's his. And he'd give the world to make her happy.

You can see it in the way he watches her when she laughs, in how he listens to every word she says, even when she's not talking to him. He'd hand her the whole damn world just to see her smile. These days, when Xander walks into a room, there's an ease about him, a calm I never saw before.

I kick the fridge door shut and head to the table, handing beers to Scarlet and Ace before dropping into the seat across from Nate. Alex climbs into the chair beside me, still dripping pool water, grinning like the world's never touched him.

The room hums with easy noise. Xander and Ace bickering over nothing while Scarlet rolls her eyes and steals food off his plate. Alex crams way too much into his mouth, as if chewing is optional.

It's chaos. It's family. Messy, loud, imperfect as fuck, but mine. And I wouldn't trade a second of it.

I glance around the table and catch the quiet hiding beneath the noise. Xander leans into Poppy, murmuring something only she'll ever hear. Scarlet and Ace are wrapped up in their own world—half teasing, half tangled in something that runs deep.

And then there's me and Nate.

I shift my gaze to him, and he's already watching, like he feels it too. The way we hover on the edge of this life. Close enough to touch it, never far enough inside.

Everyone else has found their people. Their peace. And us...we're still stuck. Still waiting on something we lost a long time ago. Something that's never coming back.

I blink, shake it off, and drag myself out of it. The table's still loud, still alive, and I force myself to tune back in.

Ace is elbow-deep in some rant about a new bridge he's written. Xander's giving him shit about the chord change, and Scarlet's throwing in comments between bites. Alex is trying to stack grapes on top of each other, determined, like the fate of the world depends on it.

Xander finally raises his voice, just enough to cut through and get us back on track. "Kit wants to see us in the morning. Meeting's at ten."

"What about?" Nate asks.

Xander doesn't answer right away. He takes a sip of his beer, eyes flicking between the few of us still half-listening.

"She wants to give the fans more," he says finally. "Not just the music. Everything around it. The process. A glimpse inside what we're building this time."

Ace raises an eyebrow. "What the fuck does that mean?"

Xander shrugs. "I doubt even she knows yet. Something about documenting all of it—the writing, the recording, the lead-up to the tour."

Ace groans. "Fuck me. Next we'll be doing TikTok dances." His eyes flick to Alex. "Shit. I mean... fudge me."

Scarlet shakes her head, muttering under her breath. "Real smooth."

I smirk. "You? Please. You've got the rhythm of a drunk giraffe on roller skates. We'd go viral for all the wrong reasons."

Poppy snorts into her drink. Scarlet laughs so hard she nearly drops her fork. Xander grins, biting back a comment, while Ace flips me off across the table.

I take a slow sip of beer. Someone laughs. Cutlery scrapes against a plate. Ace leans back in his chair, balancing on two legs like a kid asking for trouble, while Xander murmurs something into Poppy's ear that makes her smile without even looking at him. No one's in a rush. No one's checking the time.

It's the last calm before the storm. Tomorrow brings early mornings, long hours, and Xander in our ears, pushing harder. Chasing something that doesn't exist until we bleed for it. We'll lock ourselves in that recording studio and build it piece by piece.

But not yet.

Today, the air is light, the voices steady, and for a little while we let ourselves breathe in the quiet.

CHAPTER 13

Nate

My head's fucking pounding, throat dry like I've been swallowing glass. I drank myself into the void last night, chasing numbness, trying to shut my brain the fuck off.

For years, every time Theo mentioned Bianca, I killed the conversation. Closed the door. Pretended I didn't hear. As if ignoring it long enough would make the pain give up and leave me alone. Burying her was easier than letting her rip me apart all over again.

But seeing Quinn...

The trip to her place didn't mess me up the way Theo believes. Hell, it was the first time in years I could actually breathe. Being with her was like waking into a life I'd forgotten I ever lived. Same smile, same voice—only older now. Softer in some ways, sharper in others. She's grown into a woman I can't stop fucking thinking about. And none of this is new.

There's always been something about her. The way she moved. The way she took everything in without needing to be the loudest in the room. She'd sit back, watching, seeing more than she ever said. She was the first one who ever really caught my attention.

Bianca tore through everything. Loud, magnetic, impossible to ignore. She didn't walk into a room, she stormed in and flipped it on its head. All energy, all chaos, all color.

And now... Quinn's still here. Still breathing. And Bianca isn't.

I don't know what the fuck that makes me. Feeling something again isn't supposed to happen. It feels wrong. Disloyal. As if even after all this time, letting someone else in means erasing what I had with Bianca.

But seeing Quinn after all these years stirred something I thought was gone. Something I hadn't let myself touch in years.

And now it's fucking with my head.

There's something between us. There always has been.

I hear the soft creak of my bedroom door and crack one eye open in time to catch Theo's head in the doorway. He doesn't say a word, just grips the frame, fingers tight, as if he's not sure he's allowed in.

Most mornings, though, he's already here, buried under the blanket, breathing steady beside me, like this room is the only place his nightmares can't reach. He never knocks, never pauses. He comes in, climbs into my bed, and waits for the panic to pass.

But this morning he's different. His eyes flick around the room as if searching for something to hold onto. His shoulders are tense, his stance tight in a way I haven't seen in years.

It drags me straight back to those first weeks after he came to live with us. The way he lingered in doorways, never sure if he was allowed in, never sure if the food on the table was meant for him.

That's what I see now. The same hesitation. And I fucking hate myself for making him feel that way again.

I need to talk to him. I need to get out what's been sitting heavy on my chest since we left Quinn's, but the words won't move yet.

"Hey," I say.

That one word is enough. His shoulders ease, the tension slipping from his frame, and his face softens just enough to breathe again.

He crosses the room and lies down beside me, eyes on the ceiling. The silence stretches between us, heavy with everything we're not saying.

Then he turns onto his side, facing me. His eyes lock on mine, deep brown and steady, carrying a worry he doesn't bother to hide. It shows in the crease of his brow, in the way he waits for me to be okay without knowing if I ever will be.

Without a thought, I wrap my fingers around his, holding on. Just enough pressure to tell him I'm still trying. I lift our hands between us, elbows bent, and stare at them.

"I need to tell you something," I say, my grip tightening as I pull in a steadying breath. My heart's pounding, and for a second I almost don't let it out. But the words break free. "I felt something when I was with Quinn the other day, and it's been fucking with my head ever since."

I turn toward him. He's already watching.

Theo exhales. "I thought you were gonna say something worse."

"Like?"

"That you couldn't even look at me without thinking of everything we lost."

The words hit harder than I expect. My throat tightens, but I manage a dry laugh and nudge his arm.

"Never," I say. "You don't get rid of me that easy."

Silence settles between us again until Theo says, "I felt something too."

I turn to face him, but he doesn't meet my eyes. He keeps his gaze on the ceiling, as if the words come easier when he doesn't have to look at me.

"Last week... when we saw her again," he says, voice low. "There were these moments. Little things. She's still beautiful. Fuck, she's more than that now. It's not just her looks—it's the way her nose scrunches when she's concentrating. That tiny scar near her eyebrow. I forgot how she got it, but it caught my eye and I couldn't look away. She still bites her bottom lip when she's thinking too hard. Still rolls her eyes at me like I'm a fucking idiot." He exhales, slow. "I don't know if it's because we haven't seen her in years, or if it's something else. Something new. But there was comfort there...like my chest stopped hurting for a minute."

I say nothing. I just let it hang between us.

"She's still her," he goes on. "Tough as hell. Smarter than all of us. And somehow she made everything seem okay, even if only for a little while." He finally glances over at me. "I don't know what it means. But I noticed. And it stuck."

"Have you spoken to her since we left?" I ask.

"I texted her," Theo says. "Thanked her for the box. Told her I'd get someone to put together a collage, or whatever the fuck it's called, to hang on the wall."

Theo goes quiet again before adding, "You should call her."

I shake my head, exhaling.

"I wouldn't know what the fuck to say."

Theo smirks. "Well, don't lead with one of your lame-ass one-liners, hot-shot. She'll shut you down in two seconds flat."

I laugh. "Yeah, she used to do that, didn't she?"

Theo chuckles, grin wide. "Remember when you told her her ass should come with a warning label? She shot back, 'This ass has higher standards than a guy who can't even find a clit with Google Maps.'"

I can't help but grin. "God, she never let me get away with that shit."

Theo practically wheezes. "Bro. She said it loud enough the lunch tables went silent. You just stood there holding your Gatorade like your dick shriveled on command. Even Coach nearly choked on his sandwich."

I groan, dragging a hand over my face. "She didn't even blink. Just nailed me with that stare, dropped the line, and kept walking like she hadn't straight-up murdered me in front of half the school. I swear my balls actually retracted."

"She was a menace. And you loved every second of it."

I grin. "Yeah. I really fucking did."

We stay quiet for a second, letting the memory sit.

Theo claps his hands and springs to his feet.

"Let's go. If we're late, Ace'll act like someone pissed in his coffee, and Xander'll pull out the whiteboard."

I blink. "He has a whiteboard now?"

"Had it couriered to the studio. Swear on my life. Came with color-coded markers and an actual fucking pointer."

It won't be Ace with his grumpy-ass glare, or Xander barking orders like we're in some Boyband bootcamp and he's one meltdown away from shaving his head. No, it'll be Kit. And that's worse.

She won't scream or slam doors. She'll just stare at us with that unimpressed look that could vaporize egos, all five feet of fury dressed in black and platform boots.

We'll crumble faster than Theo pretending he didn't eat the last slice of pizza.

One sarcastic clap. One perfectly timed eyebrow raise. And suddenly I'm volunteering to sweep the tour bus and write a formal apology for existing.

We're at Ace's place, guitars out and ready, working on the new songs. Surprisingly, Kit's not here yet, which is rare.

We love her. Fuck, we respect the hell out of her. She's the one who keeps us grounded, who stops the chaos from swallowing us whole. That's the reason she's still with us, the reason we asked her to come when we started our own label.

Without her, we'd be five missed flights deep, buried under unread emails, and fighting over who left their socks on the amp. She's our compass in all this madness. Smallest one in the room, but somehow she holds the whole damn thing together.

The music pounds through the walls, and it feels so fucking good. Out of the corner of my eye, I catch Theo grinning, that wide, reckless one he only wears when he's finally breathing again or plotting new ways to piss off Ace.

Xander's running through a few lyrics while Ace leans over, showing Theo the bass line he wrote. It's tight, clean, solid as fuck, and for a second I let it take me under.

"After a few chords from Theo, Nate, you come in with the beat," Ace says, sharp focus in his voice.

I lean back, watching Ace and Xander work, and fuck, they get it. The way they build songs from the ground up, like it's instinct, like it's in their blood. Before Ace showed up at our door, I had options. A few bands were interested, mostly in me and Theo knew it. He told me I'd be an idiot to pass it up, said it might be my only shot. But there was no fucking way I was doing this without him.

So I waited. Held out for the right thing. And damn, I'm glad I did. Because if I hadn't—if I'd jumped into some half-assed setup with people who didn't get us. Who the fuck knows where Theo and I would be now?

That first night, when Theo and Xander sat on the couch jamming, it clicked. Not only the sound, but the way Xander treated Theo. He didn't talk over him or try to one-up him. He listened. Nodded when Theo landed something sick on the strings. Smiled in a way that said he saw him, not just the music, but the person behind it. And for someone who'd spent most of his life being told he wasn't enough, that kind of respect meant everything. That's when I knew we'd found the right fit. Not only for the music, but for us.

Ace counts us in. Theo starts first, fingers dragging over the strings, every pluck sharp. Ace joins next, his guitar growling through the speakers. I come in last, hitting hard, the crash of my drums rattling through my chest. It's loud. Raw. Alive. The kind of sound that takes over your body and wipes everything else out.

We run it a few times, tightening the edges, tweaking the rough spots, and fuck, it sounds good.

Movement at the doorway catches my eye. Kit's there, arms folded, eyes locked on us. Watching. Her presence shifts the room in that quiet, commanding way only she can.

Xander breaks first, striding over to talk to her, while Ace keeps us driving through the next set of chords. We hammer it out three more times before Ace and Theo finally unstrap their guitars and set them down in their usual spots.

"Hey, guys," Kit says, stepping inside.

Theo doesn't hesitate.

"Hey, Kitstar," he grins, scooping her clean off the ground.

"Long time no see, short stack," he says, spinning her once before setting her down. "Miss me, or just here to stop us idiots from burning the place down?"

Kit rolls her eyes, but she's smiling, and Theo's already backing off with that shit-eating grin, proud of himself.

It's been two long fucking months. Long enough for Kit's hair to grow out, no longer the sharp pixie cut she usually rocks with those bright pink highlights. Now it's longer, softer. Pinker. Almost unfamiliar. But then she smiles, and there she is. Still Kit. Still ours.

We don't say much as we drift out of the studio and into the break space Ace set up for when we're not behind the mics or tangled in wires. The fridge hums quietly in the corner, always stocked. A round table sits in the center, cluttered with half-empty bottles and scraps of paper covered in lyrics and chord changes from whatever late-night session bled into morning. In the corner, a beat-up old sofa slouches against the wall—the kind that's soaked up too many hours of sleep, sweat, and silence from bodies too worn out to make it home.

Xander yanks open the fridge, pulls out a few waters, and tosses them around without a word. I catch mine, twist the cap, and take a long swig as we drop into our seats around the table.

Kit reaches for the folder on the table—the one she must have dropped there earlier. She flips it open, pages spilling out, corners bent and worn. Every inch is covered in scribbled notes, the kind of messy, frantic handwriting that only happens when your brain is racing and you're trying to pin an idea down before it slips away.

"I know it looks like a lot," Kit says. Her voice is steady, but there's a flicker underneath, that spark she gets when her mind's running a million miles an hour.

She glances at each of us, making sure we're locked in. "I've been looking at the website. Our socials. Those ridiculous photos Theo made me post, the ones where he thought he was God's gift in that leatherjacket."

Theo grins. "I was."

Kit ignores him. "Those posts got more comments, more interaction than anything else we've done. People want the music, sure, but what they really want is you guys, the real shit. The chaos behind the scenes. The moments in between the music."

She spreads a few pages across the table.

"So I've been thinking. We don't just toss out updates or random posts. We build something that celebrates the band, something that reminds people why they fell for you in the first place."

She pauses, then adds, "Forget the posters. They're stiff. Polished. They don't say anything."

I lean in, curiosity sparking. "So what are you thinking?"

Kit grins, the kind that says she's already thought this through. "We bring someone in. A photographer. Someone who can capture everything... rehearsals, writing sessions, the shit that happens in between."

Silence hangs for a beat.

"You mean like a coffee table book or something?" Xander asks, tipping his chair back.

Ace shoots him a look like he just suggested we start a knitting club. "What the fuck is a coffee book?"

Xander smirks. "Poppy did something like that at her academy. Put together a twenty-eight-page book for investors."

Kit nods, eyes lighting up. "I'm thinking bigger. Something that feels real, something people will want to keep. Not throwaway promo crap, but something that lasts. A way to give back to the fans."

She spreads the printed pages across the table, the behind-the-scenes shots she posted, the ones that blew up online. Late-night writing sessions. Theo passed out with his guitar still strapped on. Me, hair sticking up like I'd been electrocuted. Ace flipping someone off mid-solo. Xander locked in one of his hyper-focused moods. All the messy stuff. The real stuff.

"These weren't just liked," she says, tapping each photo. "They connected. Made people feel like they're part of what we're building."

She looks up. "Picture it as a souvenir book. A way to bring them closer. Not as fans, but as part of the story. What do you say?"

We glance at each other and nod. No hesitation. We trust Kit. If she says this will work—if she believes it'll help get us in front of more people—we don't question it. It's happening.

"I'm all in," Xander says, looking at the rest of us.

I give a nod.

"Why not," Theo says before turning to Ace. "Well, what about it, Hotshot. Want to show your sparkling personality to the world."

Ace doesn't even look at him, just flips him the finger.

"Fine," he mutters.

"Perfect," Kit says, flipping through her notes, eyes skimming fast. "I'll see what I can do about getting a photographer in. They need to be here while you're learning the new songs, catching all the behind-the-scenes chaos the fans eat up. But on short notice... it might be tricky."

Theo kicks his feet up on the chair beside him, arms behind his head like the smug bastard he is.

"I might know someone," he says.

Kit looks up, one eyebrow arched. "Of course you do. Who?"

Theo grins. "You do realize I'm a man of many connections."

Ace snorts. "Yeah, mostly bartenders and groupies."

Theo waves a hand. "Details. But this time, I actually know someone legit. She takes photos, owns a camera, knows where the shutter button is. What more do you want?"

Kit pinches the bridge of her nose. "Are they good, Theo?"

"Do you trust me?"

"No."

"Well, that's fucking rude," he mutters, pulling out his phone. "Fine. I'll call her. If she sucks, you can throw a drink in my face."

"Deal."

"Not beer, though," he adds quickly. "That shit's sacred. Aim for water. Or better yet, Xander's green juice. That shit is just swamp water filtered through gym socks. I can't believe people drink that shit."

Kit watches him, arms crossed, unimpressed.

"If you call some random chick you hooked up with once who owns a Polaroid, I swear to God, Theo."

Theo holds up a finger, cutting Kit off. "First of all, rude. Second, this person is legit."

He taps his screen and lifts the phone to his ear.

We all hear it ringing, once, twice, then the sound of a voice. It's a little muffled but clear enough for all of us to catch it.

"Hey, Theo," Quinn says on the other end of the line.

The sound of her voice does something to me. It's as if the air has become dense.

"What's up, superstar?" he says, grinning. "Got a job for you, if you're not too busy shooting moody black-and-white photos of sad trees or abandoned shoes or whatever the hell it is you do these days."

There's a pause, and then Quinn's voice cuts through. "Funny. I was just editing a close-up of your ego."

Theo barks out a laugh. "Still savage. I respect that."

I grin, that firecracker mouth hitting me square in the chest. God, I miss this—the way Quinn fires back without blinking, quick as hell. I'd forgotten how good it feels.

Ace crosses his arms and raises a brow. "I like her already," he mutters. "She can stay."

Even Xander lets out a low chuckle, shaking his head.

"So..." Theo says, drawing it out. "You got anything on over the next—" He pauses, eyes flicking to Kit, brows raised, waiting for the cue.

Kit sighs, rubbing her temple. "Two weeks."

Theo nods, as if that's exactly what he was about to say. "Right. Two weeks. You busy?"

Silence follows.

Then Quinn laughs. "Two weeks... Theo, that's not a job. That's a hostage situation?"

Theo grins. "A sexy one. With benefits."

Kit groans. "I regret everything."

Xander mutters, "I regret knowing him," shaking his head, even though he's grinning now.

Even Ace, who hasn't cracked a smile since 2015, lets out a grunt that might actually be a laugh.

Before anyone can fire back, Theo shoves the phone toward Kit. "Here. Talk to her."

Kit eyes the phone like he's just handed her a live grenade. "If this is some girl you banged in a dressing room and only remembered now, I swear to God—"

"Relax," Theo says, grinning all innocent. "Her name's Quinn. Just take the call."

Kit sighs, snatches the phone, and covers the mic with her hand. "If she asks for child support, I'm hanging up." Then she turns away, pressing it to her ear. "Hey, Quinn. Yeah, don't worry. I'll give you the sane version."

We watch as Kit starts pacing slow circles near the beat-up couch, phone pressed tight. She's explaining everything properly now, walking Quinn through the details instead of Theo's bullshit sales pitch.

Kit hangs up, strides back over, and drops the phone into Theo's hand.

"She's sending me her portfolio tonight. I'll take a look and decide from there." She narrows her eyes at him. "If this is some elaborate plan to get laid, Theo, do us all a favor and download a dating app."

Theo flashes that cocky grin. "What, and miss out on you micromanaging my sex life? Where's the fun in that?"

Kit groans. Ace mutters something about needing earplugs for the whole tour.

I laugh, already knowing this is gonna be one hell of a ride.

CHAPTER 14

Quinn

My nerves have been shot for the last forty-eight hours. Ever since I hit send on those photos, I've been stuck in this endless loop—second-guessing every frame, every angle, wondering if what I gave Kit was enough. Wondering if I'm enough.

Soon after, Kit called. There was no small talk. No drawn-out waiting game. She went straight to the point, rattling off flight details and timelines as if this wasn't the biggest fucking moment of my career. Two weeks to capture the behind-the-scenes while they record the album. Two weeks of living in their space, watching through my lens, pretending my hands don't shake every time I lift the camera.

I half expected to wake up the second I hung up. Part of me still does.

Photography has always been my escape. A way to leave fingerprints on the world without saying a word. But this gig is different. From the way Kit laid it out, these photos could go everywhere. My name on something real. Something massive. It's thrilling and terrifying all at once. Everything I've ever wanted.

I just hope I don't fuck this up.

The plane landed twenty minutes ago, and I've been hiding in the airport bathroom ever since, gripping the edge of the sink like it's the only thing keeping me steady.

My reflection doesn't help. I look flushed, nervous, hair refusing to stay down no matter how many times I try to flatten it. I drag my fingers through it again anyway, pretending it'll make a difference. Pretending I come across as someone who's got her shit together.

But I don't.

I tell myself it's only Nate and Theo. The same boys from high school. Theo, the one who used to sit beside me at parties, trading bullshit theories about the universe until sunrise. Nate with that dumbass smirk and even dumber pickup lines I shut down every time without blinking.

Bianca's boys.

But that was before.

Now they're the walking wet dream of every girl with a pulse. All bad-boy swagger and tattooed charm, with that too-cool, too-famous shine that makes you forget they were ever only boys you shared smokes with behind a gym.

They're larger than life now. Nate and Theo, front and center of the hottest fucking band on the planet.

So yeah... I think I've earned this minor breakdown in an airport bathroom. Because I'm not simply photographing two guys I used to know. I'm stepping into the eye of the storm and praying I don't get swallowed whole.

I wanted to crawl out of my own skin when they saw where I lived.

The cracked walls. The thrifted couch with one leg that wobbled every time someone sat down. The stack of ramen boxes shoved into a corner pretending to be a pantry. It wasn't only small; it screamed survival. I caught it in their faces the second they stepped inside—that flicker of pity, guilt, surprise.

For one sharp, breathless second, I almost told them to leave. Almost let the shame take over and drive me straight into an excuse. But I didn't. Because I know who I am. I'm not chasing pay checks, comfort, or some polished version of success. I'm chasing moments. That click of the shutter when the world holds its breath. That rush when I catch something too honest to fake.

Photography isn't my job. It's the only thing I've ever loved.

So yeah, my place is a dump. But it's mine. And they weren't there to judge me. They were there for Bianca.

After that day in my apartment, after the beers went warm and the pizza went cold, when we sat there drowning in memories of the girl who once held all our broken pieces together, I thought I'd get a call from them. I hoped those hours meant more than a trip down memory lane. That we weren't strangers anymore.

But only Theo texted.

A simple thank you for the box of memories I'd handed him.

And that was it.

No call or message from Nate. No sign that either of them was still sitting in that moment the way I was.

I'd be lying if I said it didn't sting. I wanted to believe we'd found our way back to something real, even if only for a moment.

But the truth is, they're in a different world now. One with sold-out shows, flashing lights, and people screaming their names. A world too loud to catch the echoes of what we used to be.

They moved on.

And me... I'm still here. Still clinging to the ghosts. Still remembering for all of us.

I lift my head and stare at my reflection.

Get your shit together, Quinn. It's only a job. A normal, totally casual, not-at-all nerve-wracking job that happens to involve four of the most recognizable faces in the music industry.

I square my shoulders, study my reflection again, and pretend I don't resemble someone two seconds away from hurling into the sink.

Clothes... fine.

Hair... mostly co-operating.

Sanity... questionable.

I glance down and sigh. Of course. These cheap-ass laces have come undone again.

I crouch and yank them tight, double-knotting as if my life depends on it. The last thing I need is to face-plant in front of them. Tripping over my own feet all the time is humiliating enough.

One more fall and someone will start a GoFundMe for my coordination.

I take a breath, shake out my hands, and head for baggage claim. Simply grab the suitcase, walk out, act like a functioning adult. Easy.

And that's when I spot it.

Or more accurately, I spot the disaster riding the conveyor belt as if it's proud of itself.

My suitcase.

Wide open. Zipper blown. My entire life spilling out in slow, mortifying motion. A bra dangles from the side, practically waving to the crowd. A pair of socks cling to a rolled-up t-shirt. My underwear takes a full runway lap under the fluorescent lights.

People are watching— and I can hear it. The soft laughter, whispered jokes, a low chuckle from somewhere behind me. A guy elbows his friend, both of them grinning as if my personal nightmare is their after-flight entertainment.

My black lace bra hangs off the edge of the conveyor, swinging with every bump as if it's taking a final bow.

Kill me. Right here, right now on this sticky airport floor. End it already.

I shove through the crowd, heat crawling up my neck, and lunge for the suitcase. The second I grab it, the weight shifts. And of course, half my underwear spills out. A handful of panties hit the floor, right on top of some guy's boots.

He looks down. After that, his gaze lifts straight to me.

A strangled sound slips out of me, caught between a gasp and a groan. I snatch up the lacy evidence of my suffering and shove everything back into the suitcase as if I'm cramming my dignity in with it.

People are watching. I catch a few snickers, some muffled laughs, and soon a guy calls out something crude behind me. I want to turn around and tell him to fuck off, to choke on his own tongue, but I don't. I'm too mortified to even lift my head.

I knot my hoodie around the suitcase, praying it holds. It doesn't. Not really. The corners still gape open, a sock rebelliously poking out as if it's ready to make another run for it.

I keep my eyes forward and speed-walk out of baggage claim, dragging my disaster of a suitcase behind me. Each wheel thumps against the tiles, a fucking drumbeat announcing my shame to the world.

I keep my chin up and pretend I'm not dying inside. Even though I absolutely am.

I don't stop. I don't glance back. If I pretend this never happened, perhaps it'll disappear from existence.

Unlikely. But a girl can dream.

I keep my head down as I move through the airport, gripping my half-destroyed suitcase as if it's not actively trying to humiliate me again. Kit told me where to find my driver, and that's exactly where I'm going. No detours. No eye contact. No more moments that'll haunt me at three in the morning for the rest of my life.

And that's when I see them.

I freeze, my pulse kicking up as my eyes lock onto Nate and Theo standing only a few feet ahead. Their heads are tilted close, attention fixed on Theo's phone. They haven't noticed me yet, and I know I should keep moving before they raise their heads and catch me staring.

But I don't.

I can't.

Because fuck. They're gorgeous. Both of them.

I forgot how good they look together. How they carry that effortless, bad-boy energy, as if it's stitched into their DNA.

Theo grips his phone in one hand, the other flexing at his side, veins pronounced, ink shifting with every subtle movement. His hair is wild and untamed, and that mouth... God, that mouth, the way it curves into a smirk so slow and smug it's practically foreplay. He carries himself differently now.

Broader. Looser. The hoodie-wearing boy who once disappeared into shadows learned how to own the room instead. Fame didn't only give him confidence, it carved it into every inch of him. And fuck if it doesn't suit him too well.

And Nate, fuck. He's all angles and sin, sharp jawline cut from arrogance, a mouth set in that half-smirk that's wrecked a hundred girls before breakfast. That blonde hair... a mess of fingers and recklessness, tousled enough to make you wonder who got to touch it last. He carries a presence that makes rooms fall silent and pulses race. Black ripped jeans cling to long legs, a fitted tee stretched across his chest, silver rings flashing on his fingers...trouble you want to taste. The tattoos climbing his arms don't merely peek, they tease, bold and unapologetic. When he moves, it's with a swagger that erases the possibility of seeing anyone else.

They're rockstars now. Untouchable. Larger than life.

And here I am, standing in an airport with my dignity stuffed into a half-broken suitcase and my nerves shot to hell.

Awesome.

Heat curls low in my gut as I watch them, my body betraying me with every second I keep staring. Because fuck. I want them both.

Bianca used to whisper things about the three of them. She'd lean in close, voice low, teasing. I'd roll my eyes and pretend I didn't care, but I wanted to know.

I wanted to ask her how it started. What they did. What it was like. How good the boys were at it.

But I never asked. I didn't want to pry.

Still, I used to think about Nate. About those hands. I caught the stories back in school, the whispers from girls who swore he could pull an orgasm from them without even trying. A single look, a touch, a few filthy words in the right tone and they were done.

And Theo. I wondered about him too. If the boy who once hid under a hoodie came alive in the dark. If he knew how to take his time. If he could wreck someone with nothing more than his mouth and a grin.

I knew I wasn't supposed to think about them that way. They were Bianca's boys.

But fuck—I was jealous.

I still am.

Not only for the way they made her ache. Though that alone was enough to burn itself into my memory and stay there. It was more than that. I envied the way they looked at her, the way they reached for her, gave her their time, their focus, their everything. She got to be the center of that storm, caught between them, while I stood on the sidelines and watched. Always the best friend. Always looking in.

Back in those days, I told myself it didn't matter. That I wasn't into Nate. But the truth is, I liked the energy that simmered between us—the teasing, the smirks, the way he always had something cocky to throw my way so I could shoot him down. It meant something, even if I pretended it didn't.

But once Bianca came into the picture, everything shifted. Nate stopped with the flirting. Pulled back, shut it down. And I missed it. I missed Theo too. Missed the easy rhythm between us, the way we'd talk for hours about nothing, how he'd always say something dumb simply to make me laugh.

She was my best friend. I kept telling myself I was fine, that having them in my life was enough. I was happy being near them. Being part of their orbit. Even if I wanted more. And hated myself for it.

But seeing them now...

Nate's watching the phone, head tilted, that smirk tugging at his mouth, the one that always got under my skin.

Theo has that same wicked spark he always carried, but now it's carved deeper. More dangerous. He doesn't fidget or glance around the way he used to. He stands steady, sure of himself.

Nate lifts his head first. His sharp blue eyes catch mine, and that lazy, confident smirk pulls at the corner of his mouth. It's pure sin, slow and full of promise, the kind of smile that unravels common sense and replaces it with heat.

My stomach clenches, and I shift my weight to hide the way my thighs tighten. He doesn't need words to make me feel it. That mouth alone could wreck me.

I grip the handle of my suitcase harder, forcing myself to stay grounded.

That's when Theo moves. He slides his phone into his pocket, eyes locked on me, a wicked grin spreading across his face. His tattooed arms flex as he steps forward, broad shoulders rolling with a confidence that steals the breath from my lungs.

I should walk over, say something, close the space between us. But my feet stay planted. My heart pounds, each beat louder than the last. Every part of me betrays the logic I carried in here, heat crawling through me from the inside out.

Because it's them. And my body remembers.

Heat rolls low, straight to my pussy, a slow, relentless throb that makes my legs seem less like limbs and more like caution signs. I should say something. Do something. Move. For fuck's sake, blink at least. But no. I only grip the handle of my suitcase harder, heart pounding like it's trying to stage an escape, fully aware I'm in way over my fucking head.

Nate steps up first, closing the distance with zero effort, as if he hasn't already turned my brain into a puddle with one cocky glance.

"Hey, Q," he says, voice smooth and familiar.

And suddenly... fuck, he hugs me.

He straight-up pulls me into him, arms wrapping around me. His chest collides with mine and my entire body short-circuits. I have a full-blown internal meltdown while outwardly pretending I'm totally chill and not currently soaking through my underwear.

He smells unreal. Spice, leather, and something warm that screams bad decisions and orgasmic regret. His fingers press into the small of my back, holding me in place as if he has no intention of letting go. I want to bury my face in his shirt and stay there.

Keep it together, Quinn. It's only a hug. A normal, friendly, platonic fucking hug. Nothing more. But my body clearly didn't get the memo. Heat crashes through me, pulse racing as if I've gone headfirst into Nate Reynolds. And for a second—one single fucking second—I let myself lean into it, sink into the solid weight of him.

He steps back, that smug smirk tugging at his lips as his hands fall casually to his sides, as if he didn't leave me one breath away from moaning in a goddamn airport.

I'm still trying to reboot my brain when Theo moves in.

"C'mon, Quinn," he says, voice low and full of that teasing warmth I remember far too well. "Where's my hug?"

And fuck... if Nate was heat, Theo is fire.

He pulls me close, one arm slung low around my waist, the other pressing against me as if he's testing how many laws of personal space he can break before I pass out. His body is solid, all lean muscle and unfair heat, and his scent is nothing like Nate's. Darker. Heavier. Cedar and sin. The kind of cologne that clings to your clothes and haunts your pillows for a week.

My hands press against his chest, not to push him away, but more a "please God, don't let me melt into a horny puddle right here" movement.

For a second, I forget how to speak, because Theo's grip is a little too tight to be innocent.

I clear my throat, loudly, as if that will reset the hormones or something. After that, I step back before I end up dry humping him in front of everyone here at the airport.

Theo only grins, eyes dragging over me in a slow, filthy way that says he knows exactly what he's doing.

I want to slap him, but knowing my luck, that might only make me hornier.

"You speechless?" Theo smirks, too pleased with himself.

I finally manage to speak. "You wish."

He laughs, all teeth and trouble, and takes my camera bag without asking before slinging his arm around my shoulders.

The sudden weight of his arm catches me off guard. His warmth seeps into my skin, and my brain decides to stop working entirely. I tell myself to pull away. Instead, I stand there, stiff as hell, pretending I don't notice his thumb brushing the edge of my shoulder.

God help me, I am in so much fucking trouble.

Before I can process what's happening, Nate grabs my suitcase, fingers curling around the handle as he starts to wheel it forward. He barely makes it two steps before stopping, his brows pulling together as he takes it in properly.

"Jesus, Q. This thing's being held together by pure willpower."

I sigh. "Yeah, well, half my shit did a full runway lap on the conveyor belt. I'm pretty sure my panties were the headliners."

Theo snorts. "Damn. Did they at least get a callback?"

I shoot him a glare. "Fuck you."

He grins, hand still on my shoulder. "Perhaps later, sweetheart."

I narrow my eyes at him. "Since when are you such a flirt? I remember you used to flinch when I stared at you too long."

He leans in, voice low and smug. "Maybe I was trying not to pop a boner."

I blink. "Jesus, Theo."

"What?" He shrugs, all innocence. "I'm only saying, teenage me had eyes."

"And apparently no shame."

"None," he agrees, eyes dropping briefly to my mouth before dragging back up.

I roll my eyes. "God, your ego."

He grins. "Please, you love it."

"I tolerate it."

He pulls me tight against his side, resting his cheek on the top of my head. "God, I've missed this."

I swallow hard.

"Missed annoying the shit out of me?"

His laugh rumbles through me. "No, Quinn. I missed you."

Up ahead, Nate takes hold of my disaster of a suitcase and wheels it forward, moving ahead while Theo and I fall in behind him.

And fuck, my eyes go to Nate. I can't stop them.

The way he moves. That body. Those shoulders. His jeans hang low on his hips, fabric worn and tight in all the right places, clinging to an ass that should be illegal. Muscles shift beneath his shirt, tattoos winding up his arms and spilling from his sleeves. Silver rings flash on his fingers. Every inch of him screams trouble.

Back in the day, he almost broke me.

One night. One look. That's all it took to make me falter. I nearly gave in when he stared too long, when his mouth curled the right way.

I'd heard the rumors. They were everywhere.

Girls whispered about him in the bathrooms, in the halls, drunk and glassy-eyed after a night tangled up with Nate Reynolds. They said he fucked with purpose, with something to prove. That he needed to own you. That he got off on watching you fall apart beneath him. That the sound of his name on your lips was what he wanted more than anything.

Others said he was unforgettable. The kind of fuck that brands itself into your memory and ruins every other man who comes after.

And for one fleeting second, I wanted to know what it was like to have him.

But I didn't go there. Because I knew exactly what I'd be after it was over. Another fuck. Another girl forgotten by Nate Reynolds.

Theo's voice cuts through my Nate-induced coma, low and smug against my ear.

"You gonna need a minute, or should I start wiping the drool now?"

The heat in his tone catches me off guard. I glance over, and there it is—that fucking smirk.

"I guess being in a band gave you a whole new personality," I say, arching a brow. "The Theo I remember didn't flirt as if he were trying to land in someone's panties."

"I'm still the same guy, Quinn. I only upgraded. I still talk shit, and now I can multi-task too."

I laugh, shaking my head at how fucking confident he is. It's effortless now, the way he carries himself, how he fucking owns it.

We step into the car park, late afternoon sun glaring off the pavement. Nate grabs my suitcase, still barely holding itself together, and hauls it into the trunk like it isn't seconds from exploding again.

"You sure this thing's safe to be out in public?" he asks, shutting the lid.

"No," I say. "But I'm hoping it doesn't flash anyone else today."

Theo swings my camera bag off his shoulder. "What a shame. I was looking forward to Act Two: The Panty Parade."

"Keep dreaming," I mutter.

He opens the passenger door with a flourish. "Your throne, my lady."

I raise a brow. "What are you doing?"

"Multi-tasking," he says, giving me a wink.

I climb in and mutter something about idiots and dignity. He shuts the door behind me with far too much enthusiasm before climbing into the back-seat as if we're chauffeuring him to a red carpet.

Nate slides behind the wheel and starts the engine.

Theo sprawls out behind me, one arm slung over the headrest like he's in the middle of a moody rockstar promo shoot.

"So, Quinn," he says, voice smooth as fucking silk, "you ever been to LA before?"

I catch his dark eyes glinting in the rearview mirror.

"No," I answer, shifting in my seat. "Not really."

Theo tilts his head. "Not really? What does that mean? You drove past it once and waved?"

"I watched Clueless on repeat. Pretty much a local now."

Nate snorts as he pulls out of the lot. "Hope LA's ready."

I roll my eyes and stare out the windshield as the skyline sharpens ahead.

Day one, and they're already pushing every fucking button I've got.

This is going to be hell.

Chapter 15

Theo

She's stunning. Always fucking has been. But now she's more. Something that hits harder, knocking me sideways in ways I never saw coming.

That wild hair, still a mess of chaos and don't-give-a-shit attitude. Those green eyes, sharper than I remember, deeper too. They've witnessed more. Endured more. Lived through hell and come out the other side stronger for it. She's always carried herself as if the world didn't get a say in who she was, but now a stillness sits beneath the fire, a steadiness that shows she's survived more than she ever let on.

This isn't only the Quinn I grew up with. This is the woman time carved out of her, the one life shaped through every scar and quiet moments she never talked about. And fuck, I want to know all of it. Every second that built her into this beautiful woman. Every ache she never shared.

I saw how nervous she was when we walked up to her. The way she tried to keep her shit together, holding her head high the way she always does, but her fingers gave her away. Gripping the handle of that beat-to-shit suitcase, knuckles white, jaw locked.

So I did the only thing I know how to do. I played it cool. Tossed in a smirk. Dropped a line. Tried to take the edge off, distract her from whatever the fuck was running through her head.

I've never flirted with Quinn Thomas. Not once. That was always Nate's game.

But now I can't fucking stop.

The words fall out before I can stop them. My eyes refuse to stay where they're supposed to. Every glance, every shift in the seat, every breath she takes messes with my head in ways I wasn't ready for.

As Nate turns into the driveway, I catch her gaze in the mirror.

Her eyes widen when the gates swing open, revealing a long stretch of road that pulls us deeper into a world far removed from hers. Trees rise on both sides, shadows sliding across the hood as the car drifts through.

We first pass Ace's house. It's a striking two-story structure, crafted from rich, dark brick that gleams subtly in the sunlight. Lush green hedges frame the house, providing both privacy and a touch of natural beauty. Majestic white pillars rise gracefully, supporting a broad porch that extends invitingly to the second floor.

It's the kind of house that never sits quiet. Music always spilling out, people coming and going. The porch is scattered with guitars, half-drunk coffee cups, and that beautiful kind of chaos that somehow holds steady. It's all Ace and Scarlet. Messy, loud, but impossible not to love.

We roll past Xander's place. Golden light pours through wide windows, casting a warm glow that dances across the wrap-around veranda. Alex's bike lies abandoned at the foot of the steps. The front garden is alive with color, always something blooming. Poppy's touch is everywhere, in the flowers arranged with care and the neat pathways she tends so meticulously. Every detail radiates family, warmth, and belonging.

And finally, our place.

A double-story farmhouse with a wide porch and a front door that always sticks when it rains. The lawn gets mowed often, though it never looks perfect. Every board, every nail, every corner of the house was built from scratch. Every inch was earned. This is the only home I've ever really known apart from Rose and Wes's. But this one I can proudly claim as mine. As ours.

This is where we return after every tour. After we've stood at Bianca's graveside, broken and barely holding ourselves together. Here is where we learn how to breathe again, where the silence isn't so fucking heavy. Where we keep each other upright when the grief gets too loud.

I watch Quinn in the mirror.

She doesn't speak. Doesn't smile. Only stares out the window, her face unreadable, hands resting in her lap. The car keeps moving forward, past everything we've become, and I can't tell if she's impressed or uncomfortable. If she's holding her breath or has nothing left to say.

I wonder whether she's taking everything in—the gates, the houses, the kind of life people dream about. I wonder if she's sitting there, tallying every way we don't belong side by side anymore.

Because Quinn Thomas will always belong in my life. No matter how different everything seems now.

I'm only sorry that it took us so fucking long to see her again. To find our way back to something that once seemed so easy.

Perhaps we didn't know how to face each other after losing Bianca.

Maybe we still don't.

But at least together we can try.

Quinn chased her dreams through a lens, always hunting with that quiet kind of hunger. She found beauty where most people never thought to look. Scraping by with almost nothing, she turned silence into moments that carried weight, fragments of time that actually meant something.

And us... we ran headfirst into the noise. Let the music swallow us whole. Chased the spotlight because that was the only thing that ever came close to Bianca. Played louder, moved faster, hoping if we kept going, we might catch a fragment of her in the chaos.

By the time the garage door opens and Nate steers the car inside, Quinn glances at me—and I catch the flicker in her eyes. The way she goes still, as if her brain's scrambling to keep up with everything she's seeing.

Polished floors gleam under the garage lights. A wall of guitars mounted as though they're art. Cars lined up as if they're trophies. Cabinets worth more than most people make in a year. The kind of space that doesn't only show money, it screams it.

It's a lot, I know.

But what else do you do with money on this scale? We barely spend any of it. Nate and I hand most of the cash over now—charities, foundations, kids trapped in the kind of places I once was.

And yet... standing here, in this showroom of a garage, watching Quinn try to make sense of all this, it still feels like too much. The kind you never talk about, because nothing could ever make it sound normal.

When we first started touring, opening for bands that are no longer together, we crashed on floors, barely scraping by, the whole thing was survival. Once the album hit, the checks started rolling in. Fast. Big. And one of the first things Nate and I agreed on was getting Wes and Rose a new house. Something bigger. Something they deserved.

But they wouldn't take it.

Rose just smiled and said, "Too many memories."

She said no amount of money could replace the creaky hallway where Nate and I used to race each other barefoot. The kitchen where we burned pancakes and argued over nothing. The living room that held every Christmas morning and every fight that always ended with someone laughing.

That house raised us.

And fuck, I understood. Some walls aren't only wood and paint. They carry ghosts of love and warmth, of hate, hurt, and abuse. Every trace of who you were before the world reshaped us into something different.

Some things are never meant to be replaced. Not even with all the money in the world.

The three of us climb out of the car and step inside, Nate leading the way with Quinn's suitcase, flicking on lights as we go. Quinn walks between us, her head turning, eyes wide, taking everything around her in. I follow with her camera bag, careful not to knock it against the wall.

"Wow," she breathes, stopping short. "This house, you guys—"

She doesn't even finish the thought. She only stares, her gaze sweeping over the space as we step into the kitchen and living room. High ceilings. Exposed beams. Windows that stretch nearly floor to ceiling, that scream we made it.

Quinn just stands still, taking everything in. A flicker crosses her expression. She's seeing a version of us that doesn't quite match the memory, and for a second, the past and present seem to circle each other, unsure which one will hold.

"Come on, I'll show you your room," Nate says, already heading down the hall with her suitcase.

I step forward, holding out her camera bag. "You might want to take this too before I drop the damn thing and ruin her career."

I turn back toward Quinn, catching the way she's still staring, lips parted, hands loose at her sides.

"I'll grab us a drink," I say, already moving toward the kitchen. "Before your head explodes from how fancy this place feels."

Her eyes snap to mine, that smile twitching at the corners of her mouth.

I move past her, yank open the fridge and grab a few beers as she trails Nate down the hall. My hands work on autopilot, muscle memory kicking in as I pop the tops.

I take a long pull from the bottle, the cold settling in my chest.

The moment footsteps echo on the marble tiles, I turn.

Nate comes into the room and grabs a beer off the counter. He doesn't drink, only stands rigid with the bottle in his hand, his eyes locked on me.

"What's the matter?" he asks.

He's doing that thing again—watching too closely. Not only looking at me, but studying every detail.

"What'd she think of the room?" I shoot back, dodging the question the same way I'd dodge an ex-girlfriend waving a baby scan and swearing the kid was mine.

I down half the beer, hoping it will drown the truth I don't want to face.

But Nate doesn't budge. He sets his bottle down, the soft clink against the counter sounding a whole lot louder than it has any right to.

"Theo," he says, stepping closer.

Just my name. No bullshit, no buildup. Nothing but the weight behind the word.

I exhale hard through my nose. "Christ, Reynolds. Want to dim the lights while you're at it? Maybe throw on some slow music before you interrogate me?"

He doesn't blink. He keeps staring, cutting through every wall I've ever built.

I swallow, jaw tight.

Fuck.

How the fuck do I tell him that this pull I have toward Quinn hits wrong in a way I can't shake. That every time my mind drifts back, that voice cuts in, telling me I shouldn't. She was Bianca's best friend. They were inseparable. Every memory I carry of her has Quinn stitched into the edges, tied to her, woven into the mess of what the four of us used to be. That every time I let myself think about what it means to want Quinn, the weight slams into my chest. That sting you can't explain but can't escape. The betrayal that lodges in your bones no matter how much time has passed.

But I don't get the chance to say a damn word, because Quinn walks in.

The second her eyes land on us, she stops cold. She doesn't move. She only watches, eyes flicking between us.

"Sorry," she says, finally. "I didn't mean to interrupt."

I do what I always do—pretend. That smile I've mastered over the years, the one that says I'm good and everything's fucking perfect, slides on without effort. A reflex. A lie with teeth.

"You didn't interrupt anything," I say, too fast, too smooth.

I don't look at Nate because I already know what I'll see. Him still staring. Still reading every goddamn crack I'm trying to hide.

I turn slightly toward the counter.

"Your beer's here," I say, grabbing the bottle and passing it to her, anything to break the weight of this moment.

Quinn steps forward and takes the drink.

As she moves, Nate lifts his arm. His hand clamps onto mine, giving a quick squeeze. The gesture is subtle, but the impact hits hard. A silent message. I see you.

Quinn circles the bench and drops onto one of the stools.

"Kit said to come with you guys to the studio," she says. "What time do you usually start?"

"Hold on," I mutter, pulling out my phone. I scroll through the messages until I find Xander's note with this week's schedule. The time shifts now and then.

He planned the whole thing around Poppy and Alex. Makes sure he can drop Alex off at school when Poppy has early mornings at the academy. He's fully committed when it comes to them.

Even when he has to walk through a crowd of women at school drop-off who can't stop staring. Grown-ass women swooning as if they're still sixteen. The attention drives him insane. He's never been one for small talk, and he sure as hell isn't the type to smile and charm his way through the moment.

But he goes through it anyway, because he loves being a dad.

I tease him about it sometimes. Call him the local MILF magnet, all to get a rise out of him.

He doesn't bite. He only snorts, gives me that deadpan stare, and lifts his coffee for a slow sip, as if I'm the dumbest person in the room.

That's Xander. No bullshit. No temptation. Loves Poppy and Alex in this fierce, all-consuming way that never needs to be proven.

I skim the message before glancing up at Quinn.

"Nine. But we don't actually do anything until ten."

Nate huffs out a quiet laugh. "He's not wrong. We usually talk shit for the first hour. Xander puts up with the nonsense, but he still expects us to show when it counts. Always has. He's the kind of guy who never stops pushing himself."

Quinn nods, taking a sip of her beer.

I smirk. "Don't stress. Xander's cool, obsessive about getting things right. Now, Ace... that's a whole different problem. The guy wakes up pissed off. I don't even think he sleeps. He powers down and reboots angrier."

Quinn snorts, laughter breaking loose as she sets her beer down. "God, you're such an idiot, Theo."

And fuck, that sound... the impact lands harder than it should.

I can't stop the smile tugging at my mouth. It's been a while since I heard her laugh that way. Since any of us managed to. For a moment, the world almost seems normal.

I watch her for a beat longer before taking a sip of my beer, trying to settle whatever the hell is stirring in my chest.

She leans in, elbow on the bench, eyes flicking to mine. "So how'd you guys meet Xander and Ace anyway?"

I glance over at Nate, catching the shift in his expression. His jaw tics ever so slightly before he exhales through his nose and scrubs a hand down his face.

"This is gonna take a while," he mutters, pushing off the bench.

He heads for the fridge, grabbing ingredients. Pulls out some chicken, throws open the pantry door, snatches a packet of pasta, whatever sauce is at the front. He moves around the kitchen like a man who needs something to do with his hands, as if staying still might let all that old shit crawl back in.

I shift, stepping back until I'm leaning against the sink, arms folded, beer in hand. The glass is sweating. So am I.

Quinn waits, her eyes moving between us.

And fuck, I go all in.

"We were fucked," I say finally, my voice lower than I mean for it to be. "After Bianca... everything cracked."

I stare ahead, not really seeing the kitchen. Only her. Bianca. That goddamn smile, that laugh that used to rattle through my chest, the way she'd throw her head back and make you believe nothing bad ever touched her.

"We couldn't stay in that town. Every street, every room, every fucking shadow had her name carved into the walls. The stupid amp cable she left in our room. Her sweater still hanging over the back of the chair. Even the air carried her presence."

I take a long pull of my beer. It doesn't help. Nothing ever does. My throat tightens anyway.

"Nate kept trying to hold everything together. He was better at pretending."

The knife in Nate's hand hits the cutting board a little harder now.

"There were days I'd vanish. Wouldn't answer calls, wouldn't show up. He would always find me though. Every time. Sitting by her grave like some lost fucking kid, trying to talk to someone who wasn't ever gonna answer. Asking why the fuck she left us." My voice drops. "We couldn't breathe in that place. Everywhere we turned, her shadow was waiting. So we left."

Quinn's voice is soft when the words leave her. "Yeah. I remember. You guys just vanished."

I look at her. So does Nate. I meet Nate's eyes across the kitchen, and in that look sits the flicker of guilt neither of us can wash off. We left her behind. Alone. Her with Bianca's ghosts.

"We didn't know how to stay, Quinn," I tell her. "Didn't know how to face you without falling apart. You and that damn camera reminded us of her. It was always the four of us."

"I know," she whispers. "But I was still stuck in that place."

I drain the last of my beer, set the bottle down harder than I need to, grab another, and move back over. My eyes follow Nate as he grabs a pan and sets it on the stove.

"It was a year," I say. "A year of nothing but surviving. Playing anywhere that would take us, scribbling down lyrics that didn't mean a damn thing. Nate hammering the drums like he was trying to split his own chest open. Me drinking too much, sleeping too little. All of it was just us trying to erase her without ever admitting that's what we were doing."

Quinn speaks up, gentle but steady. "But you didn't forget."

"No," I admit. "We never did. We only got better at pretending."

Nate drops the chicken into the pan with a splash of oil. The sizzle cuts through the silence for a moment.

"And one night there's a knock at the door. Nate opens it, expecting cops or some pissed-off neighbor ready to complain about the noise." I pause, letting the memory sink in. "But it's Ace. Said he heard Nate on the drums."

Nate turns down the stove before speaking. "Next night, he brings Xander with him. He and Theo clicked instantly."

I glance over, but he's not looking at me. His eyes are on Quinn.

"I watched them that night," Nate goes on. "Xander didn't say much at first. Theo and him jammed for hours. Then they talked like they'd known each other for years."

He finally glances at me, and I catch something in his eyes that hits me square in the fucking chest.

"And I knew," he says. "We both did. That this was the moment. That we'd found the thing we'd been missing. Everything moved forward from that point."

I don't say a word. I don't need to.

Quinn stays quiet for a beat, her gaze flicking between us. "So that's how Broken Oasis started?"

I nod slowly. "Yeah. Four guys with too much baggage and no clue what the hell they were doing."

"Still don't," Nate mutters.

I shoot him a look. "Speak for yourself, Reynolds. I'm a fucking professional."

Quinn laughs under her breath. "You think Bianca would've liked the band?"

Nate stares down at the plates in his hands. I keep my eyes on the floor. The question has haunted us more times than I can count. But hearing her say it guts us both. I glance up.

"She would've loved the band," I say finally, voice rough. "Would have told me to smile more and Nate to stop showing off his arms in every damn photo."

Nate exhales a soft laugh. "She would have called Xander the 'hottie,' only to watch me lose my shit."

Quinn smiles too, but the smile aches—the kind that remembers.

"She believed in you guys," she says quietly. "Even before you had a name."

"Yeah," I say, lifting my beer. "She always fucking did."

I glance at Nate and catch him in the moment. His lips twitch, eyes softer than usual.

For once, he's letting himself enjoy it.

For a moment, we're only three people in a kitchen. No baggage. No sharp edges pressing in from the past. And for once, the ease feels better than I ever expected.

The conversation slips back into an old rhythm.

Nate throws together a salad while Quinn and I watch, tossing out smart-ass comments between sips of beer. The banter comes easy, the kind of flow that used to be second nature. Something in the air whispers we haven't lost everything.

Time has moved on, but it hasn't erased us.

When dinner's ready, we carry the plates out to the patio. The sky stretches dark above, the air still warm and heavy from the day. We eat, drink too many beers, and talk about nothing that matters and everything that does.

For a little while, we are who we used to be.

Almost.

Because the girl who once anchored all of this—the one who made us more than we ever were on our own—isn't here. Her absence is quiet, but it never fades. It lingers in the empty spaces, in the words left unsaid, in the way we sometimes fall silent at the exact same moment.

Still, we keep going. We let the laughter last a little longer. We fill the gaps with stories and shared glances. Maybe this is what it means to keep living after someone you love is gone.

Maybe this is what healing really is.

Not forgetting. Not fixing.

Just finding each other again, even while knowing a piece of us will always be missing.

Chapter 16

Quinn

My nerves are a fucking mess. I didn't sleep. Not properly. I must've closed my eyes a hundred times, but my brain wouldn't shut up long enough to let it count. It kept circling. Over and over. This job, this chance. This one shot I can't afford to mess up.

I lay in bed staring at the ceiling, running through camera settings in my head, reminding myself how to blend in, how to stay quiet, how to catch the real moments without disrupting the guys. I kept repeating that I need to focus and remember why I'm here.

But none of that stuck. Because my head was somewhere else entirely.

Back on that patio. Back in the dark with a beer in my hand and two boys sitting beside me, their laughter curling around the night as if it had never left. And all I could think about was how easy it seemed.

And how much I wanted to be closer.

All I can fucking think about when I look at them, talk to them, laugh with them, sit beside them on that patio as if it's another ordinary night, is how much I want them.

Both of them.

Pressed against me. One behind, one in front. Theo's mouth rough and greedy against my throat while Nate's hands slide up under my shirt, as though he already knows every place I need to be touched. Their bodies surrounding me, pinning me, their heat, their strength, their weight driving me right to the edge.

I imagine Theo gripping my hips, dragging my ass back against his cock while Nate palms my tits and sucks at my neck, whispering filthy things in that low, gravel voice that always makes me squirm. I imagine their fingers tangled in my hair, their hands pushing my thighs apart, forcing space for everything I've been trying so fucking hard not to crave.

I picture them taking turns. Or maybe not even bothering with turns—both of them at once. Their mouths on my skin, lips trailing down my chest, my stomach, my thighs. Nate muttering about how wet I am while Theo smirks against my inner thigh, eyes dark and starved, like he's been waiting years to taste me.

The image alone sends a bolt of heat straight to my core. My thighs clench. My breath hitches. Suddenly, I'm not thinking about the job anymore. All I register is the throb between my legs, the ache in my chest, and the way my body is screaming to let go. To stop pretending. To let them ruin me. Beautiful, filthy, no-coming-back-from-this kind of destruction. And fuck, I'd welcome it.

When I finally crawled into bed last night, I gave myself a good, long talking to. Reminded myself why I was here and why this job matters. Kit took a chance on me. If I screw it up, I don't get another shot. No do-overs. No second fucking chances.

But my body didn't give a fuck about professionalism or boundaries or any of the responsible shit I tried throwing at it. I wanted. I ached. No amount of tossing, turning, or screaming into my pillow could quiet the pulse between my thighs or ease the way my skin seemed too tight for my body.

All I could see when I closed my eyes were their faces lit by the patio lights—Nate with that stupid crooked grin, and Theo leaning back with his beer, eyes glinting with mischief. Both of them laughing, teasing me, pulling me in without even trying.

It became too much.

So I did what I had to do.

I shoved my hand between my legs, pressed down hard, and chased the edge like my sanity depended on it. Rubbed myself raw, biting back their names as wave after wave crashed through me. I came fast. Pathetically fast. And then again, slower, grinding my hips against my fingers, picturing Theo's voice in my ear and Nate's hands holding me open, telling me not to stop.

When it was over, I lay still. Panting. A fucking mess of sweat, shame, and satisfaction.

And the worst part... it didn't help.

I tell myself I have to get it together. Meeting the rest of the band is a big deal. This isn't some open mic night at the back of a bar or a favor from a friend. This is Broken Oasis. Headliners. Rock legends. Guys who are so far out of my league it's laughable.

I've seen the headlines. Their faces are plastered over magazine covers. Jawlines sharp enough to cut glass. Tattoos peeking out from behind unbuttoned shirts. Eyes that smolder straight through camera lenses. They look like sin and sound even better. Together, they're sex on stage, swagger in interviews, trouble behind the scenes. And the world cannot get enough.

Broken Oasis isn't a band. They're a goddamn phenomenon. Fans sob at their shows. Paparazzi stalk them across continents. There are viral compilations of Ace losing his temper, hundreds of thirst traps of Theo, entire subreddits dedicated to Nate's arms. And then there's Xander, the one they write fantasies about. The brooding frontman with a voice full of gravel and heartbreak, and a mouth every girl wants between her thighs.

They don't enter a room. They claim it. And now I'm supposed to be around them every day, camera in hand, documenting the madness.

But I'm not stupid. I've seen the clips. I understand what they're capable of.

I watched Xander tell a reporter to go fuck himself on live TV for spreading shit about Poppy—and that clip practically broke the internet. That glare alone could curdle milk.

And Ace. Jesus Christ. That camera incident last year. The one where he got out of the car, ripped the camera straight out of a paparazzi's hand, and simply stared at the guy with murderous intent. I watched that on repeat. Not because I enjoyed the violence, but because he didn't even flinch. He stood there, daring the world to try him.

It was brutal. And kind of hot.

Not the point.

The point is, I can't tell who I should be more nervous about meeting, Xander or Ace. Both of them carry that edge. Still, Nate and Theo swear by them, call them family, insist they'd bleed for each other. So perhaps they aren't what the media portrays.

I check my watch for what seems like the hundredth time, as if the damn numbers might rearrange themselves if I glare hard enough.

5:57 AM.

Too early to be this amped up. Too late to back out. No point worrying about chasing sleep when I've barely closed my eyes.

I exhale, running my hands down my face, trying to get my body to finally relax for a few hours, but my brain is still too wired.

A noise from the other room catches my attention. It's soft, but enough to make my ears perk up. Light spills under my closed door from the hallway.

I wonder which one of them is awake. Do they share the same room, or do they each have their own? Do they sleep together?

Not only passing out in the same bed after a long night. I'm talking about fucking. The kind of sex that strips you bare and leaves you vulnerable.

I'm not talking about lazy mornings tangled in sheets. Not only the brotherhood, the bond, the ease that comes with years of sharing the same space. But mouths on skin. Hands gripping hard. Theo pushing into Nate, or Nate taking him apart with nothing but his mouth and a fist in his hair. Perhaps they've never crossed that line, or they have and never speak about it.

God, what the hell is wrong with me?

I bury my face in the pillow, trying to breathe through it, but the image is burned into my brain now... Theo's hands gripping Nate's hips, Nate whispering filth into his ear while one of them bites back a moan.

I squeeze my thighs together. Pull it together, Quinn. Get your shit straight. I'm supposed to be working with them, not fantasizing about them. Not craving what it would be to fall apart between them.

But fuck, I do. That kind of intimacy makes you want in.

I shove the covers aside and swing my legs over the edge of the bed. The floor is cold beneath my feet, jolting my sluggish body awake.

Coffee. That's the only thought cutting through the haze.

Someone's already up. Maybe they've made a pot.

I stand, stretch the tension from my spine, and cross the room. My hand closes around the doorknob. A moment passes before I twist it open and step out.

The house is still, the only sound drifting from the kitchen. I step into the hallway, nerves simmering beneath my skin. My feet move on instinct, pulled forward by the sound, and soon I see him.

Theo.

He's standing in the kitchen, wearing nothing but a pair of black boxers, the soft light from above catching every inch of him. Broad chest, tight abs, every line of muscle flexing with the smallest movement. His back is strong, tapering down to a narrow waist.

His body isn't only fit. It's brutal. Built from pain and purpose. The kind of physique you get when control over your body is the only thing left to hold onto while everything else falls apart.

Tattooed angel wings spread across his chest, massive and detailed, each feather etched with a precision that looks painful. They frame the words: Freedom. Hope. Loyalty.

That tattoo does something to me. Not only because of how fucking good it looks on him, but because I understand the weight of it. Bianca wore those angel wings around her neck every single day. Now Theo carries the same wings on his skin, inked right over his heart.

My gaze dips lower, following the hard lines of his abs, the deep cut of muscle leading down to the sharp V that disappears beneath the waistband of his boxers. They hang low on his hips, offering only enough of a tease to make my stomach clench. My eyes drop further and fuck me... there it is.

The thick outline of his cock strains against the fabric. Even soft, he's impressive—the kind of size that makes you ache before he's ever touched you.

I should look away.

Instead, heat crawls up my spine, my pulse hammering in places that have no business waking up this early. Hunger spreads, sharp and steady. All I can think about is how much I want to run my hands over that ink, trace every curve of muscle, feel the weight of him under me, over me, inside me.

Nate might've been the guy who made girls weak in high school, but Theo... Theo could make a girl forget how to fucking breathe.

He grabs a mug and turns, setting it on the counter before nudging it toward one of the stools.

"I didn't put sugar in," he says, his eyes flicking up to mine. "Wasn't sure how you take it."

And after that, he smirks. That smug, all-seeing, cocky bastard smirk. The kind that says: *Yeah, I saw you staring and I'm fully aware of what you were thinking.*

I stand frozen. Motionless. Useless. Brain fried. Eyes wide. Probably drooling.

Jesus Christ. Was I drooling?

I blink and try to act normal. Apparently, that means continuing to stare at him like he's the main course and I've skipped breakfast, lunch, and every moral boundary I've ever had.

Did I have my tongue out? Fuck. I might have. I might have even made a sound. Some needy little moan or something equally tragic.

My whole body is radiating "thirsty girl at a frat party" energy, while he stands there shirtless, glistening under kitchen lights, handing me caffeine like a goddamn lingerie ad come to life.

I can't even blame him for that stare. The one that says, *are you good? Do you need a cold shower... maybe a priest?* Because he fucking knows exactly where my mind went.

Now I'm not sure what's worse. The fact that I got caught full-on eye-fucking him, or that part of me that wants him aware of it.

He turns back, reaching for another cup from the cupboard, and fuck, that alone should be my cue to move. Do something. Stop standing here, useless and overheating with my dignity circling the drain while he exists in nothing but boxers and cockiness.

I shove air into my lungs and will my feet to cooperate. One step. Followed by another.

By the time I slide onto the stool, Theo's already moving. Unbothered. Smooth. Acting as though he hadn't caught me practically drooling over him.

He strolls over and drops a few sugar packets on the counter. He doesn't say a word, only stands close enough that the heat from his skin seeps into mine.

I keep my gaze down, because I can't risk looking at him. Not when the image of him half-naked is still burned into the backs of my eyelids.

My fingers shake as I tear the packet open. Sugar scatters in a clumsy little trail across the counter, and I don't bother brushing it away. My hands keep moving, desperate for something to do. Stir, stir, stir. Sip. Repeat.

We've never had anything between us this heavy. Now the weight of it is deafening.

This is Theo, for fuck's sake.

The same guy who used to steal fries off my plate with a shit-eating grin and zero shame. The same guy who once confessed, drunk off his ass, that he taught himself guitar because the sound kept the dark out.

Now he's standing close enough to kiss, and I can't tell who we are anymore.

But he isn't just Theo now. He's Theo fucking Kade. Rockstar. Bass slung low, head down, fingers sliding over strings, lost in the rhythm while thousands of fans scream his name. Magazines plaster him across glossy covers. Giant posters hang in record stores and bedroom walls. Fans lose their minds when he so much as glances at a camera, and every move he makes ends up replayed in slow motion on TikTok.

And I should know.

I watched them. Bought the magazines and hid them away like stupid little treasures. They were the only pieces of Nate and Theo I could still touch, some fragile thread tying me back to the boys I used to know. Every time I saw their faces in print, I thought about the nights we stayed up talking shit and raiding snacks from Nate's kitchen. About the way they smiled when they played, before the rest of the world realized how fucking good they were.

It was never about wanting a piece of their fame. It was about our friendship. About not wanting to lose what we had, while clinging to any small fragment of the past I could hold on to.

But sitting here now, the distance between who we were and who we are feels impossible to ignore.

When Theo's coffee is ready, he turns back toward me, lifting the cup to his mouth. He takes a slow sip, dragging it out as though he's got nowhere to be and nothing better to do than watch me squirm.

He doesn't speak. He only stands there on the other side of the counter, his eyes locked on mine.

Then his gaze dips lower and stays there. It drags over my chest, lingering, settling on my tits like they've got something to say. Heat sparks in places I don't need igniting. And fuck, he's not even trying to hide it.

How the hell did he change? Back then, Theo barely made eye contact. Always in a hoodie, hands shoved in his pockets, carrying that damn stress ball he squeezed the life out of whenever someone talked too fast or stood too close.

Now he stands tall. Skin, ink, and enough tension to make my breath stutter in my throat.

I cross my arms, shifting my weight as I raise a brow. "Hey, buddy, eyes up here."

He smirks into his cup, not the least bit sorry. "I'm just multitasking. Admiring while I'm having my morning coffee. It's called efficiency."

"Oh, is that what we're calling perving now?"

He takes a slow sip, eyes never leaving mine. "Can't help it. They were practically waving good morning."

I scoff. "Jesus. You've been awake five minutes and you're already a walking HR violation."

He shrugs. "What can I say? If there's a view, I'm gonna look. That's basic hospitality."

"Well, let me know when you start asking for reviews. I'll be sure to leave a complaint."

He leans against the counter, that lazy smile spreading across his face. "I'd like to see where you'd stick that complaint."

I launch a sugar packet at his head. "You're disgusting."

He laughs, full and unbothered. "You've missed me."

"Missed insulting you, maybe."

He taps his chest. "That's still love in my book."

I take a slow sip of my coffee, stalling. Letting the bitterness coat my tongue so I don't say something I'll regret. Or let myself stare too long. Or both.

"You want something to eat?" Theo asks, stepping toward the fridge. He pulls it open, cold air spilling out and sweeping across his chest and abs. And fuck, my eyes dip again before I can stop them.

Behind me, the soft slap of bare feet against marble steals my attention. I turn toward the sound, heart already racing.

Nate.

Bare-chested.

Jeans slung low, clinging just above that sharp V. His arms stretch overhead in a lazy yawn, muscles flexing, back arching, and I swear if I were standing, my knees would give out. Sunlight pours through the glass doors behind him, threading through his hair, kissing the hard lines of his body, turning him into something close to holy.

My mouth goes dry. My pulse kicks. Coffee stalls halfway to my lips, and I freeze, staring at him like I've never seen a man before.

And then I see it.

The tattoo on the right side of his chest.

Bianca.

Her name inked over his heart in delicate script.

My breath snags. Guilt slams into me, a cold punch to the ribs that hollows me out from the inside. Because this isn't just lust. It's betrayal. Twisted. Wrong. A sickness I can't shake.

They were Bianca's. Both of them. She loved them in that impossible, all consuming way only she could. And they loved her right back.

And here I am, heartbeat skittering in my chest, wanting something that was never meant to be mine.

The ink on Nate's chest burns itself into my mind, branded into his skin like a promise he'll never stop carrying.

I used to watch them with her—how their hands lingered, how their eyes softened with love. I wanted to be loved like that so badly it made my chest ache. I still do.

God, what's wrong with me?

She was my best friend. My other half. The one person who knew every ugly part of me and never turned away. And now here I am, wanting the two people who still belong to her.

I tear my gaze away, forcing my eyes back to my coffee, fingers gripping the cup as if it's the only thing keeping me grounded. What the fuck am I even thinking? They were Bianca's. Not mine.

"Hey, Quinn," Nate says.

I lift my head, heart stuttering as I meet his gaze. That fucking smile. He has no idea what it does to me.

"Hey, Nate," I manage, forcing my voice steady even though everything inside me is shaking.

He moves past me toward Theo, who's still standing in front of the open fridge, rummaging like he's forgotten what food even looks like.

Nate steps in behind him, arm slipping around, hand brushing across bare skin. He leans in, chest pressed to Theo's back, face tucked close. A small hug.

"Morning," Nate says.

Theo leans back into the touch for a second before muttering something about eggs.

I tear my gaze away, staring down at the coffee gone cold in my hands.

Theo shuts the fridge and crosses the kitchen with a carton of eggs in one hand. Nate heads for the coffee machine, pouring himself a mug like this is any ordinary morning and not a goddamn test of my willpower.

"You want some eggs?" Theo asks, cracking one single-handed like it's nothing.

"No, I'm not really hungry."

A lie.

My appetite's shifted somewhere else entirely.

The testosterone in this room is suffocating. It's thick in the air, clinging to the walls, curling in my lungs. It should be a crime to look that good before seven in the morning. And the worst part? There are two of them. Double the sin. Double the distraction. Double the fucking problem.

How the hell is anyone supposed to stay sane around that?

I tip back the rest of my coffee. I need to get out of here before I do something stupid. Before I forget what the hell I'm here for and start acting out every filthy fantasy still echoing in my head.

I drag the back of my hand across my mouth, as if that'll erase the drool I'm half afraid is actually there. Then I push back from the stool, legs too shaky, pulse still racing.

"I might jump in the shower," I say, trying for casual as I circle the counter, pretending I don't feel both of their eyes on me.

I make a quick stop at the dishwasher, drop in my cup, and shut it harder than I mean to.

If I don't put some distance between me and those two, I'm going to combust.

Bad fucking idea.

Because the second I move closer, the heat pouring off them slams into me like a wave. The scent wrecks me. Lust claws beneath my skin as if it owns me. My body aches to be touched. To be handled. To be fucked until I forget why this is wrong.

I need to keep my focus. Prove to Kit that I'm not some starry-eyed idiot who can't handle herself around a couple of rockstars. I'm here to work. To be professional. Not to drool over abs and tattoos. I have to prove I can do this, because girls like me don't get second chances.

I've seen the women who usually surround them. Tall. Confident. The kind who glide into a room like they own it. Women who wear sex like perfume and don't flinch under the weight of attention. The kind who belong in the spotlight.

Me... I'm none of that.

I blend in. Fade out. Overthink every damn word before I say it. I'm the girl in the shadows. The one who keeps her head down and her guard up, hoping no one notices how badly she wants to be wanted.

"Towels are in the bathroom cupboard," Nate calls after me, voice smooth, relaxed, completely unaware that I'm two seconds from falling apart. "Grab whichever you want, Quinn."

Theo says my name next.

Not loud. Enough to claim it.

I freeze. My lungs forget how to work. Slowly, I turn.

And there they are.

Side by side at the counter. Watching me.

They're nothing alike. Opposites in every way. Night and day. Smoke and sunlight. But together, they're lethal.

Nate, the angel on my shoulder—heat and comfort, tempting me to play it safe. Theo, the devil on the other, staring through me as if he already knows the exact way I'll break.

Every glance they throw me drips with a challenge I'm not sure I can survive.

Be my good girl, Q.

No. Be my bad girl, Quinn.

And I'm stuck in the middle, wanting both. Caught between heaven and hell, already half in love with the burn.

I swallow hard, forcing down the lump in my throat, trying to ignore the pulse hammering between my legs. Every inch of me is buzzing, desperate, out of control. I need to get the fuck out of here.

"Yeah," I say, and it comes out weak, pathetic. I hear it. I know they do too. But I stand my ground, pretending I haven't noticed a thing, praying they'll play along.

Theo offers me a small smile. "It's good having you here, Quinn. You'll be fine today. No need to stress."

Perfect. They think I'm nervous about the job. Thank fuck for that. They don't have a clue I'm spiraling in real time just by looking at them.

"Okay," I manage, forcing a smile before turning on shaky legs and walking fast.

I make it back to my room and shut the door behind me, my pulse a wild, erratic thing under my skin. Two weeks in this house—that's all I have to survive this temptation. Two weeks of pretending I don't want to drop to my knees.

It's not hell. It's fire.

I'm living in the blaze, skin scorching, thoughts unraveling. And my pussy? Already begging. Aching.

And when it's over, they won't need a headstone. Just carve it into the floorboards and leave me here.

Here lies Quinn Thomas. Died of excessive eye-fucking. Pussy never stood a chance. Cause of death: two sinfully hot bastards with too many abs and not enough fucking shirts.

CHAPTER 17

Nate

What the fuck is wrong with Quinn? I know she's nervous, but that was some fucking Oscar-worthy, full-throttle meltdown. One second she's standing in front of me, stiff and twitchy like she's buffering in real time, and the next she's tearing out of the room so fast you'd swear I'd dropped my pants and asked her to rate my cock on a scale from one to ten.

Honestly, I've seen drunk fans hold themselves together better, and they're usually wearing my face on a T-shirt and crying into their vodka Red Bull.

I glance at Theo.

He's still planted in the kitchen, staring after Quinn like she hadn't launched herself into the hallway with the grace of a drunk gazelle. A smirk tugs at his mouth, the kind of smug, shit-eating curve that makes my hands itch to lob something at his stupid head.

He finally turns and locks eyes with me.

"What?" I ask, lifting my cup. I go to take a sip but freeze halfway when I catch the way his grin deepens, savoring some private joke where I'm the punchline. My eyes narrow. "What the fuck are you smiling at?"

"Nothing," he says, still smirking like the asshole he is. "Just an interesting morning, that's all."

"Yeah. No fucking shit. You know what that was all about?" I nod toward the door, eyes locked on Theo, hoping he'll quit dragging things out and finally tell me what the hell went down with Quinn.

He takes a slow sip of his coffee, acting as if he's got all the time in the world to be a smug little shit.

I grit my teeth. "Theo."

"What?"

I scoff. "What the fuck does that mean?"

His grin stretches, and I swear to God, if I didn't have this cup in my hand I'd be ready to punch him.

"You really don't know?" he says, clearly enjoying himself. "This from the guy who spent high school fucking his way through every girl with a pulse."

"Yeah, and?"

"And now a girl's practically short-circuiting in front of you, and you're standing here blinking like a confused golden retriever. What happened to the guy who could smell a crush from a mile away and seal the deal before lunch?"

I glare at him. "You done?"

"Not even close," Theo retorts, laughing. "Either you lost your game or your dick's out of service. Might wanna get that shit checked."

I stand frozen, confused as fuck. I wait for him to explain, but he remains there, grinning as if this is the goddamn highlight of his week.

"You're enjoying this, aren't you?"

He doesn't bother hiding a thing. "Immensely. Honestly, I haven't had this much fun since that groupie called you my name mid-blowjob."

I blink. "That never happened."

He shrugs, smug as ever. "You were too busy choking on your ego to catch it."

I take a sip from my cup and move around the bench, dropping onto one of the stools. Theo goes back to cracking eggs into a bowl, calm as ever. My eyes track him as he fishes out a piece of shell and flicks the fragment into the sink before he finally looks up.

"How do you think she'll go today?" I ask.

"Quinn will be fine," Theo says. "You've seen the way she captures shit. Moments no one else even notices. She'll get one of Ace being the usual grumpy bastard that he is. His resting asshole face will do half the work for her. What I'm really hoping for is that she finally gets a shot of Pretty-boy that makes him look like the rest of us. Sweaty. Slightly pissed off. Maybe caught mid-sneeze."

I shake my head, laughing now. "You really want to knock Xander off his pedestal."

"Someone's got to do it," Theo says, dead serious. "Every time I see one of those glossy posters, I give him a makeover. Dicks on the jawline, devil horns, the occasional lazy eye. You know, artistic expression."

I grin, already picturing it. Theo's been on a quiet mission for years to take Xander down a peg, usually by defiling his posters with dicks in various positions.

Theo grins. "It's a public service, really. Makes people stop treating him like he pisses Chanel."

I snort into my cup. "So are you going to tell me what you said to make Quinn freak the fuck out?"

He doesn't flinch, just keeps whisking. "Nah. You'll work it out soon enough. These are ready to cook now."

I eye the eggs, after that I eye him. I know Theo. Give it five seconds and he'll get distracted by something shiny and burn the whole damn pan. So I slide off the stool and take over, cracking the skillet to life.

We move around each other easily. No words needed. It's been that way for years. Through the chaos, the tours, the late-night arguments that nearly split us down the middle, we always find our way back to this—breakfast, eggs, coffee, smartass comments, and a rhythm that works.

Still, I glance toward the hallway, wondering what the fuck Quinn sees that I don't.

It's 9:03.

We're three minutes late, and I already know Kit or Xander will be riding our asses for it. Probably both.

We head toward Ace's place, the morning heat pressing down, clinging to my skin. Today's going to be a long one in the studio—the kind that scrapes at your patience and doesn't let up.

Our sound isn't what it was when we first started. It's rougher now, jagged in places, tighter in others. It hits harder. There's grit in every note. That's what happens when time beats the shit out of you. Things shift. Bands either evolve or burn out trying to stay the same.

Still, underneath all of it, the foundation holds. The rhythm, the weight, the pulse—it's all there. Wrapped in newer scars and louder truths.

Quinn walks between us, quiet, eyes on the ground, stuck deep in her own head. Her camera bounces against her chest with every step, fingers twitching against the strap. She's nervous. Anyone with half a brain could see that.

I should be focused on the day. On the music. On the set list and the shit we still need to tighten. But all I can think about is her.

I shouldn't be looking at Quinn the way I am. Shouldn't be catching how her tank top hugs her tits beneath that open shirt, or how those fucking cutoffs cling to her hips, riding high, showing off legs a man could spend all fucking day between.

But I do. And once the thought lands, it doesn't fade. It multiplies. Fucks with my focus. Strips everything else down to static.

I picture her stripped bare, laid out between me and Theo, skin flushed, chest rising fast, those pretty lips parted on a gasp as we touch her. My hands gripping her thighs, holding her open, spreading her wide. Theo's mouth trailing down her body, dragging every shiver out of her with nothing but his tongue and that cocky grin he wears when he knows he's got someone right on the edge.

He'd start with her nipple, teasing it, sucking it into his mouth while she moans, hands fisting in the sheets, begging for more. And I'd be taking in every second. Seeing her come apart under him. Catching the way he drags it out.

My hand wrapped around my cock, stroking slowly, keeping pace with every sound she makes. Theo's mouth would move lower, kissing across her stomach, grinning against her skin when she whimpers. And I'd be right there, hard as fuck, knowing exactly what's coming.

Theo would tease her first. Of course he would. The fucker lives for that. That smug bastard would make her beg, hold back to watch her unravel.

His fingers would ghost over her clit, barely grazing, enough to make her squirm, to make her hips lift off the bed in a silent plea for more. He'd smirk, knowing exactly what he's doing, and drag it out even longer. Whispering filth in her ear, telling her how fucking beautiful she looks when she's needy, when she's right there on the edge, falling apart for us.

I'd slide my fingers inside her, taking in the way her body grips me, tight and wet. She'd be so fucking soft, so ready, and I'd take my time with it. Curling my fingers perfectly, dragging over every spot that makes her gasp. Her legs would open wider, thighs trembling, mouth parting with those little breathless sounds that drive me fucking insane. She wouldn't need words. Her body would say it all.

Theo wouldn't leave her hanging for long. He'd kiss his way down her body, dragging his mouth over every inch of skin he can reach, sucking bruises into her thigh purely to watch her squirm. After that he'd settle between her legs, eyes dark, fingers digging into her hips to hold her in place while his mouth hovers, close enough that she can sense the heat of it but not close enough to give her what she needs.

When he finally does, he wouldn't be gentle. He'd groan into her, licking her clit like he owns her, as if it's his favorite fucking meal. Wet, messy, relentless.

I'd be right there beside him, fucking her with my fingers, keeping perfect rhythm with his mouth, watching the way her whole body responds. Taking in every twist and pant, her hands clawing at his hair, head thrown back as she gets closer and closer.

And right when she's on the fucking edge, we'd stop. Pull back. Make her feel the loss, make her whimper for it, make her ache so bad she forgets how to think.

Because we don't want her merely coming. We want her feral for it. Needy. Shaking. Broken open and begging for more. And she will. Fuck, she will.

I bite down hard on the inside of my cheek, cock already fucking throbbing simply from the thought. I know I shouldn't be thinking about Quinn this way. Shouldn't let it crawl under my skin and take over. But fuck, if she gave me even the smallest sign she wanted it, I'd make every filthy thought I've kept locked away since high school come true.

This is Quinn Thomas.

The girl I've wanted to fuck since I was seventeen.

The one I used to think about in the shower, hand wrapped tight around my cock, groaning her name while I picture her on her knees, lips parted, eyes wide, looking up at me as if I was the only thing she ever fucking needed.

Back before Bianca turned my world upside down. Before I learned how fast the ground can vanish beneath you when you get too close to something that is real.

We hit the front steps of Ace's place.

Theo reaches the door first, shoves it open, and tips his head toward Quinn. She steps inside, eyes already scanning the space, cataloguing the light, the angles, the shadows curling in the corners. Her hand rests on her camera strap, fingers twitching against it, ready.

I move to follow, but Theo cuts me a look. He caught the way I was eye fucking her.

A smirk pulls at his mouth as he leans closer, amusement lacing his voice.

"You keep staring at her like that, she'll catch fire."

I don't say shit, shouldering past him. Then I come to a stop when I see her. Standing near the far wall, lip caught between her teeth in focus. Shirt slipping off one shoulder. Those goddamn cutoffs showing off skin that drags my thoughts straight to hell.

And I know I'm totally fucked.

Theo nudges my shoulder, grinning. "You planning to make a move, Loverboy, or stand there and drool?"

I exhale hard, drag a hand through my hair, trying to shake the heat crawling up the back of my neck. He's loving this shit, drinking it in as if it's the best part of his morning.

"Come on," I mutter, voice rougher than I intend. "Studio's this way."

She startles, barely, as though she forgot we were even here. After that she turns.

And fuck.

Her green eyes hit mine and everything stops. The breath I was pulling in never makes it past my throat. It dies there, trapped behind the sudden punch of her gaze, wide and bright and locked on me.

The impact runs through me everywhere.

I force my legs to move, stepping past her, ignoring the way Theo snickers behind us. Prick's enjoying this way too much.

The hallway's dim, shadows clinging to the walls, the only light bleeding through the half-drawn curtains Ace never bothers with. If Scarlet were here, it'd be a different story. Windows open. Sunlight pouring in. That sharp, clean smell of fresh air cutting through the thick, stale heat. But she's off with her band, filming some music video I haven't bothered to ask about.

Even with me leading, I sense Quinn right behind me.

Too fucking close.

Her footsteps are light, almost soundless, but I swear I catch the warmth of her body at my back, the hum of her breath filling the space between us.

I reach the studio and shove the door open. The familiar hit of stale beer, sweat, and too many years spent chasing sound smacks me in the face. It's the same as always, cluttered with cables and amps, the kind of place that carries more memory than a room. Every surface has a story.

Xander's leaning against the far wall, arms crossed and unreadable. Ace is slouched in one of the chairs, boots kicked out, expression caught somewhere between half-asleep and seconds from tearing someone a new one.

The second we step in, both of them look up.

I step aside, clearing the path as Quinn and Theo move in behind me.

"This is Quinn," I say, keeping my voice steady, pretending this is another day. Another fucking introduction.

But when I glance at her, I see it.

The way her feet shift, uncertain. The twitch of her fingers against the camera strap, gripping it as if it's the only steady thing in the room. Her eyes flicker, never landing, scanning the space as though she's mapping every corner, every possible exit.

She's nervous as fuck, and now that I've noticed, I can't look away.

Xander pushes off the wall, his expression unreadable as he moves forward with that calm, controlled energy he always carries, the kind that makes it hard to tell if he's sizing someone up or already three steps ahead.

Ace lets out a long breath as though we've ruined the sacred ritual of him doing absolutely fuck all. His eyes drag over Quinn before he finally stands. He stretches like he's been asked to do something outrageously difficult, arms over his head, shirt riding up enough to flash the ink on his stomach.

"Hey, Quinn," Xander says, stepping forward, smooth as ever. "Kit showed me some of your photos. Gotta say, I'm impressed."

Quinn blinks, caught off guard for a second before her mouth curves. "Oh. Thanks," she says, a little surprised, but there's something proud tucked into her voice.

Theo claps a hand on Quinn's shoulder, eyes gleaming, then throws an exaggerated gesture toward Ace as if he's unveiling a statue in a museum.

"And this ray of fucking sunshine right here... That's Ace," he announces, voice full of mock reverence. "Big deal, apparently. Rockstar. Legend. God among men and all that bullshit. Also grumpier than a guy who discovered his favorite porn got scrubbed off the internet. Has the charm of a wet sock rotting in a gym bag. But hey, we still love him."

Ace lets out a long, pained sigh, the kind that makes it sound as if Theo's voice causes him physical discomfort.

"You done," he mutters, "or should I grab a fucking mic so the whole neighborhood can hear your stand-up routine?" He lifts one brow.

Quinn presses her lips together, clearly fighting a smile.

Theo grins, completely unfazed. "Nah, man. You're my muse. Trying to channel the raw magic of your sparkling fucking personality."

Ace exhales, already over it. After that his gaze shifts to Quinn.

"Hey," he says. "Welcome to the shitshow."

"Thanks," Quinn replies, stepping forward to shake his hand. "I hear you're engaged to Scar."

That's the moment it happens.

Ace's whole face shifts. Not in a big way. He's still Ace. Still got that permanent fuck-off look etched into every line of his face. But something in him softens. The hard edge dulls. His jaw loosens. That sharp, coiled tension he wears as armor slips for half a second, enough to let something real show through.

His mouth twitches, not quite a smile, but fucking close. Closer than most ever get. For a moment, he looks younger. Calmer. Fucking happy. He always changes when someone mentions Scarlet.

I was wrong about him. About them. Back when I found out they were hooking up, I thought he was another selfish bastard. Thought he was using her. Thought it would crash and burn, leave her gutted. But now I see it. Every time her name comes up, he softens in ways I didn't think he could. Turns out, she doesn't merely matter to him. She's the only thing that does.

"Yeah," he says, and the pride in his voice is impossible to miss. "Scar said you two used to hang out when you were younger."

"Yeah," Quinn nods, shifting her camera strap higher on her shoulder.

Theo's already grabbing his bass, sliding into place without hesitation. I move toward my drumkit, drop onto the stool, and grip the sticks.

Everything's still for a second. Quiet. After that, Ace starts playing, the kind of guitar work that hits more as a warning than a melody.

It's different. Jagged, fucked up in the best way. More chaos than control. The kind of sound that punches you in the ribs and leaves a bruise you can't stop pressing on.

Ace nods toward me, gives me the rough shape of the beat. No drawn-out explanation. No slowing down to make it easier. Only the bare bones and a glare that says, keep the fuck up.

I fuck it up the first time. Miss the cue. My timing's off. Doesn't matter. I don't stop. I grit my teeth and hit again. Harder. My whole body locked in, chasing the rhythm down as if it owes me something.

The second run comes out stronger. On the third, I hit it right. It slides into place, not perfect, but close enough to catch the rush of it. The crash, the pulse, the weight of every sound. I don't even notice when I stop thinking. The rhythm takes over. My hands move on instinct, every beat crawling through my veins and setting shit on fire.

Theo drops into sync with me. Xander starts humming under his breath, pacing, eyes closed, already hearing the finished version in his head before the rest of us even get close. It's loud, dirty, and raw. And everything about it lands so fucking good.

The room shifts.

Not in a big way. Just this slow tightening beneath the surface, the kind that creeps into your chest before your head even catches up. The energy pulls taut, every sound snapping into place. Under it all, I sense her. Quinn. Moving through the space. Camera in hand, eyes sharp, silent. She circles the room, locking this chaos into something still. Something permanent.

I catch her out of the corner of my eye more than once. The soft click of the shutter somehow louder than it should be. She crouches near Theo, gets a shot of his fingers flying over the strings, then moves around behind me. I register her presence more than I see her. The air shifts when she's close. My skin prickles. My focus wavers, then resets, harder than before.

We spend the next few hours tearing through the track, pulling it apart and building it back up. Again and again until it stops sounding messy and starts sounding alive. Ace stands next to me, guitar slung low, mouth tight with concentration. He runs through the rhythm section, calling things out in that clipped way of his, not wasting a single word.

I keep pace. Every beat I land digs deeper into me, crawling up my arms, into my spine, rooting itself there. This isn't sound anymore. It's muscle memory. It's blood. Ace leans over at one point, barely audible over the noise, muttering a quick adjustment. I shift the pattern, hit again. This time it lands. His head lifts in that sharp nod that means I got it right.

He turns to Theo, tapping out the rhythm against the body of his guitar while Theo listens, brows drawn, adjusting the bassline until it grooves the way it's meant to. The sound thickens, grows heavier, layered. It builds into something that could tear you apart if you weren't ready.

We don't stop. Not for drinks. Not for air. It's work, and it's fucking brutal—the kind that burns behind your ribs and makes the rest of the world fall away.

And when we finally nail it, when the rhythm locks in and every crash and pulse wires itself into our bodies, Xander steps forward.

He's been quiet the whole time, pacing near the mic, running through the lines under his breath, watching us. He grips the mic stand, closes his eyes for a long second, then opens his mouth.

And fuck. It hits. His voice is rough at first, frayed at the edges from hours of silence, but then it opens up. Raw. Magnetic. Every word dripping with that ache he carries so fucking well, that fury buried under the calm.

The room bends around it. Every sound we've built locks beneath his voice, lifting it higher, driving it harder. I feel it in my chest. In the weight of my hands. In the space between my breaths.

Quinn's still moving. Still working. But slower now, sharper. I catch the way she lifts the camera, framing Xander in the shot, her eyes wide with something close to awe.

Then she lowers the camera, arms falling slack, and her eyes catch mine.

And I'm not in the studio anymore.

I'm back in that beat-up bedroom I used to share with Theo. Posters curling off the walls, the constant stink of that cheap deodorant he refused to stop using. Bianca pulling her guitar from its case. Quinn on my bed, knees drawn up, camera around her neck, quiet, always watching.

She was always there. Part of those long-gone nights. One of the last true pieces of it—the music, the laughter, the late hours that didn't carry guilt. Before Bianca's name turned sharp, cutting into the back of our throats.

And now she's here again, camera in hand, pulling it all back without even trying. Every memory I've spent years shoving down, locking away, pretending never existed, she carries it with her. In the way she stands. In the way her eyes find mine.

Maybe that's why I can't stop watching her. Because when she's near, time seems to fold in on itself. Nothing broken. Nothing missing. For a moment, everything lines up again. Bianca's still alive. We're still laughing. And somehow, we're all still whole.

Chapter 18

Theo

I'm sitting next to Quinn on the back patio, watching as she flicks through her camera, scrolling through the shots from today. Her fingers move fast, pausing only when one of the images grabs her. Every few seconds she tilts the screen toward me, waiting for some kind of reaction.

Kit's gonna lose her mind over these. I'm honestly surprised she didn't crash the session with coffee and chaos to hover over Quinn's shoulder the whole time.

Every frame is sharp. No bullshit in her work. She catches the in-between moments—sweat on a brow, fingers mid-strike, Xander pacing as though the lyrics are chasing him instead of the other way around.

And I've got to admit, I'm a little annoyed Xander doesn't come off rough in any of them. Not even one. The man's still brooding around in tight jeans and layered necklaces, and somehow every photo makes him appear as though he stepped off a fucking billboard.

"They say the camera adds ten pounds," I mutter, squinting at a shot of him gripping the mic stand, shirt clinging to his chest. "What, does yours work in reverse?"

Quinn laughs softly, nudging me with her shoulder. "He's photogenic. That's not on me."

"He's a smug bastard, that's what he is."

"You love him," she says, shifting her attention back to the camera.

"Yeah, I do," I add, before shooting her a sideways glance. "But if you tell anyone I said something bordering on sincere, that'll be the end of you, Thomas. I'll deny the whole thing until the day I die. Hell, I'll take you down with me."

Quinn laughs, eyes still on the camera screen. "Your secret's safe with me."

"Better be. I've got a reputation to uphold. Can't have people thinking I've got feelings and shit."

"God forbid," she says, biting back a grin.

She taps through a few more shots, stopping on one of Ace leaning back in his chair, guitar in his lap, mouth parted mid-yawn or perhaps mid-growl. Hard to tell with him.

"That one's my favorite," she says, thumb hovering over the screen.

I tilt my head. "Why?"

"He looks real. Not polished. Not perfect. Simply tired. Honest."

I study the photo again, this time seeing what she means.

His jaw's tight, shadows cling under his eyes, but a trace of vulnerability cuts through.

"You've got a good eye," I tell her.

She glances at me, a flicker of surprise in her expression, before offering a small smile. "Thanks."

I reach down, adjust the volume on the shitty Bluetooth speaker humming low in the background.

Quinn shifts beside me, pulling her knees up, camera resting in her lap. She doesn't say anything else, only leans back. And for a second, everything feels easy. Calm. The way it has always been between us. The kind of quiet that settles deep.

But my head is spinning.

I shouldn't be sitting this close. Shouldn't let the scent of her shampoo slip beneath my skin, or notice the heat radiating off her as though it's crawling across the space between us, burrowing deep. But I'm here anyway. I breathe her in. The silence settles. And for a moment, it feels good.

Falling into a rhythm I know better than to trust.

I've carried this before. That warmth. That pull.

I didn't tell Nate what happened this morning. He'll figure it out. He's not an idiot. I wasn't about to say the words out loud. Didn't want to put a label on something I've been trying to pretend doesn't exist.

Because once you name the truth, you can't take it back.

Whatever this thing with Quinn is, it's already too much. A pull drags at me I can't shake. A wanting that refuses to ease no matter how hard I try to drown the hunger.

I know how this ends.

Getting close always fucks you up.

You let someone in, hand over pieces of yourself you never planned to give. You carve out space for them without even realizing it. And then something fucking happens, and you're left standing in the rubble, trying to remember how to breathe without them.

I won't let that happen again. No way I can risk letting this turn into something I need.

This has to stay in the now. Nothing more. You don't lose what you never allow yourself to feel.

She flicks to another photo and holds the screen toward me, casual as anything.

I barely have time to process what I'm seeing before I choke on my beer and spit half of it across the table.

"Holy fuck," I cough, wiping my mouth with the back of my hand, eyes locked on the image.

The shot is brutal. I'm mid-comment, lips caught mid-sentence, probably saying some dumb shit I'll never remember, while Ace sits across from me, eyes narrowed, jaw clenched, looking one second away from launching over the table and choking the life out of me. The angle is ridiculous. The tension practically leaks off the screen.

If Quinn had waited half a breath longer, she probably would've caught me dodging a flying bottle.

I wipe my mouth again with the back of my hand, still wheezing through a laugh. "Can you send me a copy of that one?"

Quinn doesn't answer right away. She looks up, her mouth twitching as though she's fighting a grin, but failing hard. "What's the go with you two?"

I take another sip of my beer. Slower this time. Let the taste linger in my mouth before swallowing and setting the bottle back on the table with a soft clunk.

"I can't explain," I say, eyes still on the screen. "Xander and I clicked from day one, you could tell. It was easy."

Another pause. Not because I don't have more to say, but because my mind drifts back to that day.

My eyes flick to the photo again. Something in the shot cuts deeper than it should. The tension. The rawness. The part no one outside the band would ever understand. People see us as a bunch of guys who got lucky. They don't notice the weight trailing behind the music. The ghosts that show up every time the room goes quiet.

"Ace had this sadness about him," I say finally, quieter than before. "And it reminded me of how I grew up."

Quinn doesn't move. She just watches me.

"Did he grow up the same way as you?" she asks.

I glance at her, and I remember that night at the party. Three beers deep, pretending I didn't care about anything. The music was too loud, the room pressed in too tight, and Nate was off getting his dick sucked in a hallway while I sat in a corner trying to disappear. That was when I told her where I came from. The kind of house that teaches you how to dodge fists before you can even read.

I remember how her face didn't change. Quinn didn't look at me with pity. She understood. Somehow, she fucking understood. No awkward apology, no scrambling for an excuse to get the hell away from me.

I swallow hard, reaching for the beer again so I have something solid in my hand.

"I figured you'd see me differently," I say, voice low. "After I told you that night, I thought you'd pity me or pull away. But you didn't."

Quinn shifts, tucking one leg beneath her, camera still in her hands.

"That's because I've seen it," she says softly. "And I don't believe in treating people as broken just because someone else fucked them up."

The words hit harder than I expect. I glance at her again, and she meets my stare without flinching.

"You're the first person I told outside of Nate's family," I admit.

"I figured."

Silence settles between us, heavier this time.

"Ace was different," I say, steering the conversation back before it sinks too deep. "He never told me what he went through, but I saw it. You don't carry that kind of weight unless you've lived through hell. I recognized it that day—the pressure behind his eyes, the way it sat on him, heavy, like the whole world was pressing down and he couldn't catch a breath."

"Has he ever talked to you about it?" she asks.

"No," I say. "He doesn't have to."

And that's the truth. Words aren't what we rely on. The rhythm speaks for us. The silence fills in the rest.

"You and Ace fight a lot," she says, nudging the conversation somewhere lighter.

"Only when he breathes," I shoot back, smirking.

She laughs, and the sound slices through the heaviness, pulling me back into the moment, and for a second I forget the weight in my chest.

"I'm serious," she says, smiling now.

"He's easy to rile up," I say, smirking. "And I'm a natural-born instigator. It's a gift. That's how we work. We go head-to-head all the time. He pisses me off, I piss him off. It looks intense, but there's never a moment I don't trust him with everything."

My fingers drum against the side of my beer bottle.

"I figure we do it on purpose. The arguing, the shots we take at each other. It's easier than talking. Safer than digging into the shit we've both worked too hard to bury. We keep things loud and sarcastic so we never have to say the real stuff." I glance at her. "That's the kind of friendship this is. One where you don't have to explain why you are the way you are, you just keep the surface moving so nobody drowns."

Quinn turns the camera back on and flips through a few more photos. I watch her hands, the way her fingers move over the buttons, sure and practiced. Everything she does has that same quiet precision.

A shot of Nate flashes across the screen. Her thumb pauses over the image.

I lean in, glancing down. "That one's good."

Nate steps through the open doors, moving onto the patio with a plate in his hands. The thing's piled high with steaks, all marinated and glistening, stacked with the kind of care that screams he's been working on them all afternoon. While Quinn and I have been out here knocking back beers, Nate's been in the kitchen, mixing whatever the fuck's in those secret marinades, chopping herbs with surgical precision, throwing salads together without breaking a sweat.

The whole scene is domestic as hell, and somehow, he looks completely at ease doing the work. Relaxed in a way most people don't expect from him.

I'd help, but we've been through that shit before. History's proven that the outcome is better for everyone if I keep the fuck out of his way. Nate's not just particular in the kitchen, he's obsessive. He's got rules, systems, methods that make sense only to him. The second you step into that space, you're a threat. You're throwing off his rhythm, fucking with his balance. You're risking your hand if you reach for the wrong spoon.

And honestly, he loves the whole world of it. The prep, the order, the control. He doesn't just enjoy the process, he disappears into the ritual. If music hadn't claimed him first, food would've taken him instead. No question. I can see the picture clear as day—Nate with his own restaurant, apron tied around his waist, scowling at line cooks while Gordon Ramsay–style yelling at someone for burning the fucking sauce.

He'd probably name the place something ridiculous. One word. Pretentious as shit. All clean lines and moody lighting. Menus with no prices.

Steaks cooked to perfection for assholes in designer shirts who couldn't tell the difference between rare and raw if it punched them in the face.

Still, when I watch him out here, with his shirt sleeves pushed up, jaw relaxed, face flushed from the heat of the grill, it makes me wonder if he ever imagines that life. If he ever lets himself picture a version with less noise. Less chaos.

I glance at Quinn. She's watching him too, eyes following every movement as Nate tends to the grill.

"Did you get some good shots today, Q?" Nate asks once the flames catch.

"Yeah," she says. "Let me show you."

She starts scrolling through the photos, and Nate steps closer without hesitation, his focus pulled straight to her.

I push up from my chair, scoop up my empty beer bottle and hers, and head inside for a refill. The kitchen is still warm from earlier, the scent of garlic clinging to the air. I pop the fridge open, grab three beers, and when I shut the door, something catches my eye.

Through the open window, I catch a glimpse of them. Nate's leaning in, one hand braced on the edge of the table, his body angled toward her. Quinn's showing him something on the screen, her finger tracing across the photos while her mouth moves in quiet explanation. Their heads are close. Shoulders brushing.

There's a stillness between them. A gravity I wasn't ready for.

And then it slams into me.

I know Nate. Every mood, every shift in his voice. Every wall he's built since Bianca. And right now, those walls aren't up. He's open in a way I haven't seen in years. Not with anyone and yet he's letting Quinn in.

There's something in the way Quinn looks at him, open, easy, familiar. Maybe she's the one he'd risk everything for again.

I grab the beers and head back out before I start thinking too much.

Nate looks up as I hand him one. He cracks it open without a word, takes a long drink, then nods toward Quinn. "She got some good shots. Kit's gonna lose her shit."

Quinn shrugs, thumb still moving over the screen. "I hope so."

It catches me off guard.

This is the same girl with sarcasm on her tongue. The same girl who never seemed to flinch, no matter what was thrown at her. Back then, she carried a kind of confidence that made you pay attention. Not loud or showy. Just steady and fucking unshakable. She was certain of who she was. What the fuck happened to her?

Nate moves to the grill, loading it with steaks as he talks shit about Ace's inability to cook anything that isn't frozen. Quinn laughs and for a second it all seems too easy. Too familiar.

I sit back in my chair and take a long pull of my beer, eyes drifting to her again. That same twist coils through me, heavier now. I tell myself it's nothing, but the burn in my chest says otherwise.

I meet Quinn's eyes, and fuck me, there's something there. Her gaze lingers on mine longer than it should. I toss her a slow, smug smirk, letting her know I see it. I see her and every bit of that charged silence hanging between us.

My cock stirs at the thought, my mind already painting the picture in high-definition. Her, naked and spread out, thighs open, mouth parted. Me and Nate taking our time, working her over, giving her no room to think. Just pleasure. Just us. I wonder what the fuck she sounds like when she comes. Does she fall apart fast or make us earn it? Is she loud? Does she take control or let herself be ruined?

I snap out of the spiral when she suddenly stands, camera clutched tight in her hand.

"I'm just gonna take this inside," she says, voice a little too quick. "Won't be a minute."

She walks past me, and her scent slams into me. Sweet, warm, something soft I can't name but want to drown in. My fingers twitch against the bottle in my hand, fighting the pull to reach out and make her stop. But I don't.

She disappears through the door, and the second she's gone, a weight settles on my skin. Nate's eyes are on me.

I turn and meet Nate's stare, lifting one shoulder in a half-assed shrug. I don't say shit. Don't admit I was staring too long, mind already crossing a fucking line I won't be able to step back from.

Nate checks the grill first, turning one of the steaks before stepping back. He grabs his beer from the table, eyes still fixed on the door she slipped through.

"Is she alright?"

"Yeah," I say, scratching the back of my neck. "I think so."

"She did good with those photos," he says.

"She did." I take a drink, forcing my thoughts somewhere safer. "Did she show you the one of me and Ace?"

Nate lets out a low laugh. "Yeah. You look like you're halfway through saying something that might've gotten you killed. She's got good timing. Caught the whole mood."

Silence drifts in for a beat. I watch him, the way I always do.

He stands at the grill, steady and focused, turning the steaks with that quiet intensity he brings to everything. Subtle but solid. Every move has weight. Nate's never been the type to waste movement.

He grabs the empty plate he brought out earlier, the one that held the raw meat, balancing it easily in one hand. On his way to the door, his other hand lands on my shoulder. Just a quick touch. Barely there. Easy. Thoughtless.

But it wrecks me.

He doesn't know what that touch does. Doesn't know I hold onto it longer than I should. Has no idea how it steadies me in ways nothing else ever has.

I welcome it. I live for it. I fucking crave it.

Because I love him.

Not the watered-down version people throw around to make themselves feel better. This is the kind of love that lives in your bones. The kind that aches with every breath. The kind that never lets you forget.

He's been my anchor ever since that afternoon he found me sitting on the side of the road, bleeding out in places no one could see. From that moment, he became my safety. My constant. My gravity in a world that never made any fucking sense.

And I could never risk losing him with the truth. Not with a confession that might turn everything we have into ash.

I've told him I love him, but never the way it's meant. Tossed it out casually, the way guys do between beers and bruises. "Love ya, man." Covered it with a smirk, a punch to the shoulder, a laugh that made it sound harmless.

But it's not harmless or nothing. He doesn't know that it eats me alive. He doesn't know that every time the words leave my mouth, I mean them with every fucked-up part of me. He doesn't know how raw my throat feels afterward, how it burns to swallow it back down, how it nearly kills me to keep it buried.

There was a night I can't forget. A few years back, when I almost told him. We'd just finished moving into this house. It was late. We were on the couch, beers in hand, bodies half-sprawled from exhaustion. Shoulder to shoulder. Music low. The air still sharp with fresh paint and sawdust.

We sat there, taking in the house we had designed. The walls. The kitchen Nate had always wanted, all steel and dark counters. Eight fucking burners. A monster of a stove he'd gone on about for months before we bought it. Said a man wasn't a real cook until he could command a range that big.

Boxes lined the edges of the room, still half-unpacked. Shit we'd collected over the years—band posters, beat-up vinyls, that dented kettle we shared. All stacked and labeled in Nate's handwriting. Every piece proof of a life we built without ever having to say that's what it was. The history of every fucked-up version of ourselves that somehow found something steady.

Watching Nate sip his beer and glance around as if he was letting himself breathe for the first time in years, I felt it hit me hard.

I felt the need to say it. That I loved him. Not the way you love a best friend. Not the way you love a brother. Something heavier. Messier. Something that's lived in my chest since we were sixteen, before I even had the words for it.

The confession sat behind my teeth. I opened my mouth. Then I shut it.

Because what if it destroyed everything? What if he looked at me and saw something he couldn't unsee? What if he walked away? I wouldn't survive that. Not when he's my entire fucking world.

So I swallowed it. One more secret. Another piece of myself buried with the rest. Maybe it will always stay there. It's safer that way.

When we fuck, it's always about the girl. We share them, pass them between us, the same way we always have. The rules never change. She's the focus. The center of it. Never us. It's never us.

But there are moments when I sense him. In the way he moves. In the way our bodies fall into rhythm without thought.

He fucks with control. With intent. He always has. And somehow, I always fall into sync with him every single time.

Every first that ever mattered, Nate was there. The first time I fucked, Bianca. Both of us tangled in her body, her breath, that single moment where everything seemed right. Him on one side, me on the other. Hands, mouths, sweat. Chaos and beauty all at once.

He's threaded through every memory worth holding. Every scar I carry from the life I crawled out of, he softened just by standing next to me. Every win I've ever had, he's been in the room.

And I've never told him, because I'm terrified of what it would change. Of what it would ruin.

So I stay quiet.

I let it bleed through every smile I throw his way. Every joke I crack. Every night we sit together, pretending this isn't something more.

I watch him. I love him. And I keep my mouth shut. He's my everything, and yet I'm too fucking scared to let the words out.

CHAPTER 19

Quinn

Theo and Nate move around the kitchen, clearing plates, stacking dishes, wiping down counters. Every step seems to anticipate the other, their bodies syncing until it comes across less as cleaning and more as some quiet, practiced ritual. Nate reaches for the dish towel at the exact second Theo passes it over without even glancing. Seamless. A rhythm built over years of knowing each other's every move.

I sit on the couch, beer sweating against my palm, one leg hooked over the other. From the outside I probably look relaxed, bored even.

Except my body is wound so fucking tight it hurts to breathe. I'm staring.

My beer's gone warm in my hand and I don't even care. My eyes keep finding Nate. He's locked in that quiet focus he slips into when he's working. Shoulders squared, forearms flexing each time his grip tightens on something. His shirt sticks to the shape of his back, the fabric damp near the collar from the heat spilling through the open doors.

Theo's beside him, humming under his breath the way he always does when he disappears into the task. His hair falls into his eyes, and I catch the way he pushes it back with his fingers. Then he reaches up to slide a bowl onto the top shelf, that narrow line of muscle vanishing into his jeans.

Every detail pulls me further under.

I tell myself to look away, but my eyes won't obey.

Nate leans in behind him, saying something I can't catch. Whatever it is makes Theo grin. The easy way they shift around each other, all that history folded into muscle memory, is too much.

If they turned right now, if either of them caught me staring, I wouldn't even have an excuse.

I take a sip of my beer to cover the way my pulse is thundering. My breath goes shallow as my mind drifts where it shouldn't, slipping straight into places I've been trying to avoid since I got here. What would it be to stand in that space between them, pressed into their bodies while they moved around me with that same effortless rhythm? Hands, mouths, cocks working me open until I couldn't tell where one ended and the other began.

Heat crawls over my skin, wrong as hell but so fucking good I can't swallow it down.

Theo slides another plate into the dishwasher, water dripping down his wrist as he murmurs something to Nate. Mid-laugh, Theo glances up and catches me staring.

The grin spreads slow across his face, and my stomach drops. His gaze holds mine, and it tells me he knows exactly where my heads at.

I drag my eyes to the beer in my hand, desperate for a distraction, but his stare pins me in place. My chest hammers, breath shallow, every beat too loud in my ears.

I curse under my breath. Get your shit together, Quinn. Stop being pathetic.

You're here to capture the band. Do the job. Not to sit here stripping them bare in your head while they rinse out the fucking sink.

Because if he knew… if either of them knew, that I've been imagining both of them pinning me down, cocks hard, mouths on my skin, he'd either laugh his ass off or drag me in there and fuck me until I couldn't walk.

I tip back the last of my beer and push to my feet, clinging to some illusion of control.

"I think I might call it a night," I say, trying for breezy but landing somewhere between shaky and strained.

Nate's mouth curves, subtle but knowing. "What? Q, you don't have to go yet. We haven't even caught up."

Theo drops the dish towel, eyes cutting to mine with that wicked glint. His mouth hooks into a smirk.

"If you're heading to bed, we could, you know… keep you company. Warm the sheets. Test the mattress. Strictly quality control, of course."

Heat slams through me so fast it knocks the breath from my lungs. My heart kicks hard against my ribs, and my mouth moves before my brain catches up.

I laugh, shaking my head.

"Please. You'd trip over your own ego before you even made it to the bed." My gaze lingers on him, lips curving slow. "You honestly think you could handle me in bed, Kade?"

Something sharpens in his eyes. That lazy grin twists into something feral.

"Oh, sweetheart," he murmurs, voice dropping low and rough. "I wouldn't just handle you. I'd ruin you."

My knees nearly buckle.

Nate hasn't said a word, but when I glance at him, his face tells me everything. His eyes are darker now, fixed on me with a weight that makes my skin prickle.

Theo moves closer. One step. Then another. Slow. Measured. Each one pulling something tighter inside me until I'm wound so tight I could snap.

He stops just behind me. His body radiates heat, wrapping around my back before he's even touched me. My breath falters, my grip on the beer bottle tightening until my knuckles ache.

Theo leans in, mouth grazing the shell of my ear. His voice is low, threaded with something dangerous. "You say I couldn't handle you. But I see you."

His breath drifts down my neck, and my body betrays me. "I see the way your thighs press together when I talk to you. The way you squirm when Nate brushes your arm."

Each word carves into me, heat flooding through my veins. My spine goes rigid, but my body betrays me again, tilting toward him. He hasn't laid a hand on me, and still I'm trembling, my breaths short and uneven, chest rising in quick bursts as the air between us burns thin.

Behind me, his fingers brush the bare skin of my lower back, and the single touch has every muscle in my body tightening. My eyes flutter shut. I should step forward, put distance between us.

But I don't.

Because some part of me needs to hear what else he has to say.

"I wouldn't just handle you, Quinn," Theo murmurs. "I'd have you begging. And I wouldn't stop until you forgot how to speak."

My breath snags, breaking into a sound I can't take back. A soft, desperate noise that betrays me completely.

Then Nate's voice cuts through the haze, making my pulse spike so hard it hurts.

"He will. We both will."

My head jerks up. Nate's right there. He steps in closer. The room tilts, my world narrowing to nothing but the two of them closing in. Theo stays rooted at my back, a wall of heat and muscle that locks me in place while Nate pins me from the front.

The air between us crackles, and my heart hammers against my ribs.

Nate's fingers slide up, curling around my throat with care. His palm is warm, steady, and the slow drag of his thumb over my pulse makes my legs almost give out.

"She's shaking," Nate mutters, the sound scraping through me. "You feel that?"

Theo's grip on my hip tightens, pulling me back until I'm pressed flush against him. The hard line of his cock digs into my ass, and a broken gasp punches past my lips. The pure fucking intent in the way he holds me makes my mouth go dry.

"Yeah," he growls against my ear. "She's soaked. I'd bet my fucking life on it."

The sound that rips out of me isn't a word. It's raw, filthy, a desperate whimper that shatters every wall I've tried to hold in place.

Nate exhales slowly, his breath warm against my cheek. His hand stays firm on my throat, not squeezing, only holding, claiming. His forehead lowers until it almost touches mine, his eyes burning straight through me.

Theo's breath drifts over the curve of my neck, hot and steady. His fingers press against my hip, thumb sliding beneath the hem of my shirt, just enough to send a shiver through me.

I am caught between them, trapped and trembling. My body aches with a need so sharp it borders on pain.

For the first time in years, I don't want to run.

I want to fall. I want to fucking burn.

Nate kisses me. It isn't soft. Nothing about it pretends to be gentle. His mouth crashes into mine with years of silence burning behind it. His hand tightens on my neck, holding me there, dragging me into him as if letting go would mean losing me. It isn't lips brushing. It's a storm breaking open, the taste of him flooding my mouth, stealing my breath, tearing apart every piece of control I thought I had.

Theo's hands slide beneath my shirt, rough fingers carving fire across my skin with every slow drag upward. He finds the edge of my bra and pushes past it, knuckles grazing the curve of my breast. My back arches into him before I can stop myself, my body betraying me, giving in.

When Nate finally pulls back, his breath lingers at my mouth. His lips are swollen, his eyes dark with something that shatters through my chest.

Theo's mouth finds the tender spot beneath my ear, and the sound that rips out of me is a broken moan I can't hold back.

"Fuck, listen to her," Theo growls against my skin, his breath hot as his thumbs sweep over my nipples, dragging the ache sharper. "She's already falling apart and we haven't even started."

Nate's hand tightens slightly on my throat, just enough to make my pulse pound against his palm. His eyes lock on mine, steady and dark.

"You hear that?" he murmurs to Theo. "That's the sound of her needing us."

He's not wrong. My thoughts are gone. All that remains is Theo's hands under my shirt, Nate's mouth crushing into mine, the slow drag of his breath against my lips when he pulls back just enough to speak.

My back arches, a strangled sound ripping out of me the second Theo pinches one nipple.

"Fuck," Theo whispers against my neck, his voice thick with want. "She's perfect. So fucking perfect. You can see how hard she's shaking for us."

Nate's lips brush the corner of my mouth. "You want us to ruin you, Q?"

"Yes," I gasp, the word shattering under the weight of it. "Please."

Theo's chuckle rumbles low, dark and sinful against my ear. "Begging already, and we haven't even gotten our cocks out."

Nate drags me into another kiss, deeper this time, his tongue pushing against mine until my whole body clenches tight. Theo's mouth trails down my neck, teeth scraping before he sucks a mark into the soft skin above my collarbone. My fingers twist into Nate's shirt, holding on as they both pull me deeper under.

"Look at you," Theo murmurs, his voice thick with heat as his hands close around my breasts, thumbs rolling over my nipples until I cry out. "Already wet for us. I can smell it, Quinn. Fucking desperate."

"You sure you want this, Q?" Nate asks, voice rough and low, every word dripping with tension. His lips trail along my jaw, breath scorching my skin. "Tell us what you want."

I try to speak, but what escapes is broken, more moan than word.

Theo's hand leaves my chest and slides down my stomach, fingers skimming the waistband of my shorts. The rough pads trace slow circles at my hips, teasing, making my breath falter.

"You want my cock first, baby? Or do you want Nate to split you open?" Theo whispers, mouth grazing mine. "Want us to stretch your pussy until you forget who you are? Until you scream for us?"

My knees nearly give, a raw sound tearing out of me as his fingers slip just beneath the band, close but not where I need them.

"Answer him," Nate demands, his hand steady at my throat, his gaze locked on mine.

"Yes," I choke out, thighs trembling, heat throbbing between them until it's unbearable. "I want it," I whisper. "I fucking want you."

Theo's teeth catch my earlobe, a low groan vibrating against my skin. "Good girl. We'll give you everything. We'll wreck that pretty little cunt."

Nate crushes his mouth to mine again, rougher this time, his free hand gripping my waist and dragging me tight against him. His cock presses hard against my stomach, heat and promise radiating through the thin space between us.

Theo's fingers slide lower, brushing over the damp fabric of my panties. My whole body jerks, a loud, desperate moan tearing free.

"Fuck," Theo growls into my neck. "Soaked. Just like I said. You want us to fill you up, don't you? Two cocks stretching you until you can't take anymore?"

"Yes," I cry out, the word ripping through me with no shame left to hold it back. "Please. Fuck, yes."

Nate's thumb strokes over my pulse, his voice dropping to a dangerous murmur. "You're ours now, Q. Every single fucking inch of you."

Theo presses his thumb to my clit, rubbing tight circles that send fire racing through every nerve. My body buckles, head falling back against his shoulder as another helpless moan spills out.

"Say it," Theo whispers at my ear, his tone dark and commanding. "Tell us you're ours."

My hips stutter forward, legs shaking, breath catching, and then I'm gone.

"I'm yours," I breathe. "Both of you. Fuck. I'm yours."

CHAPTER 20

Nate

The second that yes leaves her mouth, everything ends. The sound isn't soft or shy. The word lands with teeth, sharp enough to tear through me and drag every filthy thought I've buried right to the surface. That single word sinks in, claws deep, and I swear the impact lives in my bones.

Quinn fucking Thomas, saying yes.

To me.

To us.

I never thought I'd hear those words. Not in this life. Not from her mouth, wet and swollen from kissing me, whispering a surrender that's been years in the making.

It isn't just a yes. It's a fucking gift, handed over like she's been aching to give it since the first time I threw a cocky line her way. Seventeen, all mouth and no fucking clue what I was playing with. A dare. That's all it was back then. Praying she'd crack, praying she'd break and let me have her. Let me touch, savor that sweetness. Let me own every inch of her until it consumes her, until it makes breathing impossible without my name in her head.

And now here it is.

That little yes. But the sound is more than a word. The plea comes wrapped in fire. The promise is desperate, proof she's already halfway undone and waiting for us to finish the job.

My cock's hard enough to hurt. Pressing against denim, throbbing, demanding to be inside her before I even have the chance to blink. She's in front of me, a goddamn masterpiece in ruin. Lips kiss-bruised, chest rising too fast, breaths coming shallow and uneven.

And fuck me, if that isn't the hottest fucking thing I've ever seen.

Theo's hands are on her first. Possessive. Greedy. Sliding under her shirt. He peels the fabric up inch by inch, as if he's unwrapping something sacred, a favorite present he's waited years to open. Her skin glows under his touch, his fingers dragging over her ribs with the kind of slowness that makes my teeth grind.

He plays dirty. Always has. He's patient, loves drawing everything out until they're fucking begging, their thighs shaking and their voices nothing but broken little sounds they can't bite back. He loves the tease, the power in making them squirm, making them ache, holding them at the edge until they're dripping, grinding, desperate to be filled.

What never stops turning me on is watching him work, seeing that focus, that slow control. The whole thing feels like a goddamn art form, and every time he pulls it off, I get harder. He's slow, cruel in the best fucking way. Every drag of his fingers is a promise.

And tonight the one caught between us is Quinn.

Our Quinn.

A sweet little mess, ready to be broken in all the right ways.

I can already see her, body bent and begging, that tight little pussy stretched, soaking our cocks while she moans for more. We'll take her apart piece by fucking piece, drag her open until she's trembling and crying our names. Not just a fuck. Not just a quick get off. We're going to own her, every sound, every twitch, every filthy little plea.

Theo meets my eyes over her shoulder, a wicked fucking glint sparking in his gaze. The look tells me this isn't just sex. This is destruction, worship, taking every fucking inch of her and making her ours.

Her shirt hits the floor, and Theo's hands are on her tits instantly, squeezing hard enough to draw a gasp. His thumbs roll over her nipples, pulling the sound straight from her throat.

I catch her jaw in my grip, fingers digging in as I tilt her head until those eyes are locked on mine.

"Watch me," I growl, voice low enough to make her chest stutter. "Keep your eyes right here while he plays with you. While he makes you fucking ache for us."

She whimpers, the sound shooting straight to my cock. Her lips part, trembling. Theo squeezes her tits again, leaning close to her ear, whispering something that has her knees threatening to give out.

I keep my grip on her jaw, firm enough that she has no choice but to look at me. My thumb brushes over her bottom lip before I push into her mouth, watching every second as her lips close around my skin.

She sucks, and fuck, I have to shut my eyes for a beat, just to take the rush of heat tearing through me. That mouth. The same one that's had teenage me jerking off in the shower, imagining this exact moment. Her lips. Her tongue. The filthy sound she'd make if she ever had me between them for real.

"Good girl," I rasp, voice rough as her tongue curls over my skin. The heat of her mouth has my cock throbbing so hard it hurts. I force my eyes open again because I can't miss a second of this. Not when this moment is everything I've fucking dreamt of.

Theo grins, the devil dressed in soft touches and slow torture. His fingers drift down her stomach, tracing a lazy path that makes her whole body shiver. He knows exactly how to build the tension, how to stretch the ache until she's ready to sob for release.

And fuck me, I can't wait to hear her sob.

That weak, helpless little sound that tears free when pleasure owns every inch of her. When her voice collapses and her body trembles too hard to tell us to stop even if she wanted to. We'll push her past every limit, stretch her until her pussy quivers around nothing, then fill her until sweat slides down her spine and she's wearing our cum, so far gone she won't know whose cock she's begging for.

"Q," I rasp, my grip tightening on her jaw. My thumb drags over the soft swell of her bottom lip, pressing in again just enough to make her mouth part. "Eyes on me. I want to see every fucking second of what this does to you."

Her pupils are blown, lips wet and parted, chest rising fast like she can't catch her breath. That look fucks me from the inside out. What I see in her eyes is more than want—it's need, pure surrender, every filthy, impossible fantasy I've ever had of her crashing into one moment.

"Good girl," I murmur, leaning in, my voice rough against her skin.

I press my lips to her cheek, soft for a second before letting my mouth ghost over the corner of hers. Close enough to taste the heat of her breath but not giving her the kiss she's desperate for. She tilts her head, leaning in, chasing the space, already desperate, and we haven't even started.

"You have no idea what's coming, baby," I breathe onto her mouth.

My hand slides to the back of her neck, holding her in place, grounding her in the storm we're about to pull her into.

"We're gonna make you feel so fucking good you won't know if you're begging for my cock or his by the time we're through with you," I add.

Theo growls against her neck, his mouth closing hard, his teeth grazing before he sucks a mark into her skin that's going to stain her for days. His lips drag, pulling blood to the surface until it blooms deep under her flesh. He growls again. The mark is more than a bruise. That mark is a claim. He wants her to wear us on her skin, every inch of her screaming that she's been touched and fucked by our hands.

She arches between us, her spine curving in a perfect, desperate bow, head tipping back until her throat is bared, chest thrust forward in an offering. Her nipples stand hard, begging for my tongue. Her hips move in small, hungry rolls, every shift screaming that her pussy is already slick, already aching for one of our cocks.

I pop the button on her jeans, my fingers fumbling for a second because my hands won't fucking stop shaking. Not nerves—just years of caged-up want breaking loose. I've never needed anyone stripped bare this badly.

My chest is tight, my throat raw, my cock pounding so hard I swear I could come from anticipation alone. I need her naked the way I need to breathe. Maybe more.

I drop to my knees, greed crawling under my skin, and peel the denim down her legs. My knuckles scrape soft skin as I drag them off, my mouth watering with every inch of thigh I uncover. She's soft and perfect, begging for teeth, for marks, for my fucking tongue. Her thighs part slightly, unsteady on her feet, and my hands lock around them, steadying her as I strip away the last barrier between me and everything I've craved.

She sways, trembling, as I toss the jeans aside.

"Holy fuck," I groan, my voice breaking.

Red lace. High-cut, clinging to the curve of her hips in a way that makes my chest tight. The fabric is barely holding together, a scrap standing between me and heaven. It clings to her, soaked through, a dark wet patch spread across the center where her pussy is leaking for us. My jaw locks, my cock throbs violently against my jeans, and a guttural sound rips out of me. I drag my fingers up the curve of her thigh, pausing at the edge of that soaked lace, and my hand trembles as I hook a finger under the fabric.

I pull the lace to the side slowly, torturously slow, and when the wet heat of her folds comes into view, the sight rips the fucking air from my lungs. A thin strip of soft hair at the top her folds bare. My tongue drags over my bottom lip without a single conscious thought, hunger twisting so deep in my gut it hurts.

Her pussy glistens, every inch swollen and drenched, slick painting her skin in wet, perfect shine. I wonder if her clit throbs for me, desperate, aching for a mouth to close around her.

I want my tongue on her, the pulse hammering against me, sucking until she's crying and dripping down my face. I want her taste coating my tongue, sweet and filthy as fuck.

The thought slams through me so hard I don't even register my own hand moving. Instinct drives the action. My palm outlines the bulge in my jeans, fingers wrapping around my cock through the denim, giving myself a slow stroke just to keep from losing my fucking mind. The pressure isn't enough, not even close, but this is all I can do to stop myself from shoving her to the floor and burying my face between her legs right fucking now. The scent of her hits, and everything outside this moment dies. All that exists is this dripping cunt and the feral, starving need to taste every drop of her.

I spread her open with my fingers, dragging the slick folds apart. The sight is fucking savage. Shining. Dripping. My breath catches hard enough to burn. My mouth waters so bad I can already sense her on my tongue. My cock pulses, a brutal, aching throb that has me biting back a groan. Every part of me strains toward her, chest tight, lungs raw, the need to get my tongue in her so heavy the pressure borders on pain. I want her flavor smeared over my lips, running down my chin, soaking my tongue until I can't breathe without her. I want her shaking apart on my face, sobbing my name into the air while I drag every filthy sound out of her body.

"Fuck," I rasp, the words shredded and low as I glance up at Theo. "You see this shit. She's dripping. This greedy little pussy is begging to be split wide open and fucked so deep she won't walk tomorrow."

Theo peels his mouth from her neck, lips wet, eyes black with want. A dark, filthy grin curves his mouth.

"Lick her," Theo snarls, his voice full of filth, every word vibrating against her skin. "Get your fucking tongue in that pussy. Make her scream for more. Make her come so hard she forgets her own name. I want to see her dripping down your face, shaking all over you while I hold her open. Go on, Nate. Taste her. Take everything Quinn's pussy gives when she's already cock-drunk before either of us have even fucked her."

Her whole body jerks at his words, a soft, broken whimper spilling out, and that's all the permission I need.

I grab the thin lace at her hips and tear. The fabric rips away under my hands, and the second the barrier is gone, her hips jerk instinctively. A soft, startled sound escapes her throat.

Theo doesn't say a fucking word. He doesn't have to. Hunger takes over his body, pure instinct, and before I can breathe, he's bending low, his palms sliding under the backs of her thighs. His hands grip her tight, rough enough to make her whimper, and then he lifts her clean off the floor, effortless in his strength.

Quinn lets out another gasp. Her head tips back, neck arching, her face turning into the crook of Theo's neck as he locks her in his grip. His hands are clamped around her thighs, fingers digging into soft skin, holding her wide and open for me.

Her arms scramble, reaching for something to steady herself, but Theo has her caged against him, her back molded to his chest. She's not going anywhere. His hands tighten, pulling her thighs further apart until she whimpers, that high, wrecked sound that makes my pulse crash against my ribs.

And then I see her.

Spread open for me. Slick. Every glistening inch of her cunt exposed. Her pussy looks fucking sinful, soft flesh wet and swollen, shining with the kind of need you can smell in the air. The sight is primal, crawling under my skin until the burn tears straight through me.

She's not just a girl right now. She's a fucking offering. A gift from the heavens.

Theo's chest rises hard behind her, breath scraping through his teeth as he leans his head against hers, his mouth grazing her temple. His eyes lower, meeting mine over her open body, and nothing in them is soft. Nothing hesitant. Just pure fucking want.

The room falls away. No longer walls and air and space—only her. Theo holds her wide and trembling. I'm on my knees between her thighs, hands shaking as if I've been starving for years and someone finally threw me a taste.

I drag my fingers up the inside of her thighs, slow enough to feel every tremor in her muscles. My fingers move closer until I ghost over the heat of her, and my vision fucking blurs. My mouth's already watering.

I look up again, my eyes drifting between hers and Theo's stare over her shoulder. The three of us caught in this filthy, feral moment.

"She's all yours, Nate," Theo growls.

His fingers dig harder into her thighs, forcing her wide. He looks at me over her open body, pupils black, jaw tight, and the hunger in his gaze isn't just for her. That hunger is for me too.

"Fuck... let me watch you," he snarls, the words dripping in filth and need. "I want to see your tongue all over her. I want to watch her scream with your mouth on her pussy. Do it, Nate. Ruin her for the both of us. Show me how you make her come so hard she forgets her own name. I want to see you tear her apart."

Quinn's head tips back, lips parted as if she's trying to catch her breath. Her eyes are blown and glassy.

Then my gaze drags to him. Theo's stare is locked on me over her trembling body, pupils dark, his chest rising sharp against her back. Nothing hides in his eyes.

I hold his gaze for a beat longer than I should. His eyes are locked on mine, and fuck... this is a line we've never crossed. The one we've both danced around for years but never dared to touch. And now we're here, toeing that edge together, and the worst part is not knowing what the fuck happens if we finally cross it.

I drop my head, dragging my tongue up her pussy in one slow, deliberate stroke that leaves her trembling in Theo's grip. The first rush floods my tongue and tears the air out of my chest. Hot and sweet. A sharp tang of her arousal sliding over my tongue, making my whole body tighten.

Her slick coats my lips, seeps into my mouth, and clings to the back of my throat until she's all I can breathe.

Her moan rips out loud. There's no holding that sound back. It spills out of her. Every drag of my tongue tears it from her body.

I keep my eyes on Quinn as I push in deeper, forcing my tongue inside her until I'm savoring her from the inside out. The heat of her pussy wraps around me, and fuck, she's so tight the sensation makes my whole body jolt. She pulses against my tongue, a desperate, frantic clench that drags a groan straight out of my chest. The pull has me devouring her harder, needing every drop of her across my lips.

I fuck her with my mouth, curling my tongue deep until I can sense every tiny flutter inside her cunt. The wet sounds spilling out, the taste of her coating my lips, dripping down my chin, drowning me in everything she is.

I lift my eyes and see Theo watching me over her trembling body, his lips parted against her shoulder. With his eyes locked on me while I'm buried between her legs, the moment feels filthy in a way that makes my whole body burn.

Every flick of my tongue isn't just for her—it's for him. Every wet stroke is me showing him how I'll ruin her, letting him see it.

Her moans spill out louder, needier with every second. Each time my tongue drags over her clit, she jerks hard in Theo's arms.

But Theo only tightens his grip on her thighs, holding her steady while her body trembles between us. A growl rumbles out of him. "Fuck, Nate... make her come all over your fucking mouth."

"Do you feel that, baby?" he murmurs, lips brushing her ear. "That tongue dragging through your pussy like it fucking owns you. That's what being wanted is, what it means to be devoured, to be used exactly the way this greedy little cunt's been begging for."

I seal my mouth over her clit, sucking hard, pulling the swollen bud deep between my lips until a moan rips from her throat. I let go only to drag my tongue over her again. I circle her clit, teasing, then swipe the tip over that perfect spot that makes her legs jerk violently in Theo's grip.

Her whimper hits my ears and fuck, I do the same thing again. Faster. Rougher. Messier. My mouth moves on her like she's my last fucking meal.

"Fuck her with your fingers," Theo orders.

I push two fingers into her while I eat her. My tongue flicking her clit while my fingers curl inside her.

"Come for us," Theo growls, his lips dragging along the shell of her ear. "Soak his tongue. Drench his fucking face. Let that needy little pussy scream for both our cocks."

Her moans come out broken. Desperate little sounds that tell me she's hanging on by a single frayed thread. Every flick of my tongue rips another twitch from her thighs, another gasp, another flood of slick heat spilling straight down my throat.

I flatten my tongue against her clit and grind, dragging over that swollen bundle of nerves. She bucks hard, her hips jerking in Theo's grip, her whole body begging to snap under us.

"Fuck, Nate... do you know how fucking hot this is, watching you eat pussy?" Theo's voice is rough, cracking at the edges, and the words hit me like a match to gasoline.

He's never said anything that raw to me before. Never stepped over that kind of line. The weight of it sinks under my skin, and for a split second I can't tell if Quinn's heat between us is what's driving him, or if having her here is the thing that finally makes him let go in a way he never has.

Theo's grip clamps down, his hands digging into her thighs, locking her to him.

"You hear that?" he growls, breath hot against her ear. "Those wet, sloppy sounds. That's a man starving for your pussy. You're gonna come for him. You're gonna soak his face, flood his mouth, because that's what he fucking wants."

She lets out a broken whimper and then the release tears through her. Her body seizes in Theo's arms, back bowing, tits thrust up as if offering herself to the moment. The sound that rips out of her throat isn't pretty—it's guttural. She's gone, unraveling against us, coming so hard the rush turns violent, her pussy clenching around my fingers, pulsing against my tongue.

She's dripping everywhere, spilling down my chin as her hips twitch helplessly. I growl into her, eating her through the storm, dragging my tongue over every trembling inch of her cunt. I don't let her breathe through the waves—I take the air from her, stroke by stroke, sucking every last drop until she's wrung out and shaking, nothing but a perfect mess in Theo's arms.

I keep licking her. Pinning her right in that peak, holding her in the aftershock where every nerve screams and every inch of her begs.

She tries to twist away, hips jerking, her body desperate to escape the overload, but Theo's grip just clamps harder.

"Take it," he growls against her ear. "Take every fucking thing he's giving you. Ride the rush. Feel every second burn."

She whimpers, gasping like she's drowning in the pleasure. Her breath stutters, catching on a sob that sounds too close to breaking, but her pussy doesn't stop. The spasms clamp around my fingers, pulsing against my tongue.

"That's it," Theo mutters, his eyes locked on my mouth working her pussy. He watches my tongue flick her clit slow and mean, dragging her back under until she's shaking in his arms. "Let the release keep tearing through you. That pretty little pussy isn't finished. Not until we say she's done."

I sense Theo's eyes on me, and I meet them. We've never done this before, not with the groupies, not with anyone who came and went without mattering. But this isn't some backstage fuck we'll forget tomorrow, and we both know that. This is Quinn.

And that makes everything different.

I can read it in his stare, the same thought ripping through him that's clawing through me: drag this out. Burn her into our skin. Into our memory. Make it last all fucking night, because we don't know if we'll ever get to touch her this way again.

Her scream rips through the air, and my eyes snap back to her.

She's not just coming. She's unraveling, falling apart in the most fucking beautiful way I've ever seen. Her head tips back against Theo's shoulder, mouth open on a cry that sounds more like surrender than pleasure. Her cheeks are flushed, her whole body shakes between us as if she's coming undone from the inside out.

Soft whimpers climb into high, shattered moans, every pulse of her orgasm stealing the breath right from her lungs. Her thighs quiver in Theo's grip, while her nails dig into his arms, scraping his skin.

I finally pull back, my tongue wet, my face soaked in her juices. My jaw aches, my cock throbs hard enough to hurt, but none of that fucking matters.

I look up at her, and fuck me... she's gone. Completely destroyed in the most perfect way possible.

I drag the back of my hand across my mouth, smearing the mess she left on me before licking her taste off my lips.

Theo catches my eye and grins. All teeth and heat. That cocky edge sliding back into his face. His mouth drops to her neck, lips brushing over her flushed, trembling skin, and she twitches in his hold. She's a live wire in his arms, still sparking, still reeling, and he's soaking up every second of the aftermath.

"How about we take this to the bedroom?" His voice scrapes out. "Let her take both our cocks like a good fucking girl. Let's see how many ways we can split her open before she breaks."

Her breath hitches, and Theo smirks against her neck. He sets her down gently, his arm locked tight around her waist to keep her from stumbling on shaky legs. Then he leans in, brushing his lips over hers in the softest kiss, a contrast to the words that just left his mouth.

"Come on, sexy girl," he murmurs against her lips. "That was just Nate's entrée. I haven't had mine yet."

Before she can even catch her breath, he hooks an arm under her thighs and scoops her clean off the floor. She lets out a soft gasp, limp and boneless in his hold, her head falling against his shoulder as if her whole body has given up on holding itself upright.

I follow them out into the hallway. Watching her draped in Theo's arms, my chest tightens in a way I haven't experienced since Bianca.

But with Quinn, everything feels different. As I look at her, I don't think I have ever seen her more beautiful than in this moment.

CHAPTER 21
Theo

The hall seems longer than normal. I can smell her on my skin as I carry her toward my room because if I'm gonna fuck her, it's not happening on some random couch or someone else's bed. It's going to be in my room so I will never forget it.

Nate and I never bring chicks here. That's the rule. No groupies. No randoms. This is our house. Private. But Quinn isn't some girl I picked out of the crowd with smeared lipstick and fake moans. She's... more. I don't know what the fuck that means yet. All I know is she belongs in my bed.

But my mind isn't on her right now. It's on Nate trailing behind us. On the words I let slip as if they weren't a fucking bomb waiting to go off.

I can still hear my own voice in my head, telling him how fucking hot he looked eating her pussy.

I've never said anything like that before, never crossed that fucking line. We've been shoulder to shoulder for years, toeing the edge, dancing around it without ever stepping over. The moment I saw him between Quinn's legs, his mouth wet, his jaw working like he was trying to wreck her with his tongue alone, the words ripped out of me.

Because he looked fucking unreal. The focus in his eyes, the hunger bleeding through every move he made. It wasn't Nate getting off on some girl. It was him, stripped down to the bone, giving himself to her completely. And it destroyed me.

Now my chest's tight for a different reason, because I don't know what the fuck that means for us.

Does it change anything... or does it change everything?

When I turn my head, Nate's there. His face is still wet with her, his lips slick and parted, and something tears through my chest so hard it almost hurts. His eyes are locked, burning with a hunger I've never seen in him. Not even with Bianca.

What we had with her was young love. Full of firsts and maybes. But this... carries more weight. A need etched into bone, older than lust and deeper than want. I don't know if I'm ready for what that means... for him, for me, for whatever the fuck this is turning into.

I turn back around and lower my head, letting my lips brush over her forehead. "Still with us, baby? Or did Nate's tongue already fuck your brains out?"

She hums something soft, a little broken sound that vibrates against my chest, and the sound makes me smile.

My shoulder hits the door. The lights flicker on like always. It's always like that. They stay on. Even when I fucking sleep.

Darkness is a trap. A trick. A setup for shit you can't see coming.

I can't risk the dark, not anymore. Not when it still smells of dust and fear and my own breath trapped in my chest. Not when I can still hear the floorboards groan under his boots, sense the weight of the silence before he'd start shouting my name.

I hid under beds. Cramped myself into closets so tight my ribs ached. Held still, held my breath, and waited to find out if tonight was the night I became a goddamn bargaining chip for whatever debt he owed.

Every time I hear a door slam, a voice raise, my stomach still knots the same way it did back in those days. Those scars don't fade. They linger under your skin, waiting to be ripped open.

I lay Quinn down on the bed, her back sinking into the mattress, her light brown hair spilling over the dark sheets in a messy halo.

I step back for a second, because fuck, I need to see her. All of her. My eyes drag slowly over her body, tracing every inch. Her tits rise and fall with each shaky breath, nipples tight and begging to be in someone's mouth. Her stomach's flushed, her skin glowing with heat, every curve screaming to be touched, begging for hands to grip and mark.

Nate steps up beside me, and I sense him staring too, carrying that same silent hunger. Together, we stand there and fucking look at her. She's fucking beautiful spread out this way, every part of her needing to be touched, kissed, and fucked.

She shifts slightly, her thighs edging together as if she's trying to hide the one thing we want most.

"Nah," I rasp. "Keep them open, Quinn. Let us fucking look at that perfect pussy. Let us see exactly what we're about to ruin."

And that's the moment I notice it—the shift, the flicker in her eyes, the insecurity.

She was never like this before. Quinn Thomas was the girl who'd flip you off before you even opened your mouth. The one who walked through high school without giving a single fuck what anyone thought. The girl who never treated me as some broken asshole. Who saw through all the bullshit and never once judged me or turned away. She was my friend. Always beautiful.

And now... her laying here, naked and open, and somewhere along the line, some fuckhead made her doubt herself.

Rage surges hot in my chest but I force it down. Whoever did this to her... whoever made her question her worth should have their face smashed into a fucking wall until there's nothing left.

I drop to my knees at the edge of the bed, hands sliding slow up her thighs, every tremor under my palms sinking into my skin.

"You have no idea how fucking beautiful you look right now."

"He's right," Nate says beside me. "You're so fucking beautiful, Q."

And I wonder if he sees it too. The cracks she never had before. The shadows that weren't there when we were crazy teens. The way some asshole left fingerprints on her confidence and made her forget what she is.

She swallows hard, lips parting slightly, chest rising as though she's trying to hold herself together.

I lean in, dragging my mouth along her skin. The scent of her arousal wraps around my head and sinks into my blood. It's a drug. One hit and I'm fucking gone.

"Fuck," I whisper, more confession than sound. "I want to fucking devour you."

She moans, the sound spilling from her lips before she can bite it back. That helpless little slip shreds the last of my control.

Nate steps in closer and peels his shirt over his head. His jeans follow, hitting the floor in one smooth motion, and when he straightens, he's completely naked. His cock stands thick and hard, veins tracing along the shaft, pre-cum beading at the swollen tip, taunting me with the thought of how it would taste on my tongue.

He's fucking beautiful. All hard muscle and heat, jaw tight like he's holding back more than a groan. My stomach twists, and for a second, I forget everything else.

I've seen him with groupies. We've done this before. Shared bodies, sweat, moans, fucked until we're exhausted, a hundred times over until it became habit. But this... this is a live wire under my skin.

Because I've pictured this a hundred times. Too many fucking nights when the house was quiet, my hand wrapped around my cock while I thought about all the things I'll never say out loud.

It isn't some faceless girl in those thoughts. It isn't her moaning or crying out. It's him. It's Nate.

Naked. Flushed. That cock thick and leaking, aching for a hand that isn't his.

I can almost feel him—his hard cock filling my palm, my fingers wrapped tight around him, my thumb dragging over the slick head. The twitch in his hips when I squeeze too hard and he can't hold the sound back.

Fuck, I want to see him unravel in my grip. Not for her. Not for anyone else. For me.

I bet his voice changes when it's me. Bet it drops low, goes rough, gets desperate when I twist my wrist and find that perfect rhythm. I want to stroke him slow, then faster, until the sound spills from his throat, something raw and needy he's never let me hear. I want to drag him over the edge, watch the tension ripple through his abs, watch his thighs lock, that split second of stillness right before he spills hot and messy over my hand. His mouth open, his eyes locked on mine, every filthy, fucked-up second screaming all the things we've never been brave enough to say out loud.

My gaze shifts, and Quinn is staring at me. Fuck. Did she catch it? The way I couldn't stop watching Nate, my eyes locked on his cock like I wanted to wrap my mouth around him and take every inch?

Shit. My throat goes bone-dry, pulse pounding hard enough to rattle my ribs.

Nate's hands close on her, his grip so firm it pulls a gasp from her chest. He drags her across the sheets in one rough, greedy pull until she's right at the edge of the bed. Her head drops back over the side, hair spilling wild toward the floor, throat arching into a perfect line.

I crawl up onto the bed, the mattress dipping under my weight as I slide between her legs. My hands grip her thighs, spreading her wide. I lower my head, ready to bury my tongue in her, to taste every filthy drop she's got for me—but my eyes suddenly snap to Nate.

He stands over her, cock thick and hard, pre-cum sliding down the flushed head. His fist wraps around the base, stroking once, as his eyes lock on her mouth and the curve of her throat stretched bare beneath him.

I lean in and drag my tongue over her clit, soft at first, harder the next pass, slow enough to savor the first hit of her on my tongue.

Fuck.

It's instant, hot and sweet all at once. A low groan rips from my throat, vibrating against her pussy as I press in deeper, tasting her like I've been starving for it.

Her hips jerk in my grip, a desperate little twitch that makes my fingers tighten around her thighs.

I go again, dragging my tongue over that swollen bud, firmer this time, and she gasps, the sound spilling into the air as Nate watches, stroking his cock.

He leans over her, the head of his cock brushing her lips, smearing himself across her mouth.

"Open," he growls. "Open that mouth and let me fuck it."

Quinn whimpers, lips parting, her breath hitching against the tip of his cock.

I shift my eyes to Nate as he lines himself up. My tongue flicks against her clit again, and the second that desperate moan rips out of her, I feel it everywhere.

The way her mouth opens obediently, tongue flicking out to taste the tip of his cock as if she's been dying for it, makes my own cock throb so hard it's painful.

Nate groans under his breath, as though that single swipe of her tongue might already take him out.

She opens wider for him, her lips wet and shining.

Nate wastes no time, pushing in slow, savoring the first tight slide of her lips wrapping around him.

"Fuck..." His voice cracks on the word, chest rising hard as he shuts his eyes for half a second.

She takes him deeper, her lips stretched around him, every inch of her wet heat pulling him in as if her mouth was made for his cock. My tongue drags over her clit again and she moans around him. The sound pours straight into him, straight into me, and fuck, it's a sound I want burned into my head forever.

Nate's hand finds the edge of the bed, fingers gripping the sheets, holding onto something as though if he doesn't, he'll fucking lose it right there.

"Fuck yeah... exactly like that, Q," he mutters, as his eyes drop to watch her. "Take it. Take all of it. You look so fucking pretty with my cock down your throat."

Her throat works around him and the sight of it is pure fucking filth.

I suck her clit into my mouth. She moans again, a wrecked, needy sound, and it hits Nate so hard his hips jerk forward.

"Shit," he hisses through his teeth, the sound dragging from somewhere deep in his chest. His grip on the sheets tightens as he pauses for a moment before moving into a slow, controlled rhythm, sliding his cock over her tongue, letting the head press to the back of her throat before pulling out enough to watch the wet shaft, then sinking back in.

I can't stop watching. Every inch of him disappearing into her mouth, every slick sound of her sucking him, while my tongue circles her clit, has my chest tight and my head fucked.

Nate groans again, his voice rough, nearly broken. "Don't stop. Fuck, don't fucking stop."

He slides in deeper, the wet, obscene sound of her throat taking him filling the room.

Heat coils hard in my gut as I watch them, every part of me wound tight with want. It's fucking beautiful and dirty all at once, the way she gives herself to him, the way he holds his cock in the back of her throat as though he's afraid to let go. My tongue drags over her clit and I let my teeth scrape, enough to make her jolt.

The sound she makes when I do is desperate. A long filthy moan.

Nate groans when the vibration runs through him, his hips jerking against her mouth. His jaw tightens and a filthy growl spills from between his teeth.

"Fuck, baby... you feel that? That pretty little moan running down my cock? Do it again. Moan for me. Make my cock fucking throb in your throat."

My tongue drags over her clit again, teeth scraping enough to make her moan, and that sound spills out of her throat and onto him exactly the way he asked for.

Nate curses under his breath, head tipping back for half a second as though he's losing it, then his eyes snap open and land on me.

And fuck. That look. That hunger. It's scorching, and for one insane second, I swear this isn't about her at all.

I do it again, dragging my teeth over her clit to give him exactly what he wants. Her whole body arches, caught between us, the perfect mix of heat and desperation. Her moan rips out, vibrating around his cock as I drive her insane with every fucking lick.

Nate's groan tears through the room, his hips twitching as her sound shudders down his length. He reaches down, both hands gripping her hair. His abs go rigid, his eyes closing for half a second, lost in the pleasure, and I swear I sense the tremor of him fighting not to lose control right here.

It's chaos, pure and fucking beautiful. Every wet sound, every gasp, every tremble of her body in my hold and his. Every second is a perfect mess of want, and I don't ever want it to end.

I watch as Nate fucks her mouth with purpose, that intensity he always has when he fucks, each roll of his hips owning her in a way that has my cock throbbing so hard I swear it hurts.

If this keeps going, if I keep hearing those little moans vibrating around his cock while tasting her on my tongue, I'll blow my fucking load without ever getting inside her.

My hand moves and I press my fingers straight to her entrance. Her heat pulses against my touch, and I push inside her soaked pussy.

"Fuck," I groan as that tight, hot grip closes around me. My fingers sink in slow, stretching her, curling deep until I find that soft spot that makes girls lose their fucking minds.

Her back arches the second I'm inside.

I watch Nate, drinking in every detail. The way his brows pinch together, that perfect crease of raw pleasure etched into his face. His eyes roll half-shut, lashes low as his mouth parts on a guttural breath. He's fucking gorgeous in this state, caught in the moment, unraveling while she's strung tight between us, stretched and trembling, every inch of her giving in.

"You feel that?" My voice drops low. "My fingers in your tight little pussy while your mouth's stuffed full of cock?"

She moans again, louder this time, a sound that makes Nate release a groan from deep in his chest. His hips jerk forward, a rough, hungry thrust that has her gag slightly.

"Fuck..." Nate's voice is raw as hell, his hips grinding in like he can't decide if he wants to drag this out or lose it right here. His breath comes harsher now, sharp, broken gasps spilling out—the kind that mean he's too far gone to hold back anymore.

His rhythm falters for a split second before he drives in again, faster, harder. His cock slides deep, his hips rolling with every thrust like he's chasing the edge he can't escape.

"Fuck... fuck, Q..." he groans, voice cracking, every word a punch of want and pleasure. "Fuck, I'm gonna come. Gonna come in that filthy little mouth of yours."

I pump my fingers harder, curling them deep as my tongue lashes her clit, and she screams around his cock, the sound nearly fucking killing me.

Nate lets out a guttural moan, his head snapping back, neck tight as his whole body locks up. His hips slam forward once, twice, before he spills into her mouth.

"Fuck!" he growls. His body jerks with each pulse of release, his breath coming hard and broken as she swallows every drop down like it's the easiest fucking thing in the world.

I don't stop. My fingers keep fucking her, my mouth still working her clit, sucking and licking her through every twitch and spasm. Her thighs clamp weakly around my head, her whole body jerking between us, and all I can think is how much this is going to ruin her.

Nate finally pulls back, his cock sliding from her lips with a wet, obscene sound that twists my gut. He's breathing as if he's been running, his hand still buried in her hair, staring down at her fucked-out face. Her lips are swollen, wet, and her eyes glassy as she tries to breathe around what we've both put her through.

I push my fingers deeper, twisting them exactly right, and her body bows off the bed again, a hoarse, broken moan spilling from her throat.

"Good fucking girl," Nate rasps above her. He leans down and presses a soft kiss to her lips. Afterward his eyes lift to mine. That look. It slams into me harder than anything. Dark, heated, and full of something I don't have a name for. "Make her come, Theo. I wanna watch her fucking fall apart."

It isn't only the words. It's the fact that he's the one saying them to me. Wanting me to shatter her while he's right there.

A sound rips from my chest, half-groan, half-growl, vibrating against her soaked skin as I double the pace—faster, harder, relentless—until every flick of my tongue has her hips jerking, while every curl of my fingers inside her drags another cry from her throat.

"Fuck..." I mutter against her. She's dripping all over my hand, slick running down my wrist, and still her body keeps clenching, squeezing me in desperate, pulsing waves.

Her moans splinter into raw little sobs. Her thighs try to snap shut, shaking so hard I can barely hold them apart, but Nate's hands move on instinct, keeping her spread wide for me.

I suck her clit between my lips, hard and filthy, tongue grinding against that swollen nub while my fingers fuck her mercilessly. Her entire body bows tight, spine snapping off the bed as a strangled scream tears from her throat.

And then she breaks.

She comes hard, soaking my hand, wet heat spilling over my fingers as her pussy clenches and convulses. A sudden rush hits, spraying across my wrist, splattering down my arm. She's squirting, coming so fucking hard it's pouring out of her, and I groan into her cunt, licking her through it, desperate to taste every drop of her while she comes apart on my hand.

"Holy fuck," Nate growls. His fingers dig into her thighs, keeping her open while Quinn gushes all over me.

It's everywhere, splattering against my wrist, dripping down to the sheets as her pussy pulses hard. She moans, head tipping back, body jerking with each rush that spills out of her, soaking me until I'm drenched in it.

"Jesus Christ," Nate breathes again, lower this time, almost reverent. His gaze flicks to mine and it lands. This moment isn't only her coming. It's something else.

We've fucked groupies who were wet and willing and gone before the sheets cooled. But this... This is new. We've never had anything like this.

My lips pull into a grin against her pussy as I drag my tongue slowly over her clit, tasting every drop. Pride burns through my chest. I've always wanted to make a girl snap so hard she fucking squirts. But with the others, it never mattered enough to try.

Not until Quinn.

Nate lets out a low, shaky laugh, the sound dark and hungry. "We've never... fuck, Theo... never had a girl do that before." His voice drops to a whisper, almost like he can't quite believe it.

I finally ease my fingers out of her, watching the way her pussy flutters.

"Fucking hell..." I rasp, sitting back on my heels. The sheets under her are soaked, a dark stain spreading beneath her ass and thighs. I press my palm down into the mess and it squishes warm between my fingers. "Look what you fucking did."

Quinn's cheeks flush. She lets out a soft, mortified sound and tries to close her legs, but Nate's still holding them open.

"Oh no," he says. "You don't get to hide after giving us that. That was the hottest fucking thing I've ever seen."

Her breath stutters, torn between embarrassment and the aftershocks still rolling through her body.

I run my slick fingers over the inside of her thigh, spreading the wetness further, marking her with it.

"Don't be shy," I murmur, grinning up at her as I bring my fingers to my mouth and suck them clean. "That was fucking perfect."

Nate's thumb drags over her cheek. He eases back onto his heels, breath still ragged, chest rising and falling hard, but his eyes never leave her. There's nothing gentle in that stare. It's hot and hungry.

I grab the hem of my shirt and rip it over my head, tossing it aside without a second thought. Her gaze snaps to me instantly, dragging over my chest, lingering on my stomach before dropping lower.

Nate's head turns when I hook my fingers into my jeans and shove them down in one rough pull, boxers going with them. My cock springs free, hard and leaking from every second of restraint I've been holding back.

Quinn's breath stutters. Nate's jaw goes tight. His eyes drop and I sense the way they drag over every hard inch of me.

I wrap my fist around my cock, give it one long, deliberate stroke—precum smearing thick across the swollen head. A low groan slips out of me, as if touching myself in front of them is enough to undo me.

Quinn's lips part, a soft, shaky sound escaping her, and fuck, the way she looks right now—flushed, trembling, her pussy still glistening between her thighs—makes my grip tighten on my cock.

Her eyes flick between us. Me, standing there stroking my cock, veins raised under my fist, and Nate, muscles taut, lips parted as he kneels beside her, watching me.

She swallows hard, her tongue darting out to wet her lips, voice rough when it finally spills out. "Have you two..." Her words catch for a beat, her gaze sharpening as it slides from me to Nate, "...ever done anything together?"

Nate's shoulders go tight, that tiny shift in his body changing the whole room.

"No," he says, voice low, but steady enough to cut right through the air. "Not like that."

For a second, nothing moves. No one breathes.

Quinn sits up.

Both of us follow the motion without meaning to, our eyes dragging over the way her thighs slide together, hiding that soaked, perfect pussy we just had open and dripping for us.

The loss hits like a slap.

Cockblocked.

She brushes her hair back with shaking fingers, but her chin lifts with that spark she always carries. The kind that makes you forget every fucking thing except her.

"Well," she says, her voice still shaky from everything we've done to her. "If you two want to fuck me together..."

Her gaze flicks between Nate and me. Something wicked glints there, curling the edges of her lips into a smirk. "First, you have to do something for me."

My throat goes dry. "What's that?"

Her smirk deepens, sinful as hell. "Show me something worth watching."

It hits like a crack of lightning down my spine.

I glance at Nate, and he's already locked on me. His eyes aren't soft. They're not curious. They're fucking heated, all want and no shame.

The air becomes thick enough to choke on.

Quinn leans back on her elbows, legs still pressed tight together, eyes half-lidded as she stares at us through those long lashes. Her voice is soft but cutting when she says, "Kiss."

One word. That's all.

And fuck... it slams into me. My chest seizes, my pulse kicks, and all I can think is how many years we've danced around this line. How many times I've wondered. How many nights I've buried the thought of what it would be.

Before I can take a breath, Nate moves.

One step and he's right there. Heat rolls off him, bare skin brushing mine. Our chests press together, and fuck, our cocks touch. My lungs stutter.

His hand comes up, fingers rough against my jaw, grounding and destroying me all at once. His thumb strokes my skin, and those blue eyes don't waver.

And suddenly he's on me.

Fuck. His mouth slams into mine, all hunger and heat, no pause, no question. His lips are soft, but the kiss is fucking filthy—messy, raw, desperate. Years of want pouring out in one clash of tongues and teeth.

I groan and part my lips for him. His tongue slides against mine, wet and hot, and it's everything I've ever tried to bury exploding in my chest.

We collide harder, chest to chest, cock to cock. Hard. Heavy. Throbbing. The friction makes me hiss into his mouth, fingers digging into his sides as if I can pull him closer when we're already fucking fused together.

It's rough.

It's perfect.

And all I can think is yes. Fuck yes.

His teeth catch my bottom lip, a dirty scrape before his tongue soothes over it, and I swear to God I could come from this alone. From him. From the taste of him mixed with Quinn still clinging to his mouth.

He pulls back, lips wet, breath harsh against mine. Our foreheads nearly touch, and his eyes lock onto mine, dark and so fucking sure.

For a second, the heat between us is everything. No words. No rules. Just this.

The crash hits hard. Panic pulses through my ribs.

Did we step too far over that line?

I freeze, lips parted, every muscle wound tight, waiting for him to back off. To laugh it off. To shove it back into the box we've kept locked tight for years. To pretend it doesn't mean a single fucking thing.

But Nate smiles.

It's slow and crooked. His thumb drags along my jaw, rough and steady, and he leans in close enough that his breath brushes my lips when he murmurs, low and dirty, "You taste like her..."

Heat detonates low in my gut.

And suddenly he's kissing me again.

Slower this time.

It's a different kind of hunger now. Deeper. Rawer. His hand fists in my hair, tugging hard enough to make my cock twitch, and I groan into his mouth, opening for him, letting him take whatever the fuck he wants. Our tongues clash, wet and messy, and it's not soft. It's claiming. Starving. The kind of kiss that says we've both been waiting for this without even knowing it.

I hold onto his waist, drag him closer until we're chest to chest, cock to cock, and it's too much and not nearly enough. His teeth catch my lip, biting down enough to make my hips jerk and fuck, I'm gone.

We don't stop kissing. We can't.

And that's when she touches us.

Quinn's hands slip between our bodies, soft and small and goddamn sinful. One wraps around my cock—hot, slick, perfect—and the other closes around Nate's. Her grip is confident, sure, as though she's been waiting to touch both of us at the same time.

We break the kiss on the same ragged breath, foreheads pressed together, gasping into each other's mouths as her hands start to stroke. Slow at first. Testing. Jerking us in tandem, dragging over every vein, every ridge, as though she wants to memorize the weight of us in her palms.

"Fuck," I choke out, hips jerking into her fist without shame.

Nate groans low in my ear, his lips brushing my jaw before he drags them down my neck. He sucks hard enough to make me gasp, my head tipping back on instinct to give him more. His voice is rough when he growls against my skin, "Fuck her. I wanna watch you fuck her, Theo."

It's the filthiest thing I've ever heard. My cock throbs in Quinn's hand, leaking into her grip, and his mouth crashes back onto mine, crushing and wet and desperate.

When we pull apart, our breaths are harsh and tangled, my lips brush his ear as I whisper, "Let's fuck her together."

A grin spreads across his face, all teeth and desire. He nods once.

Nate moves first, pulling the drawer open and tossing me a condom without a word. I tear the wrapper with my teeth, sliding the latex down over my thick, hard cock, giving one slow stroke, just to feel it.

Nate does the same, rolling his on. His jaw's tight, breath sharp, and fuck, it's obscene watching him like this, ready and fucking feral.

I sit on the edge of the bed and pull Quinn straight into my lap, dragging her over me until she's straddling my thighs. Her skin is hot and flushed, her breath ragged as I crush my mouth to hers. There's nothing soft in it. My tongue fucks her mouth, claiming every sound she tries to make while my hands drag over her body.

"You ready to take both of us, beautiful girl?" I growl against her lips.

My fingers slide between her legs, finding that wet, swollen spot that's been begging for us all night. My cock jerks under her the moment I touch her slick heat.

"Ready to take us, to have this perfect little pussy split wide open?" I press the words into her mouth, my fingers teasing her entrance as she shudders in my lap.

Her moan spills out. She doesn't even need to answer. That sound is all the fucking yes I'll ever need.

She lifts herself, trembling, nails digging into my shoulders as she lines herself up. The second the head of my cock presses to that slick spot, my head tips back, a guttural groan ripping out of me.

"Fuck..." The words are half-breathed, half-growled, every muscle locking tight as she sinks down, inch by slow inch, taking me inside her.

She's hot. Tight. Perfect.

Her thighs shake as she bottoms out, my cock buried to the hilt in her dripping cunt. I grip her hips hard enough to bruise, dragging her down until I'm as deep as I can go.

"Jesus, Quinn..." I rasp against her skin, my teeth catching her collarbone. "You feel so fucking good."

I lean back on my elbows, pulling her with me until she's sprawled across my chest. Nate moves in behind her, the mattress dipping as he climbs up. His lips press to her back first, sliding higher until they reach her shoulder.

"You ever been fucked in the ass, Quinn?" he murmurs against her skin. His hand trails down her side, fingers brushing the curve of her ass. "Or do you want my cock buried in that perfect pussy with Theo's?"

Her breath hitches. She freezes for a second in both our hands before whispering, "Yeah... I've been fucked up the ass." Her voice is barely a breath. "Once."

The sound Nate makes isn't human. His head drops against her shoulder as though the words punched the air from his lungs.

"Fuck, tell me you loved it." Nate rasps, his voice cracking as if the thought alone is going to push him over the fucking edge.

I know that sound. Nate lives for anal. Always says it's tighter, dirtier, the kind of fuck that brands you from the inside out. He fucking thrives on it. I've never gone there. Never had the chance. Because when we fuck together, he always claims that first.

"Yeah... I did," Quinn breathes, the words soft.

His fingers dig into her hips.

"Was it with two guys fucking you?"

Quinn's head tips back, her lips parting. She shakes her head once, breath catching as she whispers, "No."

"Holy fuck," Nate grinds out. His forehead drops to her back, lips dragging over sweat-slick skin before he sucks hard enough to leave a mark, teeth sinking in to make her jolt in his hands. His fingers clamp on her hips, digging in like he's holding back a goddamn earthquake inside himself.

Quinn rolls her hips, sliding down on my cock, and the sensation is fucking chaos. Wet. Tight. Heat wrapping around me so good it steals the breath from my lungs. A rough, broken groan tears from my chest, my whole body snapping tight under her as if it can't take another second without giving in completely.

"Shit, Q..." Nate's voice drops to something dark, laced with want. His mouth drags over her shoulder, his lips brushing her jaw as his breath shudders out hot against her skin. "You're gonna fucking love this."

Nate shifts behind her, and the brush of his fingers grazes near my cock as he drags through her slick, gathering every drop, slicking his length in her wetness. He moves up onto his knees, his palm sliding over her hip to steady her as he lines up, the thick head of his cock pressing to her tight ass.

"Deep breath, baby," I murmur against her lips, kissing her, tasting her moan before it even leaves her throat.

Nate's teeth scrape over her shoulder, his voice breaking low at her ear. "Good fucking girl."

That's when he pushes in.

Slow. Careful. The first thick inch of him breaches her ass and she gasps, her entire body jolting against mine.

"Holy shit..." Nate's groan rips through the air, cracked and filthy. "She's so fucking tight."

I thrust once—enough to make her moan—and Nate drives in deeper, the two of us moving together.

"Jesus Christ," Nate hisses, his forehead dropping to her spine. "This is... fuck, Theo, do you feel her? She's squeezing the life out of us."

I crush my mouth to hers, swallowing the little sounds spilling out of her as our hips find a rhythm. It starts slow, careful, her body adjusting around us, before building deeper, harder, until every thrust drags a moan straight from her chest. The wet slap of skin on skin fills the room, the heat between us becomes fucking unbearable.

Nate shifts closer, his chest brushing her back as his hand slides around the front of her. His fingers wrap around her throat, not squeezing, holding her steady. Claiming her.

His mouth drops to her ear. "Take it, baby. Take both our cocks. You were made for this."

Her gasp tears against my lips, and fuck, it runs down my spine. Her pussy clenches around me, while Nate groans behind her, his thrust syncing with mine until she's nothing but soft, desperate sounds and trembling limbs caught between us.

When I pull back from the kiss, Nate's hand moves from her neck and yanks me forward, dragging me down with his mouth as he kisses me. It's tongues and heat and desperation.

That's when her hands slide over us. One reaching for me, one for Nate, pulling us both down until our mouths crash into hers at the same time. I almost fucking lose it right there, buried so deep inside her.

She pulls back, breath hot against my mouth, and before I can take in the loss, Nate's lips are on mine and for a second, I forget to breathe. It's hot. Wet. Raw. Our tongues meet and fuck, that's it. Her tight little body taking our cocks while our mouths devour each other. Every thrust, every kiss, every fucking second is carved into my bones.

Her fingers fist tighter, nails scraping my scalp, tugging me back to her. She kisses me before I can even catch my breath. The three of us tangled together, lips colliding, tongues sliding, moans spilling into one another. Her mouth tastes of heat and pure fucking sin, and soon it's Nate again, his lips crashing into mine, each kiss so raw it sets my whole body alight.

"Fuck..." Nate's voice breaks into my mouth, the sound of it dragging through me, down my spine, settling right in my cock. His hips snap forward, driving into her ass, the movement forcing me deeper into her pussy at the same time. The shattered moan she makes is enough to make my whole body jolt.

My forehead presses to Nate's for half a second, our breaths colliding, sweat dripping between us. His eyes are wild, and fuck, there's no holding back now. We move together in perfect fucking sync, thrust for thrust, the wet slap of skin, the filthy mix of sounds filling the air.

"Holy shit..." I choke the words out.

Quinn's nails dig into my shoulders, her back arching, her whole body trembling between us.

Nate groans low, his hand moving back to the front of her throat. "Fuck her... Theo... fuck her harder. Make her come all over us."

I slam my hips forward, rough now, the kind of rhythm that ruins everything in its path. Nate matches me, his thrusts equally brutal, and she moans between us, her body jerking, caught in the storm we've built around her.

"Shit," Nate says, voice strained, his jaw locked as his hips stutter. "I'm fucking close. I can't... fuck..." His lips crash back onto mine mid-sentence, desperate, claiming, and that's all it takes.

The taste of him. The heat of her. The tight squeeze of her pussy pulling me under while Nate pounds into her from behind. My cock pulses, everything in me snapping, breaking, shattering in the best fucking way as I groan into his mouth, spilling inside her with a violent, shaking thrust.

Nate tears his lips from mine only long enough to growl her name, his orgasm ripping through him. I sense every jolt of it—his hips jerking, his cock twitching inside the tight grip of her ass, the guttural sound he makes as he spills deep and hard, his breath caught between my mouth and hers.

Quinn's scream crashes through the room in the same instant. Her pussy clenches so violently around me it's as if she's milking every drop of cum out of my cock. Her whole body bows, every muscle snapping tight as her orgasm detonates, soaking me, drenching us in her release.

"Fuck, baby..." Nate moans into her shoulder, his hands shaking as he holds her steady. "That's it... that's our perfect fucking girl."

Her head drops back, lips parted, sweat and tears streaking her flushed cheeks, and I swear I've never seen anything so fucking beautiful in my life. My chest heaves, hips still twitching with aftershocks as I keep my cock buried in her, unwilling to let go. Unwilling to release any part of this.

Her hands slip from my hair as she breathes out a broken little laugh, shaky and soft, before kissing me. Gentle this time. Sweet. My heart fucking cracks in half. She turns her head and kisses Nate the same way, and for a moment, the room is nothing but heat, breath, and the rhythm of three hearts trying to catch up.

Nate rests his forehead against hers, his hand sliding down to cup her cheek. His other hand finds mine over her hip, squeezing once. Silent. A promise neither of us know how to say out loud yet.

And all I can think is fuck. This isn't only the best fuck of my life. This is every forbidden thought, every late-night what-if, every aching need I've ever buried. It's everything.

The room hums in the quiet aftermath, heavy with heat and the ghost of every sound we wrung out of her. Quinn is sprawled over my chest, still trembling, her breath brushing my skin in uneven bursts. She feels soft and weightless, her hair damp and sticking to my collarbone.

Nate presses a kiss to the slope of her back, low and tender in a way that twists something deep in my gut.

"You did so fucking good," he murmurs, before sliding out of her slowly. I catch the twitch in her body at the loss. He ties off the condom and heads for the bathroom.

The sound of the water rushing to life fills the silence a second later.

Quinn and I don't move, even when my cock softens inside her. Her cheek is pressed to my chest. Her skin is warm, slick, and flushed, lips still kiss-bruised and swollen. Her breathing's uneven. My hand slides down her waist, fingers brushing over the soft skin there, still feeling the ghost of her clenching around me.

For a long beat, we just breathe. The only sound in the room is the low rush of the shower behind the door.

"I saw the way you looked at him," she whispers, her voice soft, brushing against my skin.

My chest pulls tight.

She shifts, her lips grazing my jaw as she tilts her face toward mine. "When he kissed you, Theo. It wasn't just because he wanted to fuck me."

I don't answer. My throat is raw, my voice caught somewhere deep.

Her fingers move slow over my chest, trailing through the sheen of sweat. "It was more than want. Nate felt that. So did you."

The breath I let out shakes.

"It's okay to tell him how you feel," she says softly. Her fingers trace lower, over the ink across my chest. The black feathers of my tattoo. She follows each curve, each shadowed line.

I shift my eyes to her face, and something flickers there. Barely a second, but I catch it, including the stutter in her breath,

She shifts, rolling onto her back, my cock slips free. The space between us seems bigger than it should.

"Quinn?" I murmur, the word quiet, careful.

She sits up too fast. Her eyes snap to mine, wide and wet. Glossy, blurred, a shimmer of tears pooling.

"Hey…" I start, reaching out, but she shakes her head once.

Before I can say anything else, she's sliding off the bed. Moving quick, movements jerky.

"Quinn," I say, chest tight, concern biting hard under my ribs.

Something's wrong. I can see it in the way her shoulders stiffen, in the way she won't look back at me.

I don't know what the fuck shifted. All I know is it's there, hanging in the air, heavy and cold where a second ago it was nothing but heat.

CHAPTER 22

Quinn

The steam curls off the rim of my mug as I take another slow sip, the bitter taste settling on my tongue, grounding me in the half-light of the morning. The sky is still black, edges of gray bleeding into the horizon, a faint promise of dawn that hasn't broken yet. Around me, the world rests in that rare quiet that only exists at five a.m., when no one else is awake and the air still feels untouched.

The back patio is cool as I pull my legs underneath me, laptop balanced on my thighs. The faint click of the trackpad breaks the quiet as I scroll through yesterday's work, each frame flickering across the screen.

Xander appears first. His face fills the shot in a way that demands attention, every sharp line of his jaw cutting clean through the frame. Always photogenic. He doesn't have to work for it. His smile isn't soft; it's carved, a weapon he's mastered. Even in the unguarded moments, with his head thrown back mid-laugh, lips part mid-lyric, there's something magnetic. His presence bleeds through the lens.

The next photo is Ace.

He's caught in motion, arms curved around his guitar, fingers pressing down like the strings are an extension of him. His head is tilted slightly, jaw tight, eyes shadowed under the fall of his hair. There's a challenge in his expression, that quiet, fuck off confidence that says he doesn't care what you see. There's this rawness under all that restraint. A hint of something untamed.

Then I get to them.

Theo.

His bass hangs low at his hips, his head bent enough that the light catches in his hair. That face, quiet, soft in a way most people never notice. Most see only Nate, all fire and chaos. But I see him. I always have. There's a gentleness in his eyes when he's lost in the music, something so fucking pure it hurts to stare at for too long. As if the camera has caught something it shouldn't have.

And now Nate.

Sweat slicks his temples, strands of hair clinging to his forehead. His mouth is open mid-curse or mid-laugh, impossible to tell because with him it's always both at once. He's wild in the frame, pure kinetic energy captured in a single shot. His hands blur over the drums, muscles in his forearms tight, veins standing out under the skin. There's fire in him, caught mid-motion, and he looks alive. He looks… free.

Free in a way I haven't known for years.

I swallow hard and swipe to the next photo. Another one follows, and my chest tightens with every frame, a sharp ache blooming under my ribs until it's hard to drag in air. Because staring at them now isn't only looking at photos. It's falling back into that moment—Theo's hands on my body, the way his touch burned through my skin. Nate's breath at my neck, every exhale branding me.

Every shot on the screen drags me deeper into it. The weight of them against me. The filthy words that slipped past their lips, curling into my bones. They tore me apart without hesitation, stripping me down until I wasn't Quinn anymore. Until I was nothing but sound and sensation. Until I was theirs.

And those wings.

I close my eyes, but it doesn't save me. The memory hits anyway, pulling me under. My hand on Theo's chest, fingers brushing over the ink, tracing the sharp curve of feathers etched into his skin. The way his breath hitched under my touch, that tiny shudder breaking through the wall he always carries. For a second, he wasn't Theo the smartass; he was himself. Raw. Open. After that, the weight of it crushed me.

Those wings. They aren't only ink. They are everything he can't bring himself to say out loud. Every piece of his heart carved into his skin for a girl he will love for the rest of his life. A love that runs so deep it bleeds through every line of that tattoo, every feather etched over his chest. It's devotion turned permanent, a promise he can never break, not even if he wanted to.

When my fingers lingered there, when he leaned into that touch for a single heartbeat, the guilt burned so deep it closed my throat and stole the air from my lungs. I knew every stroke of my fingers was trespassing on something sacred.

The mug rattles against the table when I set it down, coffee licking the edge, threatening to spill. My fingers won't stay steady. My chest feels caged, every breath caught halfway like my lungs forgot how to work. I don't know if it's the chill of the morning or the weight of what's sitting in my gut, pressing hard.

If Bianca were here, they wouldn't just be off limits. They'd be untouchable. A line burned into the ground that no one with a soul would ever cross.

I go to the next photo, and Nate fills the frame. Sweat still at his temple, mouth caught mid-grin, wild and alive and every fucking thing I shouldn't be staring at.

The photos burn, each one a blade twisting deeper. And I hear it in my head before the words even leave my lips.

"What the fuck am I doing?"

The door creaks behind me. I don't have to turn around to know who it is.

Cedar. Memories flood back, rushing in all at once. That earthy scent, clinging to his skin, soaked into those damn leather bracelets that never left his wrists.

Back in high school, it was the first thing I noticed about him. I remember how I used to inhale it when he walked by, or when he stopped to give me those shitty lines. He never knew he had a way of making my heart do that stupid flutter it never stopped doing. I used to tell myself it was nothing, a scent in the air. But shit, I've always liked it. And even now, all these years later, it drags me right back to those days.

"Couldn't sleep?" Nate's voice is rough with sleep, low enough that it scrapes over my skin and settles somewhere deep.

I shake my head, eyes still on the screen. "Too early to call it sleep when I never closed my eyes."

He steps into my periphery. Bare chest, Bianca tattoo right over his heart, sweatpants hanging low on his hips, hair sticking up in every direction. My pulse kicks up in my throat, remembering the press of his body against mine, his cock hard and hot, his voice whispering in my ear.

Theo follows a second later. His presence hits me in the chest the way it always does. That soft gravity he carries without meaning to. Those angel wings out on display. His gaze drops to the laptop, and I slam it shut too fast.

"Morning," he says.

I force a smile, reaching for the mug even though my hand is trembling. "Morning."

They settle around me, one on each side, as they sit. The guilt twists tight in my gut as my skin remembers every fucking thing from last night. Their hands. Their mouths. The way they broke me open and put me back together in the span of a perfect hour.

I sip the coffee to give my hands something to do. The bitter heat hits my tongue, but it doesn't drown out the ache slowly crawling under my ribs.

Theo leans forward, his arm brushing mine, and the warmth of him floods my skin.

"You okay?" he murmurs.

I nod too fast. "Yeah. Just tired."

Nate chuckles. "Tired's one word for it."

The memory flashes hard. His voice low in my ear, the weight of him behind me, Theo's hands holding me open. I stare at the smudges of purple blooming against his skin, proof of where my mouth had been, where I lost myself.

I should look away, but I don't.

The air turns heavy with so many unspoken things, and I wonder if he's thinking about how tracing that tattoo gave me a meltdown.

After a beat, he stands.

"You want a coffee?" he asks Nate, his voice too casual, as if he's trying to mask whatever this thing is between us.

"Yeah," Nate replies beside me.

"Quinn, you want a refill?" Theo asks, turning to me.

I shake my head quickly, holding the mug in my palms like it's keeping me grounded. "Nah, I'm good."

Theo heads inside. The door clicks shut, and the second it does, the air changes. Heaviness settles between Nate and me.

He doesn't say anything at first, only watches. After a moment, he leans forward, resting his elbows on his knees.

"You don't seem yourself," he says. "Did you... fuck, did you regret what we did?"

"No," I say too quickly. After that, softer, shaking my head. "Fuck no."

Nate's eyes soften. "So what is it?" he asks.

The words scrape up but die before they reach air.

How the fuck do I tell him that running my fingers over Theo's tattoo last night was betrayal bleeding under my skin? That back in those days, I wanted something with him for as long as I can remember, only Bianca got there first. That every time I shoved him back, every time I cut him down with a grin, it was me begging for more.

I know what last night was for them. Nothing more than a good time. The kind of thing two rockstars can get whenever they want.

Nate lifts his hand, brushing his knuckles softly against my jaw. That one gentle touch fucks me more than anything from last night.

"Theo told me you walked out of the room after we fucked."

I open my mouth, ready to shove the words past the knot in my throat, but the sharp creak of the door swinging open kills it instantly.

Theo returns with two steaming mugs in hand, and I see he is now wearing a shirt. He sets a mug in front of Nate and sits back down.

I grip my mug tighter, hiding in the motion of taking a sip, praying they can't see the storm still raging under my skin.

Theo nods toward my laptop on the table. "Have you been working on those photos?"

"Yeah," I answer, clearing my throat. "Kit messaged. She wants to see some of them today."

"You should be fine," Nate says after a beat. His chin tips toward the closed laptop. "From what you showed me yesterday, they're pretty good, Q."

There it is. That fucking nickname. The one that digs in and drags the past up with it. I can almost hear the echo of him saying it years ago, with that crooked grin, some cocky line tossed in just to make me roll my eyes. It lands harder than I want it to, but I shove it down, keep my face neutral.

"Yeah. Xander's easy. He's stupidly photogenic. Ace doesn't even try and still manages to look good. Theo..." My gaze drifts over to him without meaning to. "Theo's a challenge. You don't stay still."

Theo grins into his mug, unbothered. "I'm not built to sit still."

"How long does it take to get an album out?" I ask after a beat. "From start to finish."

Nate exhales through his nose, thinking it over. "Once we've got a few solid tracks, we spend a day on each one. Recording it piece by piece. Layering. Ace gets picky as hell with the riffs, so we end up redoing parts until he's satisfied."

Theo smirks and leans back in his chair. "Ace gets picky with everything. The man once threw out an entire pizza because the pepperoni wasn't evenly spaced."

The laugh escapes me before I can catch it.

"That actually fucking happened." Nate mutters into his mug, shaking his head. "We should start recording in a few days." He glances at me. "We've got three songs down now. So in the next day or two you'll see how it's done."

Nate tips back the last of his coffee, the quiet clink of the mug on the table breaking the stillness. He stands and stretches, a lazy roll of his shoulders, joints cracking faintly in the morning hush. As he steps behind my chair, his hand rests on my shoulder before his lips press gently to the top of my head. It's a soft fleeting moment, but it's enough to leave a weight behind.

When he slips inside, the screen door clicks shut with a hollow sound, and the quiet it leaves behind swells like its alive. Theo doesn't move at first. He remains there, fingers curled around his mug, watching the faint curls of steam rise and vanish into the pale morning light.

When his eyes meet mine, I'm not ready for it. The smile that touches his mouth isn't the sharp, crooked smirk I know too well. It's softer. Something private.

"What?" The word comes out thin, almost broken, and I clear my throat too late to cover it.

His smile shifts, sharpening just enough to remind me who I'm looking at. "Do you remember that time you and Bianca tried to cook pancakes and almost burned the house down?"

The memory hits me so fast it steals my breath. A laugh rips free before I can stop it, spilling out of my chest.

"Yeah," I manage between breaths. "We left the paper towel too close to the burner. The damn thing went up in flames. Wes came running in, grabbed the fire extinguisher, and—" I can see it now, the burst of white foam, the smoke curling up past the cabinets. "He didn't even yell. He told us to be more careful, then walked out and left us covered in ash while we laughed until our stomachs hurt."

The smile that spreads across Theo's face is small but real, and his eyes stay fixed on me. Watching. There's no teasing in them, no wall of sarcasm or that usual edge. Only that steady, piercing gaze that's always been able to cut right through the weight I carry. The one that makes me feel seen when no one else could.

The mug in his hand lowers to the table without a sound. He leans back in his chair, shoulders easing, but his eyes never leave mine.

The morning light brushes against the side of his face, catching in the darker strands of his hair and tracing the edges of him in soft gold. For a second, he doesn't seem like the boy who's been fighting his own head for years. He doesn't appear to be the friend who's been breaking in front of me piece by piece.

"You always did laugh with her the hardest," he whispers.

My throat closes around the words I want to say. That it wasn't only her, it's him too. That he's the only one who's ever been able to pull a real laugh out of me when the world seemed too fucking heavy. But the words don't come. They stick there, and all I can do is hold his gaze and hope he sees it anyway.

"Yeah," I finally whisper.

His lips twitch as if he wants to say something else, but instead he just sits there.

Scarlet spots me before I even have a chance to breathe. One second I'm stepping into the living room of Ace's home, the next there's a blur of blonde hair and fast feet cutting across the space.

"Holy shit. Quinn Thomas." And suddenly she's on me, arms wrapping tight, laughter breaking midway into something shaky. "You're really here."

I barely manage to suck in a breath before she pulls back enough to grab my shoulders and give me a once-over. Her blue eyes are bright, the happiness practically buzzing out of her.

"Hey, Scar," I manage.

Scarlet grins wide, her eyes lighting up. "You have no idea how much I used to beg these two idiots back in the day to bring you around more. Those were the best days."

Behind her, Nate makes a sound, almost too dramatic.

"Please, Scar. You were too wrapped up in yourself to even notice who was around."

"Oh please, Nate." Scarlet spins fast, shooting him a glare. "If it was just you and Theo, I would've died of boredom in a week."

Nate smirks.

"Yeah... Funny, you seemed pretty damn entertained when I was coaching you in those drum battles."

Scarlet rolls her eyes.

"Entertained? No. I was too busy trying to ignore the sound of your offbeat chaos. You hit hard, sure, but your timing was a fucking disaster until I stepped in and fixed it."

"She's not wrong." Theo chuckles, clearly enjoying the exchange.

"Traitor," Nate fires back, but his grin widens, that familiar spark in his eyes.

I can't help but smile, seeing that the three of them haven't changed one bit, despite all the fame they've gained.

My eyes track Ace as he steps forward. I catch a grin tugging at his mouth. It's small, but it's there, softening the usual hard edges.

Scarlet slips her arm through mine as she leans in close.

"Don't tell these two, but you were the only reason I put up with their bullshit half the time."

Theo's voice cuts in. "We heard that."

Scarlet's lips curve into a sweet, innocent smile as she fires back, "Good."

The sound of footsteps carries in from the hall. A second later, Xander and a small pink-haired woman step into the room.

The woman moves forward first, her steps steady, eyes scanning the room before they land on me. For a heartbeat, I can't move. She's composed. Her gaze dips to the camera in my hand, then back to my face, and a small smile tugs at the corner of her mouth.

"Quinn," she says, extending her hand.

My fingers hesitate before they meet hers. Her grip is firm. She holds my hand a second longer than necessary.

"It's good to finally put a face to the photos," she says.

"Yeah," I manage, my voice thinner than I want. "You too, Kit."

Ace moves forward, slipping his hands into his pockets. "We should really get started."

"What the fuck, already?" Theo groans.

Ace glances at Theo completely unbothered. "Yes. You can breathe when the album's finished."

Theo lets his head roll back with an exaggerated sigh. "Scar, remind me again, what the fuck do you see in him?"

Scarlet grins. "Forearms, and the fact he doesn't make me want to staple my ears shut when he talks."

Ace's mouth curves. "And the fact I don't sound like a rejected cartoon character going through puberty every time I speak."

Theo puts a hand to his chest, mock offended. "Wow. Did it take you all night to come up with that, or did you phone a friend?"

"Nah," Ace says. "That one's been sitting in the vault for a while."

Xander is the first to move down the hall. "Every time you two talk, I lose brain cells. Studio's waiting."

Theo calls after him. "Aw, come on, pretty boy. Don't pout because the spotlight's not on you for once."

Ace smirks, eyes still on Xander. "Pretty boy had girls lining up in high school just to watch him walk to class."

Theo lets out a laugh that bounces off the walls.

Xander doesn't even turn around. "You two done giving each other hand jobs, or do I need to come back with a towel?"

Nate groans. "Jesus Christ. Can we go five minutes without needing therapy?"

Then the door swings open and they step through. The room falls quiet.

Kit lets out a breath and drops her folder onto the table with a soft thud. "You know, managing those four is like running a daycare... if the toddlers had tattoos and unresolved trauma."

Scarlet laughs. "But you love them."

Kit lifts a brow. "Unfortunately." She raises her hand and starts counting them off one finger at a time. "Xander says two words and suddenly thinks he's carried the entire conversation. Last week, he didn't talk to anyone for an hour because someone moved his water bottle and messed with his flow."

Scarlet snorts.

"Ace communicates in grunts, head nods, one word texts and that one eyebrow twitch that means either 'I agree' or 'I hope you fall down a flight of stairs.' Still somehow knows everyone's schedule better than I do."

Scarlet's already shaking with laughter.

Kit moves on, lifting another finger. "Theo's like a drunk squirrel with a Wi-Fi connection. Always moving, always talking, always one bad idea away from a lawsuit. I once caught him googling how to stage dive off a vending machine."

Scarlet wheezes. "That sounds like Theo."

A grin pulls at my mouth before I can stop it.

Kit moves to the last finger. "And Nate. The quiet one. Golden boy. Voice of reason. Steady as hell... until he isn't. Still uses his drumsticks to stir his coffee. Once ordered three pizzas during a live radio interview because he and Theo forgot to eat breakfast and thought they might collapse mid-question."

Scarlet's crying now, doubled over with her face in her hands.

A laugh slips out of me.

Kit finally glances my way, face unreadable. "I know everything about them. Unfortunately. Intimately. Against my will."

A beat passes. After a moment, she nods toward the bag on my shoulder. "Did you get some good ones yesterday?"

I nod because my throat's too tight to speak. Reaching for the laptop, my fingers brush the zipper, and even that soft sound seems too loud in the quiet.

Everything feels louder now—my heartbeat, the blood in my ears, the weight of this moment pressing in from all sides.

I pull the laptop free, setting it on the counter in front of us. My hands aren't steady. If these photos are not exactly what Kit wants, maybe this whole thing ends right here, right now.

I flip it open. My fingers seem clumsy on the keys as the screen glows to life. I move the mouse to a folder. I don't think; I click without hesitation.

Xander fills the screen. His head is angled toward someone slightly off-frame, that half-smile bleeding through. His hair's damp, curling at the edges, neck glinting with sweat. The light hits his jaw at the perfect angle, all bone and attitude, but it's the look in his eyes that lands the blow. Unbothered. Unshaken. Fucking magnetic. The kind of shot you never get twice.

Kit steps closer. I don't meet her eyes. I keep my focus on the screen.

She hums low in her throat. "Alright..."

I click through to the next.

Ace. He's caught mid-moment, guitar slung low across his hips, hand gripping the neck, body angled just enough to catch the light on his forearm. His head's tilted slightly, hair falling over one eye, mouth parted in concentration. There's a lazy, lethal kind of heat in the shot. The kind that turns into a poster, pinned to bedroom walls while fans lie on their backs, legs parted, pretending they're not getting off to it.

Scarlet exhales. "Damn."

Kit, eyes glued to the screen, doesn't say a word.

I move to the next photo.

Theo.

He's leaning forward slightly, elbows on his knees, looking past the camera. There's a softness bleeding out of him, a quiet fucking ache in the curve of his mouth. His shirt hangs loose at the collar, sleeves shoved up his forearms. The light hits at the perfect angle, brushing against the edge of his face, catching in the strands of his hair and casting that sharp jawline in gold. He looks good. Messy in the best way, as if he rolled out of someone's bed and hasn't decided if he wants to stay or fuck them again. And still, somehow, it's the softness that lands the hardest.

That flicker of something vulnerable behind the eyes. The part of him no one ever sees unless he forgets to hide it and yet the camera caught it. Frozen, branded into the pixels.

Kit leans in, just slightly. "Shit."

Scarlet's grinning. "Shit, Quinn, you really got him."

Kit nods once. "That doesn't happen by accident."

I press my lips together and click to the last member of the band.

Nate.

He's behind his kit, caught mid-beat. One arm lifted high, muscles flexed, the other hand low against the snare. The leather straps around his wrist, the way his shirt clings to his chest. He's pure momentum in the frame, caught mid-breath, head tipped just enough that the light catches the curve of his jaw, the gleam of sweat on his neck. There's a wild joy on his face that makes him look more alive than I've ever seen him.

Kit blows out a slow breath. "He's gonna hate that one. Which means it's perfect."

Scarlet bumps her shoulder into mine. "You crushed it."

Kit nods, more serious now. "They're not just promo shots. You can really see them."

"I'm trying to," I say.

"You don't need to try," Kit says, eyes still on the laptop. "It's already there. These feel personal."

They are. They so fucking are.

She shuts the lid gently and looks at me again.

"They're good, Quinn. Theo's right. You've got a good eye."

She grabs her folder and starts toward the studio.

Scarlet calls after her. "Hey, Kit, do you mind if Quinn and I catch up for a little while before she heads down?"

Kit pauses by the door. "Yeah, that's fine, Scar. Quinn's clearly got everything under control. Judging by those shots, she doesn't need me breathing down her neck." She disappears toward the studio without waiting for a response.

Scarlet turns to me, her expression soft. "You okay?"

I nod, even though it hits like a lie. There's a tightness sitting behind my ribs. I press the heel of my hand to my chest, trying to ease the heavy thud of my heart.

Scarlet tilts her head toward the kitchen. "Coffee?"

"Yeah."

She crosses the space and reaches up into the cupboard, grabs two mugs that don't match, and sets them on the bench.

"How do you have it?" she asks, her back to me.

"Black. With sugar."

She nods and presses a button. Nothing happens. "This machine hates me," she mutters, smacking the side of the coffee maker. "But Ace said he fixed it last week. So if it explodes, it's his fault."

I huff a laugh and sink into one of the chairs.

The machine hums to life. The scent hits first, before the coffee even touches the mug.

My fingers tap against the wood, I'm restless for some reason.

"You killed it with those shots," Scarlet says. "Seriously. I don't think I've seen Kit that impressed since Theo figured out how to show up on time."

I laugh, picturing him with that smug little grin, probably late on purpose. "Thanks."

Scarlet watches me for a beat, her gaze steady before swapping out one mug for the other. When the second pour finishes, she grabs both cups and walks over.

She sets mine down in front of me, then lowers herself into the seat beside me.

"It's good having you around again," she says.

That ache behind my ribs pulses harder, and all I can manage is a nod.

She keeps going. "It's different this time. For them. Seeing Nate and Theo with you again... it's changed them."

My pulse kicks. Because it feels good to be around them too. It feels right.

I wrap my hands around the mug.

Scarlet leans in a little. "They laugh more now. They've been lighter since they came back. It's like you've made them remember who they were."

She pauses.

"I think you helped them remember Bianca," she adds.

My hands still. The mug stays warm, but I go cold all over.

I look away. The ache spreads fast. Through my chest. Into my throat. Down to the hollow place I never let anyone see.

That wasn't what I needed to hear. That I'm a trigger. A stand-in. A fucking ghost dressed in someone else's memories. That this impossible thing burning between me and Theo, between me and Nate might not be about me at all.

I take a sip of coffee, not wanting her to see how much that last comment fucking hurts. But then I catch the glint of the ring on her finger. It's easier to focus on that than the mess in my chest.

I set my cup down and reach across the table, grabbing her hand. "Are you gonna tell me about this monster?"

Scarlet's cheeks flush instantly. "Ugh. That idiot. We were in Rome. We'd had the dumbest fight over gelato, and I was still pissed. He says nothing. Not a word, only pulls this box out of his jacket, hands it to me, and walks away."

I blink. "Walks away?"

"Yeah, he didn't even wait for me to open it. Just strolled off like he was going to buy bread or something. Meanwhile I'm standing there, furious, holding a ring box and thinking, this absolute dickhead is the love of my life. I almost threw it at him."

"But you didn't."

"No." Her voice softens. "Because when I opened it, I swear to God my heart stopped. I could see everything. Who he is, who he's still trying to be. Every stupid fight, every time he showed up when he didn't have to. The way he loves me, even when I'm impossible. That ring wasn't just a promise. It was every messy, complicated part of us, and him saying he's all in."

I look down at her hand again. "I'm happy for you."

She squeezes my fingers, just once. "You know, you deserve that too."

"Yeah," I say. But it doesn't feel true. Not today.

I let go of her hand and stare into my coffee, trying to believe I'm not merely a placeholder in someone else's grief. That I'm not chasing something already broken.

I want to believe it. But that ache under my ribs won't let go.

CHAPTER 23

Nate

I t's fucked up how comforting this feels with Quinn around. Her being here, watching everything through that damn camera of hers... it's giving me a piece of myself back. Back before all the shit happened. Before the silence. Before Bianca's name started tasting like grief every time I thought about her.

There was a time when I used to laugh more. Talk shit. Throw myself into life as if it couldn't touch me. Fear was something other people carried. I was born with bare hands and a bulletproof grin. That version of me doesn't exist anymore. He's buried under the years of loss.

Now, I exist in the after.

But Quinn... she cracks something open. Brings flickers of that old me back. Little slivers of light cutting through all the dark. She doesn't know she's doing this. But she is, and I don't know whether to thank her or run until the ache in my chest stops.

I was never the serious one. That was Theo. Hood up, walls high, hiding behind silence as though it were armor. But after Bianca died, I turned into the one who couldn't talk. Couldn't breathe or register anything that didn't burn.

The steaks are already drowning in marinade. Soy. Garlic. Black vinegar. A fuck-ton of cracked pepper. My hands are deep in a bowl of marinade, coating the steaks I bought this afternoon from some overpriced butcher. The radio hums low in the background. My fingers are stained with sauce, my jaw's clenched but my thoughts are somewhere else entirely.

Theo's on the couch, locked in a heated Mario Kart race with Alex. They've been at it for half an hour. Every now and again, I hear Theo's voice rise in dramatic horror when Alex throws a banana peel at him or overtakes him before the finish line.

"You're cheating!" Theo yells, laughing. "There's no way you hit that drift by accident."

Alex cackles like a little demon. "Get better, old man."

Old man. He's six and already has Theo wrapped around his finger. The two of them are chaos and comfort in one.

I glance over my shoulder in time to see Theo leap off the couch as his kart crashes into a wall. He throws his hands up in mock despair, and Alex howls with laughter, clutching the controller above his head as if performing some kind of victory dance.

"You got lucky," Theo tells him, slumping dramatically against the cushions.

"I beat you five times. That's not luck."

Theo ruffles his hair, and Alex bats him away, still giggling.

I should be smiling, enjoying it like I always do. That scene always loosens something inside me, but not tonight.

Tonight my focus is on that fucking chair in the corner. The one Quinn usually curls up in, legs tucked, eyes watching everything like she's documenting the world. But the chair sits empty. Has been ever since we got home from Ace's.

Something's wrong. I can feel it.

Quinn's been quiet all day. Too quiet. Said she had edits to make, photos to upload, and shots to send to Kit. But I know the difference between working and hiding. I know what pulling away looks like, and I fucking hate that.

She didn't even join in earlier. All of us sitting around at Ace's, drinking, half-buzzed on that rush that hits when the prep's done and the real work begins. The first song is getting recorded tomorrow.

She didn't even take out her camera earlier or laugh at the way Theo faked pulling a hamstring after Alex made him do burpees. She only sat in the chair with her eyes miles away.

And I can't stand it.

I press the air out of the bag, seal it tight, and toss the whole thing into the fridge.

Theo curses behind me. Again.

Alex laughs so loud the sound echoes, this evil little cackle that only a six-year-old on a sugar high can pull off.

"You cheated!" Theo calls out, breathless and dramatic.

"No, you're just bad," Alex fires back, voice high and full of glee.

I turn my head to see Theo hunched over on the couch, shoulders tense, controller clenched tight, jaw locked in frustration. Alex's legs are crossed, face smug as hell, tongue peeking out the side of his mouth while his fingers blur over the buttons.

I wash my hands in the sink, watching the marinade swirl down the drain. I dry them on a towel and head for the back door, needing air.

The backyard is quiet. Only the sound of distant cars and the occasional bird cutting through the stillness. I step outside and lean against the railing, breathing in the night. The breeze carries a chill, but I don't move. I welcome the cold. Maybe the sting in the air will wake something in me. Maybe that same pull will bring her out here.

A minute passes, followed by another, before the door slides open and Theo steps out.

"You need help with the grill?" he asks, scratching the back of his neck.

I shake my head, eyes still fixed on the horizon. "I've got it."

We're both quiet for a beat, watching the dying light disappear into the night.

"Quinn okay?" he asks finally.

And fuck, there it is. That same gnawing unease I haven't been able to shake since this morning.

"She's been quiet," he adds.

I nod once. "Too quiet."

There's a pause. The kind that drags. Then—

"Come on, Uncle Theo!" Alex's voice floats through the screen door.

Theo flicks a glance toward Alex, before turning back to me. His face softens.

"Go check on her," he mutters. "I'll stay here and get my dignity shredded by a six-year-old dictator in Crocs."

And with that, he's gone, slipping back inside.

I remain where I stand a moment longer, watching the door, listening to Theo and Alex. After that, I head inside.

I move past the couch, sidestepping Alex's wild arm movements and Theo's dramatic groan as another red shell wipes him out.

I pass the laundry room, the door half open, and the place is a fucking disaster. An overflowing basket sits lopsided right inside, towels spilling over the rim. A crumpled shirt lies half in, half out of the doorway, as if someone kicked the thing and gave up. No one's touched the mess in days. Probably won't anytime soon.

I keep moving. Every step toward her room makes me nervous.

I stop at her door. Breathe in. Lift my hand. Knock once.

"Come in." Her voice is soft.

I push open the door.

She's lying on her side, one arm curled beneath her head, the other resting across her stomach. Her tights cling to her legs, her top riding up slightly to reveal a sliver of skin.

She's fucking beautiful.

She has always been.

It's in the shape of her mouth, the delicate lines of her face, the kind of symmetry that makes you pause when she laughs or pulls her hair back or stares you down like she's about to call you on your bullshit. It's in her high cheekbones. The faint freckle under her left eye I've known about since we were kids. In those lips, full, bitten raw from how she holds her bottom lip between her teeth when she's anxious. In her eyes, when they're not avoiding mine. They hold entire storms.

This isn't new. I've always known the truth. Always fucking felt that pull in my gut when she was near. I never let myself sit with that weight for too long. But now. Now I'm really looking at her. And fuck me if the hit doesn't land hard. All of it. The softness, the strength. The kind of beauty that's always made her dangerous.

To me, anyway.

"You good?" I ask, stepping inside.

She shifts slightly on the bed.

I don't wait for an answer. I move across the room, toe off my shoes, and stretch out beside her. My body sinks into the mattress, the warmth of her right beside me, close enough to touch.

Her eyes stay on the ceiling as her hands rest flat on her stomach, fingers lightly tangled. A quiet stillness lingers in her.

I watch her for a second longer. The way her lashes shadow her skin. The shape of her mouth. All those soft features I've always known but never let myself really look at.

"Quinn," I say, voice low.

I reach out, fingers brushing her chin, and tilt her face toward me. Her skin's warm under my touch. Soft. Familiar.

My gaze drags over hers, catching the subtle flicker in her eyes as they trace mine. She's reading me, same way she always has.

Without warning, she shifts. Rolls toward me. Her thigh brushes my leg, and her hair falls across the pillow in a way that makes the air hard to fucking breathe.

"I've been meaning to ask you about Theo," she says.

I roll to face her, propping my head up on my hand.

"What about Theo?" I ask, but my focus is still caught on her mouth.

She hesitates, only for a second. After a beat, her voice drops, quiet. "He's different now."

My brows twitch. "Different good, or different bad?"

She lets out a shaky breath. "Neither. Just... different."

I wait, letting her find the right words.

"I remember when he used to hide behind those awful hoodies," she says. "Used to pull the strings so tight you could barely see his face. Always had his head down, always quiet unless we were alone."

I nod. "Yeah. He was all shadows back then."

"But now he's loud, playful, and charming as hell. And he knows it. A confidence lives in him that never existed before."

I smile faintly. "That confidence is mostly bullshit."

Quinn lets out a soft laugh, but a trace of sadness lingers in the sound.

"I guess I didn't expect him to be the one who changed the most," she says. "Not in that way."

I shift a little, lying flat on the bed, staring at the ceiling for a second.

"He rose." I keep going even though I feel her eyes on me. "He doubled down after Bianca died. Made her this unspoken promise to never dim. Never apologize for who he is. He started showing the world every fucking loud, brilliant, messy piece of him. All of it."

She doesn't interrupt.

"And I... I caved inward," I admit. "He exploded out, and I folded in. We flipped."

A beat of silence stretches between us.

"I think about that a lot," she says. "How grief hits everyone differently."

"Theo wears joy like armor," I murmur. "Every joke, every flirt, every dumbass comment that comes out of his mouth, all of it's covering the same shit. He's still bleeding too. I see the truth, even when he thinks I don't."

Quinn's hand finds mine.

"You still seem the same Nate to me," she says. "Although you don't throw around those cocky pick up lines anymore."

With one brow raised, I glance over at her.

A smirk forms on her mouth. "But I guess you don't need to. Being a rockstar God and all. Must be nice that the name does the work for you now, huh?"

I bark out a laugh. "You think I've gone soft?"

"I think you've gone lazy," she shoots back, eyes sparkling. "Or maybe you've forgotten how."

I roll onto my side, facing her, a slow grin pulling at my mouth. "Careful, Quinn. You say something like that, you're practically begging for it."

She arches a brow. "Then go on. Hit me with your best. Let's see what Rockstar Nate's still got."

I pause.

And fuck... my mind goes blank. Because it's been years since I had to pull one out. Years since I felt the urge to impress anyone. Everything's been easy and meaningless. But this... Her... There's weight here. History. It's different.

My smirk falters just a touch.

She notices. "You really are out of practice."

"Give me a sec." I rub my jaw. "I've been busy headlining stadiums and avoiding emotional growth."

"Tragic."

"I've still got it," I mutter.

She grins. "Prove it."

I narrow my eyes, before letting them drop to her mouth, and back to her eyes again.

"You know," I say slowly, dropping my voice. "I was gonna tell you that your smile's always been my favorite curve on your body..."

She holds her breath.

"But then you showed up in those tights," I continue, "and I completely lost my train of thought."

Quinn's laugh explodes out of her. She swats my arm, shaking her head.

"Oh my God," she says, breathless. "That was awful."

"That was brilliant."

"That was desperate."

I grin, soaking in the sound of her laugh, the way that sound loosens something in my chest.

"Maybe," I say. "But it worked."

"Yeah," she murmurs. "It kinda did."

I watch her laugh fade into something quieter. Her eyes linger on mine, and I swear the whole fucking room shifts.

Her fingers are still brushing against mine.

I tilt my head slightly, eyes locked on hers.

"So..." I say. "Does that mean I can kiss you?"

Her lips part, only a little. That spark in her eyes doesn't waver. If anything, the fire deepens.

"When have you ever had to ask?" she whispers.

That's all it takes.

I move before I can second-guess myself, before the weight of everything we've been through has a chance to sink its claws in and pull me back. My hand buries in her hair, fingers twisting through those soft strands I've thought about too many fucking times, and I kiss her.

The kiss isn't gentle. No room exists for that. Our mouths crash, tongues sliding, the kind that scrapes something raw out of your chest and dares you to survive the force of it. Years of tension, years of want, years of everything we've never said spilling into this one brutal moment.

She groans against my mouth and the sound nearly ends me. Her hands grip my shirt, fingers fisting tight as if she's holding on for dear life. Our bodies twist together, mouths locked, breath ragged, hands tearing at fabric and skin.

She pulls me closer, grinding up against my jeans, and I register the way her body arches, begging for more. This isn't slow or sweet. This is fucking urgent.

Her top rides up as I shove my hand beneath it, palm dragging across the soft skin of her stomach, fingers searching for every place that makes her gasp. She's burning. Her whole body hums beneath mine, wound tight, ready to snap.

Her legs wrap around my waist, hips grinding against the thick outline of my cock. Every movement of her pussy against the rough denim is enough to make me grit my teeth. I've been hard since the second I walked in and saw her on that bed in those fucking tights, legs stretched out, body soft and waiting. The way they clung to her thighs, her ass, her cunt—fuck, she had to know what that did to me.

My cock throbs beneath the restraint of my jeans, tight and unforgiving, and when she moves again, pressing herself against the hard ridge, she lets out this soft, helpless moan that cuts through me. That sound. That fucking sound. The noise strikes somewhere deep and primal. It's the kind of sound I chase. The kind I've dragged from other girls before but never like this. Never with her.

I slow everything down.

Grip her hips. Hold her still.

Her eyes snap open, breath catching as I stare down at her.

"Don't move unless I tell you to," I murmur, my voice low, steady, full of warning.

She freezes and obeys like a good fucking girl.

I press my forehead to hers, breath ghosting over her lips, not giving her another kiss yet. Only holding her in place. Letting the tension stretch, coil, burn.

"You still sure?"

She nods fast, eyes wild.

"Words," I growl, tightening my hold on her waist.

"Yes." It's barely a whisper. "Fucking hell, yes."

I smirk. That mouth—so quick, so fucking sharp—and now she can't even form a sentence.

"Then you do exactly what I say." I drop my head to her neck, lips brushing her skin, letting her feel the heat of my breath as I speak. "You've heard the shit they say, haven't you?" My voice is all gravel now. "Those rumors back in the day."

She tenses, ever so slightly, but doesn't answer.

"The ones about how I fuck. How I don't rush. How I don't stop until the girl comes completely undone."

"You're such a cocky bastard," she mutters, trying to cover the way her thighs squeeze around me.

I grin against her throat, teeth scraping over her pulse.

"No," I breathe. "I'm a patient bastard. And you're about to learn the fucking difference."

I drag my mouth up the column of her throat, tongue tracing the heat of her skin. When I reach the spot right beneath her jaw, I suck hard, letting my teeth scrape over that delicate flesh until the full-body shiver rolls through her. Her nails bite through the cotton of my shirt as she arches, desperate for more contact. Her hips twitch beneath me, trying to grind against the thick, hard press of my cock still trapped in my jeans.

"Did I say you could move?" My voice scrapes low in my throat, filled with warning.

She freezes. Every muscle goes tight beneath me. Her breath catches, chest lifting fast. Her heart pounds beneath me. The rhythm is wild and frantic. She doesn't speak, doesn't move again.

That's better.

I sit back on my heels, still between her thighs, eyes dragging over her body. Her tits heave beneath the thin fabric of her top, nipples hard and straining. Her thighs are clenched tight, trying to chase friction, but I don't let her have it.

She watches me as I reach for the hem of her top, and pull it up over her head, tossing it to the floor without a word. Her bra comes next. Black lace. Thin straps. Useless fabric that's in the fucking way. I unclasp the clip at the front, pulling it away to reveal the soft swell of her tits.

"Hands above your head," I command her. "Palms flat against the headboard."

She moves instantly, obeying without a word. Her arms rise, trembling as she stretches them above her head. Nails scrape across the wood as she settles into place, fingers splayed wide, body taut with anticipation. She's wide open. Exposed. Exactly the way I want her.

"Good girl."

I lower my head, tongue flicking over one nipple before I take it into my mouth. I suck hard, lips dragging, teeth teasing the sensitive peak until her whole body jolts. A sharp gasp escapes her, her back arching. Her hands remain against the headboard but everything else is screaming for more.

I shift to the other breast, let my teeth catch the tip before biting down hard enough to make her flinch. Another broken moan slips free from her mouth. She writhes beneath me, trying to grind up against my chest, desperate for friction.

I flatten my palm against her stomach, pinning her hips to the mattress.

"You move one more time and I'll stop."

She freezes, breath caught between a moan and a plea. Her thighs press together. She's losing control already and I've barely touched her.

I trail kisses down her stomach, my wet mouth dragging heat over every inch of exposed skin. Her body quivers with each pass, soft whimpers slipping out with every exhale.

Her tights cling to her hips, stretched tight over her cunt. They are already soaked through, the outline of her pussy clear beneath the thin fabric. It's fucking perfect. Swollen. Desperate. Ready.

I kiss the top of her thigh before pressing my mouth right over the spot I know she's aching for. The fabric's damp against my lips, and her body jerks beneath me.

"Fuck," I growl, dragging my mouth across the heat of her, tongue working over the wet patch. "You're dripping."

A helpless whimper spills from her lips as she tries to lift her hips into my mouth, chasing more.

"Did I say you could move?"

She sighs again, a breathless sound of frustration and want. Her fingers curl against the headboard. But she goes still.

Right where I want her. Ready to be undone. One filthy inch at a time.

I hook my fingers into the waistband of her tights and drag them down her legs, letting the fabric catch on her skin enough to make her squirm. Every inch I reveal makes me harder. Her panties are completely soaked, clinging to her cunt, a dark patch of arousal spreading between her legs.

Fuck. I tear them without care, the ruined lace snapping in my grip before I toss them over my shoulder like they were never worth a second thought. She's laid out in front of me, flushed and glistening, her pussy wet and swollen, dripping for my mouth.

Her thighs fall open on instinct, a silent plea without a single word. I spread her wider so I can take in the full fucking view.

And fuck, the second I see her cunt clenching as though it already knows what's missing, I hiss through my teeth. My body's trying to hold back but there's no controlling this kind of hunger.

"Shit."

All I want is to bury my tongue in her until she screams.

But I don't rush.

I start with soft kisses along the inside of her thighs. Long, slow kisses that go nowhere near where she needs me. Her legs shake, hands gripping the headboard harder. I watch her face. Every time I get close and don't give her what she wants, her mouth falls open, her brows pinch together.

I'm breaking her.

Good.

I drag my tongue up the inside of her thigh, stopping just short of her pussy. The heat radiating off her skin is unreal, pulsing with how worked up she already is. Her body flinches, hips twitching, breath stalling in her throat.

I press another kiss higher before dragging my tongue along the crease where her thigh meets her pussy. Enough to make her squirm. Enough to watch her suffer.

She lets out this shaky little sound that's half moan, half protest.

I smirk against her skin. She's already losing it, and I haven't even started.

I shift lower, letting my breath ghost over her pussy. Then I give her the lightest touch. The tip of my tongue grazing her clit. Barely a whisper of contact.

Her whole body jolts. Her legs tremble, breath catching so hard it turns into a choked gasp.

One light flick of my tongue and her body comes alive. She's so fucking sensitive.

Every flick of my tongue, every breath I push across her clit, makes her hips jerk. She can't control herself. Her whole body's strung tight, teetering on a thread that's fraying more every second I keep her waiting. She's begging for more with every breath.

Finally, I fucking give her what she needs.

My tongue dips down, finding her clit, and flicks fast. The sound that tears from her throat. Fuck me. It's broken and breathless, scraped raw from somewhere too deep to even fake. The kind of sound that hits me right in the chest and drags every last scrap of control straight out of my body.

I want more. I need more.

I do it again, slower this time. Drag my tongue over her clit in a slow wet circle. I don't blink. Don't look away. I want to see what I do to her.

She's flushed from head to toe, eyes fluttering, lips parted, chest rising too fast. Her whole body jolts again. That sweet little cunt pulses under my mouth as if it's already coming, and I've barely fucking started.

And fuck, something hits me low in the gut. The weight lodges under my ribs, digging in, fucking with my head in a way I didn't ask for.

Whatever this pull is, it's not going away. Quinn was always the fantasy. A girl who got under my skin and stayed put. She was always out of reach. Untouchable.

But now... now she's spread open for me, soaked and shaking, her pussy in my mouth, her moans tearing through every shred of control I've got left. Every filthy thought I ever had about her back then, every time I stroked my cock thinking about her as a desperate, horny teenager, hard as fuck and drowning in fantasies I knew I'd never touch—none of it come close to this. Nothing I imagined even fucking compares. And I can't stop watching her now, writhing under my tongue, gasping my name without even knowing she's doing it... there's no part of me that isn't hers already.

Her head tips back. Her lips fall open. She whimpers again, a soft, shattered noise that makes my cock ache so hard it's almost unbearable. Her whole body moves with mine now, chasing every flick of my tongue, every lazy circle over her clit.

I suck her clit. A firm pull between my lips, tongue circling the swollen nub, and her whole body arches, hips lifting clean off the mattress before I slam my hands down and hold her in place.

She's so fucking close. I feel it in the way her pussy pulses against my tongue. Her breath's all over the place, stuttering in her throat, chest rising too fast to steady. Her thighs keep trying to lock around my head, desperate to hold me there, but I keep prying them apart, forcing her open like I own her body now and she fucking knows it.

I drag my tongue up through her soaked folds again. Her pussy throbs, pulsing hard, slick running down onto the sheets. The sounds coming out of her are raw little gasps and whimpers that don't even sound human anymore.

She's climbing. Too fucking fast.

I suck her clit again, harder this time, tongue flicking just right, and her whole body jolts. Her legs shake. Her moans grow louder.

Another second and she'll break.

I stop.

Pull back barely enough for the air to hit her dripping cunt, the sudden cool against all that swollen heat making her gasp. Her hips jolt, a sharp, helpless twitch before she freezes, chest heaving, body shaking with the effort it takes not to chase what I stole from her.

She's right fucking there, and I don't let her fall.

Not yet.

I wait, watching the tension ripple through her stomach, the way her legs tremble and her pussy clenches again, empty and desperate.

Good.

I lean back in and take my time. Drag my tongue along the length of her folds, collecting every drop she's given me. Her thighs twitch as I press a kiss right beneath her clit, before swirling my tongue around the swollen bud, keeping the pressure light, teasing. She moans, breath caught in her throat, legs struggling to stay open as I lick her again.

I spit on her. Let it drip. Watch it mix with everything she's already leaking. Then I suck her clit deep into my mouth, hold it there.

She cries out. The sound breaks halfway through. Her legs jerk. Her stomach pulls tight.

She's shaking now, breathless, lost in the moment. She's almost at the edge again, seconds from coming.

I pull away once more.

She lets out a strangled cry, voice cracking. "Fucking hell, Nate, stop teasing me."

I smirk and press my mouth to the inside of her thigh instead, kiss the spot slowly, before dragging my tongue along her skin while she writhes. Because I'm not here to give her a quick orgasm. I'm not here to let her come easy.

I want to build the hunger. Slowly. I want to take her apart one pulse at a time. Hold her right at the edge and make her body burn for release until she can't breathe. I want her aching in places she didn't know could ache. I want her to come so hard she doesn't only feel it in her pussy, she carries the shock in her chest, her spine, her fucking soul.

She's going to remember this. Not because I made her scream. But because I made her wait.

Her entire body is a fucking livewire, wired so tight she's shaking beneath my hands. I want her begging without shame.

Her hips lift again.

"Please," she chokes.

I smirk and then I give it to her.

I press my mouth back to her clit and suck hard. No teasing. No restraint. Just full, relentless pressure. My tongue flicks fast and ruthless, dragging across the swollen nerve again and again until she cries out, her body jolting beneath me.

I slide two fingers inside her, slow at first, only to take in the way she grabs at me. She gasps. Then I curl them. Perfectly placed. Up and forward, pressing deep into the spot I already know will undo her. And when I register that spongy swell, I fuck her there. Fast. Rough. My fingers pump hard, curling with every thrust while my tongue stays locked on her clit, working her over with a pace that doesn't give her a second to breathe.

She fucking breaks all at once.

Her body arches so high it leaves the mattress, a scream ripping from her throat. Her pussy clamps down around my fingers like a vice, pulsing in violent, rhythmic spasms. She's coming so hard her entire body shakes, her hands clawing at the sheets.

It tears through her. Wave after wave after wave.

Not one orgasm. Not two. But a constant, unending crash that hits again and again as I keep curling my fingers, keep sucking her clit until she's sobbing from how hard and how good the release is.

She doesn't moan my name, she screams it. Her legs go limp. Her whole body trembles. And still, she pulses around me.

This is the hottest fucking thing I've ever seen.

I don't stop until I feel her give out. Until her back drops to the bed, thighs twitching.

I slow my touch. Ease my fingers out of her before leaning back, wiping the back of my hand across my chin. My mouth's soaked with her, my jaw aches, and my cock is straining so hard it hurts, but fuck, I've never been this wired in my life.

She doesn't speak. Doesn't move. She just lies there. Chest rising hard, eyes glazed and unfocused.

Exactly how I wanted her. Exactly how I imagined her all those years ago. Only now, she's mine.

And she knows it. Every fucking inch of her knows it.

CHAPTER 24

Quinn

My entire body won't stop trembling. Every nerve is alive, charged, stretched thin from the intense orgasm he just tore out of me with his mouth and those fucking fingers. It wasn't gentle. It wasn't sweet, it was brutal. Fucking relentless. The kind of climax that doesn't fade quietly but crashes through you, tears you apart, and leaves you gasping for more.

My heart slams against my ribs in a wild and unforgiving rhythm. My thighs are soaked. I'm still twitching, everything inside me pulled tight and still sparking. And he's kneeling between my legs, shirt clinging to his body, chest heaving. His mouth is slick with me, lips red from the effort it took to ruin me. His jaw clenches when I meet his stare.

Those fucking dark eyes are locked on me, devouring everything I am.

I try to hold his gaze, try to stay with him, but it's too much. I'm not shaking from what he did to my body. I'm shaking because I want more. This was never just need. It's something else. Something heavier that's been waiting years to take shape.

My body screams for him. My skin begs for more. There is nothing careful left in me, and this time, I'm not running from it.

"Come here," I whisper.

He yanks his shirt over his head, tossing it aside without taking his eyes off me. Then he crawls up the bed. The muscles in his arms shift as he cages me in, his body heat wrapping around me before he even touches me. My hands move on instinct, gliding up his chest, feeling the ridges of each flexed muscle. His pulse pounds hard under my fingertips. His breath is shallow, dragging through parted lips as he stares down at me.

I reach for his jeans, unbuttoning them with shaking fingers. The zipper slides down with a sound that's too loud in the silence between us. His cock is already hard, thick, straining for release. I slide my hand inside. His whole body reacts. A sharp inhale. A broken breath.

"Quinn..." It's a warning and a plea in one.

I stroke him once, and watch as it takes him apart. His head falls forward, eyes squeezed shut, jaw clenched. His arms tremble where they're braced above me, forehead dipping until his lips brush mine. Close, but not kissing me yet. Not giving in. Not fully.

"You gonna fuck me now?" I ask. "Or are you gonna stare at me all night and pretend this isn't happening?"

He smirks. That cocky, smart-ass smirk that has always turned my insides molten. It makes my breath hitch. And in that moment, I already know the answer.

"Fuck," he mutters, pulling back far enough to meet my eyes. "I don't have a condom. It's in the other room."

I should be the responsible one and tell him to get it. But the way he's looking at me, chest rising, skin flushed, jaw tight, I'm not going to miss this.

"I'm on birth control," I whisper. "When was the last time you got tested?"

His brow furrows. A flicker of hesitation touches his features.

"Last month," he says. "Kit always makes us get tested. Me and Theo..."

He trails off. He doesn't need to say the rest. I know what it means. They're the only two who still fuck groupies.

"But I'm clean," he finishes. "She still makes me get tested even though I've never fucked anyone bare before."

"Ever?" I ask, the word breaking through the quiet.

He nods, still above me. One arm braced beside my head, the other trembling slightly beneath the strain of holding himself up. His cock lies heavy on my stomach, glistening, flushed. His eyes drag across my face, searching, waiting, his jaw tight enough to crack. Every inch of him is wired with control, with restraint, with something he hasn't said out loud. But I feel it.

He's waiting for me to say it. To give him permission. To let him have this, have me.

I swallow. My fingers slide up his chest again, and I give the smallest nod. That's all it takes.

He pushes off the bed. The muscles in his chest flex as he drags his jeans down his legs. He kicks them away, his boxers with them.

He's standing there.

Naked.

And it's fucking breathtaking.

Every part of him is carved and solid, his abs, his chest rising and falling in shallow, uneven breaths. His cock stands thick and ready, swollen and leaking at the tip. I can't stop staring. He's so fucking perfect.

He watches my face as he crawls back onto the bed, his knees pushing mine wider as he moves over me again. His hands roam my body with purpose, dragging over my skin, memorizing every part of me all over again. His breath brushes my jaw as his body settles into mine, every inch of him burning against me.

"Fuck," he mutters. "You have no idea how long I've fucking wanted this."

He dips his head, mouth pressing against the hollow of my throat, and I register the weight of him everywhere. His cock drags through my folds; it makes me ache all over again.

He lifts his head, his eyes meeting mine.

He lines the head of his cock to my entrance and pushes in slowly, stretching me until I swear I can't take any more. My body arches as I take in every fucking inch of him sliding in deeper. The pressure is insane, a brutal invasion that burns in the best fucking way. I breathe through it until he bottoms out, cock buried to the base, and everything goes still.

His hips press flush against mine. His hands tighten on my thighs, the tendons in his forearms pulled tight. He doesn't move, doesn't even breathe at first. He stares down at me.

Watching.

I see something flicker behind his eyes. It's not only heat or lust, it's something dangerous that makes my heart slam hard against my ribs.

My pussy clenches around him, desperate for him to move, but he holds still, only watching.

"Fuck, Q," he breathes. "You feel so fucking good I can't even think straight."

He pulls out slow, dragging every inch from my body until only the thick tip of his cock remains inside me. The stretch lingers, heat coiling tight in my belly, my walls clenching with the loss. Then he sinks back in with a deep, guttural groan that vibrates through his chest. The sound alone makes my pussy tighten, makes my breath catch.

My head falls back against the pillow, lips parted, a sharp gasp slipping out as I feel him fill me again. His thick and hard and fucking perfect. Every nerve in my body lights up. I swear I can feel the shape of him inside me, every vein, every inch, pressing deep against places no one's ever reached.

His hips meet mine with a soft slap of skin, and still he doesn't rush.

His gaze drops.

He watches his cock slide back in, eyes dark with something feral. Watching my cunt take him. Watching the way I open for him, stretch for him, throb around every inch.

His jaw clenches. His breath stutters.

"Fuck, Quinn... I want to rail you so hard you forget your fucking name." His fingers squeeze my hips tighter. "But if I do, I'm gonna blow the second I start. You feel that fucking good."

He drags his cock out again, before drives back in harder. My whole body jolts, thighs tightening around his hips.

I can't stop watching him.

He's fucking breathtaking. Beautiful. All muscle, his jaw tight, veins thick in his forearms as they hold my hips. His abs flex with every thrust, the lines of his body catching the light. His mouth hangs open, breath coming hard, the edge of restraint twitching in his throat.

His cock slides into me again, deeper, harder this time, stealing the breath from my lungs. The stretch of him is too much and not enough, the kind of pressure that builds and builds until it takes over everything.

He groans through his teeth, every muscle in his body stretched tight with restraint. The sounds he makes aren't soft. They're guttural. Primal. As if he's right on the edge of breaking and holding himself there to punish us both.

"You've got no fucking idea what you're doing to me." His voice is rough, torn from somewhere deep inside him. His hands grip my hips, his pace never speeding up. Every thrust hits deep, heavy, bruising.

"Touch yourself," he commands.

My heart stutters.

"I want to feel your pussy squeeze around my cock while you rub that pretty clit."

A noise rips from my throat. A broken, desperate sound I've never made before. I nod without speaking, because words are useless when your body is burning this hard.

My hand shakes as I reach down between us. My fingers find the aching bundle of nerves already swollen and throbbing from the way he's been fucking me.

The first touch makes my eyes slam shut. Pressure coils hard behind my ribs. My pussy clenches so tight around him that he lets out a strangled groan, hips stuttering for half a second before he grips my waist harder and starts fucking into me again.

"Don't stop," he growls. "Play with that clit for me."

He watches everything. His eyes burn into the place where my fingers work myself and his cock stretches me open. I'm soaked. My slick coats my fingers, dripping between my thighs. My body is a livewire. Every nerve ending is lit up. The tension builds so fast it knocks the breath out of my lungs.

I moan louder as my hand moves faster. The orgasm is already clawing at me, violent and sharp, ready to break. My whole body is braced, back arched, fingers shaking, breath catching in my chest.

"That's it," he rasps. "Come on, Q. Let me feel it. Fucking come while I fuck you."

The pressure builds fast, sharp, and vicious. It crawls up my spine and coils behind my ribs, heavy and hot, until it's all I can take in. My clit throbs under my fingers.

Then it happens.

Everything breaks at once.

The orgasm rips through me so hard my vision blurs. My mouth opens in a scream I can't hold in if I tried. It tears out of me, high and frantic. My pussy clenches in tight rhythmic spasms. He swears under his breath, hips faltering for a second before slamming back into me.

My legs lock around his waist, holding him there, needing him deeper.

My fingers jerk against my clit, twitching against the slick, swollen nub as the pleasure spirals out, fast and cruel. The muscles in my stomach seize. My nipples ache. Every nerve is wide open and screaming.

He keeps fucking me through it.

His cock drives into me again and again. Every thrust sends another jolt of pleasure through my oversensitive body.

I can't think. I can't speak.

All I can do is take it.

I'm dripping. Soaking. The sheets are wet under my ass. His cock slides through it all, thick and perfect, hitting that place inside me that makes me see stars. My moans fall into breathless gasps. My body locks up again, tighter this time.

He growls something I can't even register over the sound of my own moans. He fucks me through the orgasm, until I'm twitching, overstimulated, wrecked beyond recognition.

And even then, I still want more. Because nothing has ever felt this good.

He pulls out, leaving me trembling. My body is desperate with everything he's taken from me. There's no warning, no pause. Just his hands grabbing my hips and flipping me over.

My cheek hits the pillow. His hand fists in my hair, dragging my head back until my spine bows. I gasp.

His hand slides lower. Rough palm on the curve of my ass. Fingers slipping down, parting me without hesitation. I suck in a breath as my body braces, ready to take him where he fucked me yesterday.

Instead, his hand moves down lower. Spreading me open until the swollen heat of my pussy is bared to him completely.

A growl tears from his throat.

"Fucking hell," he mutters.

I whimper as his fingers stroke once, teasing my entrance. After that, the head of his cock presses where I need him most. Not against my ass but pressed to my pussy.

He groans. "Fucking hell, you're so fucking wet."

He holds himself there for a beat. Long enough to make me ache, to make me beg again if he wanted. His cock teases the swollen entrance of my pussy, the tip nudging in enough to tease me with the stretch.

"You want this?" he asks, voice filthy. "You want my cock again?"

"Yes," I breathe out.

He slams into me.

There's no easing in. No building up. Only the brutal thrust of his cock filling me in one hard, unforgiving drive. My whole body jolts forward. My breath leaves me in a broken scream.

He fucks me hard. The sound of skin on skin is deafening. Wet. Loud. Feral.

He leans forward, slipping his arm tight around my stomach, lifting me in one smooth, brutal motion. My back crashes against his chest, slick with sweat, his skin burning against mine. His cock never leaves me. He's still buried, fucking me hard. I gasp, head falling back onto his shoulder as he forces me upright on his cock, speared open and held there like I belong to him.

His breath fans hot against the shell of my ear, as his hand slides around, rough and possessive, gripping the front of my throat. Not enough to hurt, enough to claim. To make sure I know I'm his.

"You've already come," he growls in my ear. "Now I'm gonna take what I fucking need."

He thrusts up, hard and deep, and I moan so loud it tears from my throat raw. My hands scramble for something to hold onto, but there's nothing—only him. Only this. His cock slamming into me again and again with a pace that's feral and possessive. No rhythm, no mercy, nothing but pure, filthy intent.

"I swear to God," he hisses against my ear, fucking me harder. "You come again before I do, and I'll bend you over and start all over again."

He shifts behind me. His legs spread wider, his thrusts deeper now, grinding into the place that makes my entire body seize up. His hand stays locked at my throat, not choking, but holding, owning, reminding me that I'm his to use.

My moans are helpless and broken. There's no pride left in me. No shame. Only need.

His breath scorches the shell of my ear, each brutal thrust tearing a sound from my throat, a half-moan, half whimper.

"Look at you," he breathes. "Fucked out. All from my cock."

His hand slides from my throat, trailing down to my chest. He grabs my breast hard, his palm rough, his fingers pinching my nipple. I cry out, the sting blurring with the pleasure building from the inside.

"You love this," he whispers. "You love being used. Being mine. Say it."

"Yes," I gasp. "Fuck, yes."

He laughs behind me. "Good girl."

He thrusts into me again, harder, deeper, driving everything else out of my mind. Over and over, I'm falling and he's the only thing keeping me tethered to this world.

His body presses tighter against mine, his skin slick with sweat, his breath dragging ragged across the side of my neck. Every thrust rocks me forward, my breath catching, my thoughts scattering.

His hand moves lower, skimming down my stomach, lighting every nerve on fire. I can't breathe or think. My thighs are wide open, aching, slick, trembling. I should care, should be embarrassed by how much I want him. But I'm not. I want him deeper. I want him to tear the rest of me apart.

"You're shaking. Fucking desperate. Say it." He growls into my ear, voice thick with need. "Say your cock filled pussy wants to fucking come again."

And I can't deny it. Not with the way my body is already unraveling again. Not with the way he knows exactly how to break me open and keep going until I forget my own name.

The only sound I manage is a whimper. He laughs. It's dark and breathless and his hand is between my legs, fingers moving over my clit while his cock drives into me with a ruthless rhythm.

"I'll let you come on my cock," he growls, dragging his mouth along my neck. "I'm gonna fill you so fucking deep you'll feel it tomorrow. You'll feel me when you walk. When you sit. Every time you close your legs, you'll remember this. How hard I fucked you and how you begged for it."

His fingers flick my clit.

"That's what I want," he mutters darkly. "To know that when you touch yourself tomorrow, when your fingers slide over this swollen little clit, you'll remember exactly how it felt. My hands. My mouth. My cock. All of it. And you'll fucking cry because you'll know nothing you do will ever come close to this."

He presses in harder, circles tightening. My mouth opens on a gasp I can't catch.

I break.

The orgasm hits so hard I scream. My body clamps down, spasming around his cock. He fucks me through it, harder, filthier, until I'm gasping.

"That's it," he breathes. "You're mine now."

My legs shake under me. My entire body is twitching, destroyed and yet I still want more. I don't even recognize the sound that leaves my throat.

He leans forward, dragging his mouth down my neck, teeth grazing before his lips close hard around my skin. One mark. Then another. And another. Each one darker than the last until I'm left bruised and burning everywhere his mouth claims me.

He thrusts, sudden and deep, and I feel his whole body lock behind me. Every ridge of his abs strains tight against my back, his chest heaving with the force of it. His thighs drive hard into the backs of mine as his hand slides back to my throat, tightening just enough to trap me in that perfect place between submission and madness.

He comes with a sound I'll never forget. A broken groan, torn from somewhere deep inside him. His body locks, cock buried to the hilt, pulsing as he spills inside me. Hot. Thick. Endless. My pussy clenches greedily around every drop, every throb of him setting off aftershocks that leave my legs trembling.

He yanks me flush against his chest, holding me there while his cock drives into me through every clenching wave. Each thrust drags out the high, every inch of him claiming more as he empties inside me. His teeth bite into the curve of my neck. The sting burns through the haze, and then he seals it with his mouth, sucking until the blood surges to the surface, until the pain blooms. I cry out, my head falling back against his shoulder, body trembling.

And still he doesn't let go.

He licks the spot he just marked. His tongue dragging over the sting until I'm panting again, the heat between my legs reigniting even though I'm already spent. He kisses the side of my neck. Softer this time. But the edge is still there. The hunger, the claim, that possessive, filthy growl still buried under his breath.

"Mine," he whispers, voice rough against my skin.

And fuck, there's no doubt in my mind.

I am his. I always fucking was.

His arms stay locked around me. One across my stomach, the other still cradling my throat. His body pressed into every inch of mine, keeping me there, keeping me his.

And for the first time in years, I feel complete.

Even if I know it won't last. Even if we break apart again tomorrow.

Right now, at this moment, he's mine. And I'm his.

Because now I know exactly what it feels like to be fucked by Nate Reynolds until I come so hard I forget my own fucking name.

And I'll never stop chasing it.

CHAPTER 25

Theo

The pizza's cold. Limp and greasy, but I'm still shoving it into my mouth. I'm not starving. I just don't have the energy to care.

I'm stretched out on the couch, half-dead and sauce-stained, one foot hooked on the coffee table, the other planted flat on the floor. The pizza box sits open on the table, grease bleeding through the cardboard, crusts scattered across the lid in lazy disarray, each one a sad little tombstone for my self-respect.

The cheese has gone rubbery. Each bite clings, stretching between my fingers and my face as though the stringy mess is trying to escape the slow descent into hell.

The TV's on.

Real Housewives of Somewhere Plastic.

Poppy and Xander's favourite disaster. I keep the noise running to pretend they're here. Screaming women, flinging martinis and accusations, twisting themselves into verbal gymnastics over who slept with whose husband during what charity gala. One of them hurls a diamond-encrusted shoe and I don't even blink.

Because the rest of the house... yeah, that's not quiet either.

Somewhere down the hall, Nate's busy fucking Quinn as if the world's ending. Again... Loudly.

There's nothing subtle about it. The walls might as well be made of tissue paper.

I chew slowly because what else am I meant to do while our past catches fire in the other room.

I pretend the screeching blonde on screen is why my head's fucked. That it's the show unraveling me, not the sound of Quinn moaning Nate's name three doors down.

It's easier to lie to myself.

Easier than admitting that one night, back before Bianca, when Quinn and I sat on the porch at some party, both drunk enough to be honest.

She was talking. I don't even remember what about. I just remember thinking what would it feel like to touch her.

I'd never wanted to touch anyone. Not back in those days. Not after what happened to me. But for a split second, I did.

And now Nate's in that room doing all the things I never let myself imagine.

I toss another crust onto the lid right as the silence finally hits. Miracle of the fucking year. The quiet presses in now, unnatural, eerie after what felt like hours of Quinn sounding like she was auditioning for a porno, and Nate. Fuck, those moans of his weren't the usual kind either. They were guttural. The kind a man makes when he's not just getting laid. He's being fucking exorcised.

I let the silence settle into the space as I wipe my fingers on my pants because the napkins are all the way across the room and I'm too fucking emotionally drained right now to move.

I glance over as Nate strolls in, all smug, hair wet from the shower. His sweatpants hang low. Chest bare and unfairly fucking perfect. A towel draped around his neck like he thinks he's shooting for the next Calvin Klein campaign instead of just blowing out Quinn's back in the next room.

Of course he looks good. Smug bastard.

He walks into the kitchen and yanks the fridge open, staring into it like he's genuinely surprised the steaks didn't cook themselves.

He grabs two beers, pops both caps off, then strolls over and drops onto the couch beside me. Without a word, he hands one over and tosses the towel onto the floor.

"Sorry, man," he mutters, reaching for a slice of cold pizza. "I realize we were supposed to have steaks tonight, but—"

"But you got distracted," I say, lifting the beer in mock salute.

He smiles.

Not the fake shit he throws on stage. Not the dead-eyed version he uses when cameras flash or fans scream his name. This one's real. Slow. Lopsided. The kind of smile that doesn't fight its way through him first.

And fuck, it's been a long time since I've seen that.

His eyes spark with something that looks a hell of a lot like peace.

That used to be him. Before the world fucking shattered and grief took to us with a sledgehammer.

But now. Now I'm watching that version crawl its way back through the cracks. One breath at a time.

It's Quinn. She's doing that.

She's reaching into places he swore were dead and pulling the pieces out.

She's bringing him back. To himself. To us.

"Thought I might have to call the cops," I mutter, smirking over the rim of my beer. "With all the screaming going on in that room."

Nate takes a bite of pizza and grins around the mouthful. "You're one to talk. You treat sex like a fucking competition. Half the time, I swear you're only trying to see who can make them scream louder."

"Oh, please." I scoff, waving pizza crust in his direction. "That's not a competition. That's a public service."

He laughs, mouth still full. "Honestly... I'm shocked you didn't come knocking. Moaning girls are usually your bat signal."

I lean back, take another sip of beer, and nod solemnly. "My dick and I had a very serious talk. He wanted to help. I told him no."

Nate laughs and some fucked-up part of me loosens at the sound.

"Why didn't you?" he asks, licking sauce off his thumb like we're not talking about the girl he's always wanted to fuck.

I pause. Not because I'm unsure, but giving the truth its space.

"I know you've wanted that since the day she shut you down with all those pick up lines," I say, tilting my head toward him. "Don't bother lying. You smiled through every rejection."

That grin spreads again. All teeth, mischief, and yeah, the nostalgia. He remembers.

"Was it everything you imagined?" I ask.

Nate leans back, pizza still in hand, eyes on the ceiling like it's got answers he never thought to ask.

"You know, back then, my teenage brain had it all mapped out. Quick. Messy. Loud." He huffs a laugh. "Probably would've lasted all of thirty seconds and still thought I'd nailed it."

He glances over, and something shifts behind his eyes.

"I wouldn't have known how to fuck her like that. Wouldn't have known how to pull an orgasm out of her so hard she'd forget her own name." His voice dips. "Back then, I would've just screwed the whole thing up. So yeah. I'm glad she shut me down."

I nod, lips twitching. "Look at you. All grown up and sentimental. Do we get you a little trophy? Or perhaps a condom wrapper with 'well done' stamped across the front?"

He snorts, head tipping back against the couch as he lets out a short laugh. "Fuck off."

But he's smiling, and he doesn't deny a thing.

After that, the room goes quiet. Not awkward. Only the kind of silence that settles in when you've both said enough for a minute.

I take a breath and let the silence sit for a moment more before I say: "I feel bad for her, man."

Nate turns toward me, one brow lifted.

"You know... the way we left her there. In that fucked-up town. After everything." My jaw tightens. "Bianca dies, and we run. Meanwhile, Quinn stays behind, carrying it all."

He doesn't answer right away. Just continues chewing before swallowing hard.

"Yeah," he finally says, voice quieter now. "But you know why we had to go."

I do. Of course I do.

We weren't just running. We were crawling toward something that didn't hurt to look at. The dream we both promised Bianca we'd follow. That town was a fucking graveyard. Every street, every beat of every song had her ghost stitched into it. Staying would've gutted us.

So we left. Packed up our grief with our gear and ran.

And Quinn. She fucking stayed in the ashes. In the silence. In the shadow of every place Bianca ever smiled.

"Where is she?" I ask, dragging my thumb along the label of my beer.

Nate runs a hand through his damp hair. "Shower."

I nod. Cool. Casual. Pretending the word doesn't hit low and dirty. That I'm not picturing her naked, dripping, soap sliding over that skin. Pretending I didn't hear her scream his name so loud the neighbours probably need a cigarette.

"You're falling for her," I say.

The words come out low, barely a breath. No smirk. No sarcasm. Only the truth, stripped bare and dropped between us as though meaningless. When in reality, the truth is everything.

Nate freezes.

He turns his head, and meets my eyes.

And in that split second, I see everything. The weight pressing heavy in his chest. Not fear or doubt. Only the quiet fucking truth.

He's already gone. Already fucked. The kind of fucked that rearranges your whole damn wiring.

And I understand. God, I fucking understand.

Because saying the words out loud, that's what makes everything real. That's when the clock starts ticking. That's when the universe starts looking for ways to rip it away from you, because nothing good ever lasts.

He probably won't say the words. That's easier. He'll bury the truth. Shove the feeling down somewhere it can't be seen or touched or stolen. Somewhere nothing can shatter the parts of us that are still bleeding.

But before I can get another word out, Quinn walks in.

And fuck me... everything stops. My pulse. My breath. Even the fucking earth stops spinning.

Her hair's still wet, hanging in tangled strands that cling to her skin like they know how lucky they are. A loose oversized shirt hangs off one shoulder teasing the line of her chest, hitched just high enough to show the tops of her thighs.

Bare legs. Long, toned, but still slick in places the towel didn't catch. And those fucking thighs my head was between days ago, my mouth buried in her like I needed the taste of her to stay alive.

Her eyes cut straight to us, pinning us both like she knows what we've been talking about.

She's not just beautiful, she's fucking lethal. And right now, she's the most dangerous thing I've ever seen.

Nate doesn't say a word. Only fucking stares at her like his body forgot how to move.

She walks in slow, bare feet whispering against the tiles, skin still dewy from the heat of the shower. Her eyes flick to the pizza box, casual as if she didn't just walk in here looking like sin itself.

"You want pizza?" I ask, my voice rough, catching in my throat before I can smooth it out.

Her lips curl with that dangerous little smirk as she steps closer. She slips down between us on the couch. Her thigh presses into mine.

And fuck, she smells so good. The same scent that's been clinging to the air since Nate walked out of that bedroom.

The rush sinks into my blood, curling through my chest until my ribs ache with the weight of it. Some part of me wants to push her away, because I can't let myself endure something this sharp again, while the rest wants to drag her closer and never let her go.

She leans forward, brushing against my arm as she reaches for a slice of pizza from the box on the table. Her bare shoulder grazes mine, and even that tiny touch carries weight. My nerves short out under the contact. My body forgets every rule I've made about keeping her at a distance.

She takes a bite.

And then fucking moans.

The sound is soft, breathy, but it tears through me. Her head tips back, lashes fluttering, and I swear to God, she makes that piece of cold pizza sound better than anything I've ever done to a woman in bed. My dick twitches to attention before I can even curse the reaction. No loyalty. No shame.

She chews slow, as though she's savoring every bite, as if this is some kind of religious experience. And maybe that's true. Because watching her sit beside me, damp hair falling around her face, flushed, soft and glowing from whatever the fuck Nate did to her, the sight tears something loose in me.

She leans back, chewing like she hasn't shattered my entire nervous system. She tilts her head until her temple rests against my shoulder.

Just Quinn. Curled into my side, her head resting against my shoulder like she's always belonged there.

Her fingers lift the crust to her lips again, teeth tugging gently, lazy from whatever bliss still lingers in her bloodstream. She makes a quiet little sound, nothing more than a hum of contentment, but it wraps around my chest and squeezes. That sound is peace. And I didn't even realize how much I missed hearing it in her.

Her head shifts slightly, cheek brushing my arm. Her breath is steady. Soft.

And she looks up at me.

That sleepy, gentle smile still tugs at the corners of her mouth, as if she hasn't fully come back to earth yet. A strand of damp hair slips loose, brushing her cheek, catching in her lashes.

My hand moves before I can stop it, fingers brushing the strand away from her face, my knuckles linger longer than they should.

She doesn't flinch. Doesn't pull away. She holds my gaze.

Her eyes are unguarded, the kind that pull truth out of you without asking for it. And fuck me, the impact hits hard.

Dead center. Deep in my chest.

That ache.

The one I buried so far down I stopped believing it could surface again. The one I wrapped in barbed wire and concrete and left to rot beneath all the noise and grief. I've kept people out for so fucking long, the moment doesn't even feel real—watching her melt into me as if I'm safe.

I can't breathe right.

Because there it is.

That thing I've been running from.

The weight presses against my ribs. The sharpness slides beneath my skin with the way her steady energy is filling cracks I swore I'd sealed shut.

Something is shifting. Something that hits a hell of a lot like falling.

And fuck I didn't see none of that coming.

I thought I was done with that part of myself. That whatever I carried for Bianca all those years ago had taken every last piece of my heart with her. I thought that kind of love only comes once, and when it's gone, it drags the fucking light out with it.

But Quinn... She's already starting to matter. She's threading herself into places I swore were dead.

And for the first time since Bianca, something stirs inside me.

Bianca's not being replaced. She'll always live in every scar, every silence. But she's shifting. Making space. Moving aside in my heart without resistance or pain. As if she knows it's time.

And in that space, Quinn is settling. Quietly, and the ache that used to live in every breath... the edge doesn't cut as deep anymore.

I swallow hard, trying to look away and gain control of my thoughts, my body, the way my heart beats, but I can't.

She turns her head again, rests it back against my shoulder, and exhales softly. I catch the warmth of her breath, the weight of her, the quiet trust she's giving me.

I don't move. Don't blink. Because right here—this moment—is when I know I'm fucked.

My gaze lifts on instinct, when I realize Nate's watching me.

Pizza half-eaten in his hand, a faint crease between his brows. He doesn't say a word, because I know what he sees.

I'm falling. Same as him. Maybe not as deep, not as hard, but it's happening—and he knows.

And that's what terrifies me.

Because loving something only ends one way.

It gets ripped away. No warning. No reason.

One day she's in your arms, and the next, she's a memory that tears you open every time you breathe too deep.

And I've only barely started breathing again.

Because if I let her in...

And if I lose her...

I'm not sure I'll survive it twice.

CHAPTER 26
Quinn

The door swings open, and I trail after the guys, stepping into the house. My camera bag is on my shoulder, the strap digging deep into a muscle already tender from the weight of the day. The ache is a brand now, proof of the hours that have passed. Proof that I stood there for every second of it.

It's the third day of recording the album, and I had no fucking clue how much work went into making one until now. Not the kind people see, anyway. Not the sweat and grind that lives behind the music. I've watched them push themselves until there was nothing left, and push again because almost perfect wasn't good enough.

I spent the day on the other side of the glass, because I couldn't step inside while the red light was on. The shutter of my camera would bleed into the sound and ruin the take. So I stood there silent, my lens pressed to the glass, watching them work together in a rhythm that was its own language.

Ace sat at the soundboard for hours, his hands a blur over buttons and dials, adjusting, layering, chasing some invisible edge only he could hear. When it was finally his turn to play alongside Nate and Theo, Xander took over his spot at the board, his eyes locked on the three of them as they lost themselves in the music.

By the end of it, the guys looked like they'd run a marathon in a rainstorm. Sweat plastered their shirts to their backs, strands of hair sticking to damp skin, hands flexing as if they still felt the instruments in their grip. They work fucking hard. Harder than anyone out there with a ticket in their hand will ever know. No one sees this part. No one sees what it costs them.

During the breaks, they let me in. For a few minutes at a time, long enough for me to steal the kind of shots their fans would kill for. Sweat-slick, eyes glassy with focus, their edges softened by exhaustion until they looked almost dreamlike. The kind of shots that would have panties dropping and thighs pressing together in bedrooms all over the world.

The smell hits me first. Not pure sweat, though there's enough of it to cling to the air. It's Theo, close enough that a trace of his cologne brushes over me, that same earthy scent he's always worn. It's him, stripped down to the core.

The house is quiet. The kind of hush that settles when there's nothing left to give. Outside, the last rays of sunlight sink into the trees. Inside, shadows take their place.

Nate drags his shirt over his head, the fabric clinging before it finally gives. His back shifts, muscles pulling tight, the sheen of sweat catching what little light is left. The day's stamped on him. The flush along his neck, the faint slump in his shoulders from hours bent over his drum kit, driving every beat to perfection.

"I'm gonna hit the shower," Nate says, voice rough, worn down. He walks off without looking back, disappearing into the dark at the end of the hall.

I set my camera bag on the kitchen bench, the strap slipping from my shoulder with a dull thud. My hands feel empty without it. I move to the fridge.

"Do you want a water?" I ask Theo, pulling the door open. The cold air instantly chills my skin.

Theo's head tilts enough to show he heard me, but he doesn't turn.

"Nah," he says, voice flat, before walking toward the hallway.

It's been three days since I fucked Nate. Since I let my body answer questions, my heart's still too much of a coward to touch. And Theo hasn't been the same since. Not in ways most people would notice. He still throws out those cheeky one-liners in that Theo way. Still laughs with the others when someone fucks up a take. Still hums under his breath when he thinks no one's listening. But he's quieter.

The spark that usually lights him up? Gone. Like someone reached in and yanked the plug.

Even Ace noticed. Earlier today, from behind the soundboard, he looked at Theo and said, "You've got the spark of a guy whose favourite hand just broke up with him."

It got a few snorts from the guys, but Theo didn't fire back. No smirk. No comeback. He kept playing. And all I could hear was the truth under it—something's up with him.

Last night I pulled Nate aside, hoping for answers, but all he gave me was, "He's going through something. That's all."

Which, coming from Nate, means it's the kind of shit buried too deep for me to touch. The kind that closes doors and keeps me on the wrong side of them.

I stand there for a second, a cold bottle of water sweating in my hand, the fridge door still hanging open. My eyes stay fixed on the empty space where Theo disappeared. My feet don't move, even though something in my chest is already halfway down that hallway, pulling hard.

I don't know if this is the right move. If I'm about to step into something I've got no business touching. But I go anyway.

I move down the hallway, passing the room I've been staying in. When I reach the bathroom, the steady splash of water against tile fills the air. Steam drifts from the gap beneath the door. Nate is in there naked under the spray, water running over hard muscle and the kind of body built to fuck for hours. For a second, I picture his hands braced against the wall, head tipped back, water sliding over his cock.

I stop in front of Theo's door and lift my hand. I knock once.

"It's open," he says.

I push the door open gently, and the first thing I see is him, sitting on the edge of the bed, head buried in his hands. His shirt is gone, lying crumpled on the floor. His chest rises and falls in slow, uneven breaths that look heavier than they should.

Outside, the last of the daylight bleeds into the room through the window, casting faint, fractured shadows over the tattoo that spreads across his chest. Those wings that sent me spiralling, bolting out of the room when my fingers traced them.

The guilt still comes, at the thought of what I've done with Bianca's boys. But I shove it down. In less than a week, I'll be gone. They'll go back to their usual lives, back to being the untouchable rockstars everyone else sees, and I'll be nothing more than a memory of someone they used to know. Much like before, when they left the first time.

So I might as well take what's here now. Every benefit. Every stolen second. Live out the fantasy while I can, before it fades into something that used to be. Two weeks of my life tangled up with two rockstars who were once my friends.

Theo's head lifts when I step inside. And fuck.

There's something about him at this moment that steals the air from my lungs. There are no walls. No jokes or smirks to hide behind. Theo, unguarded, the fight gone from his eyes. He looks like someone who's been carrying too much for too long, and it's dragging him under. I can see he's in his fucking head again, turning over whatever's been eating at him until it's worn him down.

I want to ask and tear it out of him, if only to hold it for a while, so he doesn't have to. But I know better. Push him and he'll retreat. I've watched that happen. Bianca and I used to talk about how he'd make himself small when things got bad, curling in on himself until there was nothing left for anyone to grab onto. Back then, Nate was the one who could cut through all that mess, drag him back into the light.

And standing here now, I know I'm not Nate. All I can do is watch him fold in on himself and pretend it doesn't break something in me.

I cross the room, the carpet soft under my feet. Guitars lean against the wall, some in stands, others resting where they've been left after a late-night play. A laptop sits open on the desk beside a scattering of guitar picks, empty coffee cups, and a mess of crumpled set lists. There's a hoodie draped over the back of the chair, a phone charger coiled on the floor, and a pile of clothes kicked half under the bed.

When I sit beside him, our thighs brush. Neither of us says anything at first. He only watches me. My eyes flicker to his, and it fucking breaks something in me to see him like this, stripped of the spark that usually lives there. I hold the water bottle out to him. He takes it without a word, but doesn't drink. Instead, he tosses it onto the bed beside him as if it weighs too much to bother with.

My eyes drift around the room, catching on details I never noticed before. When I was in this bed with both of them, I wasn't looking. I was too busy being touched, coming apart under two mouths, two cocks, two bodies that knew exactly how to tear orgasms out of me.

On his dresser sits a small ball, the kind he used to throw against the wall or squeeze in his hand when his anxiety got the better of him. This one is a different color, but it proves that some things never change, no matter how many arenas you sell out.

Beside it, a gold photo frame pulls my attention. I rise from the bed and cross the room.

It's the four of us. Nate. Theo. Bianca. And me. We look stupid-happy, all sun-drenched smiles and bare, golden skin. The kind of photo that makes your chest ache with everything it holds and everything it reminds you of.

It isn't one I took, which makes it unfamiliar, almost foreign, yet still loaded. The background looks like Nate and Theo's old room with rumpled sheets, posters curling at the edges, the faint chaos that was always theirs.

I reach for it, lifting it carefully into my hands. My fingers trace the cool metal, brushing over the fine layer of dust along the frame, proof it has been sitting here a long time, waiting to be noticed.

"Who took this?" I ask without turning.

"Scarlet, I think."

His voice comes from right behind me. Closer than I realized. Close enough that I can sense the faint heat of him at my back.

I don't move. My gaze stays locked on the photo, my eyes tracing every detail. The way Theo's arm is looped around me, holding me without thinking. The way Bianca's smile spills light into everything around her, bright enough to burn. The way Nate's hand rests on Theo's shoulder, steady and sure, as if he's anchoring him to the moment.

Something inside my chest pulls tight until it hurts.

I know Theo's eyes are on me before I even look up. His gaze is steady, carrying a heat that pulls me in without a word.

He moves closer, until he's standing beside me. I watch his eyes drop to the photo in my hands, the faint crease appearing between his brows. The grief in him is obvious, written in the way his mouth tightens for a moment.

"That was the day Bianca tried to teach Nate how to skateboard," he says, a half-smirk tugging at his lips. "Didn't even last thirty seconds before he ate shit."

He looks back up at me, the smirk still there, though it doesn't quite reach his eyes. His gaze dips to my mouth, lingering there for a fraction too long before it flashes back up to meet mine.

"I'm sorry," I say, setting the photo down gently, as if it might break.

"What for?"

"For bringing up the past. I know it hurts."

Silence stretches between us. When I glance up, he's already watching me.

"You never have to apologize for remembering her," he says quietly. "Or for remembering us."

He steps in, close enough that the faint heat from his body brushes against my skin. My grip tightens around the edge of the dresser because I don't know what to do with the weight of his stare. It pins me in place.

His hand lifts, his gaze never wavering. Fingers slide into my hair, brushing it back from my face. The touch lingers, enough to feel intentional, enough to make my pulse skip.

The pads of his fingers graze the curve of my jaw. It's so faint it's almost not there, yet the spark it sets off is immediate.

"You know," he murmurs, his voice low enough that it curls right into my chest, "back at those parties... the only reason I went was to talk to you."

For a second, I blink, the words hitting harder than I'm ready for. "What?"

He leans back half a step, his hand falling away, rubbing at the back of his neck. His eyes dart aside, like maybe he already regrets letting it slip. "I didn't give a shit about Nate disappearing to get his dick sucked, leaving me stuck with those idiots running their mouths. I just... I went so I could sit and talk to you."

My mouth opens, but nothing comes out.

I don't know how to say it—that the only reason I ever went was to sit and talk to him too. If he hadn't been there, I wouldn't have walked in. No fucking way I'd step into a party to deal with guys trying to corner me, trying to get into my pants, running their mouths about how they'd fucked Quinn Thomas. None of them knew back then that I was still a virgin, and I wasn't about to give that to some cockhead who only wanted pussy and not the person attached to it.

When I don't answer, he turns away and walks back to the bed, sitting down like he didn't drop something I've been dying to hear for years. The fact that he shuts me out that easily makes my heart break.

I follow him. "Why the hell do you do that?"

His gaze stays on some point past me. "Do what?"

"This." I motion between us. "Shut down right after you tell me something you've never said before."

Silence.

His eyes finally meet mine. The expression makes it impossible to tell whether he's about to kiss me or walk away.

"Theo," I say, stepping closer. "Talk to me."

I reach out, my fingers wrapping around his forearm. The muscle is solid and warm, heat rolling off him in steady waves. The moment my skin meets his, something in him shifts. His breath hitches, eyes closing for a beat like he's holding himself back.

When they open again, he's already closing the distance.

His hand lifts slow, giving me every chance to stop him. Fingers skim my cheek, the rough pads grazing skin that suddenly burns with sensitivity, before his palm curves around the side of my face. A breath later, his mouth crashes onto mine.

It starts soft, but fuck, the filth is in the way he moves—his lips coaxing mine open, tongue sliding in like he's here to claim me. He tastes me slowly, as if he wants every inch of me mapped on his tongue before he's done. It's a kiss that lands like a warning, the kind a man gives when he plans to fuck you until no one else can touch you without finding his fingerprints.

My hands find his chest before I even register moving. Hard muscle under my palms, his heartbeat pounding fast enough to match mine. My thighs press together under the pull of it, heat sparking low and deep. My nipples tighten under the thin fabric of my shirt, aching, while every slow grind of his mouth over mine turns the air between us molten.

Every pass of his tongue says I want to fuck you, but every careful tilt of his mouth says I'm not letting you go.

When he finally pulls back, his breath drags hot over my lips, his forehead resting close enough that I can feel the faint tremor in him.

Theo's arms come around me, drawing me in. He turns us toward the bed and lowers me down, the mattress dipping beneath our weight. He stays there, close enough for his breath to ghost my mouth, but he doesn't close the gap. Not yet. He looks at me... really looks, his gaze roaming over my face as if he's committing every detail to memory before he lets himself take more.

His hands slide to the hem of my shirt. The fabric gathers in his fingers, rising slow over my stomach, ribs, and breasts. He sits me up only long enough to peel it over my head, tossing it aside before laying me back down.

The clasp of my bra snaps open beneath his fingers. The straps slide from my shoulders, and his head dips, his mouth brushing the newly bared skin in slow, claiming kisses. His tongue traces the curve beneath my breast, and his lips close over the tight peak. The pull of his mouth sends a sharp rush of heat straight between my legs, causing my back to arch into him.

He doesn't rush. He takes his fucking time. He moves from one breast to the other, leaving my skin damp from his mouth, lips dragging lazy and wet, sucking and teasing until my breath becomes uneven.

"Beautiful," he murmurs against me.

He tips his head, meets my eyes, and doesn't look away. There's a softness that rattles something deep in me, something I'm not ready to name. He isn't performing. He isn't hiding behind some flirty grin or careless lines. He's right here, anchored in this moment with me, and he wants me to see it.

His mouth moves lower, lips brushing my stomach in slow, open-mouthed kisses, each one landing further south than the last. His breath skims my skin, warm enough to make me shiver. His fingers find the button on my jeans. The metal pops under his touch. He draws the zipper down in a steady pull, the sound of it dragging over my nerves, making my pulse slam.

He grips the waistband and eases them down my hips. The denim drags against my skin, slow enough that I feel every inch of it leaving me. My panties go with them, the lace catching for a heartbeat before he works them past my knees, down my calves, until I'm bare in front of him.

Theo straightens, standing at the edge of the bed, his gaze fixed between my thighs. His throat works as he swallows, his jaw flexing once. There's hunger in his eyes, but also something patient—as if he's taking his time because he knows he'll never forget the sight of me spread out for him.

The weight of that stare shoots straight through me. My clit pulses, an ache blooming until I'm squirming under it, needing him to close the distance.

"Spread for me," he says, voice threaded with that filthy command I've always been powerless against. "I want to see everything I get to touch."

I let my knees fall open, and watch the way his gaze drags down to where I'm already wet for him. His breath leaves him in a slow exhale.

"Fuck," he murmurs, almost to himself. "You're perfect."

He drops to his knees between my thighs, and the sight alone sends a rush through my veins. His hands drag up my legs in a slow, claiming sweep, the heat of his palms branding me as his.

He's so fucking close I can sense the heat of his mouth, but he doesn't touch where I need him most. Not yet. He holds me open, forcing me to take the weight of his control, making it clear this isn't about me telling him what I want—this is about him giving it when he's ready.

His breath hits the crease of my thigh, hot and teasing, and then his mouth is on me, pressing a slow kiss into my skin. My nails dig into the sheets. He moves to the other side, doing it again, sucking hard enough to leave heat behind. By the time his mouth drags higher, my hips are arching without my permission, chasing him like I'm already addicted.

And fuck, his tongue is between my folds, tracing me in one long, wet stroke from my entrance to my clit. I twitch under him, a soft moan catching in my throat. He stays low, circling my entrance with slow, lazy swirls before pushing his tongue inside. The wet slide of it makes my pussy squeeze around him, desperate for more, and he groans like he fucking feels it.

When he pulls out, I'm seconds from begging, but he moves higher, finally finding my clit. He flattens his tongue over it, dragging slow, heavy strokes that make my back arch. Every pass is deliberate, controlled—enough to get me shaking, nowhere near enough to let me come.

"Fuck, you taste good," he murmurs against me, before his mouth seals over my clit. He sucks deep, like he's trying to drink me down. My hips jerk into his face, but his hands are already gripping my thighs, pinning me to the mattress.

Theo's tongue flicks in short, perfect strokes before circling my clit in tight, ruthless loops that make my voice break on his name. The heat builds sharp and fast, the kind that makes my thighs tremble and my pussy ache to be fucked.

He groans again, the vibration shooting through my core. "Yeah… give me that. Get my face wet."

His tongue fucks me harder now, faster, his lips sucking around my clit until the pressure turns unbearable.

It's dirty. Obscene. So fucking good I'd stay here all night, letting him tear me apart, just to feel him crawl up my body and fuck me with that same ruthless precision.

Every now and then he pulls back, chin slick with my wetness, eyes locked on mine with that unblinking, predatory focus.

My body arches toward him, desperate to fuck myself on his mouth, and he answers with a deeper suck on my clit that has me moaning loud enough to echo in this quiet room.

"Good," he growls against me. "That's it. Give it to me. I want every fucking drop."

The words make my nipples tighten and my pussy flood. He doesn't break his pace. Every pass is deliberate, unhurried, his mouth owning every inch of me while the pressure builds into something sharp and unbearable. My hips jerk, chasing harder contact, but he's already holding me down. One arm hooked around my thigh, keeping me open for him, the other pressing hard into my stomach, pinning me to the bed like he owns my body.

The control makes it hotter. Dirtier. I can't grind against him or speed him up. I can't do anything but take what he's giving me.

Then it comes. The knot inside me snaps. My back bows off the bed, a choked cry ripping out of me as the orgasm tears through me so hard it nearly blanks my vision. My pussy spasms, clenching again and again around nothing, each pulse wetter than the last while he keeps his mouth locked on me. He doesn't just lick—he drinks me in, swallowing every bit of it like I'm something he's been starving for.

I'm shaking uncontrollably, my toes curling, my hands gripping his hair hard enough to hurt, but he still doesn't let go. He works me through every wave, every aftershock, until my body starts to jolt from overstimulation, my thighs trying to clamp shut. He forces them open, holding me there until he's satisfied. He finally gives me one last filthy, open-mouthed suck on my clit before lifting his head.

When he crawls up my body, his mouth crashes to mine, and I taste myself thick on his tongue.

"Tell me what you need," he whispers, forehead pressed to mine, his breath warm and thick against my lips.

"You," I breathe, voice cracking. "Inside me."

Something shifts in his eyes. He doesn't only hear it—he feels it. His jaw flexes once before he nods.

He pushes up onto his knees, the mattress dipping under his weight. He shoves his jeans down his thighs, briefs going with them, his cock springing free, hard, heavy, the thick length flushed and glistening at the tip.

Fuck.

It's perfect, big enough to make me ache with the stretch in my head before he's even inside me. Veins run along the shaft, his hand wrapping around them as he gives one slow, lazy stroke from base to tip, smearing pre-come over the head while never breaking eye contact. This isn't for show—he's making it clear exactly what I'm about to get.

He leans forward, kissing the inside of my knee, his mouth soft but full of promise. After that, he reaches for the drawer.

"Condom," he murmurs.

The foil tears between his teeth. He rolls it down his cock with steady hands, and my eyes follow every movement, watching the latex stretch over that thick length until he's fully sheathed.

He settles between my legs, one hand gripping my hip hard enough to bruise, the other wrapped around his cock. He drags it through my slick, the ridge catching on my clit in a slow grind before sliding lower again. My hips twitch, chasing him without thinking.

"Greedy," he mutters, smirking like it turns him on.

He bends down, pressing a kiss to my stomach, his lips hot against my skin, before straightening and locking eyes with me. He stays there, the head of his cock resting right at my entrance making me ache.

Then he pushes in.

The stretch is obscene. My pussy grips him instantly, the first thick inch making me gasp, my hands curling into the sheets. He keeps going, until my body is stuffed full of him, the head nudging so deep it steals the breath from my lungs.

"Fuck," he groans, his eyes dropping to where I'm stretched tight around him. "Look at that pussy, taking every fucking inch of me."

The stretch tears the breath from my lungs, my walls clamping down as if they're desperate to drag him deeper. Heat races up my spine while his eyes stay fixed on me, catching every flicker—my parted lips, the flutter of my lashes when he pushes further. Inch by inch, he buries himself inside me until he's balls deep.

His jaw flexes, a groan rumbling up from deep in his chest.

"Fuck," he breathes, voice rough. "You feel fucking perfect. So tight I'm scared to fucking move."

When he moves, it's slow enough to make me ache and clench for more. Long, deep thrusts drag over every sensitive ridge inside me, forcing my thighs to lock tighter around his hips. Each push is deliberate, measured, making sure I register every vein, every inch, every hard withdrawal and slow slide back in.

His hands won't stay still. One roams over my waist, the other traces down my hip, then skates along the inside of my thigh until his fingertips are brushing dangerously close to where I'm stretched around him. It's claiming.

"Look at me," he murmurs, his voice all command. "Don't drift, Quinn. I want you here for every fucking second."

I try to hold his gaze, but the way he moves makes my eyes flutter, my breath stutter. He thrusts deeper, finding that spot that makes my spine bow and my fists hold tight onto the sheets.

"Fuck," he groans, watching my mouth fall open, my chest heave. "You feel so fucking good, so hot, so wet for me. That's it, baby... grip my cock. Show me how much you fucking need it."

Every stroke builds the heat low in my belly, winding it tighter with each slow grind of his hips. He doesn't rush, doesn't chase it, keeps that unhurried rhythm, letting the friction make me shake and burn under him until I'm right on the edge.

"Yeah," he whispers, a dark curve to his mouth. "There she is. Look at you taking my cock so fucking well. This pussy was made for me."

He sits back on his knees, the ink sprawled across his chest catching my eyes.

My palm skims up the solid plane of muscle until it rests over his heart. It's pounding hard and fast, each beat thudding against my hand like it's trying to break free.

He catches my wrist, brings my fingers to his mouth, and drags his tongue over them before sucking one between his lips, before he kisses it. He pulls my hand away, presses it back over the frantic hammer of his heart.

"Tell me what you feel," he growls.

"You," I whisper.

That word rips a feral sound from his chest, and he's on me again, forearms braced on either side, caging me in. His hips roll in slow, punishing strokes, cock grinding deep. The stretch steals my breath, every thrust leaving me tighter, my walls clenching around him with each deliberate pull and push.

He kisses me, mouth hot and wet, swallowing the desperate fucks and ragged yeses that spill out of my mouth.

"That's it," he murmurs against my lips. "This pussy's already so fucking close. I can feel it. It's begging me to fill you. But first I want you to come all over my cock."

A sharp, deep thrust makes me cry out, my nails raking down his back. He smirks against my mouth as if he owns me for pulling that sound out.

The rhythm stays slow. Deep rolls that drag his cock over every swollen, sensitive nerve before sinking back inside me to the hilt. He shifts, angling just right, and pleasure detonates so hard my head tips back, a choked moan spilling out.

His mouth is on my throat, tongue and teeth marking my skin. His hand slides under my thigh, hauling my leg higher around his waist. The new depth is obscene.

"Better?" he says, his cock grinding in deep.

"Yes," I gasp, clinging to him like I'll come apart if I let go. "So fucking good. Please...don't stop."

His eyes go dark. He doesn't break eye contact as he rolls his hips. The rhythm is steady but punishing in its precision. Each thrust leaves me stretched to the edge.

"Fuck... look at you," he growls, thumb dragging down my cheek to my jaw.

The headboard bumps against the wall with every slide in of his cock. My thighs grip around his waist, not letting him pull back far, keeping him buried where I need him.

"You're so fucking perfect. Every little moan, every twitch of this greedy pussy... fuck, I see all of it." His fingers slide down the column of my throat, wrapping around it just enough to make my breath hitch. "I could fuck you until your body forgets how to do anything but come for me."

I moan from the way his pelvis grinds my clit, the friction sending a rush of heat through my stomach.

His mouth curves faintly, dark with satisfaction. "Come for me. Eyes on me while I watch you fall apart."

My thighs lock around his hips, holding him to me as my breath breaks into filthy, helpless sounds. Every grind of his pelvis against my clit lights me up until I can't take it—

And suddenly the orgasm rips through me. It's so brutal it steals every breath until I'm gasping into the heat between us. Every slow drag out and hard push back feels so fucking good. Then he stills, stays buried to the hilt, cock locked inside me while I pulse around him, making sure he catches every single spasm. After a beat he starts to move again, long, ruthless thrusts that drag over every raw, over sensitive nerve until I'm squirming under him again.

"Yeah," he breathes against my mouth, the words almost a growl. "Take it... fuck, you're perfect."

I moan into the kiss. Every nerve feels frayed, begging for more even while my body fights to keep up.

He pulls almost all the way out, before he buries himself to the hilt again with a groan that sounds torn in half. His hips jerk once, twice, then lock, every muscle in his body tensing. Shoulders rigid, stomach drawn tight, thighs steel against mine. His eyes screw shut, brow furrowed, mouth falling open in a silent gasp before a broken, guttural sound tears free.

The hot, rhythmic throb of his cock pulses deep, spilling into the condom in thick, heavy bursts.

"Fuck... Quinn..." The sound of my name leaves him in a raw groan, rough and frayed.

He stays there, for a moment not moving, buried deep, jaw locked, face caught between strain and surrender. Slowly, the tension starts to bleed out of him, and his hips begin to move again.

He fucks me through it, keeping me pinned in that haze where pleasure and oversensitivity blur, drawing it out until I'm breathless beneath him.

His forehead rests against mine, his breath hot. He keeps the rhythm unhurried, as if wringing every last drop of pleasure from what we've already given each other.

Only when my nails dig into his back in a silent plea does he finally still, holding there, chest slick against mine, the weight of him pressing me into the mattress while faint twitches still run through both our bodies.

Nate fucks with a force that owns me from the first thrust. But Theo builds it. He doesn't simply take me, he shapes every move. Each slow drive is measured to wind me tighter, to pull every nerve in my body into a sharp, aching point. And when he finally lets me fall, it isn't an orgasm—it's a detonation.

After a long minute, he eases out of me, both of us still trembling in the aftershocks. He ties off the condom, tosses it into the trash by the bed, then comes back immediately.

The sheet whispers over our sweat-slick skin as he pulls me into him. His heat closes around me until the world narrows into this cocoon. Only his body, his scent.

He shifts onto his side, facing me. His fingers find my face, tracing over it with a quiet certainty, the pad of his thumb brushing beneath my eye in a way that steals my breath. His hair is mussed, mouth flushed and swollen, eyes carrying a softness I've never seen in them before.

Theo has always been the restless one. The quick grin, the smart line, never lets anyone get too close. But here, he's still. Quiet. Every touch from him tells me this wasn't only sex for him. It was something he needed. Something I'm not sure he's ever let himself have before.

This side of him is new, unsettling in its gentleness. And in this moment, it's more intoxicating than anything that came before.

"You okay?" His voice is quiet.

I nod, still catching my breath, my lips curving without thought. "More than okay."

A kiss lands on his collarbone. I let the silence cradle whatever it is he is not ready to say.

His arm comes around me, pulling me close, his grip steady as though he fears I might slip through his fingers. The beat of his heart under my cheek is almost too much; it carries trust and something deeper than I can name, and it terrifies me.

The room holds its stillness, broken only by the sound of our shared breaths. His fingers trace a slow path along my spine, every touch unhurried, almost reverent. My eyes close, and I let the warmth of him pull me toward sleep, knowing I have never felt him this way before... and uncertain if I ever will again.

CHAPTER 27

Theo

Two weeks vanish in a blur of sweat, shitty coffee, and Xander riding our asses like it's a sport he's training for. Ace is one bad take away from going full WWE on the sound board, while Nate and I spend half our time pretending it's all good and the other half planning each other's funerals, anything to break the monotony.

And Quinn—she fucking fits. One day she's a stranger with a camera, the next she's wedged into the middle of our chaos, like she's always been here.

Even Xander talks to her, which is saying something, because the guy barely says a word unless there's a riff involved. And Ace, he gets that forehead vein going, the one that screams somebody's about to die, and she lifts her camera, snaps a shot, then tilts the screen his way. Whatever she shows him, it hits. The vein eases, his shoulders drop, and the murder drains out of his eyes.

Quinn's got this freaky sixth sense for reading people. She knows when to push, when to back off, and exactly when to pull out the camera. I've caught both Ace and Xander leaning in when she tilts the screen toward them, staring at whatever shot she's captured. Then comes that quiet, almost smug look on both of their faces, the kind that says *"oh yeah, this is the dream we swore we'd bleed for."*

And Nate and me? We're both just stuck in her gravity, and I'm not entirely sure I want to crawl out of it.

A couple of days ago, we were at Xander's for one of his pool barbecue things. Those were his exact words, because apparently "party" is too mainstream for him. I was halfway through a beer when I realized I had lost sight of Quinn.

I found her and Poppy tucked away on the far side of the deck, clinging to each other and laughing their asses off. This wasn't a chuckle. This was full-on, can't-breathe, tears-running, completely-fucking-gone laughter. Poppy hit that high-pitched snort she does, the one that sounds like a dying kettle, and it set

Quinn off even harder. That, in turn, set the rest of us off, even though we had no fucking clue what was so funny.

That is the thing about Quinn. She slides into our chaotic lives so effortlessly that one day you look around and realise she belongs here.

I'm not sure when the days started speeding up, but it's hitting me now that time is running out. Soon the nights will be gone of her curled up on the couch with her laptop, making those soft humming noises she probably doesn't even realize slip out when she's editing photos. No more midnight arguments about whether pineapple belongs on pizza. No more watching her grin at Nate like he's said the funniest shit in the world, even though we both know he hasn't.

She is part of the rhythm here now, woven into the noise and the quiet in a way that makes it hard to picture our lives without her. And I am not ready for it to change.

The days are loud. Guitars. Drums. Xander's voice tearing across the booth.

But the nights? We fuck.

The two of us get lost in her. She's pulling Nate and me closer too, tying us together in ways I never saw coming.

Nate always goes first. To him, the whole thing is a game. He gets off on being the one to break her open. Fingers, tongue, cock. He wrecks her, and he knows exactly what he is doing. And I love watching him do it.

After he's done, it's my turn. My mouth on her tits while he's buried deep inside her, her head thrown back, nails clawing for something to hold. Sometimes she's on her knees, swallowing my cock while Nate fucks her from behind, both of us watching her fall apart. I love dragging my mouth over her nipples, sucking until she's squirming, my fingers finding that spot between her legs where Nate's cock splits her wide open.

Other nights, she rides us both, one after the other. Soaked. Screaming. Wild-eyed. Her nails leaving marks on our skin, as if she's afraid letting go would mean losing this entirely.

She has changed us. Changed everything.

Before Quinn, fucking a woman together was simple. We knew the rhythm. In. Out. Swap. Done. No eye contact. No lingering touch beyond the quick graze of a hand. We got off, pulled out, zipped up, and walked away. It was sex stripped of anything that could matter.

Now Nate's hand finds me mid-thrust. When she's on her knees, my cock in her mouth, he comes up behind me, mouth hot on mine, his palms sliding over my chest before he moves around to bury himself in her from behind.

When she's bouncing on my cock, he grips her hips and fucks her ass while his eyes stay locked on me. His mouth claims hers, shifts to mine, and returns to hers again. Every touch drags us closer into something I don't know how to name.

After we have Quinn flat on the bed, hair damp against her face, skin flushed, cunt still leaking both of us, I'll be lying with Nate close beside me, sometimes with me caught between them. His fingers slide up my spine, heat blooming under every slow stroke. The sensation burns into me before his mouth follows, pressing soft kisses into my back. Afterward he shifts, moving over me to give Quinn the same.

No longer is it only about fucking her. This is about the way she's pulled the three of us into a closed orbit where nothing exists outside this bed, this heat, this tangle of skin and breath.

That night I fucked her without Nate, something in me cracked wide open. It wasn't the way I usually fuck. No mindless pounding until she broke apart. I took my time, watching every twist of her face when a moan slipped free. My hands covered every inch of her, committing it to memory, tracing her curves as if I could etch her into my skin. Every sound she made slammed into my chest, sinking deep like it was meant to stay.

I've never had that shit hit me before. Not even with Bianca. I'll always love her—she was my first, my girl, the one who taught me to love and left me bleeding. I thought that was the end, that what we had was the peak, the only kind of love I'd ever know. But nothing compares to this. Bianca made me feel alive. Quinn makes me feel owned.

I'm certain this is love. That truth scares the fuck out of me. I haven't let myself love another woman since Bianca. Haven't even let the thought in. But that night with Quinn stripped me bare, and now the door won't close on what I feel.

Nate loves her too. I see it in the way his eyes lock on her, in the clench of his jaw, in the stillness that takes over when she laughs. That sound pulls a smile out of him, cuts straight through whatever noise is in his chest. He's every bit as fucked as I am, just as scared to let the words out. He still carries the weight of never telling Bianca he loved her before she was gone, and now he's fighting the same war I am—wanting her, loving her, and knowing exactly how much it costs to live with love you can't bring yourself to speak.

And tomorrow?

Quinn is leaving.

I can already feel that shift in the air.

Poppy threw a lunch today to say goodbye. Xander's place smelled of garlic bread and that vanilla candle Poppy burns until the wick's nothing but ash. The table was buried under bright flowers, crooked paper crowns, and enough food to feed half the street. Poppy kept topping up Quinn's glass, telling her she had to drink enough for both of them now she couldn't. Her hand lingered on her belly when she spoke, eyes warm in that way Poppy makes everyone instantly at home.

When Quinn laughed, Poppy laughed louder, and snorted of course, and Scarlet joined in until the whole table cracked up.

A moment later Quinn's voice snagged on something she couldn't swallow. Poppy didn't hesitate, she grabbed her hand and held on, thumb running over her knuckles until her smile steadied.

And fuck, Quinn looked beautiful. Cheeks flushed, eyes wet but steady, holding herself together enough to make the rest of us believe she wasn't breaking. All I wanted was to pull her into my chest, tell her she didn't have to be fine. But I didn't. I sat at the table, chewing garlic bread and pretending I wasn't falling apart watching her.

Later, Nate and I dragged her to this dusty little photography store she'd sniffed out online. The place smelled of old film, the air heavy with decades of people trying to trap their memories before they bled away. She disappeared inside, already lit up in that way she gets when the world makes sense to her.

Nate and I ended up in the department store next door, hunting for a suitcase that didn't need a hoodie to keep it together. We stood in the middle of the aisle, two idiots surrounded by luggage.

Nate was adamant on black. "Timeless," he said, like she was about to walk down the aisle at a funeral.

I went for the obnoxious neon pink, the kind that screamed emotionally unstable but great at parties. He said the color looked as though Barbie had puked. I told him that was exactly why she would love it.

But through all the bickering and bad color commentary, I kept wanting to ask him if he feels the same. That ache. That hollow pull in the chest that never loosens, as though something's clawing at the ribs from the inside out. The thought of Quinn not being here after tomorrow guts me.

No more laughter spilling down the hall at two in the morning, loud enough to wake the dead because she's never learned how to whisper. I wish I could freeze it, trap it in a bottle, keep her here.

She's messy, wild, impossible. A beautiful kind of chaos that somehow made our broken pieces seem like they were finally close to fitting.

And now she's leaving. The world is already quieter without her. Too fucking quiet.

It's our last night. No one says a word, but the truth hangs heavy, thick as smoke. Every movement comes slower, softer, as if time's trying to drag its feet, handing us a few more stolen seconds before she goes.

She's curled up on the floor in one of Nate's hoodies, legs folded tight, hair falling loose around her face. Old prints from that photography shop are spread out in front of her, and she's holding them the way most people hold treasure. She looks so fucking at home it punches something sharp through my chest.

I nudge Nate.

He disappears down the hall without a word and comes back with the suitcase. No wrap, no card, only us standing like a couple of idiots holding a gift we wish we didn't have to give.

Her eyes land on the suitcase. "What's this?"

Nate jerks his chin. "One that closes without a hoodie doing all the work."

Her laugh fills the room, same as always, only this time the sound cuts.

She stands and runs her hand along the handle. "Thank you. It's so bright. I love this. You guys didn't have to."

"We did," I tell her, my mouth twitching into a smirk I can't fully fake. "Your old one was more fucked than a Vegas pro on a double shift. It was practically stripping in public."

She pauses, giving me that maddening smile, all soft edges with something dangerous buried underneath. "Never change, Theo."

Three simple words, yet they hit with the force of a freight train.

She goes to Nate first. Wraps her arms around his neck in that easy way that says she trusts him. His arms come around, holding her as if loosening his grip might split him open. His jaw tightens, eyes dropping, shoulders refusing to let go even when the moment starts to stretch. I watch him, every muscle in me screaming for him to ask the thing I can't get out. Ask her to stay. Because maybe if he does, she will.

But, he doesn't.

She turns to me, and my arms close around her before my head catches up. I keep her there, locked against me, memorizing the feel of her. The line of her shoulder under my palm, the warmth bleeding through my shirt, the way her breath moves against me. If I could hold her long enough to make time stall, I would.

Her hair brushes my jaw, carrying the soft scent of vanilla shampoo and something that is only hers. The ache spreads through my chest, until I swear it might crush me.

"You're squishing me," she murmurs into my shirt.

I smirk, resting my chin on her head. "Please. After putting up with you, this is the least painful part of my week."

She laughs, but doesn't pull away. My eyes flick to Nate. He's watching us.

She shifts. Her arms loosen. She eases back enough to draw a breath, and her fingers swipe at the corner of her eye in a quick motion.

"I have something for both of you," she says. Her voice is light, but there's a flicker behind her eyes, half mischief, half nerves.

Before either of us can ask, she spins on her heels and bolts down the hall. Bare feet slapping against the tiles.

Nate and I stand still, watching where she vanished.

"Should we be worried?" Nate mutters.

"Only if she comes back with glitter or a live chicken," I say. "If it's handcuffs, I'm not asking questions."

Nate groans. "You need therapy."

"Probably," I reply, because we both know that will never happen.

We are both smirking, because Quinn has a way of turning any quiet moment into a small-scale disaster. Her footsteps reach us before she does. Quick, uneven, almost tripping over her own excitement.

Nate and I exchange a look.

"Brace yourself," I tell him.

She skids into the doorway, cheeks flushed, hair a little wilder than before, holding something behind her back.

She remains silent, grinning as if she is guarding a secret big enough to blow the roof off the place.

"Well, I don't hear a chicken," I say, giving her a slow once-over. "We're off to a strong start."

Her brows draw together. "A chicken?"

I jerk my chin toward Nate. "He's gutted. Already had a name picked out. Was gonna call it Cluck Norris."

Nate groans and rubs his forehead. "I swear to God, Theo."

Quinn takes a small step forward, her hands still tucked behind her back. She hesitates, eyes moving between us. There's a flicker of nerves in her smile, the kind you get when you're about to hand over something that you're unsure about.

"I wanted to give you this," she says quietly.

A pause stretches long enough for my stomach to knot. Her hands shift and she brings the gift forward. My gaze drops to the dark sheen of a plain wooden photo frame.

I have no idea what I expected, but it isn't this. The image is from the studio. Nate and I are shoulder to shoulder, caught mid-laugh, eyes locked on each other. The rest of the room fades into a soft blur, every detail except us slipping out of focus.

The grin tugging at my mouth, the spark in Nate's eyes, the way his head tips toward mine. All of it caught. Not posed, not planned. The truth, wide open.

I see it now.

The way I look at him, the way he looks at me. Words have never touched it, but the truth bleeds through every line of that photo. The kind of thing you can't fake, no matter how hard you try.

Her voice breaks through the quiet. "This is you. This is what I see."

Nate stands still for a long moment, the frame in his hand, his eyes softer than I've seen in months. He studies the photo quietly, his jaw working once before he draws in a slow breath. After that, he steps forward and wraps his arm around Quinn. His hold is firm, almost protective, the kind of embrace that carries a whole conversation without a single word.

I stay where I am, letting the scene breathe. A part of me wants to tell him to say it—to ask her to stay—but the words sit heavy in my throat and never make it out.

After a moment I close the distance and slide an arm around her and Nate, and suddenly the three of us are pressed together, close enough to catch each other's breath. The weight that has been pressing down on me today lifts a fraction. The heaviness isn't gone, but for a heartbeat, the ache almost seems manageable.

I am the first to let go, ruffling her hair as I step back. "Thanks, Quinn. But seriously, next time I'm holding out for the chicken. Would have really tied the room together."

She laughs, shaking her head. "Theo, I have no idea what the fuck you are talking about half the time."

I grin, tipping my head toward her. "That's fine. Most people do not understand me fully clothed either."

Before she can fire back, I hook my hands around her waist and lift her clean off the ground. Startled, she squeals, her laughter spilling into the air as I start carrying her toward the bedroom. The hoodie she's wearing bunches in my grip, her legs kicking lightly against me.

"Come on, Nate," I call over my shoulder. "Let's give our girl one last night to remember."

The words hang for a beat, hitting me harder than I expect. Our girl.

And fuck... did I really say that?

The ride to the airport is fucking suffocating.

Nate's in the driver seat, knuckles white around the steering wheel, his whole body wound tight enough to snap. He keeps his eyes on the road, jaw locked, every muscle screaming that he's holding himself together by force.

Quinn sits in the back seat, forehead near the window, eyes on the blur of buildings and streetlights outside. Her reflection stares back at her, the glass catching every blink.

I sit in the passenger seat, the words pressing against my teeth. I could tell her. I could spill everything and beg her to stay. But I won't. I know where that road ends. I've been down that path before, and the loss carved me out from the inside. There's no way I would survive if something happened to her.

So I let the silence win. The clawing pain builds until it hurts more than I thought possible. It's easier to watch her go knowing she'll still be somewhere in the world. But fuck, it's still tearing me apart.

Nate turns off the highway, sliding into the lane for the airport. When he finds a spot and kills the engine, none of us move. For a second, it's as if staying still might stop the clock.

The door slams harder than I mean when I get out. I circle to the trunk, pop it open, and grab the handle of her new suitcase. The weight bites into my hand, not from what's packed inside but from what the bag represents—her leaving.

I don't hand the suitcase to her. I start walking toward the terminal, wheels dragging behind me. Quinn follows, with Nate beside her.

Inside the terminal, the air changes. Fluorescent lights hum overhead, making everything feel too bright. The suitcase wheels thump over the tiles, each uneven seam in the floor sending a little shudder through the handle.

Quinn's close enough now that I keep stealing glances, memorising what I can before she's gone. She has her head down lost in her own thoughts. Her hair is tucked behind one ear, her mouth fixed in a way that tells me she's swallowing words she won't let herself speak.

The crowd doesn't slow for us, but it parts. People glance up, eyes flicking between Nate and me, phones sliding into hands. I don't need the whispers to understand what they're saying. Normally, I'd smirk, maybe even play along, tossing out flirty lines. But today, I keep my head down. The attention sits wrong. This isn't a moment I want the world to see.

We stand off to the side while Quinn checks her suitcase in. The conveyor swallows the bag whole, and for a second I hate how easily it disappears, like the universe is reminding me how simple losing something can be when you're not ready to let go.

When she turns toward us, her steps are slower than they should be. Her shoulders are too stiff, her eyes fixed on the floor as though looking up might split her open. Every line in her body screams restraint, that desperate grip on control you only get when you know you're a second away from breaking.

She stops in front of us and finally lifts her head.

Fuck.

Tears are sliding down her cheeks. She doesn't wipe them away. She lets them fall, thin silver trails catching the harsh airport light, proof she's bleeding from the inside out.

It hits me hard enough to steal the air from my lungs. Because I have seen her this way before.

The day she turned up at Nate's door, her face pale, hands trembling, eyes already emptied of light. Her voice was small when she told us Bianca was gone. And in those seconds, I swear I felt the ground split open beneath my feet, swallowing whatever part of me still believed we were untouchable.

Now the feeling is back. That same hollow punch to the gut that leaves you reeling, waiting for the world to tilt back into place, knowing it never will.

She steps in close and hugs Nate first, her arms clinging to him for half a breath before she lets go. After that she's in my arms, smelling faintly of my shampoo I washed her hair with this morning. My fingers press into her back, memorizing the shape of her before she slips through my hands.

"Goodbye," she says, quietly. "Take care of each other."

And then she's gone. Moving through the crowd, away from us.

My chest is carved out, scraped raw. The ache doesn't fade, only waits for the next hit. And fuck me, that's exactly why I can't let myself love her the way I already fucking do.

CHAPTER 28

Theo

The house is too fucking quiet for how loud everything inside me is. Every tick of the clock slams like a hammer to the skull. Even the distant hum from the fridge cuts too sharp, too clean, in a world that's supposed to stay messy.

Sunlight filters through the slats of the blinds, breaking into long, gold bars across the floor. It's warm, delicate, beautiful in a way that almost makes me want to tear the blinds down. Because nothing about me is delicate right now. Nothing is fucking beautiful.

There's a faint trace of her perfume that's somehow still here, three days later. Or perhaps that's just in my head. I don't even trust my senses anymore.

My heart's a fucking wrecking ball, smashing against my ribs like it's trying to tear its way out. Every beat is a reminder that I can't stay in this house another second without losing it. Quinn's everywhere in here. The air tastes like her, the walls hum with her voice, and I can't breathe without feeling her fingerprints on my skin.

I need out. I need to move before I drown in it. I have to find someone to talk to. Or sink into the couch with Alex and let an animal documentary pull me under until the noise in my head thins to nothing.

The front door shuts behind me with a click. The sky is too goddamn blue for the way I feel. It digs at me, makes me want to spit at it for daring to look perfect when everything in me is a fucking storm.

I head to Xander's.

Not because he'll fix it. Fuck no.

He's the only one who'll let me fall apart without trying to clean it up. The only one who won't flinch when I tell him the noise in my head is louder than anything else. That's always been his way.

Nate isn't an option. Not for this. Not with Quinn between us like a fucking shadow neither of us can shake. He's bleeding out the same as me, but he's gone quiet, pulled so far in that the air between us has turned cold. If we keep drifting this way, I'll lose him.

I can't even name what we are anymore. It's not simple. He's been there my whole damn life. My anchor. My constant. The one person I never had to doubt. Now everything's shifted. It lives in the way his eyes find mine and hold there, in the silence that stretches too far, in the way my chest aches when I think about the lines we've already crossed. And if losing him is the price for whatever the hell this is now...

I won't survive.

I move up Xander's driveway too fast, chest tight, breath ragged as though I've been running for miles. I take the porch steps two at a time, and shove the door open and step inside, a man on a mission.

Alex's squeal cuts through from the back patio. I head for the window. Xander's out there floating on the water, stretched out like some retired rock god on a spa day, head tilted back, sunglasses catching the light.

I watch Alex, as the kid launches himself off the ledge, backflips and splashes, pure dolphin-on-crack energy. Every jump sends another wave crashing toward Xander, who doesn't even flinch, until the next one soaks him completely.

That's when he's up, grinning, and in two strokes he's catching Alex mid-laugh.

He dunks him under, the kid's muffled yells bubbling through the water. When they resurface, they laugh. Alex says something, and Xander answers with a lazy grin, sending a playful splash his way. Alex fires back, the water exploding between them until they're both laughing harder, their voices carrying out across the pool.

They're loud. They're happy. The air outside is all sunlight and unbroken days. I'm glad he has this — that broken guy I met all those years ago, finally content with life.

I scan for Poppy. I expect her curled in a deck chair with a book or whatever the fuck that glorified Etch A Sketch thing she reads on is called. Or sitting in the water on the pool steps, smiling, watching the way she always does when Xander and Alex are in their own little world.

But she's not there.

I move further into the house, and that's when I see her.

Poppy.

Sprawled on the couch like a pregnant queen who's been ruling the kingdom of cushions since sunrise. Legs kicked out, one hand on her belly like she's guarding a treasure, the other dangling off the armrest like she fell asleep mid-thought. Her long blonde hair's a glorious, knotted mess that says she either just woke up or fought off an intruder with her bare hands.

"You asleep," I ask, "or marinating in your own ass air and calling it aromatherapy?"

One eye cracks open. "I was asleep, asshole."

"Could've fooled me. It kinda had that angry goose in a wind tunnel vibe."

"I don't snore."

I lean against the doorway, grinning. "Tell that to the fucking moose you scared off."

"Fuck off. This coming from a man who sounds like a cat coughing up a hairball when he laughs."

I grin. There she is. That smart-mouthed girl who never let Xander get away with shit, and who sure as hell isn't letting me.

I drop onto the end of the couch and haul her legs into my lap like she's some entitled queen who's summoned her footman. She lets out a long, guttural groan when my thumbs dig into her arches.

Her head falls back like she's about to ascend into the afterlife, all that blonde hair spilling over the cushions. "Oh my god. Marry me."

I huff out a laugh, rolling my eyes as I dig a little deeper. "You only say that because I'm touching your plantar kink."

Her foot twitches, but she doesn't pull away. "Gross," she mutters. "Don't say plantar kink like it turns you on."

I smirk. "Bit late for that. You moaned like I just proposed with a ring and a foot rub."

She kicks at me half-heartedly. "Shut up and keep going. I'll sign the prenup later."

I slow it down, thumbs pressing deeper into her pressure points, working them in lazy, deliberate circles. "Pretty sure lover boy might have a problem with you coming onto me, Spitfire."

One eye cracks open. "Please. You think he's scared of a guy who once pulled a hamstring sneezing?"

I glare. "That was one time."

She opens both eyes and smirks. "And yet somehow, it still lives in my head rent-free."

The look lingers for a beat, and then her smile fades. "What's going on, Theo?"

That's the thing about Spitfire; she's always been able to slice straight through my bullshit, slip past the grin, and land right in the crack beneath it all.

"Nothing." I work my thumbs into her heel with deliberate focus, hoping the pressure there might be enough to steer her away from the truth.

"Theo." Her tone softens, carrying that edge that's always made it impossible for me to hide from her. "Is this about Quinn? I know you love her. I can see it."

She sees everything. Which is why the words come out before I can stop them, words I have never let out for anyone else.

"I do love her, Spitfire," I whisper.

Her eyes stay on mine.

"I love her, and I hate it," I tell her, my voice fraying until it sounds foreign in my own ears. "Because the last time I felt something this big... this real... we buried her."

Her gaze does not falter. She waits, peeling me apart without touching me.

"I keep thinking that if I give myself over to this, the universe will notice. It will take her the way it took Bianca. I walked through years where every heartbeat was a punishment. I can't do that again."

"The universe isn't some sick fuck playing Russian roulette with your heart," she says.

"Says who?"

"Me. The all-knowing, hormone-fueled goddess currently growing a human and putting up with your shit." Her mouth curves with that smug little dare-me-to-disagree smile.

I let the quiet sit between us.

"Can I ask how Bianca died?" Poppy's voice is softer now.

I swallow, the words etched into my brain from reading them so many times on the same fucking Google page, trying to understand how she could be here one minute and gone the next.

"Brain aneurysm rupture. Massive internal brain haemorrhage. She was unresponsive by the time Quinn called for help, and the paramedics couldn't save her."

She doesn't speak. I keep my focus on rubbing her feet so she won't see the tears threatening to spill.

"That's why it seems like... if I go there, something could happen to Quinn."

"Loving Quinn doesn't curse her, Theo. And not loving her sure as shit won't protect her. That's not how life works. It's messy and brutal and unfair, but it isn't some cosmic punishment with your name written on it."

I swallow, the words scraping on the way out. "Yeah, but if something happened to her—"

She cuts in before I can finish. "Then it happens. And it'll wreck you. But I'll be here. Nate will be with you. Xander, Alex, Ace, Scarlet... every single person who gives a shit about you will help carry the pieces. You don't get to pre-grieve someone who's still here."

I open my mouth to argue, but she gives me that look, the one that could shut up a stadium.

"I haven't lived what you've lived, Theo. I can't pretend to know how that loss carved you out. But I know this... if someone told me tomorrow that I only had a year with Xander, I'd still choose him. Every time. No hesitation. I'd take that year, burn it bright, and hold on until the last second, because nothing could stop me from loving him or being with him. Those five years without him were hell. I'll never live like that again. Love is worth it, Theo, even if the clock's already ticking. Because the alternative... A life too scared to love at all. That's not living. That's hiding."

And fuck, she's right. She always is. I watch her, this Spitfire who can lace a truth bomb with sass so sharp it leaves shrapnel.

"You're a pain in the ass when you're right," I mutter.

Her mouth curves, eyes warm in that way that slips past every defense. "And you're my favorite idiot, so quit sulking."

Her words drag a smile out of me.

Xander and Alex's voices carry down the hall. The second they step into the room, Alex's face lights up. "Uncle Theo!"

He comes at me like a heat-seeking missile, water dripping from his hair. His grin is pure chaos and sunshine, and he launches himself with zero concern for human safety.

I catch him mid-air, saving Poppy's ankles. "Jesus, kid. Warn a man before you go full cannonball."

Alex wriggles out of my grip, suddenly remembering his mom exists. He backs up, still grinning at me as if I'm the main character in his favorite bedtime story.

Xander's gaze finds Poppy instantly. Her legs are still sprawled across my lap, my thumbs pressing into that sweet spot on her arch.

"Hey, Princess," he says, crossing the room. He leans over and drops a kiss on her lips. "You good?"

She hums without opening her eyes. "Better now. Theo's finally proving he has a purpose beyond being a shit-stirrer."

Xander laughs, then smooths a strand of hair away from Poppy's face.

"He lives to stir shit," he says, eyes cutting to me with that smug shine. "But we love him anyway."

"Finally," I say. "Some recognition."

Xander tips his head toward the kitchen. "You wanna beer?"

I shake my head. "Nah. I've got to talk to Nate."

My chest squeezes at the thought. I need answers to the questions that have been running through my head about what we are now. The kind I am not sure I want to hear.

I ease Poppy's feet from my lap and stand, setting them down with all the care of someone handling live explosives.

She blinks up at me.

I lean in, press a quick kiss to her cheek, and murmur, "Thank you. For giving me the kick up the ass I didn't know I needed."

Her fingers curl around my wrist before I can pull away.

"Call her, Theo," she says, no hesitation.

That pull in my chest hits hard. I hold her gaze. "Yeah, I will."

She lets me go, and I turn to Alex, holding out my hand. "Later, little man."

He grins wide, slapping my palm before we launch into our secret hand-shake—three quick claps, a finger gun, and the ridiculous hip bump he insists is essential.

I catch Xander's eye. He is still holding that lazy grin.

"Don't worry, pretty boy," I say, moving towards the front door, saying it loud enough that my voice carries. "She turned me down earlier. You get to keep your crown for another day."

Xander's snorts. "Pretty sure she turned you down because she's got standards, not because I'm in the way."

I can't help the laugh that slips out. I fucking love it. Nothing better than watching a man defend his girl with a grin sharp enough to draw blood.

Now it's time to track down Nate and have the hardest fucking heart-to-heart of my life. Part of me hopes we can claw our way back to what we were. The other part knows I might be walking straight into the truth that there's no going back. I have no idea what the fuck I'm going to say to Nate. Only that if I don't do it now, I never will.

I shove the front door open and step inside. The air carries the faint smell of burnt toast, which is nothing at all like Nate. He never burns anything.

I find him in the living room, sitting on the couch, TV muted, eyes pinned to the floor. His head lifts when he hears me, but there is no shift in his face.

I stop in the doorway, hands jammed deep in my pockets. My shoulders feel wired tight enough to snap. My hair is a wreck from dragging my hands through it the whole walk over, trying to rip the thoughts out of my head. It didn't fucking work.

He leans forward, elbows leaning on his knees. "You good?"

A sound escapes that's supposed to be a laugh, but it's hollow. Fragile like something broken trying to pass for fine.

I take a few steps in, the air heavy enough to slow me down. My feet plant halfway across the room, as though the next move could set off a chain reaction. My hands stay buried, because if I let them loose, I'm not sure if I'll start talking or start tearing the place apart.

"Can I ask you something?"

He nods. "Yeah, what's up?"

My jaw flexes, teeth grinding until bone threatens to crack. The words scrape their way out, sharp enough to bleed on.

"What am I to you?"

The air goes heavy, pressing in on my ribs until breathing feels optional. I ask it the way you ask a question you already know could shatter you, but you need the answer anyway.

He stands up slowly. The kind of slowness that says he knows I am seconds from falling apart.

"Theo—"

"No." My voice rips through the space, raw and shaking. "Don't feed me any of that vague bullshit, Nate."

I'm coming apart under his stare, threads snapping one by one. I have never been this exposed, not even when Bianca died and he was the only thing keeping me from drowning. He has been my fucking rock since we were kids, and the thought of losing him now terrifies me.

"Because we kissed, Nate," I say, stepping back to get oxygen I cannot seem to pull in. "And it wasn't nothing. Don't you fucking dare tell me it was comfort, or some other fucking excuse where we pretend it didn't happen. It was real. And I don't know what the fuck to do with that."

Nate closes the distance until his breath brushes my cheek. Heat radiates off him, thick with the tension that's been clawing at both of us. The weight settles in my chest, the fucking ache that's been building for weeks.

"I know things have changed," he says, his voice threaded with something I can't name.

My jaw locks. My throat strains around a swallow that lodges halfway down.

"Yeah," I mutter. "They've fucking changed."

"Quinn changed everything for both of us."

The words land hard, a clean shot to the ribs that knocks the breath out of me. My lungs seize, desperate for air that refuses to come. I hold his stare.

"But not everything was because of her."

That one cuts deeper, tearing through something I have been holding together for too long. My jaw twitches. My chest locks so tight it's as if I am holding back a scream that would strip my throat raw. I do not blink. I do not breathe.

He keeps going.

"I haven't said this before, Theo, but I think you see it. You fucking feel the same way I do. Quinn's the one I want. I didn't know how to say it without tearing everything apart. I haven't been the same since she left, and she might be the one I see a future with..."

He stops. The pause stretches, until his next words hit like a wrecking ball.

"But you..." His voice splinters. "You've always been mine. Even before I knew what that fucking meant and I didn't have the guts to admit it."

I exhale hard, as if he has torn open something I have been holding together with duct tape and silence for years. The kind of break that lets the cold rush in.

"I didn't plan this," he says, his voice steady. "But the second I kissed you, everything shifted. And fuck, I felt it. That thing I have been burying so deep I thought it would rot before I ever touched it. I was scared, Theo. I thought if I said anything, if I let myself go there with you, I'd destroy what we had. So I stayed silent. But that kiss... it ripped the fucking silence to pieces."

My eyes close for a heartbeat. He is not wrong. That same fear has been living in me, coiled, waiting for the moment it could break us.

"This is new ground," he continues, his voice softer now. "It's not about the band anymore. It's us. You and me. We've been moving around this for so fucking long without naming it."

The words I want to say reach my throat but die there.

He steps in, his palm pressing flat to my chest, heat searing through the fabric of my shirt. My heart pounds hard against his hand.

"I want whatever the fuck this is," he says. "I want you. But I also need the softness of a woman between us. I need Quinn too. I'm done standing on the sidelines while life belongs to everyone else. Xander and Poppy have something real. Ace and Scarlet are heading toward it too. I fucking want that. I want what they have. And I'm done pretending my life is enough when it isn't. You have been the one constant in my fucked-up world."

I swallow hard. The burn catches in my throat, refusing to let go.

"I'm not doing this halfway anymore, Theo." His voice drops. "No more hiding. I want you. I fucking love you. And I love Quinn too."

My vision stings, my eyes turning glassy with something I have no chance of hiding.

"I'm scared, Nate," I admit, my voice breaking low. "What if I break what we have?"

"You won't."

"What if I can't be what you need?"

"You already fucking are."

My mouth trembles. His forehead comes to rest against mine, anchoring me to something solid when the ground beneath me threatens to give way. He has always done this. Always known when the tide in my chest is about to pull me under.

"I think I have always loved you, Theo." His voice carries no hesitation, only truth. "You are carved into my world. You will never lose me. Because I would not fucking survive if I had to breathe in a world without you in it. You think you need me, but I fucking need you too."

The words land heavy, filling every hollow place I have kept hidden. His breath brushes my lips, and the space between us hums with something dangerous and alive. My hand curls into his shirt, not to pull him closer, but because I am afraid of what will happen if I let go.

He exhales, the kind of breath that scrapes out of his chest as if it's been trapped there for years. "We should never have let Quinn go. I should've told her I loved her. I didn't get to say it to Bianca, and that's a weight I'll carry until my dying fucking day. And now I've done the same thing with Quinn and I hate myself for doing it."

"I love her, too," I say, the words sound almost strangled.

His gaze locks on mine, unflinching. "Yeah, I know you fucking do. I saw it every damn time you looked at her. But we were too fucked up from what happened before to let the words breathe. We've been living in this cage we built for ourselves, Theo, and if we don't tear it apart now, we'll lose her too."

Before I can answer, Nate's hand slides up, gripping the side of my neck. He stares into my eyes for a long beat, jaw tight, eyes burning with every unspoken thing we've both carried for years. Then he leans in and kisses me. It isn't gentle. It's the kind of kiss that tastes of battle scars and promises we'll claw our way out together, no matter what it takes. When he pulls back, his hand stays on my neck, thumb brushing my jaw.

"Then let's go get our fucking girl." I say, my hand staying locked around his arm, holding him there with me. "But first, I need to do something."

"What's that?" Nate says.

"I need to go to Bianca's grave. Are you okay with that?"

"Yes." His thumb brushes across my jaw. His eyes soften, the fight draining into something heavier. "I need to say something to her too."

The car is too quiet. Nate's hands are fixed on the wheel, his jaw set the way it always is when there's too much on his mind. I haven't driven since the accident last year. Since he got hurt. My gaze stays fixed on the road ahead while my hand stays buried in my pocket, fingers curled around the necklace that has never been far from me.

It has been through every city. Sat against my skin on every stage, every sleepless night where I've stared at the ceiling trying not to fall apart. It has seen me at my highest, and it has stayed with me when I've been on the floor, drowning in my lowest.

The original chain is long gone.

I wore it until it broke, from the weight of years I refused to take it off. Now the angel wings hang from a black cord, the threads worn thin and rough against my skin from too many days of pulling it on, too many nights of holding it in my fist.

There's a jagged half-pick on there too. The one Bianca broke by accident during a jam session in our room. I remember that day when she pressed it into my palm, her fingers curling around mine. "Keep it. So you don't forget to feel when you play."

I told myself it was luck, that it had something to do with the music. But the truth is, it was her. It was always her. The last piece I could still hold.

Today I'm keeping the promise I made to her that day. Not because the love for her has faded. It never will, but because I'm done letting the grief hollow me out. There's finally something in my life worth holding onto. And I know in my heart if she were here, she'd tell me to stop hiding behind her memory and start fucking living.

We pull into the cemetery just after noon. The sun is high, burning down so bright it borders on cruel. Heat shimmers off the cracked pavement as we pass through the rusted gate. That crooked tree stands in its usual place, limbs twisted up towards the sky, its leaves brittle and brown. It's been dying for years, same as us.

Nate's carrying flowers. Bright ones, the same kind I pick every single time we come here. The colors are too vivid for this place, almost jarring against the washed-out headstones and faded grass. They feel alive, and maybe that's the point.

Neither of us speaks. Our footsteps crunch against the gravel, each sound loud in the heavy quiet. The wind moves slowly through the rows, brushing over the headstones like it's memorizing their names.

And then we're there.

Bianca Rose Laker
1999–2018
Bright, Wild, Unforgettable

It's the same punch to the gut it's been for seven fucking years. It still doesn't feel real. Maybe it never will.

There's already a fresh bunch of flowers resting at the base of her headstone, the same kind Quinn brought the last time we were here. Their stems are bound with a thin white ribbon. Beside them sits a new photograph, edges tucked under a small stone to keep it from blowing away. It's Quinn and Bianca, shoulders pressed together, both with streaks of glitter running along their cheekbones, lipstick shades too bold for anywhere but a bedroom mirror. I can almost hear their laughter and see them leaning in toward each other, faces lit up by something only they found funny.

It's proof that Quinn was here. I wonder if it was earlier this morning, yesterday, or whether we just missed her by mere minutes.

Both Nate and I stare at the photograph, caught in that frozen slice of time, until Nate finally moves. He steps forward, drops to one knee, and sets our flowers beside hers. The bright petals brush against Quinn's bouquet, colors bleeding together against the grass.

Nate stays there for a long while, his head bowed, shoulders still. The wind catches his hair, lifting it from his face. From where I stand, it looks as though he's speaking to her, words too soft for me to hear. I wonder if he's telling her goodbye. If he's telling her he loves her, and that he'll carry her with us no matter where we go. Maybe he's promising her that it's time for us to keep moving, even if we're still taking her with us in everything we do.

Nate rises slowly, brushing his palms against his jeans before stepping up beside me. He doesn't speak, doesn't need to. The silence between us is thick enough to say everything.

I move forward. My hand slips into my jeans pocket, fingers brushing over the curve of metal I've carried for far too long. The angel wings rest against my palm. They still hold a weight that never seems to fade. I lift them into the light, and for a second, they glint in a way that makes my chest ache.

As I stare at the wings, her voice drifts back in fragments.

"I want you to be exactly who you are... spectacular, beautiful... all of it."

I can still feel the brush of her knuckles against my neck as she fastened the chain. She made me feel seen in a way no one else ever has.

"Every time you feel yourself shrinking. Every time you want to fade. This is proof that someone fucking sees you."

The words land heavier now than they ever did then, pressing into me until my lungs ache. Because I have been all of those things since—shrinking, fading, hiding in plain sight. And somehow, through the wreckage, I've found my way back to the surface.

My thumb drifts over the metal, following the gentle curve of each wing. The clasp comes apart easily beneath my fingers, and I work the broken guitar pick free before slipping it into my pocket. The wings rest in my palm, light but carrying every ounce of her weight. They were always hers. I was only keeping them safe until I could finally see myself the way she saw me.

I step forward until I'm close enough for my shadow to spill over her name. My knees almost give out before I make the decision to kneel. The still air here sits wrong, like even the wind knows it should keep its distance.

My thumbs follow the curve of one wing before I set them down against the base of the stone, the cord necklace pooling between my fingers. For a second, I keep my hand there. It almost feels as though I'm passing them to her, as if she might curl her fingers around mine and take them back.

My throat burns. I try to swallow, but it's useless.

"You told me once that I'd give this back when I finally believed I was worth more than I thought," I say, my voice low, scraped raw. "I guess this is me saying you were right."

The words hang, heavy enough that I can't move past them. I stare at the wings until my vision blurs.

"I'm not that scared kid anymore," I manage, softer now. "When no one else saw me, you did. You taught me how to let someone in... how to love without hiding. And fuck, Bianca, you gave me more than I ever deserved."

I stay there longer than my knees want me to, the ache working its way up my legs, but I can't walk away yet. My hand hovers over the stone, close enough to touch, but I don't. If I do, I might not let go.

"I'll always love you," I whisper. "You're in every chord I ever play. You're part of every goddamn thing that I am."

The chord slips fully from my hand, pooling against the granite. The wings look small there. Fragile. But I know better. They're stronger than anything I've ever known.

I lean back on my heels, wiping at my eyes before the tears can spill all the way. But one still escapes, sliding hot down my cheek. I let it fall.

Finally, I push myself up, my fingers brushing the pick in my pocket, holding onto the last piece of her I can't leave behind. I turn away before doubt can pull me back.

I move to Nate and stop beside him, both of us staring down at her name carved into the stone. Without looking, he finds my hand, his grip strong, steady. For a long moment, we stay here. Two people bound by the same loss, the same love, finally saying our goodbyes in the silence she left behind.

Chapter 29

Quinn

The first knock nearly folds into the background. This apartment's always humming with its own kind of chaos—the fridge rattling before it kicks in with a low growl, the fan coughing in its corner, the sirens bleeding through the thin glass and sinking into the walls. The floorboards creak when the neighbours upstairs stomp around, probably arguing again, but I've learned to stop hearing it.

Then comes the second knock.

Heavier. Then softer, a second rhythm chasing the first. One confident, one almost tentative.

I remain still, camera in hand.

Nobody comes here. That's not me being dramatic, that's a fact. My phone barely rings unless someone's chasing up an order from my website, and even then it's almost always an email because no one bothers with phone calls anymore. I don't have drop-ins. I don't have the kind of friends who show up without warning.

It couldn't be my neighbor Mrs Brickmore, either. She left this morning, dragging Charlie and Milly toward the bus stop while I was heading in the opposite direction toward the cemetery. She's predictable. Shopping on Wednesdays, bingo on Thursdays, gossip every other day.

My stomach drops.

That leaves my landlord.

The sleazy fuck's been circling for weeks now, finding excuses to "check the pipes" or "inspect the locks," always with that smirk like he's picturing me on my knees instead of fixing whatever's broken. He's the type who thinks because the place is cheap and falling apart, I should be grateful enough to put up with his wandering eyes.

Another knock sounds.

I cross the cramped space, avoiding the peeling patch of lino in front of the sink. My pulse hammers in my throat as I set my camera on the table, the strap sliding until it hangs over the edge of the chipped table.

The peephole's clouded from years of dust, but I can still make out the shapes—two tall figures, filling the hall.

It's not my landlord. My heart does that thing it always does when I see them—trips, stumbles, forgets the rhythm meant to keep me alive.

Nate with his cap backwards, shoulders squared as if the hallway isn't big enough to hold him. Beside him, Theo, standing too close in that way he always does, restless energy written in every line of him.

I step back, my fingers lift on instinct, combing through my hair to smooth out the worst of the mess. Hours in the darkroom mean chemicals and heat have had their way with my hair, and frizz is the price I always pay for my craft. Not that either of them have ever cared how I look, but something in me still wants to meet them on even ground.

But I stop short. What the fuck are they doing here? I haven't heard a thing from either of them in days. Three, to be exact. Three days since I walked away from them at the airport, red-eyed and blotchy, snot running, mortified that I couldn't hold it together. No texts. No calls. No sign they even noticed I was gone.

To be fair, I didn't reach out to them either. A few times I almost did. I had the words sitting on my screen—some funny joke or ridiculous meme for Theo, a quick check-in with Nate asking how things were going. My thumb would hover over send before I backspaced everything into nothing. No way was I going to make a fool of myself, acting like some clingy girl desperate to hold onto a fortnight of fun with old friends. Or worse, chasing after rockstars who have the world at their feet while I'm just someone they entertained for a while before going back to lives that barely have room for me.

Still, seeing them here now, so close I could reach out and touch them through the wood, twists something deep in my chest.

I open the door, pulling it wider with a smile.

"What are you guys doing here?"

Nate steps forward without answering. His hands cradle my face with the kind of certainty that makes my knees want to give way. He studies me for a beat, eyes running over every inch, as if he is checking I am still the same. Then his mouth is on mine.

His lips move in slow, measured strokes, coaxing rather than taking. He breathes into it, and my body betrays me, leaning closer, letting the kiss catch me completely. His thumbs stroke over my cheeks, gentle enough to make me want to close my eyes and stay here forever.

It is too much and not enough all at once. That kiss holds things I do not dare name, but the truth burns in the heat between us, in the way he drags the moment out until my pulse is a drumbeat in my ears.

When he finally pulls back, his lips curve into that sexy, dangerous grin.

"Missed you," he says, the words carrying a heavy weight.

I try to breathe, but the sound slips out as a whisper. "Missed you too."

Then my eyes shift to Theo.

He moves closer, every line of his body wound tight. His mouth twitches as if he has a smart-ass remark loaded, but nothing comes out.

And for one ridiculous second, I wonder if they came here for something else entirely. A quick fuck. A warm body between them. A way to work out the tension they carry everywhere. Because I am not some booty call. I am not someone they can show up on the doorstep after three days of silence expecting me to spread my legs.

Although, if they gave me those looks that make my knees weak, I'd probably think about it.

Fuck, who am I kidding of course I would.

Theo finally steps in, closing the gap. His hug is quick and tight, his chest solid against me, his breath warm against my hair. But there's a care to it, almost cautious, as if one wrong move might splinter whatever fragile, unspoken thing is holding us together.

I stay in his arms, letting the weight of him settle over me. Whatever brought them here, I still have no answer. The question burns hotter than the kiss Nate left behind, but I bite it back. The longer he holds me, the less I care about anything except the steady press of him against me and the strange, fragile thread binding us together.

He pulls back. "Hey, sunshine."

The smile he gives me isn't the one I remember. It stops short, hanging in place without the heat he usually carries.

"Still haven't torched this place, huh?"

"Tempting," I tell him, lips curving even while I'm studying him too closely. "You two planning to come in or stand out here acting like emotionally unstable door-to-door salesmen?"

Nate crosses the threshold first. Theo trails after him, his shoulders drawn tight. His eyes sweep the room in a slow pass, pausing at corners, at the cluttered shelves, at the stack of laundry I didn't have time to hide.

Theo is closed off, guarded in a way I've never seen with him before. Whatever he's carrying has nothing to do with my apartment. The weight runs deeper than that.

Nate drops onto the couch, settling in without a single flicker of guilt for the mess in his wake.

Theo doesn't follow. He stays on his feet, arms folded, shoulder leaning against the wall. His eyes shift to the table, lingering on the mess of prints I've developed since I got back. Too many. Evidence of hours in the darkroom, of the rabbit hole I disappear into until time stops meaning anything. Where the chemical smell clings to my skin and my fingers prune from the rinse water, and I only come up for air when the real world forces its way back in.

There are candid ones, where they didn't know I was watching. Shots of them caught mid-smile, unaware of the lens. Others where I set the timer and ran into the frame where Theo would find some way to ruin it, pulling a face or making me laugh so hard my eyes squeezed shut.

I hate that they are seeing this. The parts of them I kept.

I clear my throat, grateful for the excuse to move.

"Water? Tea? Coffee? The kind of wine that could strip the paint off the walls?"

"Water," Nate says.

Theo tilts his head.

"Water," he repeats, then lets a slow smirk creep in. "If I drink paint-stripper, I'll end up challenging the fan to a fight. And we both know the fan's undefeated."

I bite back a laugh, because that's Theo, throwing out something ridiculous to cover whatever the hell's running through his head. But it's there, in the way his eyes don't stay on me for long. He's hiding something under the joke.

I make my way to the fridge, grateful I filled the water shelf yesterday. The cold seeps through the plastic as I grab two bottles. When I turn back, I freeze. Nate is at the table, leaning over my prints. His hands move, lifting one photograph, studying it for longer than I can stand, then setting it aside for the next.

I pass Theo his water on the way by, catching the glint of his rings in the light as he takes it. My focus drifts back to Nate. He lifts another print, his brow drawn, the edge of his mouth unreadable. I wish for one fleeting second that the stacks scattered across the table were filled with shots of the band. Something I could point to and shrug off as work.

Instead, it is of them. Theo in profile, his jaw caught in a shaft of light. Nate laughing at something I said off-camera. The three of us in frames I set on timers, moments where they didn't realize they were mine to keep.

I had printed too many. I was aware of that. But missing them had sunk into my bones, and I needed them in my orbit again. This was the only way I could trap us in these small, frozen seconds and keep them where I could reach them.

I drift towards Nate as he studies another photograph. The fridge hum falls away. The whole room narrows to the table, the prints, his hands. To his fingertips skimming the border, almost reverent. A breath slides out of him. The vein at his temple ticks.

"Those are from the last day," I say, not sure why but feel the need to say it even though I am sure he already knows.

He sets that print down and reaches for another. This one is of the three of us, timer-shot, my mouth open mid-laugh, Nate's head tipped, Theo's eyes on me instead of the lens. Heat crawls up my throat. I should have hidden these. I should have pretended I am less obvious than I am.

He places the print back on the table and straightens. His gaze shifts to Theo. My eyes follow for a moment, catching the smallest movement of Theo giving him a nod. Subtle, but enough to send something skittering in my chest. The exchange carries a weight I haven't been invited into, as though some conversation I'm not privy too.

What the fuck is going on?

I turn my head back, tilting my chin up until my eyes meet Nate's. Nothing about his look is casual now. The stare pins me in place, a warning that something is about to shift and can't be undone.

He steps in, close enough that the heat rolling off him grazes my skin. His fingers brush mine as he takes the water bottle, eyes briefly scanning the cluttered table beside him. Not a scrap of bare wood from the weathered table shows beneath the scattered mess of prints. With nowhere to set it down, he turns, tossing the bottle onto the couch. It lands with a dull thud, forgotten.

I flick a nervous glance toward Theo. He hasn't moved from his place against the wall, but his eyes are locked on us with the kind of focus that makes the air press heavier. The way he's watching, it's almost as if I've been pulled into the middle of a moment they started without me.

When Nate faces me again, his focus pins me in place. The noise from the street fades, the air pulls tight until it feels too small to hold the both of us.

Nate's voice is quiet when he speaks, but an edge cuts through—one I've only ever heard when he's close to breaking. "I never got a chance to say this before... when I had to. I should have said it before you left, but I was a coward."

The words hang in the air, heavy, like they're afraid to move too fast. Then he closes the last of the distance between us. His hand comes up, cupping my jaw. His thumb rests under my cheekbone, holding me as if he's terrified I'll disappear if he lets go. His gaze doesn't waver.

"I love you," he says. The words aren't rushed, not thrown out to fill the silence. Every syllable sounds carved from something deep, years in the making. "I love you in a way I never believed I could again. I wake up wanting you. I fall asleep thinking about you. Every fucking day you're not near me leaves me hollow, like I'm missing my own heart. And that scares the fucking shit out of me, Q. I thought I understood what you meant to me before, but these last two weeks have changed everything. You've always been a part of me, but now you're the one part I can't live without."

My pulse is pure chaos. My chest feels too tight to hold everything that's trying to get out. He's looking at me as though I'm the place he's been trying to find his whole life—as though every road has led him here, to me, to home.

"I've spent years keeping everyone at arm's length," he continues, voice low, almost careful, as if the words might break if he's not gentle with them. "After Bianca... after losing her, I thought that was how you survive. You keep moving, keep smiling. You never let anyone close enough to see how much you're still bleeding. But you... you shattered all of that. You made me believe I could be more than what loss turned me into. You made me believe there's still something in me worth loving. And for the first time since she died... I want to let someone in."

His hand slides to the back of my neck, pulling me in until his breath brushes mine.

"I can't promise I won't screw up," he says. "I'll say the wrong thing, get stuck in my head, push when I should hold on. I'll fuck it up sometimes. But I'm done keeping my distance, Q. I'm done letting fear win. You're the one I want to fight for. I'll love you on the easy days, and I'll love you harder on the days that scare the shit out of me. Because losing you..." His thumb grazes my jaw. "Losing you would be the one thing I wouldn't come back from."

My throat aches. I want to answer, to tell him that every word he just gave me is buried so deep in my bones that he's always been part of who I am, but my voice won't work. My chest is too tight. My eyes sting. And the way he's looking at me splinters whatever walls I had left.

So I do the only thing I can.

I move. My hand curls into his shirt, bunching the fabric between my fingers as I pull myself into him. I press my mouth to his, soft at first, because anything harder might break me wide open. He exhales into me, as though he's been holding his breath for years.

Then he kisses me back. Gone is the carefulness. His hand at my neck tightens, his thumb brushing my jaw, tilting me just enough so he can take the kiss deeper. It's all heat and desperation, a clash of breath and pulse and the sharp taste of want. He kisses me like he's making a promise, and maybe he is, one he doesn't need words for.

When I finally pull back, it's only enough to breathe. My forehead rests against his and both of us pant. His eyes search mine, and his confession still thrums through me, waiting for my answer.

"I love you too," I whisper.

His eyes close like the words hit somewhere deep, somewhere he's been afraid to touch for a long time. The corners of his mouth curve, not into a smile, but into something softer. He presses a kiss to my temple, lingering against my skin, and I swear the relief shows in the way his body loosens against mine.

For a moment, the world narrows to only us, full of all the things we've never said until now. I want to stay inside that space, let the feeling wrap around us until nothing else exists. But the world still presses in. And a piece of it stands only a few feet away.

I turn my head, and find Theo watching. He's not smirking, not making a joke or hiding behind that cocky grin he uses when he wants to pretend nothing gets to him.

I turn my attention back to Nate. The weight of what he just said is still vibrating through me. He leans in, his mouth grazing my lips, and murmurs something too soft for me to catch.

His attention shifts to Theo. The air between them changes without a single word spoken. Nate's fingers slide down my arm, catching my hand before releasing it, the warmth lingering even after it's gone. He steps forward and stops in front of Theo, close enough that the rest of the room seems to fall away.

I can't hear what is said, but I see Theo's jaw tighten, then he gives a small, certain nod. Nate's hand finds his shoulder, a brief squeeze that says more than words ever could. I've always known something unshakable binds them, but at this moment it's written in every line of their faces.

When Nate turns back to me, the edges of his mouth curve in that way that always knocks the breath from my chest.

"I'm heading to Marino's," he says. "Haven't been there in forever. I'll grab us a couple of pizza's and let you two talk. Remember how they would always burn the crust but we still ate the whole damn thing anyway?"

The corner of my mouth lifts before I can stop it. "You mean before you drowned every slice in chilli flakes?"

His grin deepens. "That's the one."

He then moves toward the door.

Theo hasn't moved, but his gaze is still on me. Out of the corner of my eye, I see Nate pause at the doorway, glance back at us, and then leave without another word.

The room seems smaller once he's gone, though his presence still clings to the space. Theo takes a slow step forward, and I know something is coming. I sense it building.

CHAPTER 30

Theo

Nate and I mapped everything out in the car for ten minutes, parked in the shadow of Quinn's apartment block, rehearsing how to tell the one woman we both love that we fucking do. We agreed he'd go first when the moment came. I understood how hard that was for him, because saying the words has never been his thing. But that was one hell of a moment when he finally told her.

My eyes have been on her since we stepped into this shoebox she calls an apartment. She's still too fucking beautiful for my sanity, and she's nervous, which bugs the shit out of me. This is Quinn Thomas. The girl who went head-to-head with half the assholes in our year and made them regret it. I watched her take on a quarterback back in school, and the guy walked away nursing more than his ego.

She's standing there, arms crossed tight, chewing her lip hard enough that I'm half tempted to tell her she's going to chew the damn thing off. Quinn Thomas. The same girl who once made a full-grown teacher cry for trying to take her camera. Now she's holding herself small in her own place. Doesn't she know she could own the whole damn room with a single look.

This is supposed to be my turn to tell her how I feel, but my head's gone sideways, stuck on the question of what the hell happened to her. Did some prick make her shrink in on herself the way they tried to do to me back in school? Did someone cut her down enough that she stopped seeing who she really is?

Because the Quinn I remember never hid from anyone. The fact that she's here now, holding herself like she's afraid to spill over, makes me want to track down every single person who ever made her seem small and show them exactly how much damage I can do when I'm pissed.

I take a step closer, close enough that I can count every damn freckle dusting her nose.

"What happened to you, Quinn?" I ask.

"What do you mean?"

"What made you change?"

"Nothing made me change, Theo."

"Sure," I say, stepping closer. "And I'm a fucking nun."

Her mouth twitches, but the smile dies fast. She lifts a shoulder, casual in a way that's too practiced.

"People change."

"Quinn," I say.

"No one did anything to me." Her voice is flat, but I see her throat work hard around the words.

I close the gap by a step.

"You gonna tell me, or am I supposed to start guessing? Because I've got all night and an impressive track record of being annoyingly persistent."

Her arms tighten over her chest. "I told you. No one did anything to me."

"That's cute. Wrong, but cute." I let the silence sit, heavy enough that she feels it, but not so heavy she bolts.

She exhales through her nose, eyes still fixed somewhere past my shoulder.

"Maybe... Bianca's death changed who I am," she says, her voice careful, like each word could splinter. "But you wouldn't know... because I never saw you again."

Her eyes drop, lashes shadowing her cheeks as if she's bracing for me to argue.

But I don't. I can't.

Guilt digs in deep, cruel and unrelenting. I'd never considered what she must have gone through until she brought it up at our house.

"I'm sorry... I didn't think about you back then," I admit, the words tasting bitter in my mouth. "I couldn't. I was drowning and I didn't even try to look for anyone else in the water. That's on me."

Her chin trembles, and she shakes her head slightly. "You don't understand, Theo. I had no one. Not one person who could grasp what it was like to lose her and still have to walk past the bench where we used to sit. Or step into the shop where she always laughed too loud. I faced that every single day."

A tear slips down over her cheek and it breaks me to see the strong invincible Quinn falling still like Nate and I have these past seven fucking years.

"Everyone talked about how you and Nate were holding up, but no one asked me. No one even considered..." her throat tightens. "...no one thought I mattered in that grief. So yeah, maybe I have changed."

I can't stand that she's hurting. I take her hand gently, pulling up the sleeve until I find her wrist, planting a soft kiss there, like I'm making a promise straight into her pulse.

"I remembered her every day," I murmur against her skin, "but I should've thought about you too. You mattered, Quinn. You always did."

When I lift my head, her eyes are glassy, and I know it's not enough to fix the years we lost, but perhaps this is a start.

My mouth's dry. I want to crack a joke, turn the moment into something stupid and harmless, but pressure builds in my chest and won't let me go. It's sitting there like a fist, squeezing tighter every second, and I know if I don't speak now the words will choke me.

I drag in a breath that doesn't do shit to steady me. She stands in front of me, eyes seeing more than I ever want anyone to see. I've spent years perfecting the art of being untouchable—loud, reckless, always moving, making jokes before anyone can get close enough to spot the cracks. And somehow, Quinn has always been the one staring straight into them, as if they're the only parts of me worth looking at.

My fingers twitch on her wrist. I want to grab her, pull her in and hold her, anything to close this distance. But I don't. Not yet.

"I've told a girl I loved her before." I swallow hard. "Bianca. With her it was easy. The words fell out of my mouth without thought, as if they'd been waiting the whole time for me to catch up and finally say them."

I glance away for a second because looking at her is too much. She's got a stillness about her now.

"With you..." I take a breath before lifting my gaze back to hers. "This is different. Harder. Not because I don't already know it's there—fuck, I do. The weight is real. And it's because I know what comes after."

The memories come quick and sharp. The funeral flowers, Nate's silence, the way music stopped sounding like music. The kind of ache you don't walk away from.

"I hate that you went through the worst alone," I tell her. My voice drops, emotion edging every word, but I push through. "I hate that I let you. That I wasn't beside you when the grief cracked you open and turned you quieter. You're not the same Quinn I used to know. But under all that..." I take a step closer. "...you're still you. The girl who called me out on my shit without blinking. The one who could make Bianca laugh so hard her muscles ached for days. The one who made me believe I wasn't some walking mistake."

Her throat works like she's swallowing something down, but she doesn't say a word.

"And I love you for that," I go on, because if I stop now, I'll never start again. "God, I fucking love you for that, Quinn."

The silence that follows is thick enough to touch. I reach up and cup the side of her face. My pulse roars in my ears.

"I've tried to be the guy who never says those words again," I admit, voice low, rough. "The guy who keeps things light, stays loud, stays sarcastic. The one always cracking a joke before anyone can spot the cracks. Because if I hand you this part of me, there's no taking it back."

Her eyes drop for a moment and then glance back up.

"I have no fucking idea how to do this," I confess. "I don't know how to stand here and not hide. But every time you look at me, I feel it. The way you see me. The way you don't flinch at the fucking mess I am. I've been a hurricane my whole life, Quinn, and you..." My throat chokes up, but I force the words out. "You were one of the few who ever walked straight into the storm instead of running."

Her eyes soften, but that doesn't make standing here with my chest cracked open any easier.

"You've got to understand something," I say, my voice low, the words spilling before I can catch them. "Every joke, every smart-ass line—they've all been armour, and you already know that. My way of keeping the world from touching what matters. But you..."

I swallow hard, my thumb brushing her cheekbone as if letting go would erase her from the moment. "You've been slipping past my walls since the first time we talked at those parties. And I've fought against this, Quinn. Christ, I've resisted with everything in me, because loving someone this much is terrifying. It means standing here stripped down to the bone and praying you don't turn away."

My grip on her wrist tightens, slightly. "But if you asked me right now to be that guy—the one who risks everything for you—I'd do it without hesitation. Because I love you in the way storms love the sea. Wild. Relentless. The kind that doesn't end because the world tells it to."

Her lips part, but no sound comes out. I tuck a strand of hair behind her ear, letting my fingers linger against her skin until I can feel the shiver run through her. She's caught in the same undertow that's been dragging me under for months.

"I fucking love you, Quinn," I whisper, barely more than breath, but every syllable wrecked and real. "Not the version I show the world. Not the one who makes people laugh to keep them from seeing too much. You've got the version no one ever sees. The one who doesn't hide when everything hurts."

I shift closer, until no air remains between us.

"I'm yours," I say. "Every fucked-up, broken part of me. If you want me... I'm already yours."

She lifts her hand, resting her palm over my chest.

I don't pull back. I let her touch the pieces I've spent years pretending didn't exist.

"You think you've been hiding," she says softly, voice brushing against the cracks in me, "but I've seen you since day one."

The ground turns unsteady, but she's still holding me.

"You mean everything to me, Theo. You always have. And I've watched how your jokes light up everyone's world even when you're hurting. You make people laugh like it costs you nothing, but I understand it costs you everything. And still, you hold space for everyone else when no one ever did for you."

Her thumb drags over my chest, right where the beat of my heart stutters beneath her palm.

"You've always burned bright to me. Even in the dark. Especially in the dark."

I can barely breathe. A lump swells in my throat that won't go down, and something stings behind my eyes I don't want to admit to.

Because damn it, I've waited my whole fucking life to hear I'm not some mess people tolerate. Like someone finally sees through all the noise and still wants what's left.

I don't breathe. I don't blink.

"You are the storm," she says. "But you're also the calm after. And I love you, Theo. I love you in every form you've ever taken. The loud. The quiet. The chaos. All of you."

Then she surges forward and kisses me.

Not soft. Not sweet.

It's a fucking collision—mouths crashing, breath stolen, her hands in my hair like she needs to anchor herself to something real. I stagger, grabbing her waist with one hand and the back of her neck with the other, kissing her back like I've been starving for this.

Because I fucking have.

I lose the world in her. Everything blurs except for her mouth on mine, her body pressed close, and the way my chest aches from trying to hold this moment still.

By the time she pulls back, my lungs are useless. My knees are a mess. And my heart... It's fucking shattered in all the right places.

I blink, dazed. "Jesus, Quinn... if that's what loving me looks like, I'm gonna need a defibrillator and a helmet."

Breathless, she laughs, her forehead resting against mine, and it's the most beautiful sound I've ever heard.

A knock sounds at the door.

Quinn pulls back, her fingers still tangled in my hair, lips swollen, eyes bright and wrecked in the most beautiful way. She doesn't move for a second, still breathing hard, still pressed to me like she's not ready to let go.

"That'll be Nate," she whispers.

I groan, dragging my hands down her waist and muttering, "His timing's always shit."

She laughs under her breath and slips from my arms. I watch her cross the room, barefoot, her shirt slipping off one shoulder, hair a fucking mess from my hands. I've never seen anything more perfect.

She opens the door, and Nate is standing in the hallway like some cocky bastard sent to interrupt the best moment of my life.

He doesn't say a word at first. Just steps inside, quiet and watchful, his eyes flicking between me and Quinn like he's trying to figure out if I have told her what we came here to say.

A pizza box in one hand, a six-pack of beer in the other, and that raised eyebrow I've known for years. The look he gives when I've done something reckless.

Which, to be fair, is often.

I meet his stare and nod once.

"Yeah," I say. "I fucking told her, man."

Something shifts in his face. Pride. The kind of silent Nate approval that speaks louder than any bullshit words ever could.

He places the pizzas and beer on the kitchen countertop. He goes to lift the lid to grab a slice, but before he does, Quinn's hand settles gently over his.

"Fuck the pizza," she says, her voice low, thick with heat. There's a wicked glint in her eye that punches the air straight out of my lungs.

Then she reaches for my hand, her palm hot, wrapping around my wrist before sliding down to lace through my fingers. The feel of her skin against mine is enough to make my thoughts splinter.

We follow.

I trail a step behind, watching the sway of her hips in those tiny fucking shorts, the hem riding higher with every step. Her shirt's slipping off one shoulder, hanging loose enough to tease the curve of her tits. No bra. Nothing but temptation painted in every goddamn inch of her.

Nate walks beside her, his jaw flexing the way it always does when he's fighting the urge to lose control. I understand that pull. I carry the same tension, coiling tighter with every step toward her room. Every heartbeat slams harder in my chest.

She's not walking, she's fucking leading us to our knees. To her bed, where nothing else exists but skin and sweat and every filthy, perfect way we've learned to worship her. And fuck me if I'm not ready to burn for it.

"You know," I say, as we step into her room, "we could still eat the pizza while we fuck. Bite between thrusts. Feed each other while I'm balls deep in you. Multitasking at its filthiest."

Quinn laughs, breath catching halfway through, and Nate groans beside me.

"You're impossible," he mutters.

"Yeah," I say, grinning. "But now I'm yours. Both of yours. So buckle the fuck up. I snore, hog the sheets, and come with a warning label."

The door clicks shut behind us, and for the first time, it feels as if something has truly ended.

Not in the way heartbreak does. Not in the way grief eats through you. This is quieter. Deeper. It's the end of every lie I've ever told myself just to survive.

All of it. The chaos, the shame, the years I spent trying to outrun the version of me my father built with his hurtful words. They all start to fall away. That power over me is gone.

For the first time in my life, I let myself want. I open myself to everything, the ache, the beauty, the weight of being loved this much without having to earn a single fucking second.

With Quinn holding my hand and Nate right beside me, something in my chest settles. It clicks into place.

I used to think I was made wrong. That I was too much or never enough. That I was cursed. That anyone I loved would unravel. That I dragged the wreckage behind me, bleeding worthlessness into their lives, poisoning everything I touched.

But standing here now, with them, I finally understand I'm more than the mistake my father convinced me I was. More than the shame he fed me. More than the curse he swore I'd carry until I destroyed everything I touched. He never loved me. He didn't have the capacity. All he ever managed was making me think I was born already broken, before I even had a chance to be anything else. But I'm not him. I've learned how to love.

Quinn tugs us toward the bed. We follow. Of course we fucking do. This is the moment we stop running. The moment everything that's been bruised and broken inside us finally breathes.

Three hearts. One fire.

No boundaries. No shame.

No rules, only the ones we carve with shaking hands, open mouths, and bodies finally learning what it means to belong.

This is where we begin.

Messy. Loud. Beautiful in a way I never believed could belong to someone like me. And it's ours. Every filthy, fucked-up second of it.

For the first time, I don't feel lost.

I feel found.

Epilogue

Quinn

The very next day, they moved me in. Theo stormed around my place with my suitcase slung over one shoulder, acting like he was single-handedly launching a military operation. Every few minutes, he tossed insults at Nate for standing there like some trophy husband with one hand on my hip and the other sipping coffee like he'd done his part.

"I hired movers," Nate kept saying, smug as hell. "Delegation is a skill, bro."

It didn't matter that my place was already a mess of half-packed boxes and chaos. Between Theo's dramatic commentary and Nate's calm efficiency, they had me out the door in under two hours.

Calling my landlord was the cherry on top.

He tried to guilt-trip me about the lease, whining about how little warning I'd given and some imaginary paperwork. I smiled so wide my cheeks hurt and told him I wouldn't be renewing because my boyfriends were rockstars and I had better places to be. A long pause followed, then a muttered, "Right," before he hung up. I don't think he believed me. I wouldn't have either. But I never heard from him again.

They didn't waste a second. Nate hired someone to convert the spare room into a darkroom and insisted on painting the walls himself. He got more paint on his jeans than the walls, but it was endearing. Meanwhile, Theo climbed a chair, cursed at the ceiling for twenty minutes, then strung fairy lights with the enthusiasm of a man assembling IKEA furniture blindfolded. Nate called them "fucking pointless", but Theo immediately grinned when they lit up.

Now I find myself inside, hands dipped in chemicals, seeing the images bloom under soft red light. Sometimes Nate appears, leaning against the wall, silent, eyes fixed on me like I'm the show. Drum-rough fingers twitching, lashes low, breathing slow.

Then comes Theo. Shirtless. Mouth full of chips. Demanding I print the one where he claims he looks "like a Greek god." He flexes for emphasis. Completely ridiculous. And weirdly flattering.

I never imagined life could be so damn content. So full. I have both of them. Every day. Every night. And they have each other, too. They always did. They just needed to stop pretending they didn't.

And the sex... It's fucking obscene.

They don't ease up. They push. They ruin. They fuck like it's war. All teeth and hands and sweat and cum. One of them will shatter me until I'm left trembling, and then the other's already dragging me back under, flipping me over, shoving my thighs apart, whispering all the filthy things they want to do to me while I beg them not to stop.

They're touching each other now.

Everything began with me telling them what I wanted. Showing them how fucking beautiful breaking together can be. How much it turns me on to watch them fall apart for each other.

Now it's greedier. Hungrier. No hesitation.

Theo's mouth trails down Nate's neck, biting hard enough to leave marks, while his hand pumps Nate's cock. Nate's groans shatter against my shoulder, as he comes all over Theo's hand.

Then Theo comes apart, spilling across his stomach, his body trembling from everything we've done to him, and I watch as Nate's tongue drags through the mess, licking up every drop like he's starved.

It's hot. Messy. Wild and desperate. It's fucking perfect.

They've turned my body into their playground, their battlefield, their religion. Every night, they come back hungry, greedy, determined to outdo each other. To see who can make me scream louder, fall apart faster, beg harder.

The other night, Theo pressed his mouth to my ear and growled that he was going to fuck me until I cried. Nate didn't miss a beat. He grabbed my thigh, threw it over his shoulder, and said, "Then I'll fuck her again while she's still shaking."

They meant every goddamn word. And I let them. Because nothing has ever come close to the way they make me feel.

I've been to every show. Every city. Every stadium packed so tight the air vibrates with sound. I'm backstage with my camera, passes clipped to my belt. I tell myself I'm here to work. To document everything. To stay focused. But every time they step out on that stage, I forget what the hell I'm supposed to be doing.

Because I can't take my eyes off them.

Nate behind the drums is sex on fire. His shirt clings to every hard line of his chest, sweat dripping down his neck, hair plastered to his forehead as he hammers the beat like the kit owes him something. His thighs flex wide, shoulders tense with every strike, and an unholy rhythm drives the way his body moves. Animalistic. Powerful. He throws his head back, lips parted, that wicked grin spreading across his face—the one that says he owns the fucking stage and everyone in the crowd knows it.

Theo stalks the stage with his bass slung low, hips rolling to a beat that makes the whole damn stadium feel dirty. Sweat glistens on his skin, catching in the lights as he moves. He doesn't smile. He smirks, the kind that makes girls and guys lose their minds. His fingers drag over the strings with obscene precision, coaxing a sound that thrums straight through your spine. There's no apology in the way he plays. No permission asked. He owns it. The stage. The crowd. Me.

Xander commands the crowd with nothing more than a smirk. Shirt half-open. Voice soaked in sin. One verse in and thousands are his—pulled straight into his orbit, drunk on the sound of his voice. He doesn't flirt with the spotlight. He devours it. Takes every cheer, every scream, and turns it into fire.

And then comes Ace. Always off to the side. Head bowed. Hands moving with violent grace. He doesn't look at the crowd. Doesn't need to. Every note he plays cuts deep. The sound spills out of him, gritty and bruised, music that bleeds before it burns.

Together, they're sex in stereo.

All swagger and sweat, a four-part fever dream that doesn't ask permission to crawl under your skin. This isn't a performance. This is a striptease for the soul, a slow burn scorching across soundwaves and stage lights. They walk onstage and the room tilts. Bodies lean in. Mouths part. Minds go blank. You don't witness them, you ache for them.

They aren't a band. They're a goddamn fantasy.

And I'm right in the middle of it.

You'd think I'd be jealous of the groupies. Every city, there they are, crowding barricades with glitter-splattered signs, shouting Theo's name like a battle cry, begging Nate to sign their tits while batting lashes. Some press up against them in the chaos, trailing their nails along tattooed arms or slipping hotel keys or phone numbers into their pockets.

They flirt with no intention of stopping. Laugh too loud, touch too long, make promises with their eyes and fingers. They purr compliments, pretend they're whispering secrets when they're really issuing invitations. And every single one of them thinks she'll be the one they'll remember.

It's never subtle. It's grins too wide, dresses hiked too high, and vodka-laced breath purring things no girlfriend would ever let slide. They ask Nate what he's hiding under his jeans. They pop the buttons on Theo's shirt, dragging their fingers over the ink on his chest as though reading braille. Some even have the nerve to look surprised when security escorts them out, as if grabbing at them wasn't crossing a line.

And yeah, it's a circus.

I don't know how Poppy or Scarlet can stomach it. Maybe they've taught their hearts to flinch quieter. Perhaps they've made peace with the circus.

But for me? I'm drowning in it twice. Twice the hunger clawing past security. I watch two men worshipped by strangers who want to turn screaming into something dirtier.

But I know they will never feel Nate's hands the second the door shuts or wear the bruises his mouth leaves when the crowd's roar fades.

They don't know the sound Theo makes when he's wrapped around me, breath tangled in my hair, hips pressed close, whispering broken things into the hollow of my neck.

They think the high is on that stage. They've never had the after. The sweat. The tremble. The fucking. The quiet. I get the parts no one else sees. I get the music when the stage has gone quiet.

Tour life is a beautiful chaotic mess. But in between the madness, Nate and Theo make time for me. For us. Theo takes me on the most ridiculous dates. Last night, he dragged me to an art gallery in this tiny Czech village. He looked like a delinquent shoved into a tux. I could tell he was bored out of his mind. While I explored the exhibits, Theo set his sights on the poor girl carrying around a tray of hors d'oeuvres. He kept sneaking snacks when he thought she wasn't paying attention. But when she finally caught him mid-swipe, she didn't scold him—she stayed and chatted with him for twenty minutes while he ate nearly everything on her tray. That's what I love about Theo. He doesn't bend for the world. He brings the world to him.

Nate's different. He plans things. He'll rent out a whole restaurant and tell the waitstaff to leave us alone, then spend the evening talking with his hands all over me. One time, we didn't make it out of the place before ending up in the bathroom, his mouth on mine, my back against the door, fucking, while both of us whispering that we'd missed each other even though we'd spent the whole day together.

Another night, we hit up a football game, Theo with one of those giant foam fingers, yelling insults at players he couldn't name. I don't think he even knew which team we were rooting for, but he screamed his heart out anyway. I couldn't stop laughing.

And now it's midnight in Prague. I'm sitting by the window, knees tucked to my chest, watching the city lit up like it was painted in gold. The hotel window is cool against my skin as I watch the glow of ancient streets and cathedral spires stretch out beneath the stars. The air smells of rain and heat and old stone.

The guys are asleep in the king bed in the bedroom. Nate is snoring softly, one leg hanging off the bed like always. Theo is curled around a pillow with his mouth slightly open. He's finally able to sleep in the dark now.

It's quiet here, peaceful in a way that seeps under your skin and makes you breathe slower.

This is when the truth always hits me.

Not during the chaos of the crowd screaming out their names. Not when I've got my camera raised, catching moments before they vanish.

In this stillness, the truth sinks in.

We're okay.

That ache I used to carry—the one that clung to my ribs and made every breath feel cracked—doesn't live here anymore.

It's gone. Replaced by the steady rhythm of this life we've built. The easy kind of love that doesn't need permission. The kind that doesn't question whether we've earned it.

We laugh more now. Loud, ridiculous laughter that fills the walls and drowns out every silence that used to haunt us. Nate's always in the kitchen, losing himself in recipes for Theo and me to try. Theo's always walking through the place half-naked, talking shit, leaving dirty little love notes scribbled on napkins.

And me—I wake up every morning knowing I'm safe. I'm seen. I'm loved.

But the ache isn't pain anymore. What remains is a shared memory of a beautiful, wild girl we all loved with everything we had. She brought us together in our youth. And even in her death, she brought us back.

That day at her gravesite I couldn't have predicted we'd find each other again. I had no sense that loss would lead me here, into something impossible and real all at once.

I have never loved anyone the way I love them. Not with this kind of burn. Not with this kind of ache.

I breathe them in, greedy for the taste, because I know what it means to live without. I hold that moment deep inside me, letting the weight sink into my bones. It's wild, relentless and mine.

The door creaks behind me.

Nate steps in, shirtless, rubbing the heel of his hand over one eye. "Couldn't sleep?"

"Not really," I say, my voice soft.

Theo follows. His hair is a mess, eyes hooded. He doesn't speak, just lowers himself onto the window seat beside me.

Nate slips behind me, settling against the cushions. I lean into him, my back pressing to his chest. He curls his arms around me, his lips brushing my shoulder before resting his chin on it.

Golden light from the window splashes across Theo's face. It warms the curve of his mouth, the dark lashes casting shadows beneath his eyes.

"You're beautiful," I tell him.

I always do. Every time, the weight lands in his chest like a blow he can't brace against. His lashes flicker, his breathing stumbles. I see the impact tear through him. No mask, no smirk, no quick-witted line to deflect the truth.

Because somewhere along the way, his father carved lies into his skin with every cruel word he threw at him. But I will never stop saying the truth. I'll whisper those words into his mouth with every kiss. I'll breathe them against his neck when he's asleep. I'll tattoo the promise into every silence until the belief settles deep in his bones.

Because he is beautiful, and he's mine.

His hand reaches for mine and then he leans forward and kisses me.

His lips brush mine, soft at first, nothing greedy. Nothing rushed. A kiss that says he's here.

Theo pulls back, smirking. "You know your trouble, right?"

"Obviously," I whisper.

Nate chuckles behind me, brushing a kiss to my shoulder. "She's the best kind."

They make me laugh, they make me feel. This love we've built together is louder than the silence we once drowned in.

I stay tucked between them on the window seat. Nate's fingers trace gentle lines over my hip. No one speaks.

This is what I've wanted my whole life. Arms wrapped around me. Hands I trust. Love that stays. Love that heals. A home I never thought I'd ever find. And now because of them, I have it.

Is Xander and Poppy's baby a boy or a girl?
Grab It Here –
https://evecampbellauthor.myflodesk.com/obm2tcpoge

Want more angst, more heat, more heartbreak?
Your next obsession is waiting:
Eastern High Series — an addictive bully romance, starting with
Cruel Intentions
Broken Kingdom Series — a dark, dangerous mafia romance, starting with
The Lies We Lived

About the author

Eve writes broken boys who love too hard and fuck it up anyway.
Come for the spice. Stay for the scars.

Stay connected with Eve for book updates, sneak peeks, and exclusive
extras:
Sign up for Eve's emails:
https://evecampbellauthor.myflodesk.com/thaq2q59or

Join Eve's Facebook Readers Group
Find her on Facebook and Instagram

Seven Lost Summers : ISBN — 9781923416109